ICY PASSAGE

WHERE SCIENCE FICTION AND THE OCCULT COLLIDE

ANN GIMPEL

CONTENTS

ICY PASSAGE

WHERE SCIENCE FICTION AND THE OCCULT COLLIDE

By
Ann Gimpel

A woman running from her magic.
 A man who's given up.
 Mutant culture colonies.
 A doomed ship.

AFTER VIOLENT, out of control magic killed her sister and drove her father mad, Kayna Quan ran as far and as fast as she could from the mixture of Chinese and Celtic power boiling through her blood. Fresh out of residency, she opts for a tour in Antarctica. Money is short, so she hires on as medical officer aboard a Russian research vessel headed for McMurdo Station.

Brynn McMichaels' stint on remote South Georgia Island is a fancy, probably overplayed, escape from a crappy breakup. He may have left an irate woman behind, but he could have picked somewhere closer to get away.

When cultures of the single-celled organism, archaea, begin shifting into another form, overgrowing the bins in his lab, he's convinced the isolation got to him until a call from an old buddy at McMurdo reveals a similar phenomenon. Intrigued, Brynn agrees to lend a hand. The weather's too uncertain to send a plane, so he hitches a ride aboard Kayna's ship, bringing his mutant culture colonies with him.

And that's only the beginning…

~

READER PRAISE FOR ICY PASSAGE:
The story merges science and magic in an irresistible way, as if they've always been branches of the same tree. Woven among the branches are Chinese and Celtic mythology and monsters trying to steal Kayna's magical powers for their own devious use. The science is intriguing and enhances both the adventure and the danger in "Icy Passage." Gimpel's background includes science, having worked as a research psychologist, and developing a fascination with single-celled organisms. As if the conflicts between science and magic aren't enough for Kayna and Brynn, there is also political intrigue. "Icy Passage" is a breath-holding thrill ride through Antarctic ice.

ICY PASSAGE IS a unique combination of an amazing setting, science, paranormal happenings, political events, and romance. It would appeal to you if you are a reader of Science Fiction or Paranormal fiction. Especially if you are sitting in front of a warm fire and have a glass of Irish Whiskey close by.

THE WRITING IS FLAWLESS, as usual. The story sucks you in and it won't let you go, which of course meant I couldn't put it down. I didn't know I wanted to go to Antarctica until now. And I am learning more new things with science and even different cultural mythologies. Ms Ann sure puts her knowledge out there and I LOVE!! Way to make real things so damn interesting. You know if science and math classes figured this out, more kids would love those subjects. With that said, 5 MAGNIFICENT PAWS!! I think maybe I'll have to put a trip to the bottom of the world on my bucket list.

AN UNUSUAL BUT very good story about a woman that wants to be away from it all because her life just seems to be too much for others to handle. She has PSI or an ability to venture into the otherworld. She has forgotten most of her ability because it was dormant for so long but when one person, one ship and one long journey turn it back on, it gets good. Some sex involved so I will recommend this read to 16 and over but a great read for those of us wishing for a passage away.

KAYLA IS AN INTERESTING HEROINE, and Brynn is the perfect man—both tough when it's called for, and extraordinarily thoughtful. Much of the story is about them, but not all of it, and not at the beginning. The mystery and paranormal/fantasy/sci-fi elements join and balance to keep you guessing what will happen. The final resolution of those conflicts are implied rather than spelled out, but I felt completely satisfied when I reached the end of the book (the HEA for our protagonists helped).

ICY PASSAGE by Ann Gimpel is a wild ride through stormy seas and I adored every moment. There's action, suspense, science, and mystery. There's magic, too. At the heart of the story, though, is the tender, blossoming romance between the hero and the heroine. Each is very strong, intelligent, and compassionate. Each is on his/her own path toward wholeness. Fully realized characters, Kayna and Brynn are soul mates from the very first moment they connect. I loved their romance.

PART ONE ~~ BEGINNINGS

No river can return to its source, yet all rivers must have a beginning. Proverb

The beginning and endings of all human undertakings are untidy. John Galsworthy

There are two mistakes one can make along the road to truth...not going all the way, and never starting at all.

Micah Greenwich sucked air as he pushed up from his squat, a weight bar balanced across his shoulders. He did one more squat before a wave of dizziness threatened to bring him to his knees. Gasping, he shucked the bar onto pins protruding from the back of the squat rack and grabbed one of the metal stanchions for support. A headache pounded behind one eye, and he felt nauseous.

"What the fuck is wrong with me?" he muttered, still clinging to the metal cage shoved in a back corner of the gym at McMurdo Station, Antarctica. No one was in the gym. Not at this hour. Granted, the perpetual night for part of the year, followed by perpetual day, yielded some odd circadian rhythms, but Micah rarely had competition for any of the gym machines or weight equipment late at night.

He glanced at the weight plates balanced on the ends of the forty-five pound bar, thinking perhaps he'd misjudged and put too much weight on it, but that wasn't the issue. He shrugged. Maybe he was getting sick. Something was going around. So far, he'd been lucky during his brief stint at the southern end of the

Earth and had avoided the colds and flus McMurdo residents passed among themselves like candy.

He wiped sweat from his face with a ratty towel and decided to call it a night—at least for working out. He still needed to stop by his lab. Because he was the newest and greenest microbiologist, he'd been assigned archaea, the most ancient single-celled life form on the planet. His cultures had taken a decidedly odd turn, though, a couple of weeks back—growing like mad and not looking like any prokaryote he'd ever seen. While he might have started with archaea, what was in his bins didn't look much like them anymore.

Another wave of nausea battered him, and he folded his arms around his midsection, wondering if he was going to vomit. Saliva flooded his mouth, but he choked it back. Even though he didn't feel like doing anything beyond finding his bed, he left the gym and made his way three buildings over to his lab. McMurdo was a series of prefab buildings with interconnecting doors and insulated tunnel-walkways, so you didn't have to go outside into the weather. Antarctica never got particularly warm, and nights were always bitter.

He glanced out a window at an inky sky shot with stars, and a reluctant smile split his face. It might be minus something outside, but it was beautiful too. He'd always loved wild, remote places, and Antarctica was about as wild and remote as it got—shy of signing up to be an astronaut, which was a long-standing dream of his.

Micah frowned, wondering if the astronaut gig was even possible. The United States had cut their funding for the space program rather dramatically. Besides, he needed more in the way of credentials to even be considered for something like that. With another swipe at his still sweaty face—the more he thought about it, the surer he was he was coming down with the flu—he pushed open the door to his lab and froze, not believing his eyes.

"Britta?" he called. "Marguerite!"

The women didn't answer. They sprawled face down on the floor in front of his main workbench, clearly passed out. Wondering if they'd gotten into the high-grade, ethyl alcohol he used to preserve things, he called their names again, louder this time. The longer he looked at them, the weirder he felt. They were too still. Sudden fear gripped him, making the nausea worse.

"Jesus fucking Christ. Why me?" he muttered, and raced to the women. He bent, grabbed Britta's shoulder, and shook her. When she didn't respond, he flipped her over and stared at her cherry-red face.

Fighting a deeply sinking feeling, he turned Marguerite over. She looked just like her friend and roommate. Micah squatted next to them and laid his fingers across their necks, searching for a pulse.

Nothing.

He placed his ear over their hearts, willing there to be something, anything, before he started CPR. Still nothing. He ground his teeth together, unnerved. How could there possibly be two dead women in his lab?

Even though he was pretty sure it wouldn't do any good, he tilted Marguerite's head back and breathed into her mouth before doing chest compressions. When he looked over at Britta, he understood he had to have help and lurched to his feet. Snapping up the wall phone, he punched in the after hours code for the clinic. As soon as one of the nurses answered, he screeched, "Send help now. Third micro lab."

His headache worsened. So did his twisting, roiling guts, but he went back to the women. He didn't need to be a doctor to recognize death. Despite the futility, he alternated CPR from one to the next. Five long minutes passed—but they felt like five years —before the door burst open.

"Christ!" One of the docs—Stewart maybe, Micah was too rattled to take a good look—pulled him off Marguerite. A tall, broad-shouldered woman Micah didn't recognize examined Britta.

"Looks like carbon monoxide poisoning to me," the female medic said flatly. "This one's well past CPR."

Dr. Stewart rocked back on his heels. "Yeah, her too." He trained his blue eyes on Micah. "What happened?"

Micah shook his head. "Damned if I know. I just got here. I had dinner in the mess hall, worked out in the gym, and then I swung by here to check on my cultures."

The woman narrowed her eyes and half-crawled to where Micah sat on the floor. She folded her fingers over his wrist and took him in with practiced hazel eyes. Her reddish hair was short, almost in a butch cut. She pressed her lips into a harsh line, frowning.

"I'm Ariana," she said, letting go of his wrist. "One of the nurse practitioners. How have you been feeling?"

"Bad," he admitted. "Think I finally succumbed to the community disease everyone else has."

Dr. Stewart joined them and squatted next to Micah. He ran a hand down the side of Micah's neck and listened to his chest with a stethoscope before exchanging a pointed glance with Ariana. "Where's the CO meter in here?" he asked.

Micah gestured behind him. "On that wall." He twisted to look at it, but the indicator light was green—safe. Maybe it was defective. His scientifically trained mind arranged informational bits into an unpleasant pattern. "The women," he said. "If I'd been firing on all cylinders, I'd have figured it out as soon as I looked at the color of their faces. They died from carbon monoxide poisoning, didn't they?"

"Probably," Dr. Stewart said cautiously. "But it's conjecture at this point."

"That cherry-red color is a dead giveaway," Ariana said with conviction. "Nothing else will do that."

"We'll wait for an autopsy before we make statements like that." The doctor eyed his colleague coolly.

"Yes, Doctor. Sir. King of all things medical." She set her lips in a thin line, clearly biting back further sarcasm. "Meantime," she ground out, "I'm pretty sure he—" she jabbed a finger at Micah "—has whatever killed these two." She stood and punched numbers into the wall phone. "I'm calling security."

Dr. Stewart sifted his hands through his untidy, blond hair. "Tell them to alert maintenance. Until we figure out what killed these two, we've got to get out of here. Now."

Micah straightened. "Wait a minute," he sputtered. "The meter says it's safe. For all we know, Britta and Marguerite got poisoned elsewhere and just happened to be in here cleaning when they collapsed."

Dr. Stewart got to his feet and hauled Micah upright. "For tonight, we'll put you in the infirmary and run tests to check if your hemoglobin's been compromised. I've got to alert the boss and talk with base security. We'll to get to the bottom of this."

"But my lab—"

Dr. Stewart made a chopping motion with one hand, and the rest of Micah's protest died unspoken.

Ariana hung up the phone and nodded at Dr. Stewart. "You take care of the boss. I'll deal with security and maintenance. Need to get the gas sniffer in here to make sure there's not a leak."

Micah tried to focus, but the room spun crazily. He really was wiped out. Much more tired than a thirty-year-old man had a right to feel.

"Can you walk?" Dr. Stewart nudged him.

Micah focused bleary eyes on the physician. "Yeah. I think so."

"How are you feeling?" Ariana asked the doctor.

He shrugged. "Normal. But it takes time for exposure to take a toll. Micah probably lives in this lab, except when he's asleep."

"Yeah, but," Micah pointed out, "those women didn't. They

clean all the science labs. Maybe one of the other ones is the problem."

The doctor folded an arm around Micah's waist supporting him, and led him out of the lab. "I'm on it. By the time you wake up, we'll know more."

Micah staggered through the door, flanked by Dr. Stewart and Ariana. "What are you going to do about the women?" he asked.

"You were there when I alerted base security. They'll take care of them," Ariana assured him. "For tonight, focus on getting well."

It hadn't been just that night, though. Micah spent the next three days in the infirmary sucking bottled oxygen. When that didn't clear his red blood cells fast enough, the doctors ordered chelation treatments. In the meantime, he had a chance to think, and he didn't care for what he came up with. Besides, it was so fantastic, no one would believe him.

Maintenance had given his lab, and the other three microbiology studios, a clean bill of health, which meant he could go back to work tomorrow. Even more disturbing, the entirety of the science wing where the dead women cleaned showed zip in the way of evidence of a gas leak. In the interest of thoroughness, maintenance had checked the female dorms too, and found exactly nothing. Autopsy was conclusive regarding cause of death, but no one could figure out how the women had been exposed to a big enough dose of carbon monoxide to kill them.

The same was true for him—major exposure to something pigging up his hemoglobin, but without an identifiable source. Another few hours without medical intervention and he'd have been just as dead as Britta and Marguerite.

Armed with that knowledge—and a phalanx of unanswered questions—Micah spent his downtime in the infirmary mapping out a series of tests to run on his strange archaea colonies. He had suspicions, but needed facts before he presented them to Jack DeVoe, the man in charge of McMurdo operations. If he went to him now, Jack, who had a Ph.D. in biochemistry, would laugh him right out of his office. And there would go Micah's hopes of earning his chops, so he could go on to something more prestigious than working at McMurdo Station.

CHAPTER 2

Jack DeVoe sat behind his desk staring at his computer monitor. He snagged a bottle of whiskey from a drawer and belted back a slug, but it didn't make the news any more palatable. Russia and the U.S. were at it again, arguing over Ukraine like a pack of feral dogs battling each other for a juicy bone. The U.S. threatened to send troops, and the Russian president was screaming threats over network news. Unfortunately, Jack was fluent in Russian, and the barrage of words sounded like much more than posturing.

He'd been in Antarctica for years. Maybe now was a good time to go for early retirement—before World War III stranded him at this remote outpost. The more he thought about it, the better he liked the idea, especially in light of the two dead women who'd shown up in the micro lab the other night. Despite him harassing maintenance until they ran the other way every time they saw him, they hadn't come up with a goddamned thing.

He straightened in his chair and rolled his shoulder blades to loosen the tension making his neck hurt. How in the fucking hell could two women die from carbon monoxide poisoning with no leaks? Not just two women, either. The young microbiologist would've been just as dead—but he got lucky. Jack ground his jaws until his teeth ached. He'd figure out what was killing his people. No matter what it took.

Then he'd leave Antarctica.

His phone buzzed and he picked it up, growling, "What?"

"Hey, boss. Micah here." He hesitated. "Is this an okay time? You seem miffed about something."

Nothing much. The world's imploding and a mystery gas leak is on the loose.

"Nah, I'm fine, Greenwich. You still feeling all right? What do you need? It's ten at night."

Micah cleared his throat. "Thanks for asking, but I made a good recovery." He paused a beat. "I suppose in a backhanded way, I owe my life to Britta and Marguerite. If it weren't for them, I'd be dead too."

"Get on with it." Jack rolled his eyes. "You didn't call to swap philosophies."

"Right, sir. Sorry. I know it's been a while since you did much with your biochem background, but I'd appreciate it if you could stop by the lab."

"Now?" Jack straightened in his chair and screwed the top back on the liquor bottle. "Is the lab on fire or something?" He shoved too-long blond hair out of his face and listened intently.

Micah laughed, but it sounded strained. "I've been running tests on my single-celled samples, but I keep coming up with odd results." He hesitated. "The other problem is a critical mass issue. Something bizarre happens when the colonies reach a certain size."

Jack squeezed his eyes shut. "Bizarre, how? Did you run it past the other microbiologists?" When Micah didn't answer, Jack prodded, "Well, did you?"

"Yeah. They're so freaked out by this, they don't want anything to do with it. They'd rather chalk it up to me being nuts."

Jack clicked away from Yahoo! News. He couldn't do a

damned thing about bad decisions on either side of the political fence. Or dead staff, apparently. Focusing on the phone in his hand, he said, "I still don't understand exactly why you need me," and followed up with, "Can it wait until morning?"

"I really think you should come see this, sir. If you tell me I've spent too much time at this Godforsaken outpost, I'll pick up my marbles, and no one will ever hear another word about my concerns."

Breath hissed from between Jack's teeth. "Fine. Be there in ten."

He dropped the phone into its cradle before the other man said goodbye and pushed heavily to his feet. The cold and isolation of Antarctica did things to people's minds. Maybe Micah had fallen prey to what Jack labeled the, "Aw shit, I'm stuck at the ass end of the world," syndrome.

He flexed his fingers, stretching them after long hours at the keyboard. Maybe a side trip to the lab wasn't a bad idea. He'd worked as a senior researcher in biochemistry at the National Institutes of Health before accepting the job running McMurdo, and he missed being in a lab teasing out thorny problems.

Besides, if he retreated to his quarters, he'd polish off the whiskey. A wry grin split his face. Compared with a lot of McMurdo residents, he was practically a teetotaler. The base went through buckets of booze, but it kept other problems at bay. He booted down his terminal, told the base operator he'd be on the sat phone if anyone needed him, and left his office.

The halls bustled with activity. Between the times when they had twenty-four hours of daylight, and the months of twenty-four hour darkness, no one kept much of a regular schedule. He nodded to a few folk as he passed them, clapping a shoulder here and punching an arm there as he made his way to the microbiology laboratories.

Located near the end of one of McMurdo's many wings, the labs housed state of the art equipment for studying the rich array of unicellular life forms that inhabited the Antarctic. He pushed the door open and strode inside. Not seeing Micah in the outer room, he yelled, "Greenwich!"

"In here, boss."

Following Micah's voice, Jack walked into one of four smaller rooms that shot off from the main one like wagon spokes.

The other man straightened from where he'd been bent over a binocular microscope. Tall and lanky, he wore hazmat gloves. Blond hair stuck out at crazy angles around the mask perched over a full beard. Bright blue eyes regarded Jack. "Thanks for coming."

Jack grunted and grabbed a mask and gloves of his own. "What's got you so fired up, son? And why the major hand coverings?"

Micah shook his head and twisted his stool to face Jack. "Should I start at the beginning?"

"Just hit the high points and let me ask questions." Jack hooked his foot around a stool and dropped into it.

Micah pulled his mask aside. "Okay. I've been here four months. Because I was youngest and new kid on the block, the others stuck me with archaea, you know the prokaryote colonies."

Jack snorted. "Yeah, no one's ever very interested in proks, probably because their structure's so simple." He narrowed his eyes. "You never answered me about the fancy hand coverings. Did the little bastards get away from you?"

Color stained Micah's face above his beard. "Now that you mention it, yes. Things were fine until the colonies developed a certain mass, but then things shifted."

"Are you talking about quorum sensing?" Jack asked, referring to a bacterial mechanism of population control based on density and several other factors.

"That's exactly what I'm talking about." Micah exhaled softly, fogging the lab glasses perched atop his nose. "Before we go further, come look at this." He got to his feet and pulled a sample bin across the table. Beige plastic, it was about eighteen inches long and a foot wide.

Jack got to his feet, frowning. The bin was large for bacterial colonies, which grew just fine on agar plates. Micah removed the lid, and Jack's mouth fell open when he stared at towers of cell colonies growing up the sides and along the bottom of the bin. Instead of the gray-green he'd expected, the colonies were violet, blue, red, and bright green.

"Holy crap!" He grabbed a sterile instrument off Micah's tray, pulled the plastic protector off, and gently prodded the mass in the bin. The tower nearest the tip of his instrument recoiled and flowed into a nearby glob of cells.

"I wouldn't get my hands too close," Micah cautioned.

Jack dropped the spatula back on the tray and motioned for Micah to put the lid back on the colony bin. "So instead of limiting their growth in response to quorum sensing, they're going nuts?" he asked.

"That's what it seems like to me," Micah replied. "But it gets worse. You asked about my gloves. I started feeling bad last week —a few days before I came in here and found Britta and Marguerite. Because of them, Dr. Stewart and Ariana caught my downhill slide in time to save me." He shrugged sheepishly. "The symptoms of carbon monoxide poisoning are subtle, and I'm a guy. I probably wouldn't have ever thought to turn myself in to the medics."

He shook his head. "During my stint in the infirmary, I had a lot of time to think, and I figured out what might've happened. It was pretty off-the-wall, though, and I needed to run some tests, first—"

"Cut to the chase. I'm all ears." Jack sat back on his stool. His stomach tightened, and he wished he'd either laid off the booze— or finished it.

"This will sound farfetched—"

"You already said that. Skip the fucking caveats. Just spit whatever it is out."

Micah inhaled sharply, exhaling in a rush before words tumbled past his lips. "You know how some proks have an affinity for iron?" At Jack's nod, he continued, "My best guess is I got sloppy with my gloves, and the proks worked their way through my skin, latched onto my red blood cells, and displaced their ability to bond to oxygen. It's the same mechanism carbon monoxide—and any other toxic gas—uses to kill you. Basically, you suffocate."

Jack felt like someone had sucker punched him. Before he could stop himself, a long, low whistle escaped. "I can see why the other researchers would want to discredit your theory. Distance themselves."

Micah colored again and studied his hands. "Sorry to bother you, sir. Like I said, you'll never hear another word—"

"Shut up," Jack snapped. "I didn't say I didn't believe you. Did you experiment with mice?"

The color mottling Micah's face deepened. "Er, yes. I know I'm supposed to requisition—"

"I don't give a flying fuck about that. What'd you find?"

Micah straightened his shoulders. "I introduced normal proks into a bin with two mice and these proks into a bin with two others. The mice with the normal proks are fine. The others are dead. When I examined their tissues, they died from oxygen starvation. Just like Britta and Marguerite." He stared hard at Jack. "Since maintenance couldn't find any gas leaks, my best guess is the women looked in the sample bins, were fascinated, and touched the colonies."

Jack felt old when he got to his feet and went to look into the bin with the crazily growing bacterial colonies. Micah's theory made a whole lot of sense. Plus it explained why maintenance had come up dry. After he replaced the lid, he gestured to the microscope. "What's under there is stained samples from this bin?"

"Yes."

"What's unique about them?"

"It's why I called you, sir. We finally made it to where I need your biochem background. These don't exactly look like proks anymore."

Jack strode to the microscope, adjusted it, and peered through the eyepieces. What he saw gave him pause. The prok structure was there, but these had more to them—lots more. He straightened slowly. "What happens if you separate the colonies?"

"Funny you should ask, since I already did. After a day or two, they revert to regular proks. My assumption is they'll stay that way until they divide enough to reach whatever critical mass spurs them to shift into that." He pointed at the sample bin.

"Mmph. Let's limit access to this lab to just you and me. For now, keep the colonies small, even if you have to jettison some material."

Micah shook his head. "I don't think tossing anything is smart. These guys thrive in almost any environment including extreme cold and salt water, but I'll do my best to keep the colonies under critical mass."

"Douse the ones you want to get rid of with ethyl alcohol and see how they like it." Jack stripped off his mask and gloves. "I'm going to call a friend of mine, Brynn McMichaels. He's a microbiologist I worked with at NIH. Just so happens he's stationed at South Georgia Island. Proks were a big interest of his."

"What's he doing with them?" Micah perked up, the flat, worried expression leaving his face.

"Building boutique antibiotics or some such thing. It's been a while since we've talked, so I'm not totally certain. Anyway, his contract must be close to up. If he hasn't signed on for another stint on South Georgia, maybe I can talk him into coming here.

We might be onto something fascinating with these mutant proks."

Micah smiled for the first time since Jack had entered the lab. "Thanks, sir. I appreciate it."

"Hang onto your gratitude. Let's see if we can get Brynn to come here, first. At the very least, I'm sure he'd be willing to bat ideas around on the phone or via email."

Jack headed out the door before Micah could thank him again. He remembered what it was like to have ideas no one else endorsed. The scientific community could be pretty shitty to researchers they viewed as renegades.

As he walked McMurdo's corridors, he rolled Micah's idea around in his head. Whiskey sloshed in his belly, and for the first time in years, he wished he had a pack of cigarettes. To quell his craving for tobacco, he scrolled through the contacts list on his sat phone on the way to his quarters. He had no idea if Brynn would be up yet, but it was morning on South Georgia, so he punched the buttons to put the call through.

After three rings, a sleepy-sounding Brynn said, "Hello?"

"Hey, old buddy. Jack here."

Sputtering blasted through the phone. "What the blazes are you doing calling at this hour? Must be the middle of the night there. Did McMurdo implode?"

"No, but the world might. Are you following the news?"

"Yeah, sure, but that's not what you woke me up for. Or is it? Hang on." Something clinked against the phone—probably a glass. "Damn. It's past eight. Time for me to get up anyway. Back to why you called. You speak Russian. Do I need to beat a path home?"

Jack grunted. "I was actually considering that earlier tonight, but no one's declared war—not yet, anyway. The reason I'm calling is we've got an unusual situation in the lab here with proks that've gone wild—"

"Aw, shit!" Brynn cut in. "You're kidding, right?"

"Wish I were." Jack pushed open the door to his small suite of rooms and kicked it shut behind him. Instincts working overtime, he asked, "You having the same problem?"

"Not exactly, but my colonies are acting oddly. Growing like mad. For some reason quorum sensing isn't slowing them down one whit, and once the colonies get to be a certain size, they almost demonstrate a group intelligence."

Air left Jack's lungs in a whoosh. Brynn had always been the most level-headed of researchers. "Are you certain?"

"Of course I'm certain," Brynn snapped. "What I haven't figured out is what to do about it."

"Be very careful while you're figuring it out. It's likely the proks here killed two women."

"What?" Brynn screeched. "They're single-celled life forms. How could they possibly harm a human?"

"This batch has an affinity for iron. Once they drill through the skin and get into the bloodstream, they have a heyday." Jack paused. "I've read about that phenomenon, but never come across it before."

Time dripped by before Brynn spoke again, still sounding agitated. "Maybe mine have a different problem. If they were going to get me, they've had lots of opportunity, and I feel fine."

"When's your contract with that Brit bio firm up?"

Brynn snorted. "Very soon. I already gave notice. I've had it with the southern ocean. Two years was plenty."

"Would you consider coming here and bringing your colonies with you?" Jack forged on before Brynn could protest. "It's good science to look at both mutating colonies side by side. Maybe we'll learn something critical."

A low rumble—maybe compressed frustration—preceded Brynn's next words. "I don't know, Jack. If I don't charter a flight back to Argentina, I might be stuck here if the political mess heats further."

"You could catch a plane from here to Christchurch," Jack

pointed out, not bothering to mention he'd be on it right along with Brynn.

"How would I get there? We're heading into winter, and the weather's unpredictable."

"Does that mean you'll come if I can figure out the logistics?" Jack pressed.

After a lengthy pause, Brynn said, "Yeah, I guess that's what it means, but I'll be damned if I know why I just said yes."

"Because we go back a long way, buddy."

"Yeah, we do. Keep me posted. If I don't hear from you in a few days, I'll make arrangements to get to Ushuaia or Buenos Aires."

"Fair enough. One more small favor."

"Hard to imagine it could be any bigger than what you just asked. What?"

"Can I give one of the microbiology staff your number? He'd love to have a blood brother to talk with, and the other three here have pretty much blown him off."

"Sure, Jack. No problem. As long as he waits until a little later this morning to call."

"I won't even tell him how to reach you before tomorrow morning here—and I'll remind him about the fifteen hour time difference. My admin staff will figure out how to transport you and your cultures to McMurdo. Stay tuned."

"Gosh, guess I'll make myself some breakfast now that you've given me something to look forward to. A reason to get out of bed and all that."

"Spare the sarcasm. Talk to you soon." Jack disconnected and booted up the computer in his quarters to check the weather window.

As his fingers flashed over the keys, he kept seeing the bacterial colony with its multi-hued towers of one-celled organisms. It seemed absurd, beyond the pale, that they'd attacked Micah and the two women. Regardless, Jack felt certain that if the young researcher hadn't stumbled over the lab cleaning staff, he'd be just as dead as them—and the mice in his experiment.

An uncomfortable sensation tracked down Jack's spine. It took a moment before he recognized it as fear. Thank Christ he'd warned Brynn.

The path itself changes you, shapes you, tempers you, molds you.

Not all that glitters is gold; not all who wander are lost.
~J.R.R. Tolkien

A journey is a person in itself. No two are alike, and all plans, safeguards, policies, and coercion are fruitless. We find after years of struggle that we do not take a trip; the trip takes us.
~John Steinbeck

The ship's slick decking canted under her feet, and Kayna Quan lunged for the cable strung beneath the portholes. Her fingers slipped on the ice-coated fibers before they caught, making her heart beat faster. The ship rolled the other way, challenging her to remain upright. She licked her lips, tasted salt from the spray coating everything, and gawked at misty gouts boiling upward from the restless southern ocean.

Wind tore strands of black hair from beneath the hood of her parka, half-blinding her. Rain pounded from leaden skies. Water scuttled into every opening in her supposedly waterproof jacket and dripped down her neck. She should go back inside, but she needed a respite from the stale air and mostly-seasick scientists, who were her fellow passengers aboard the *Vladimir*. A Russian research vessel, it offered bare minimums in the way of comfort, but it seemed sturdy enough. Good thing, since they'd encountered nothing but turbulent seas since she'd boarded in Buenos Aires.

Kayna blinked seawater out of her eyes and made her way forward, clinging to the cable. Her life had changed dramatically, the shift so profound it was hard to curl her mind around the freehearted, spontaneous decision that had landed her on this postage stamp-sized ship bucking its way through the South Atlantic. She'd finished her residency in internal medicine a few months before and passed her boards. Back in Minneapolis, a year's tour in Antarctica sounded like a grand adventure, much better than settling into hospital-based work.

A wave crashed over the starboard bow, dousing her, and she sputtered with annoyance. When she'd told her almost-fiancé, Derek Thompson, about her plans, he'd looked at her as if she were a candidate for the psych ward, basically told her to have a nice life, and that had been that.

"Easy come, easy go," she muttered and switched direction, working her way toward the back of the boat in hopes of finding a more protected spot. In truth, they'd had their share of rough spots. Her psi ability gave Derek the creeps, and he had a fit if she used it in his presence. Hell, she hadn't even been able to *talk* about that side of herself when he was around. And he cringed every time he caught a glimpse of her runic tattoos that offered protection from marauding spirits. Kayna thought the tats were overkill, but her Irish grandmother had insisted on them.

My problems with Derek were my own damned fault. I should've done a better job standing up for myself.

"Dr. Quan," someone screamed at her over the howl of the wind. She spun, almost lost her footing, and snapped up another cable.

"Coming." She headed in the direction of the voice and ducked through a door onto Deck Four. Inside, she bent double and shook her head briskly. Water flew everywhere. She straightened, shoved her hood aside, and more water ran down her back.

The ship's staff captain, second in command on the vessel and staunchly British, clucked in annoyance as he tugged the heavy, reinforced steel door closed, latching it securely. Muscles bulged in his arms and shoulders as he wrestled with the uncooperative door. "Thank bloody fucking God I found you," Harold Markham blurted and grabbed her arm. Panic streamed from him in waves that battered her paranormal side.

Kayna's eyes widened in surprise. She didn't know Harold well, but he'd seemed imperturbable until now. "What happened?"

"Tell you on the way." A corner of his mouth twisted downward. "Be grateful. This saves you from a harsh lecture about going outside in rough seas, without telling anyone." He yanked on her trying to jockey her down the corridor.

"Stop that!" She raised her voice for emphasis. "If there's a medical emergency, I have to know what it is because I've got to stop by the surgery to get my bag and anything else I might need."

"Oh." An uncomfortable look washed over Harold's face. Worry etched lines into the skin around his blue eyes, and he raked a hand through unevenly cut blond hair. He lowered his voice and spoke near Kayna's ear. "It's one of the Russian seamen. He caught his arm in machinery. It's bad."

"Amputation bad?"

It was a stupid question since he wouldn't know. Kayna made a dismissive gesture with one hand and said, "Don't bother trying to answer." She sprinted past him, stopping in the corridor outside the suite that contained both her surgery and living quarters. "Maybe you should have someone carry him here," she told Harold. "At least I have an exam table we can strap him to."

He shook his head. "You need to have a look before we even think about moving him. He's on the raised walkway in the engine room, and there's more blood than I've ever seen—unless the person was already dead."

Kayna keyed an electronic code and let herself in. At the beginning of the trip, she'd left the door open all the time, but drugs had practically flown out of her supply cabinet, despite its padlock. She supposed the others thought she wouldn't notice, but she had.

She shucked her soaked jacket, threw additional items into her medical bag, and raced to where Harold waited in the corridor, bristling with tension. "How do I get to the engine room?" she asked and jerked the door shut. "I walked through it at the beginning of the trip, but I don't remember—"

"There's an access door at the end of Deck Three. I'll be right behind you," he cut in, his normally cavalier voice edged with anxiety.

She fought the rocking ship, moving as fast as she could, and hustled down one flight of stairs. Once there, she ran toward the door that led into the bowels of the ship where the engine took up two decks. Harold followed hard on her heels. Her heavy bag, coupled with the ship's unpredictable motion, almost landed her on her ass—twice. When she glanced back at Harold, his face was set in grim lines. He'd given up any pretense of unnecessary conversation, but he held out a hand for her bag and opened the door just wide enough for her to squeeze through.

Adrenaline hummed along her nerves as she navigated steep, oily steps into the heart of the ship, grateful she could hang on with both hands. Her clumsy bag would've made the stairway treacherous. Engine noise hit her in the pit of her stomach, and she wished she had earplugs. Practicing medicine was frequently mundane, but when she could leverage her skill to save a life, it made everything worthwhile.

Footsteps pounded toward her, and one of the Russian engineers came into view. He motioned frantically and added a volley of Russian. Close-cropped black hair hugged his skull, and his dark eyes held a haggard edge. Blood had spattered his dirty white T-shirt, leaving a hell of a mess.

"Lead the way." Kayna didn't know if he understood, but it didn't matter because he spun and raced back in the direction he'd come from. Two more twists of the corridor and she heard screams even over the noise of the ship's enormous twin engines. Another moment and she saw a tall, bald man writhing in a pool of his own blood. A close-to-severed arm lay next to him. Kayna dropped to the metal decking and made a dive for the artery running beneath the man's arm. If she hesitated long enough to glove up, she might lose him. Straddling his body, she applied pressure while the seaman lashed his body from side to side like a bucking bronco.

"Get me a clean towel or shirt," she yelled, wondering if anyone spoke enough English to understand, but it didn't matter because Harold shouted in guttural Russian, dropped her bag by her side, and sped into a side room.

She eyed the mangled arm and cursed softly. It looked as if a giant had twisted the seaman's lower arm until the severed section hung from a slender flap of skin. Both the ulna and radius were broken, their white, jagged ends protruding through a sea of tattered flesh. Without a sophisticated operating theater, there'd be no way to save the sheared off limb. Blood poured from the injured extremity, jetting from injured arteries and flowing from torn veins, but at least the rate had slowed. She ran her free hand down the man's neck, other arm, chest, and abdomen, searching for further damage with a magical assist from her psi ability.

"Dr. Quan."

When she glanced up, Harold hunkered next to her and handed her two bath towels reeking of bleach fumes.

"Thanks." She nodded sharply. She'd been so focused on assessing if the seaman had other injuries, she'd missed the staff captain returning with towels. She folded one, tucked it into the wounded seaman's armpit, and pressed as hard as she could while the sailor shrieked and thrashed, clearly in agony. "Put your hand where mine is," she told Harold. He complied immediately, and she twisted to reach into her medical bag for a syringe and a vial of morphine. She thought about gloves again, but she was already coated in the man's blood.

She guesstimated the seaman's weight, did some quick calculations, and hoped to hell she'd gotten them right as she drew enough morphine into the syringe to dull pain, but not totally knock him out. He thrashed wildly beneath her, his blue eyes so crazed with agony they were nearly all pupil. "Hold him down so I can give him this," she said.

Harold started to move his hands. "Not you," she cried. "Keep pressure on that artery so he doesn't bleed out." Harold barked a command, and four burly seamen stabilized their wounded companion. Kayna plunged the syringe into the meaty part of his other arm and clenched her jaw as she waited for the morphine to spin its magic. Dropping the empty syringe back into her bag, she pushed Harold's hands aside, replacing them with her own.

"His arm?" the staff captain asked in a rough voice.

Kayna looked up long enough to meet his gaze. "His arm is probably toast. Right now I'm fighting to keep enough blood in him so he doesn't die. The morphine will kick in soon. At least it will give him some relief. Once he settles down, I'll give him a whopping injection of antibiotics and a tetanus shot."

"What can I do?" Harold asked.

"Where exactly are we?" she countered.

"Not far from the Falklands."

"Better news than I'd hoped for. Have someone radio for a medevac helicopter. This man needs a hospital. Actually, he needs a level one trauma center for that arm, but that's probably not going to happen."

Harold bolted from the engine room, and Kayna eyed the group of Russian seamen ringed around her. She gestured to one to keep pressure on the towel and dug in her bag for a stethoscope, blood pressure cuff, and a tourniquet. She filled another syringe with a mix of antibiotics and readied it. The man's body relaxed as the morphine did its work. Soon, she could inject her antibiotic soup without anyone holding him down. As grim and desperate as the situation was, Death was a worthy adversary.

"Bring it on," she muttered as she checked vital signs and noted them. "I'm going to win this round."

Almost as if Death had a corporeal presence and had risen to her challenge, a chilly breeze passed through the overheated engine room. She'd sensed Death before when she was pulling out all the stops to save a life, had even mentioned it to some of the other docs when she was an intern, but they gave her such odd looks, she'd never made the mistake of disclosing her paranormal abilities again. When it got right down to it, almost everyone was just as psi-phobic as her erstwhile almost-fiancé.

"Easy," she murmured and injected antibiotics. The man's eyelids flickered, and for the barest moment, he focused on her. "That's right." She patted his uninjured hand and hoped her tone would bridge their language barrier. "Help will be here soon. You're going to make it."

So many hours passed before Kayna dragged herself back to her surgery, she was surprised it was still night. The medevac chopper hadn't arrived right away. There was no place large enough on the ship's outer decks for it to land, so it hovered and dropped a basket, along with two paramedics who'd rappelled out of the bird. Between the three of them, they'd packaged the seaman into an aluminum gurney.

Her body ached and her head throbbed with exhaustion. She'd traded the pressure bandage in the seaman's armpit for a tourniquet, and dosed him with enough antibiotics to kill damn near anything. The man would lose a good part of his arm, but not his life unless something unexpected happened. She closed her teeth over her lower lip and bit hard enough to clear her head. The engine room was so far from OSHA-compliant it was a joke. What was equally amazing was that Harold told her this was the only serious accident he'd ever seen aboard this ship.

Kayna rounded the last set of stairs and ground to a halt. Someone was sitting in front of the surgery door typing away on a laptop. *Damn!* It was Chris McLaren, a paleontologist she was treating for opiate addiction. Guilt smote her. She'd made him a promise and hadn't been there to deliver. Shambling forward, she said, "I'm sorry. I—"

"None of that." He powered down his computer and got to his feet. He was tall and so thin he reminded her of Ichabod Crane. "I heard what happened. It was all everyone talked about over dinner. Other than the U.S.-Russian mess, that is. You must be trashed."

She smiled crookedly. "I've had better days. Here. I'll get you fixed up in a jiffy. Right after I wash my hands."

He glanced at her reddened fingers and said, "I can wait. Don't you guys usually wear gloves?"

"There wasn't time. He might've died if I'd taken even a few extra seconds." Kayna heard a defensive undertone in her voice, but didn't bother modulating it. "Once I was soaked in blood, it didn't matter anymore."

"I wasn't being critical." His angular face and brown eyes looked dejected, as if he were used to apologizing. Thick blond hair framed his clean-shaven face.

"Yeah, I know. I'm just tired."

She keyed the code to open her door, dropped her blood-splattered bag in a corner, and made her way to the sink. Mercifully, the seas were a bit quieter. Kayna glanced at herself and grimaced. Everything she wore was streaked with red, the coppery stench of blood still thick and cloying even hours later. She scrubbed her hands with soap and a brush and dried them on a paper towel before turning to face Chris. "How's the amount I've been giving you working?"

An uncomfortable look washed over his face. "Not bad." The words were right, but they lacked conviction.

"Are you certain?" She eyed him. "White-knuckling it won't help you stay on the wagon."

A sheepish grin softened his austere features. "You've been reading my mail."

"No. I've known a lot of addicts. I want this to work for you, and I'm too wiped out to play games."

"You're right. Okay. More would help. That last bump downward was a bitch, but I didn't want to look like a weak suck loser by admitting it."

She exhaled wearily. "If I weren't blood from stem to stern, I'd hug you. No one is a loser unless they see themselves that way." She unlocked her drug safe and counted pills into small, buff envelopes. "Take all of them. They'll help you sleep."

"Thanks, Doc. Get some sleep, yourself." He held out a hand for the envelopes and faded through the open surgery door, laptop tucked beneath one arm.

Kayna nudged the door shut and sank into a chair. She dropped an elbow onto a nearby table and used her hand to support her head. A moment slipped by and then another. Weariness tugged at her, but she forced herself upright, dropping clothes as she went and stuffing them into a bag for the ship's laundry. Once she wrapped herself in a robe, she sat at her computer and noted what she'd done for the seaman. Medical records were dicey little devils. Once you got behind, it was a bitch to catch up.

More asleep than not, she moved into her bedroom in a fog and then to her small bathroom where she stood under the shower until she couldn't smell blood anymore. She barely remembered climbing into her narrow bunk. It was good the seas had settled because she was too far gone to lash herself in.

CHAPTER 4

A Few Days Later

Brynn McMichaels strode out of his living quarters on South Georgia Island determined to do a better job figuring out what was up with the samples in his lab. A ship would arrive soon, and there was no point in freaking out the biologists aboard it any more than necessary—never mind the ones at McMurdo.

He'd spent time on the phone with Micah Greenwich and really liked the young researcher, but he understood how quickly other scientists would tune him out if his ideas—and mutant colonies—flew in the face of convention. Brynn prided himself on keeping an open mind—no matter what.

He crossed the deserted walkway separating his bedroom and study from the lab where he housed his samples and paused with his hand closed around the door latch. Micah was convinced the colonies in the McMurdo lab had turned on him, and Brynn had listened to his theory about the proks bonding to red blood cells and displacing oxygen. While it was certainly true some proks had an affinity for iron, still, the other man's beliefs were a tough nut to swallow.

People are dead. I can't ignore that—no matter how much I'd like to.

Steady old man. Nothing's happened here yet.

Steady, my ass. What's behind this door is either a modern miracle or the worst kind of disaster ever.

Micah's description of how he'd nearly died was damned sobering, never mind the two dead lab workers.

Brynn sucked cold, marine air into his lungs. Despite a heavy fleece jacket, two-layer bibs, and Arctic Pac boots, he was cold. Not an ordinary cold, but the kind that froze slowly, from the marrow of his bones outward. He'd never viewed himself as an alarmist. Far from it. He'd finished a Ph.D. in microbiology and worked as a researcher for a while before earning his M.D. Because he'd enjoyed the charged atmosphere of emergency rooms as a medical student, he opted for a residency in emergency medicine and practiced for a few years before returning to research. In the E.R. he'd been viewed as coolheaded through the worst kinds of emergencies.

What happened? Did I lose my competitive edge somewhere between taking care of people and growing cultures?

Realizing he was stalling, Brynn dragged the lab door open. Not much reason to lock anything here. For eight months of the year, he and two other scientists rattled between the buildings in Grytviken, a deserted whaling village on South Georgia Island. The other scientists were meteorologists studying Antarctic weather patterns and tracking the Antarctic Convergence, so he didn't have much interaction with them. During the brief Antarctic summer from November to February, the occasional cruise ship stopped, disgorging hardy tourists via Zodiac inflatable rafts. They walked around the island, visited Shackleton's grave, and spent money at the museum, post office, and gift shop. By March, the Brits who ran the concessions returned to the Falklands, leaving the island to make its way through another winter.

Brynn had set up his current operation two years before in barracks left over from the Falklands War, and Grytviken took some serious getting used to. He'd never lived anywhere so remote, but he'd finally almost adapted to the isolation now that his contract with a British bioresearch firm was drawing to a close. Two years was plenty long enough on South Georgia, and he was grateful there hadn't been any indication his contract would be renewed. It made him feel less guilty when he gave notice he was quitting.

He walked briskly into his lab and flicked on the overhead bank of lights. Generators powered everything on South Georgia from an inexhaustible supply of gasoline. While fuel wasn't a problem, the generators were old and needed frequent attention. Nothing beyond his capabilities, but he'd been relieved to find schematics for the cantankerous pieces of equipment to guide his repair efforts.

A low hum that had nothing to do with the generators swelled against his ears. He clamped his teeth together. Single-celled organisms weren't supposed to be capable of sound, but then these samples weren't exactly unicellular anymore. At least he didn't think they were. He hadn't done a precise evaluation, because that would entail chopping into the clumps growing up the sides of his sample chambers. Even though it bordered on the ridiculous, he was certain whatever his samples had morphed into wouldn't approve of any of their number being sacrificed in the name of science.

Who knew? They might turn on him just like Micah's colonies had.

What was worse, the low-pitched wave of sound held a hypnotic quality, almost as if the samples were trying to lull him into some kind of détente. When he'd queried Micah, the other man hadn't said anything about his colonies vocalizing.

"For Christ's sake," he muttered. "I've been by myself too long.

There's no fucking way these things can think, and I'm probably imagining that hum. It must be a product of the acoustics in this room."

Yeah, right. One I just started noticing...

He clamped his jaws together. This whole mess began when he'd done routine scrapings from the mosses and lichens that grew thickly on the steep mountainsides of the Allardyce Range rising above Grytviken. What started as unremarkable colonies of archaea—prokaryotes—had changed over time, but so gradually it hadn't commanded his attention until about a month ago, right after an enormous power surge wiped out damn near everything that was plugged into an outlet.

Luckily, he had a second adapter for his computer. Equally fortunate, his microscope hadn't been plugged in. He figured his archaea colonies in their temperature and humidity controlled storage bays would be history, but that was when they began growing like mad things.

Brynn shook his head as he gazed about his neat lab. It might look the same, but it felt different—ominous somehow. He pushed his overheated imagination aside with stern admonitions to leave him be, goddammit.

Originally, the crew at McMurdo was going to send a plane, but the weather had gone to hell. The current plan involved a ship. When he'd spoken to some of the microbiologists aboard the vessel earlier in the day, he'd hinted his samples weren't exactly normal without disclosing much in the way of details. After all, he didn't actually know anything—not for sure.

Taking a good, hard swallow of gumption, he donned gloves, yanked one of the oblong, clear plastic sample bins out of the neat line with its fellows, and carried it over to his workbench. No time like the present to determine what was going on. Scientists lived for unusual events, so why was he so suspicious of what might be a huge breakthrough worth years of journal articles?

Excellent question. Too bad I don't have any answers.

He hadn't been drinking enough to make a difference, but he swore to lay off his nightly single malt Scotch as he rummaged in a drawer for a face mask—no point in introducing further contamination if that was the problem—and shrugged off his jacket, replacing it with a lab coat. Kicking a three-legged stool into place, he sat and observed the gelatinous mass in his bin. If he cocked his head and looked from a certain angle, he was almost certain he could see the pale gray-green mounds pulsating. Thank God, Micah's colonies didn't look like his—at least not from a gross morphology perspective. They'd exchanged jpegs via email, and Micah had also sent screen shots of stained slides.

Brynn would've sent some, except he didn't have any. That was part of the reason he was hovering over his bins now. Despite the colonies not appearing to be the same, he needed to find out if what lay in front of him bore any resemblance to Micah's proks. The only way to be sure was to prep slides, stain them, and take a look.

He squeezed his eyes shut, opened them, and looked again. This time the bin's contents didn't do anything unusual. He readied his microscope and scraped a small amount of tissue off the closest clump, quickly replacing the bin's lid. Preparing a slide was second nature, and he worked with nimble dexterity, although he couldn't completely shut down his overactive thoughts.

Once the slide was stained and ready, Brynn was out of excuses. Nothing to do but study it. When he looked through the eyepieces of his microscope, his jaw tightened with surprise. The archaea looked exactly like they should, the outline of each cell distinct and the inner cellular landscape containing precisely what he expected to find. He straightened and rolled his shoulders forward and then back to displace the iron bar of tension that gripped him.

Confusion vied with relief his colonies weren't anything like Micah's—at least not yet. Had everything, including the low, hypnotic humming, been a product of his imagination? It didn't make sense. Presuming his random sample was representative of the whole, what grew in his bins were simply huge colonies of archaea. Harmless enough. Maybe his growth medium was responsible.

Except he hadn't changed it.

He replayed his conversations with Micah. Obviously whatever was growing in these bins was a different critter entirely from what the other researcher described. Brynn shook his head to clear his thoughts. The odds of having two divergent oddities was excruciatingly low. Cells mutated slowly, stimulated by environmental factors. Surely, things couldn't be that different between here and McMurdo.

Brynn stared at his gloves. Were the critters from the sample bin invading his body, like they had with Micah? Quite aside from iron, some proks had an affinity for cerebrospinal fluid and could create tumors, blindness, madness…

Stop! Just stop. I'm overreacting all over the place.

Brynn arched his back. His muscles still felt like rocks, even though his apprehension seemed groundless. His slide showed zip in the way of evidence for interconnections between the cells. Or any resemblance at all to Micah's killer proks. Not trusting his first take, he bent over his microscope for one more look, but nothing had changed.

Why would it? This should be a relief.

It would've been, but Brynn didn't have faith in what his eyes told him. He prepped and stained two more slides with material from different bins. And came up with the same result. What stared back at him from the microscope's stage were prokaryotes, pure and simple.

He blew out a tense breath, turned off his microscope, and returned the bins to their proper spots. A few scribbled notes in a lab book, and he couldn't ditch his smock and get out of the lab fast enough. What had begun as a haven gave him the creeps. Disgusted with himself, he stomped back across the breezeway and into his living quarters. He glanced at the cozy space with patched leather furniture and an overflowing bookshelf, but settling in with a book or six-month-old research journals wouldn't do a thing to address the adrenaline souring his stomach.

Because he didn't think he could sit still long enough to focus on anything, he zipped his heavy outer coat and went back outside where he kicked a rock harder than he meant to. It bounced off his boot and hit a seal lying across the roadway. The seal barked its annoyance, but didn't move.

"Whoops. Sorry, old fellow." Brynn considered walking over and patting the seal's snout, except it wasn't like a dog. The animal looked quiescent, but it was just as likely to bite him as ignore him.

Wishing he'd opted for a career studying something with less chance of mutating, like seals for example, he jumped into the old Land Rover he used to tool around Grytviken. It was the only running vehicle on the island. When it broke down, he doubted it would be replaced. There weren't more than a few miles of roadway around the deserted whaling village, and it would probably be better for him to walk, but the wind had a bite to it, and up until an hour ago, it had been snowing. He started the car and drove a hundred yards along a road fronting the sea. No reason to hurry, there weren't many places he could go.

He snorted derisively and watched the windshield fog from the warmth of his breath. In addition to his other problems, he also wasn't spending enough time at the gym. The barracks had a well-equipped weight room, but he hadn't visited it since his suspicions about the samples surfaced.

He stomped on the brake, and the rickety vehicle screeched to a halt. Brynn pounded his fist against the steering wheel. Pain ratcheted up his arm, but it was welcome because it cleared his head. He'd studied enough psychology to recognize that isolation played hell on people's minds. He'd been by himself for so long, his imagination was playing tricks on him.

It was the only rational explanation.

Is Micah's imagination out of control too?

Brynn shook his head. It'd be a hell of a lot easier to discount his unusual colonies were it not for the other man's experiences.

He got out of the car and walked to the ocean's edge where he watched the waves roll in. They held a spellbinding quality, and time dribbled past. A seal lumbered by him and into the sea. Brynn marveled at the transition from clumsy to graceful a few feet of water created. As if it sensed his approval, the seal raised its sleek head above the surf and stared right at him. Brynn grinned. The shades of aquatic life on South Georgia were incredible. He'd miss that part—a lot. During the summer months, he'd explored the island by motor launch and sea kayak and been blown away by the penguins, seals, and seabirds.

Grateful for a return of something akin to sanity, he pushed to his feet, retraced his steps to the Land Rover, and coaxed the engine to life. Maybe a spot of company would be welcome. The other resident scientists always seemed happy to see him. They had wives and families back in Norway and clucked over his bachelor status, while ribbing him about the possibilities his freedom offered. He teased right back that female seals weren't his cup of tea.

A sideline benefit of taking a break from his lab was he hadn't thought about the cultures once in the last half hour.

Better enjoy the break. Once I'm at McMurdo, I'll be back in the thick of things, at least for a while.

Brynn grimaced. He'd give McMurdo two weeks. Then he'd catch a plane out of there, so long as winter storms didn't intrude.

He brought the Land Rover to a halt in a spray of gravel and got out, whistling a tuneless ditty as he walked briskly into the

Norwegians' lab. Sven glanced up and drew a hand through his shoulder-length hair, pushing it away from his face. Both he and Lucas could be Nordic poster boys with their broad shoulders, blond good looks, and sharp features. A set of blue eyes beamed at him. "Look who's come to visit," Sven crowed.

"I can't imagine," Lucas called from the back room. "Shall I break out the akvavit?"

"I'd prefer beer if you have it." Sweating in the sudden heat of the lab, Brynn unzipped his coat and hung it on a hook.

"Whatever our guest desires." Lucas's laughter rang through the thin partition. In moments, he appeared with a bottle of akvavit and a beer.

"So, how's it going?" Brynn waved his hands expansively to encompass the lab.

Sven's smile faded. "The ship that's coming to get you and your germs needs to hurry. This lull in the weather's not going to last."

"They're not germs, they're unicellular cultures." Brynn held out a hand for the beer and twisted the cap off.

Sven shrugged sheepishly and laughed. "Don't mind me. I chose something manageable to study."

"Since when is weather manageable?" Brynn leaned against a workbench, tipped his bottle toward Sven, and said, "Cheers."

Sven grabbed the liquor bottle from Lucas and waggled it in Brynn's direction. "You'll be lucky to make McMurdo in one piece."

"Maybe you should reconsider traveling." Lucas tugged a chair over and dropped into it.

"Thanks, but all this concern is misplaced." Brynn mimed sinking under a heavy weight. "I've been doing some hard thinking, and I'm looking forward to getting back to the States. I won't be at McMurdo long."

"You've been here for what?" Sven asked. "Two years?" When Brynn nodded, he went on. "That's about the maximum any of us can stand. It's wild and lovely and all, but unless you're a true hermit, the isolation gets to everyone."

Brynn chose not to reveal just how much it had gotten to him. He took a hefty swig from his beer, enjoying the bitterness of the hops. "So tell me about this storm," he prodded, more to make conversation than because anything Sven could say would change his mind. "What makes you think it's going to be so bad?"

CHAPTER 5

Light pouring through her cabin window woke Kayna. Though she'd been exhausted after yesterday's crisis, she hadn't slept all that well. Groaning with fatigue, she rolled to a sit tangled in her duvet. By the time she found clothes, splashed water on her face, and ran her watch down, she wasn't surprised to find it was closing on ten. Meals happened at set times. She'd missed dinner last night, and now breakfast was long past too. Maybe the cook would take pity on her and either make her something, or let her fend for herself in his shiny, stainless steel kitchen. When she padded into the surgery in search of shoes, she saw a note someone had stuffed beneath her door.

Kayna snapped it up and scanned the few lines.

Didn't want to bother you. Find me when you're awake. Chris.

She smiled ruefully. Hard to say who was taking care of whom. Shoving her feet into tennis shoes, she bent to snug the laces. Before she left her surgery, she placed some pills for Chris in tiny envelopes and dropped them into her pants pocket. Even though she was starving, she stopped at Chris's door first and knocked softly.

It opened almost immediately. She dug in her pocket for the envelopes and handed them to him. "How are you?"

His smile faded, and he bit his lower lip. "Still hanging on by my toenails. It might be easier if I could go outside."

"Talk to Harold. The seas are better today."

"I already did, and he said maybe. You missed breakfast, so you won't have heard. There's been a change in plans."

She pursed her lips. "What kind of change?"

"Instead of heading straight for McMurdo, we're stopping at South Georgia Island."

The ship lurched, and she caught herself on the doorframe. "Any idea why?"

"It's pretty vague." Chris turned away from her long enough to grab a bottle of water out of a fixed ring bolted to the wall. He emptied the pills into his mouth and swallowed. "Sorry," he muttered, and his cheeks flushed with embarrassment.

"I'm the last person you need to apologize to. Vague how?" she pressed.

"A scientist at Grytviken cultured specialized scientific samples. Apparently, it's some kind of microorganism the group at McMurdo wants."

"Any idea why?" Kayna drew her brows together in thought.

"From what Harold said, McMurdo has a similar type of culture, and everyone wants to introduce them to each other. Or something like that." Chris rolled his eyes and went on. "We're the easiest courier and a hell of a lot cheaper than sending a plane—even if one could get off the ground, which isn't likely given the weather. The bottom line is we're stopping to pick up the samples and the researcher."

"What's Grytviken?"

"A deserted whaling station that got built up during the Falklands war."

"Mmph." She thought about it. "How long will that add to our ship time?"

"Funny, but I asked the same thing. Maybe four days. Longer if the sea kicks up again."

"I'm going to scare up some food." She backed into the corridor. "See you tonight."

"I'd love to say maybe you won't—" he dipped his chin "—but I know better."

"It'll be okay." She aimed for a reassuring note. "Keep telling yourself that. Don't expect too much too soon."

Kayna walked into the dining room and got a cup of hot water, stirring instant coffee, cream, and sugar into it. Even the stragglers had finished eating, and the room was empty.

"Doctor." The cook, a Brit named Robert Jones, stepped out of the kitchen and folded his arms over a substantial belly draped in a seersucker apron. His reddish hair was shaved closed to his skull, and his pale blue eyes were kind. "Bet you're hungry."

She nodded. "Whatever you have left over from breakfast would be great."

"I made you a plate and popped it in the warming oven." He smiled and disappeared back into his domain, emerging moments later with a steaming plate that he took to a table beneath a window. "I'll bring you toast and jam too."

"Thank you." Sighing with pleasure, Kayna pulled out a chair and sat. She ate methodically, working her way down to china, and was considering asking for more when a shadow fell across her.

"All recovered, Doc?" Harold settled into a chair cattycorner from her.

"Why wouldn't I be?" she countered. "It's no worse than lots of times when I worked in the E.R. as an intern."

"Yes, but then you had an entire medical team for backup. Yesterday it was just you."

Kayna eyed him warily. "I managed to do okay, and it wasn't *just me*. You and the crew helped. What's your point?"

"I'm not sure I had one. You're prickly as a winter cactus. I was trying to be supportive."

"Maybe, but you want something too." She pushed her empty plate off to the side. "I'm going to get a refill on my coffee. Be right back."

She cast a sidelong glance Harold's way as she stirred cream into her coffee. He laced his fingers together and placed his hands on the table in front of him, his expression unreadable.

"You're right," he said without preamble as she sat down. "I need your help."

"If it's about hosing that elevated walkway with disinfectant to make sure the engine room doesn't turn into a biohazard area—"

He untangled his fingers and made a chopping motion with one hand. "That was taken care of before the helicopter left. We've had a slight alteration in our plans, and I may need your help."

She nodded and took a sip of the steaming coffee thinking how much she missed brewed beans. "I already know something about it. Chris told me. We're detouring past one of the deserted whaling stations on South Georgia Island to pick up scientific samples."

"Yes, and also another microbiologist, but it's the samples I need your assistance with."

Kayna set her cup down. "There are at least three Ph.D. microbiologists on board this ship, plus the one you just mentioned from South Georgia. What could you possibly need from me?"

Harold snugged his brows together until they touched over the bridge of his aquiline nose. "I don't like bacterial colonies aboard my ship. Bad things happened to me once when they got out of control, and several people got really sick—including some of my crew. Anyway, you're the ship's doctor, so you need to be vigilant." He hesitated, "Besides, the microbiologists on board weren't certain they wanted anything to do with Dr. McMichael's colonies."

Kayna bent forward. "I still see this as more of a biological issue than a medical one. I usually wait until there's a reason before I launch countermeasures. What's the deal with the microbiologists? It's what they do."

"I'm sure I don't know the answer to that." He shrugged in a way that flagged her suspicions he might be lying. "Maybe they're still too seasick to consider much of anything."

"I can dose them with more Phenergan."

Harold shook his head. "Look, Doc, I don't think drugs will fix this one. Just say you're on board with this."

"I'll certainly treat anyone who becomes ill. I've got enough antibiotics to deal with damn near anything."

"Great! Thanks."

His expression didn't match his words, and Kayna narrowed her eyes. "What exactly is in these samples?"

An even glummer shadow crossed Harold's face. Her paranormal side blared a strident warning. She reached across the table to grip one of his hands. "That's it, isn't it? The reason the microbiologists refused to have anything to do with the samples is because they're toxic."

"They didn't refuse—not exactly. Let go of me, Doctor."

"Sorry." She withdrew her hand and tried to stuff her psi hackles back in a sack, but they refused to retreat.

The line between his brows deepened. "Ship safety is my first concern. I was stunned when the microbiologists balked."

Kayna leaned back against her chair and kept her gaze trained on his face, but didn't say anything.

Harold pursed his lips. "Mind if I change the subject?"

"It might actually be welcome." She took another sip from her almost-too-hot-to-drink coffee.

"What do you know about South Georgia Island?"

She shrugged, surprised by his abrupt shift in topics. "Very little." When he didn't offer anything further, she added, "You opened this line of conversation for a reason."

He snorted. "Did they rob you of your social skills in medical school?"

"I never had many to begin with." Curiosity surfaced, and she quirked a brow. "Why'd you ask me about South Georgia?"

A rueful grin lit his sea-tanned face. "Maybe because I hoped if I told you about the island, I could pique your curiosity enough, you'd want to see it. If I knew ahead of time, I could arrange things to have time to accompany you."

"Nice try." She sat straighter, recognizing a clear pick-up line. "But no thanks. Bad idea, Harold. I work for you."

"It's just a bit of a sightsee, not a date—" he began.

The swinging doors into the dining room whooshed open, and two middle-aged men stumbled in. Kayna recognized them as some of the microbiologists. Both had been intensely seasick, but one had made a better recovery than the other.

Stabilizing themselves with their hands on tabletops and chair backs, they made their way across the room. "Good to see you, Doctor." Abel Clarion, a tall, thin, sandy-haired man, inclined his head.

"Indeed." Zach Wiedland, shorter, burly, and bald, seconded. "From what we hear, you did a nice piece of work yesterday."

"Thanks," she murmured.

"Look, old chap," Abel said and dropped a hand on Harold's shoulder. "We've changed our minds."

"Yes," Zach chimed in. "We talked about it, and we were being drama queens." He rolled his shoulders self-consciously.

Abel shot Zach a meaningful glance from clear blue eyes before transferring his attention back to Harold. "We just got off the sat phone with Dr. McMichaels. All is well. If the new cultures need additional caretaking—beyond what McMichaels can provide—we're on board."

Harold smoothed astonishment from his face and got to his feet. "Excellent. I'll tell the captain." He trotted out of the dining room, leaving Kayna to wonder why the men's change of heart surprised the staff captain. He clearly hadn't been expecting them to capitulate.

What does he know that he's not telling me?

"We'll keep you company," Abel offered and stuck out a hand.

Zach grinned and plopped into the seat next to hers. He stared at her coffee with his sharp, green eyes. "Looks like slop, but I'd be up for tea."

"Would you like to make us some?" Abel batted his eyes.

The gesture was so out of place on Abel's long, thin face, Kayna struggled not to laugh.

"Sure, hon." Zach pushed to his feet and made his way unsteadily to the hot water carafe.

"You guys are a hoot." Kayna crossed her arms beneath her breasts and cut to the chase. "What was the problem with the samples?"

"Probably isn't anything," Zach called from across the room.

"What's in the samples?" she persisted.

"Single celled organisms, really ancient ones," Abel said without quite meeting her gaze.

"Except they might not be unicellular anymore." Zach returned with two cups and settled his bullet-shaped body into a chair. "Which is what made us nervous."

"You mean they're creating something new?"

"Hard to say. McMichaels was evasive as hell."

The same chill presence that alerted her Death—or some equally grisly disaster—lurked in the offing clutched at her stomach. "If you fellows would excuse me—" she got to her feet with a smile so fake it made her cheeks hurt "—I need to inventory my medical supplies."

To a chorus of, "No problem," and "Nice to finally meet you when I'm not sick," she walked briskly from the dining room and tried to coerce her overheated imagination into submission. It didn't work.

Her intuition shrieked a warning, one she couldn't discard out of hand. Maybe there were good reasons to keep the Grytviken samples separate from the McMurdo ones, but she couldn't see any way to suggest that to anyone without looking like a deranged fool. Kayna blew out a breath and sifted her hands through her hair. "I don't know anything," she muttered under her breath. "Not for sure. Just because my psi hackles are up, it doesn't mean anything. I could be wrong."

Not feeling even mildly better, she let herself into her surgery, fastened a clean inventory sheet to her clipboard, and put numbers in its tiny boxes while her mind raced unbridled toward what felt like Armageddon.

CHAPTER 6

Kayna stood on deck as South Georgia Island grew larger on the horizon. It had only taken three days to cross the Scotia Sea because the winds calmed, so much so it was the main topic of conversation around the ship. It was almost as if they'd sailed out of autumn and back into the northern hemisphere. The ship's captain shook his head, muttering in Russian as he shuttled between his cabin and the bridge. When she'd asked Harold what he was saying, he rolled his eyes. "No, really," she pressed, worry still dogging her. "I want to know."

"He's cursing the Norse weather gods and predicting a mother of a storm."

"Why Norse?" she'd asked. "Don't Russians have their own mythologies?"

But Harold hadn't answered. Maybe he didn't know, or maybe he didn't think it was worth the time to educate her. For about the millionth time since she'd set foot on board the ship, she missed the Internet. A few keystrokes would've brought up the underpinnings of Russian myths and legends. She already knew something about the Norse gods. Satellite coverage in the southern oceans was spotty, though—and expensive. The ship had a sat phone and minimal Internet coverage, but searches ate up bandwidth, so she was limited to short emails—without attachments.

She scanned the horizon. South Georgia was a big island, more than a hundred miles long, with a mountain range cresting at nine thousand feet running along its spine. Snowcapped peaks rose through mist, reminding her of an untamed version of the Scottish Highlands. Harold, who hadn't given up trying to seduce her, regaled her with stories of Ernest Shackleton, penguin colonies, and albatross nesting grounds, but when she pressed about opportunities to actually see something beyond Grytviken, he'd hedged.

Apparently, the seaman in him won out over his romantic inclinations. Everything was weather dependent, particularly this time of year. With the ship's captain so nervous she was tempted to spike his vodka with Valium, she doubted they'd stay in the shadow of South Georgia any longer than they had to. She'd wrangled permission to go ashore, though, and she was really looking forward to walking on land after the ship's rolling deck.

"Hey there, Doc!" Chris ducked out a door and joined her by the ship's railing. An expensive-looking camera hung around his neck, and he snapped several shots.

Grateful for a diversion, Kayna spun and looked at him. "Is it my imagination, or are you feeling better?"

He grinned sheepishly and shrugged. "I'm not sure. This will sound odd, but something inside me feels different. It's as if the drug demon packed up shop and left." Color splotched across his cheeks. "Is that even possible?"

She held his gaze. "Of course it is."

"Maybe I can skip the rest of the pill crumbles you're doling out."

He sounded so hopeful, she didn't want to do anything to shake his new-found confidence. But still, it had only been a little over a week since he'd confessed his problem and asked for her help. Antarctica would be a hell of a place to detox, and he wanted to get it over with before he reported for duty at McMurdo.

"How about this?" she suggested. "I'll give you your dose and you can decide whether or not to take it. If you make it through the day—or night—you can return the envelopes. I still want you to check in with me twice a day for at least another week, though, no matter what."

"You're smooth. What you didn't say is probably more important than what you did." He raised the camera, and the shutter clicked as he shot more pictures.

Harold tromped over. "If you want to go ashore, Doc, you need to get yourself together. We're dropping anchor very soon, and it will only take ten to fifteen minutes to get a Zodiac ready to launch."

Excitement churned through her. She was about to set foot on land again. Her uneasiness about whatever they were picking up faded from center stage. "How long will I have to look around?"

He screwed up his face, and she could almost hear gears crunch in his mind. "At least an hour."

"That's it?" She drew back, surprised it would take so little time for Dr. McMichaels to bring his materials on board.

"If we can allow you a longer walkabout, we will." Harold placed a hand on her shoulder. "Once we get to McMurdo, you'll miss the ship. I guarantee it."

Kayna opened her mouth to assure Harold she absolutely would *not* miss the rocking, pitching ship, but shut it before she said something that would probably annoy him.

"Can I go ashore too?" Chris asked.

Harold moved his hand and turned to face the paleontologist. "Huh?"

"I'd like to go ashore with Kayna," Chris repeated, enunciating the words individually as if he were talking to an idiot.

Harold blew out a snorting sigh. "It wasn't that I didn't understand you, Dr. McLaren. I was surprised by your request."

"Why?" Chris edged closer to Harold. "Do I have *remain on ship* stenciled across my forehead?"

His tone made Kayna wary he might start throwing punches.

Harold laughed uncomfortably. "Of course not. Catch the two of you later. Looks like I'm needed over there." He pointed with two fingers and loped toward the front of the boat, presumably to oversee a gaggle of Russian seamen congregated around the anchor chain.

"We're all a little edgy—" Kayna began, but Chris made a chopping motion with his hand.

"I don't need to be mollycoddled. He didn't say I couldn't go, so I'll put on more layers of clothing and meet you next to the starboard gangway in fifteen minutes. I'll bring my sample kit. You never know. Maybe I'll find some fossils worth examining."

She tossed a smile Chris's way, returned to her cabin, and bundled up. After chucking a water bottle and a snack into her backpack, she made her way to the steep, narrow gangway leading to the water, careful to rinse her waterproof boots in the tub of disinfectant located on the forward deck. The fauna and flora throughout the entire Antarctic region were delicate, and she didn't want to accidentally introduce bacteria that might cause problems.

Harold was coming into sight standing in the stern of a Zodiac raft, and Chris was already positioned next to the gangway's steps. Apparently, he was just as anxious to leave the ship as she was. Kayna glanced around, somewhat surprised to not see any of the other scientists. Had Harold not extended the offer of escape to anyone else?

Probably not. He likes it when things are easy, and rounding up a bunch of us would be a headache for him.

Mirroring her thoughts, Chris turned to her and asked, "Do you suppose Harold didn't bother to mention shore leave to anyone else?"

She rolled her eyes. "That's exactly what I think. Did you rinse your boots?"

"Of course. Last thing I want to do is drag some microbe from this ship onto South Georgia. Hell, I could wipe out an entire seal colony."

"I didn't know they were particularly sensitive to disease."

"I'm blowing smoke. I study dead things, but I don't want to add to the list by carelessness."

Harold latched the Zodiac's bow rope at the bottom of the gangway and made come-along motions. She navigated twenty slick stairs until she stood on the platform at the bottom. Harold extended a hand.

"Step on the pontoon, and then on this step—" he pointed "—and then onto the boat's floor."

She moved past him and settled on a pontoon. "That was easy."

Chris ignored Harold's hand and leapt nimbly into the boat.

The staff captain eyed them both. "Getting into the raft was only easy because the seas are calm. It can be an absolute bitch to get in and out of these things when the ship's bouncing up and down and the raft is too." Moving to the stern, he engaged the outboard motor, and nosed the raft toward shore.

"How stable are these?" Kayna asked, rather enjoying herself.

"Very in these conditions, but they can flip in rough seas."

"Mr. Cheerful," Chris muttered.

"I'm practical," Harold snapped, sounding out of sorts. "I've spent my life at sea. I wouldn't begin to presume to tell you how to practice your craft. I'd appreciate if you offered me the same courtesy."

"Touché." Chris inclined his head. "Sorry."

Harold pursed his lips into a thin line. "I am too. Don't know what's gotten into me these past few days. Maybe the captain's nervousness is catching, but I'll be very glad once we reach McMurdo."

"I thought you were sailing back to somewhere in Europe after that," Kayna said.

"That's the plan, but if the weather's hideous, we'll stay put at McMurdo until it clears."

"Just how bad is it likely to get?" Chris asked.

Kayna should've kept her mouth shut, but she wasn't thinking. "It's nearly winter. Can't we get stuck in the ice or something?" Harold's face darkened like a thundercloud, and she muttered, "Sorry."

"No need to apologize, Doctor." His words held a forced calm. "The captain and I are already at odds over what happens if—er, I mean once, we reach McMurdo."

"If?" Chris's voice came out a high-pitched squeak.

"I misspoke." Harold ground the words out. "Of course we'll see you delivered safely to your destination."

If that wasn't a piece of politically correct dialogue, I've never heard one.

She didn't want further false assurances from the ship's staff captain, so she held her peace and focused on a stretch of beach that was moving up fast.

Harold cut the engine to a purr once they were very close and strode past them to free a long rope from a box in the bow. Once he had it in hand, he hurtled over the pontoons and waded through shallow surf to guide the boat onto rocks and sand. "Swing your legs to the ocean end of the raft and time the waves before you get out," he instructed.

A tall, tawny-haired man loped toward them. Kayna did a double take and tried not to stare, but he cut such an arresting figure she couldn't tear her gaze away. He was hatless despite the chill temperature. Bright hair spilled to his shoulders and framed his high forehead, sculpted cheekbones, and strong, square jaw. When he smiled, his teeth shone very white against tanned skin. Dark glasses covered his eyes, but he had a presence that stole her breath. He had to be at least six feet four with broad shoulders and slim hips. Even buried in layers of warm clothing, his physique was impressive.

"Thanks for stopping to get me. I know it was out of your way." He stuck out a hand, shook briefly with Harold, and helped steady the Zodiac by taking hold of the anchor rope.

Kayna swung her legs toward the ocean end of the raft, but forgot the part about timing the waves. If her boots hadn't come to her knees, she would've ended up with wet feet. As it was, she felt like an ass. Was she really so devoid of a love life that the first handsome man she'd seen in ages robbed her of her wits?

Yes. The answer to that is yes.

She plodded through light surf and onto the beach. The man, presumably Dr. McMichaels, held out a hand to her. She shook it and said, "Kayna Quan. I'm the ship's doctor."

His blindingly bright smile widened. "Great. It so happens I'm an M.D. too. Nice to meet you, Kayna."

She waited, but he didn't introduce himself. Right before Chris joined her, she asked, "Are you Dr. McMichaels?"

He rolled his eyes. "Christ! I've been here too long. All the social niceties passed me by, not that they were my strong suit even when I lived around people. Yes. I'm Brynn McMichaels."

"Chris McLaren." Chris moved between them and extended a hand.

Kayna realized hers was still clasped firmly in Brynn's grasp. Self-conscious, she pulled away and hoped her cheeks weren't as red as they felt. Maybe the others would chalk up her rosiness to the cold air, but she doubted it.

"Always pleased to meet a fellow Scott." Brynn took Chris's hand.

"Actually, I'm more Irish than Scottish, but at least we're from neighboring stock." Chris looped a hand beneath Kayna's arm. "We don't have much time. We probably should get moving."

"Of course," she murmured and ripped her gaze from Brynn's face. The last thing she wanted to do was leave, but sticking around drooling like a love-struck schoolgirl wasn't a good idea, either. "Nice to meet you." She nodded briskly in Brynn's direction. "Feel free to stop by my surgery once you're aboard. It'll be great to have another physician close by." She giggled and felt like an ass, but couldn't make herself shut up. "Really could've used you a few days back."

"I haven't actually practiced medicine for a while, but I'd love to hear what happened."

He turned his smile her way again, and her knees felt rubbery. What would it be like to have him all to herself for a few hours?

Stop, Kayna's stern mind voice lectured. *Cut it out right now. He probably has a wife. Children. I need to trim my horns before I make an even bigger fool out of myself than I already have.*

Chris tugged gently on her arm, and she followed him toward a cluster of buildings. "I thought I was going to have to leave you there," he said quietly once they were well out of earshot.

"Damn! Was I that obvious?" Heat flooded her face again, doing battle with the air temperature that hovered in the low twenties.

Chris stifled a grin. "Maybe not rampantly obvious, but I'm guessing it's been a while since you had someone special in your life."

"Actually, it hasn't been all that long." She debated saying more, but didn't.

They wound their way toward a museum that had been boarded up for the season, and she stopped to look at a conglomerate of whaling implements. The harpoons were huge and made her sad for the whales. Wind whistled around her, threatening far worse to come. "Looks like our weather window is closing," she mumbled.

"I'm waiting for you to say more," Chris prodded. "But not about the weather."

She shrugged uncomfortably and led the way toward a church. Not surprisingly, it was locked tight too. "Not sure what more there is to say," she replied, aiming for a neutral tone. "I had a boyfriend, but he dumped me when I decided to go to Antarctica."

Chris swung her to face him. "Really?"

"Why would I joke about something like that?" Defensiveness made her chest tight. Apparently, she wasn't as close to being over Derek's cavalier decision to cut her out of his life as she thought.

"You misunderstood." Chris chewed on his lower lip. "I can't believe any living, breathing man would leave you because you wanted to go on an adventure."

"Believe it," she snapped, surprised by the surly undernote in those two words. Kayna shook her head. "I'm sorry. To be candid, I had a hard time wrapping my mind around it too."

"How long were you together?"

"Seven years. Look, let's not talk about Derek. It wasn't that we didn't have our problems, but we stuck it out through most of med school and residency. Once we were done, he didn't need a roommate who made sure there was food in the house. Antarctica gave him a convenient excuse." She pointed to her left, anxious to change the subject. "Shackleton's grave is over there."

"At least you have a personal life to talk about." Chris fell into step next to her. "Drugs have always been my first love. I'm not sure what it would feel like to be free to care about a person."

She eyed him. "I have a premonition you're about to find out. There must be a few females at McMurdo."

"There are." He grinned. "It was one of the things I researched once I knew I'd be going there."

Kayna had done the same research, but she'd rather die than admit it. Making sure there'd be eligible men to flirt with during her stint in Antarctica made her look old, sad, and desperate. That Chris could chat animatedly about it drove the gender gap home.

Reality intruded, slapping her hard, and she clenched her teeth together. Gender gap be damned. If her fears about McMichaels's samples and the McMurdo ones came home to roost, there'd be no flirting. Maybe not any living, either. She set her jaw in a tight line to keep from voicing her suspicions about whatever Brynn McMichaels was loading onto their ship. Chris would listen to her—and it might be good to have someone to talk with—but he'd sounded so frantic when Harold slipped up about how perilous their voyage was likely to become, the last thing she wanted was to alarm him. Anxiety could shatter his tenuous sobriety, make it hit the skids.

"Don't expect too much too soon," she cautioned. "It can take months for your body to find a balance point—for everything."

He rolled his eyes. "Spare me, Doc. That was pretty patronizing and had *I'm your M.D.* carved all over it. Just be my friend."

Kayna hesitated, knowing he'd nailed her. She had a host of handy platitudes she hid behind; they made her professional life bearable. She'd always shied away from anything that smacked of *personal* where her patients were concerned, but this was scarcely a normal environment. If she couldn't be friends with the people she treated, it would be a hell of a lonely year.

"I can do that, but feel free to hand out reminders." She opened the gate into the small graveyard, and walked to Shackleton's final resting place.

Chris ran his gloved hands down the granite headstone. "After all his years at sea, it's amazing he died here."

"They tried to send him home. I believe he got as far as Buenos Aires, but his wife told the ship to return him to South Georgia." Kayna walked around the headstone and read the inscription on the other side. "Look at this." She crooked a finger. "It's a Robert Browning quote—*I hold that a man should strive to the uttermost for his life's set prize.*'"

"His *life's set prize* certainly didn't include his wife." Chris walked to where he could inspect the backside of the gravestone. "No wonder she didn't want him back in the U.K. I read about him being unfaithful every chance he got."

Kayna shrugged. "It was a different era. Most men had

mistresses." A gaggle of seals closed on them, growling menacingly. Kayna jumped sideways. "What the hell? Do they bite?"

"How would I know?" Chris made shooing motions at the seals, and they withdrew a few inches. "Remember, I study dead things."

A battered gray Land Rover pulled as close to the cemetery as it could get, and Harold bent across Brynn to beckon her over. Kayna trotted close enough to hear what he wanted.

"When you're done here," Harold instructed, "walk back along the road that parallels the sea. Keep going until you hit the barracks. That's where we'll pick you up."

"Got it." She waved cheerily and tried to ignore Brynn in the driver's seat. It wasn't easy since it was a right-hand drive car, and he was closest to her. Her heart rate sped up. Dear God, but he was attractive, with a confident air that drew her like a lodestone.

"See you soon, Kayna." Brynn winked broadly before spinning the car in half a circle so it faced the other way. She stared after it as it disappeared in a cloud of dirty exhaust and gravel bits.

"Is there anything else you want to see here?" Chris asked, also gazing after the retreating Land Rover.

She shook her head. "If we're going to be friends," she said, "do me a favor and be plain with me when I make an idiot out of myself."

"Sure." He eyed her shrewdly. "What else are friends for?"

"I wouldn't know, I haven't had all that many."

"We're even then." The lightness left his voice. "Neither have I."

CHAPTER 7

Brynn stared after Kayna and Chris as they walked up the beach, away from him and the man who'd driven the Zodiac. The swing of Kayna's hips was mesmerizing. What a striking woman. For starters, she was tall, close to six feet. And she had Asian blood. Not full, but her eyes were a delicate almond shape and tilted slightly upward at their outer corners. Rather than brown, her irises were a startlingly clear, emerald shade. It was hard to tell how long her hair was, but it was coal black, and tendrils blew around her face from under her hood. Even beneath thick layers of clothes, he'd noted the swell of breasts and hips.

"She's quite a looker," the Zodiac driver spoke quietly. "By the way, I'm Harold Markham, ship's staff captain."

"Nice to meet you." Brynn nodded pleasantly. "Is Kayna married?"

Harold snorted laughter. "You don't waste any time. No, not according to her paperwork, but she's not overly friendly, either. I wouldn't get your hopes up if I were you, mate."

Brynn glanced sidelong at him, while still holding onto the Zodiac's anchor rope. "Sounds like she shot you down."

"I never got close enough to get *shot down*. Getting her to talk with me without ripping my head off has been a challenge. She has a hell of a short fuse." Harold shrugged. "Maybe she likes girls. It's the modern way. We blokes are becoming anachronisms."

"Speak for yourself. Circling back to practical matters, it would make it easier to load my things if you brought the Zodiac to the beach next to the barracks. Everything's packed, but I have a crap load of personal gear too. Since I'm not returning to South Georgia, I'm taking everything with me."

"Not returning?" Harold furled his brows. "For some reason I thought we were bringing you along to nursemaid your samples. I assumed you'd cobble a few flights together to get back here."

"Nope. They invited me to McMurdo to help out, but once I'm done with that, I'm returning to the States." Brynn hesitated. "You do have space on the ship, right? I have a few duffels and several boxes beyond my samples. It seems like a lot to me, but it's not really all that much."

"Yeah, we have plenty of room. What about your lab equipment?"

"It's not mine. It stays here for the next sucker—er, scientist loony enough to sign on for South Georgia. It's wild and dazzling and remote, but after two years I'm done. I'd have left anyway, even if they didn't ask for my help at McMurdo."

Harold took the rope back and buried the anchor hook in rocks and sand. "I felt the same way after my first few months at sea, like I'd wither and die if I couldn't get off the boat."

Brynn narrowed his eyes. "What happened?"

"Hard to say." Harold straightened and dusted damp sand off his gloved hands. "The sea, she sort of crept up on me. Got into my blood. At first I couldn't wait for voyages to end, but then I got itchy feet back on land." He shook his head. "I tell you, it was hell. For a couple of years, I didn't want to be on a ship, but I'd lost my comfort zone back in Liverpool. Eventually, the sea won."

Brynn thought about it. He was pretty certain South Georgia wouldn't win, no matter how long he stayed, but he didn't say so.

"Why'd you anchor the raft? Do you want me to shuttle loads from the barracks?"

"No. But we need to let Dr. Quan and Dr. McLaren know what we're doing. They both wanted off the ship. It'll give them a decent walk if they meet us by the barracks."

"Come on." Brynn gestured toward the Land Rover. "Let's tell them, and then we can get down to it. Like I said, I'm packed and ready to go."

Harold grabbed his arm and walked around so he faced Brynn. "Are you certain you want to come with us? The voyage will be rough."

"Oh, you've gotten that intel on your end too?" Brynn grinned. "The only other two guys here are meteorologists, and I've already heard the whole gloom and doom saga from them. I don't get seasick, so how bad could it be?"

Harold thinned his lips into a harsh line. "Bad. The ship could sink. Those enclosed, insulated lifeboats are so claustrophobic, they'd drive anyone to the brink of insanity. Between you and me, I'm not entirely certain the captain isn't going to turn back the way we came and beat a path to Ushuaia. He was studying the wind charts when I left and said we'd discuss it once I returned."

Brynn thought about his samples. If they never made it to McMurdo, it wouldn't be the end of the world. It might actually be a blessing since his uneasy feelings hadn't totally subsided, despite the benign nature of the slides he'd studied. "Doesn't matter." He squared his shoulders. "I'm still coming with you. If I end up in Argentina, I'll get home that much sooner."

His thoughts flickered to the woman he'd just met, and he wondered if she was a permanent part of the ship's staff or headed for McMurdo. He'd sensed her interest, but maybe she had a boyfriend—or even worse, a husband—stashed somewhere and was simply sex-starved, like him.

Guess I'll find out.

At the very least, there might be a hot, shipboard romance in the offing. Brynn whistled a jaunty tune, and Harold shot an odd look his way.

"You're sounding entirely too cheerful for someone heading into the eye of a storm."

"I wasn't thinking about the storm."

"If it's Dr. Quan who's caught your eye, I tell you, she's not exactly approachable."

Brynn glanced at Harold, but didn't say anything. He'd seen Kayna's cheeks turn pink, and she hadn't been in any hurry to let go of his hand. Maybe he'd get lucky. After two years of a monastic existence, his groin tightened in anticipation of holding a woman in his arms again.

KAYNA AND CHRIS ended up with time to spare once they walked the mile to the barracks. Since the Zodiac was busy hauling Brynn's paraphernalia, they wandered past buildings left over from the Falklands War, looked at Shackleton's crosses, and explored a hillside choked with wet vegetation.

Chris found a few fossils and some bones that he dropped into sample bags. It was closing on four when Harold came looking for them. Kayna and Chris helped load the last of Brynn's things into the Zodiac and got in, working around insulated packing crates.

"Where's Dr. McMichaels?" she asked.

"I left him aboard the ship with some helpers from the crew to get the rest of his biologic material situated," Harold replied. "Figured we could manage these last few boxes without him riding herd on us."

"Sounds good to me." Kayna shivered and wrapped her arms around herself. It had been alternately sleeting and snowing for over an hour. The raft ride back was choppy, and she was drenched with seawater by the time she made her way to her quarters. She stood under a hot shower for a long time to get feeling back into her feet. When she walked into the dining room for dinner, everyone else was already eating.

Brynn sat at a table with the other microbiologists. He nodded pleasantly to her before returning to what looked like a serious conversation. She nodded back, picked a table with Chris, other paleontologists, and some geologists, and made small talk, but her heart wasn't in it.

She retreated to her quarters as soon as dinner was over, but it was hard to concentrate on the book in her hands. She fidgeted, seeking a more comfortable position on her hard, narrow bunk, but it didn't help. Rather than printed lines, she saw Brynn's face and his to-die-for body, filling in unknown details with her imagination.

Stop it! Just stop.

She propped her back against a wall and closed the book. Brynn McMichaels looked like a Greek god, but that didn't mean he had any interest in her. He hadn't invited her to sit with him at dinner.

There weren't any empty seats. This isn't like a restaurant where you can drag an extra chair over. All of them are bolted to the floor.

Kayna wrapped her arms around herself and chivied Brynn from her mind. Not much percentage in thinking about him, anyway. The *Vladimir* was still moored in the bay surrounding Grytviken. She'd heard Harold and the captain arguing earlier. Despite the language barrier, the heated tone behind their words was unmistakable. Even in their relatively protected harbor, waves slapped against the ship's hull, making an ominous, hollow, booming noise. A pervasive sense of wrongness nipped at her heels and made her want to crawl under the covers, pull them over her head, and never come out.

Appalled by her cowardice—and recognizing her fantasies about Brynn as a diversion—she tossed the book aside and stood, determined to ferret out some answers. A few steps brought her to the surgery's door, but she stopped shy of opening it. Tracking

Harold down wasn't a good idea. Assuming she found him, which wouldn't be all that hard, and demanded to know what the hell was going on, he probably wouldn't tell her anything. Breath whooshed from her tense body, and the truth she'd been ignoring ever since she got back aboard ship flattened her with all the subtlety of a steamroller.

Something had shifted. She felt it in an alteration in the weave of the air surrounding her. When she breathed in, it smelled different. If she stuck out her tongue, it even tasted different, with a tart undernote that hadn't been there before.

Kayna walked back into her bedroom and sank to the floor in a cross-legged sit. She rested her forearms on her knees, palms upward in a position she remembered from years past, and opened herself to whatever the universe chose to shove her way. She hadn't done this since well before medical school, and she wondered if her spirit guide, a shiny black raven with striking amber eyes, would show himself.

After a few calming breaths, her Irish grandmother, Nana, rushed into her mind, followed by Kiki, her sister who'd died of an overdose at seventeen. Never comfortable with the magic coursing through her, Kiki had sought refuge in drugs with disastrous consequences.

Long moments passed, and the raven formed at the periphery of her visual field. He was hazier than she remembered, maybe because it had been so long since she'd invited a trance state. Kayna straightened her spine to align her chakras and emptied her mind of all but the raven. Nothing she could do for either Nana or Kiki. Maybe there wasn't a damned thing she could do about whatever was on this ship, but she needed to understand what she faced.

Darkness swirled, sucking her into a vision. The raven stood like a sentinel in her mind while creatures floated past, odd things with glowing red eyes and scaly hides. Softer, fluffier animals followed—more mammalian than reptilian—but they all fell off the edge of something and never crawled back up. A dead ringer for the Loch Ness monster slithered after the lot that had gone before it. Before disappearing, it swiveled its black, triangular-shaped head and bared a double-toothed row of shiny fangs. Knowing, golden eyes with vertical slit pupils—lambent, ancient, and deeply disturbing—caught hers.

The raven cawed low and fluffed his feathers to make himself larger.

"Kayna." The sea serpent mouthed her name. It rang hollowly in her mind.

Shock tightened her gut. How the fuck did the thing know her? She thrashed through possibilities to ask it, but her mind was mush. Next, she tried to terminate her trance state. When she couldn't, her throat thickened with fear, and she tasted bile, sour and acrid.

The serpent shimmered before her, morphing into a Chinese man with long, dark hair and penetrating eyes. Horror slammed her hard when she understood it was her long-dead father in a borrowed body. He'd been cremated, but his energy was unmistakable, and it throbbed against her in gray-black waves with sharp, hungry edges.

"What do you want?" she squeaked out.

"You. I want you." Chill laughter followed on the heels of Guiren Quan's words.

The raven ruffled his feathers into a menacing shield and hopped between Kayna and the ghostly image of her father.

"Why?" Kayna asked. "What do you want with me?" But Guiren didn't answer. His spectral form sidled closer, so close she felt cold emanate from him. Memories from her childhood flooded her: his rages, the beatings, the black sorcery, so different from her grandmother's Celtic magic. His death had been a relief. How the hell could he be here now?

Because she couldn't look away, she squeezed her eyes shut. When she opened them, her father was gone, along with everything else including the raven. Shaking with dread, she pinched the bridge of her nose between her thumb and forefinger. Her trance states used to bring information, not this obscure swamp of imagery—laced with fear. Her head pounded, and then she separated the sound from her vision and understood someone was knocking on her door.

"Hold up." Her voice sounded raspy, rusty. "I'll be there in a minute."

Dizziness threatened to unbalance her as she dragged herself upright, using a chair for assistance. She made her way unsteadily to the door, hoping she didn't look as rough as she felt, and tugged it open.

Harold stood in the corridor. His eyes widened when he looked at her. "Are you all right? Sorry if this is a bad time, but it can't be helped."

"It's fine." She stepped aside and gestured for him to come in. "I was meditating. Sometimes I go pretty deep."

Harold shoved the door shut with his foot and plopped into a chair. Kayna stared at him. It was the first time she'd seen him sit other than during meals. Dark stains ringed the armpits of his gray T-shirt, and his face was haggard and drawn. Kayna dragged the other chair close and sat, waiting to see what the staff captain wanted.

"We never had this conversation," he growled.

She spread her hands. "Fine. You have a right to patient confidentiality like everybody—"

"Stuff it." His sharp tone made her draw back. "I'm not your patient, and this isn't about me. Or maybe it is." He closed his teeth over his lower lip and balled his hands into fists where they lay in his lap. "You know nothing about how things work on ships."

"Never claimed to." She pursed her lips, wondering what he was leading up to. When he didn't say anything else, she asked, "Are you going to tell me why you're here?"

"I thought you were smarter than that."

"Look." A bright, brittle anger displaced her earlier foreboding. "I'm not a mind reader. You don't want me to posit theories, and you don't welcome questions. Why the hell are you even here?" She raked both hands through her hair and shoved it behind her shoulders to trail down her back.

"I'm here to offer you a choice. I've already cleared it with the two men who live in Grytviken."

"Huh? What kind of choice?"

Harold exhaled noisily. "I know you heard me talking with the captain. You don't speak Russian, so you have no idea what we said."

"Oh, I have some idea," she cut in dryly. "You were furious with one another."

He cracked a bitter smile. "We both read the wind charts and checked the weather, but came up with different conclusions. I wanted to head back toward South America, but the captain disagreed. Something happened to change his mind while we were ashore, but he wouldn't tell me what." Harold's mouth worked as if he'd bitten into something rotten. "A ship's hierarchy isn't a democracy. What the captain decides trumps everything."

Understanding rocked her, and Kayna's throat tightened. "You're afraid he's compromising our safety?"

"That's one interpretation." Harold spoke carefully. "There are others, but if you'd like, I'll fire up a Zodiac and leave you, and enough of your things to get by, in Grytviken. The Norwegians thought you might be handy if one of them was injured." He hesitated a beat. "There'll be cruise ships next November, but I'm certain you could find a clear weather window before that for someone to stop for you. Hell, you probably have money. You could call in a plane or helicopter from the Falklands."

Kayna scrambled to her feet and placed her hands on her hips. She stared down at Harold. "No, I don't have money. What I have are med school loans. Is anyone else getting this special deal?" she demanded. When Harold shook his head, she asked "Why me?"

He unclenched his fists and steepled his fingers so the tips touched. "A couple reasons. Dr. McMichaels can fill in as medical officer, so you've become redundant. And if the U.S. and Russia end up at war, I'm not certain McMurdo will even let us dock. We fly a Russian flag."

Kayna bit down on her lower lip. "Has it gotten so much worse then? The news broadcasts are in Russian, so I haven't followed them."

Harold nodded. "Yeah. Bad enough I'm worried about it. Poor Ukraine. Always in the middle."

He raised his blue eyes to meet her gaze. "I'm offering you a sure chance at staying alive, Doc. At least think about it before you toss it in my face. I took a huge chance doing this. If the captain finds out, the best thing that could happen is he'd fire me."

"And the worst?"

"It doesn't matter." Harold's voice held a flat, dead quality.

"People have divergent opinions all the time," she persisted.

"It doesn't matter," he repeated. "In the old days, they keelhauled men for less." Harold stumbled to his feet, the starch drained out of him. "I told you at the front end of this you don't understand how things work on ships. Basically, the captain's word and decisions are law. It's up to ship's staff to uphold them." He pushed his shoulders straight as if the motion cost him. "The seas will be bad, but this ship has seen rough seas before. If it was my money on the line, I might've made the same call the captain did." He gripped the door latch. "Five minutes, Doc. You can find me in my cabin."

She laid a hand on his arm. "You never exactly told me why you singled me out."

"If you weren't so self-absorbed, you'd have figured it out." He wrenched away from her grip and stalked into the corridor, pulling the door shut behind him.

She made her way into her living quarters and swept the small, neat space with her gaze, but didn't see any of it. What bombarded her was the vision Harold had wrenched her from. Her father. And her raven. Even though she'd hoped the bird would materialize, its return after such a lengthy hiatus couldn't be accidental. Her paranormal ability had ratcheted into high gear, and its message was crystal clear—she was needed right where she was.

Whatever Brynn McMichaels brought aboard the ship had wrapped her in its net. She'd sensed it from the moment she heard about his cultures. And she'd seen challenge flash from the sea serpent's eyes as it turned to stare at her in her vision— before it turned into her father and upped the ante considerably. What possible link could Guiren have with the sea serpent?

Not a sea serpent, she realized in a flash of shattering awareness. A Kiao. Her father's totem animal had been the Chinese water dragon.

Crap! What the fuck is going on here?

Aside from the dark, creepy mystery she was being drawn into, she had absolutely zero desire to be dumped on South Georgia Island for the next nine months. Harold had given her five minutes to make up her mind; at least double that had passed. She made her way out her door and up to Deck Five where his cabin was. Maybe she wasn't the only prescient one because his door swung open before she had a chance to knock. He dragged her inside and closed it. The cabin was fancier than anywhere else she'd seen on the ship, with polished inlaid wooden shelves and built-ins. Every shelf was filled to within an angstrom of capacity with books, CDs, DVDs, and labeled notebooks. His bed fit neatly into a corner with a reading lamp attached to a brass swing arm affair. A closed door at the far end of the cabin probably led to a bathroom.

Kayna clasped her hands behind her and faced him. "I

appreciate your intentions—and I promise I'll keep my mouth shut—about everything."

"Not leaving, huh?" He smiled sadly.

She shook her head. "No. For a bunch of reasons I can't go into, my place is here, and I'll take my chances. You said this ship has seen rough seas. Hell, we've had them on this trip already."

"Is it because of Dr. McMichaels?" He shot a discerning glance her way that cut right through her.

"No," she sputtered. "Christ! I only met him a few hours ago." She folded her arms beneath her breasts. "It's the twenty-first century. Not everything is about boy-meets-girl."

"Really?" Harold's upper class British accent dripped sarcasm. "You could've fooled me."

Kayna winced. "While we're on that topic, I'm flattered you seem to care about me, but—"

"Don't bother," he cut her off. "I'm not quite what you had in mind for partner material." He reached around her and yanked his cabin door open. "Thanks for the house call, Doc, but I really am fine." With his other hand, he pushed her into the corridor. "Be sure to lash yourself into your bunk tonight. The seas will pick up as soon as we leave this harbor."

Shocked by how abruptly he'd dismissed her, Kayna made her way down to her deck, but then kept going. She'd picked at her dinner, and her midsection felt hollow. Maybe she could find something to snack on if she wandered through the dining room. Aside from that, Harold's current affairs update was wretchedly unsettling. Had coming on this trip been a mistake? Would she be able to get home if war broke out?

As soon as she pushed the door open, she was sorry. Brynn, Zach, Abel, and another man she didn't recognize were ringed around a table playing cards and drinking.

"It's the Doc!" Abel yelled. "Join us."

Not seeing a graceful way out, she made her way toward them. Before she sat, she glanced at the table and realized she'd need a glass if she didn't want to swill scotch right out of the bottle.

"Go on." Brynn patted an empty chair. "Sit. I'll get you a glass." He rose. "So long as I'm headed for the galley, is scotch okay, or would you prefer something else?"

"Irish whiskey. If there's not any of that, then maybe some red wine."

"You got it."

He walked briskly toward the kitchen. Absent his heavy outer clothing, his body was a work of art, and she admired the fluid way his long legs covered the length of the room. He was dressed in tight jeans that outlined his muscled thighs and neat ass. A long-sleeved black shirt made from stretchy material showcased his broad shoulders. His eyes, which had been hidden by dark glasses earlier in the day, were an unusual hazel shade, greenish in this light, but she bet they'd shade to amber outdoors. His golden-brown hair had coppery streaks running through it. She swallowed a snort. Any woman would die to have hair like that.

"Earth to Dr. Quan." Zach waved his hand in front of her face.

"Sorry." She swiveled to face the group.

Zach elbowed Abel. "She says she's sorry," he mimed.

"Yeah, I say she's smitten." Abel grinned and whistled low. "He's quite a hunk, if I say so myself."

"Watch it, sweetheart." Zach lowered his eyebrows and glowered at his partner, but the corners of his mouth twitched with repressed humor.

"The two of you are impossible." Kayna grinned back, grateful for something to take her mind out of the grim place it had settled before she'd summoned her trance state. And the even grimmer place Harold's pronouncements and her father's visit had spawned.

"Hi." The fourth man reached across the table to shake her hand. "I'm Ted Doria. Nice to meet you, Doc."

"Nice to meet you too. Guess you haven't been on my

seasickness roster, or I'd have seen you before." She took in neatly trimmed blond hair and sharp blue eyes that probably didn't miss much. Ted was short, a bit pudgy, and dressed in black sweats. Although it didn't seem possible, he appeared to be about twenty. "Child prodigy?" She quirked a brow.

"Yup, a regular Doogie Howser." He drew his hand back and smiled engagingly, showing two deep dimples, one on each cheek. "Actually, I'm twenty-eight, but I skipped a bunch of high school and graduated when I was fourteen. I've had my doctorate for almost five years. No worries about offending me. I'm used to it. You should've seen me trying to teach at Yale." He rolled his eyes. "Got lots of lines like, 'What have you done with the professor?'"

Kayna settled back against her chair. Maybe this was exactly what she needed. A break from everything. If Harold's predictions came true, soon enough there'd be no casual sitting around the ship's dining room because the ship would be moving around too much to do anything but hang on. And if her father showed up again, she had no idea how she'd deal with it. One thing was certain, she needed help from her extremely rusty magical side.

Damn!

Of all the times to be in the middle of nowhere. Maybe she could raise her grandmother again. She could also go broke using the ship's sat phone to call her mother, but Moira Quan hated her power. Kayna had no reason to believe she'd be any more forthcoming talking about it now than she'd ever been.

Because there were too many unknowns to grapple with—at least right now—she glanced from one man to the next as she waited for Brynn to return with her whiskey. "I understand the seas are about to pick up. Do any of you need anything from my surgery, or are you pretty much over being seasick?"

CHAPTER 8

Brynn moved into the well-provisioned galley. It didn't take long to locate the Irish whiskey Kayna wanted. Armed with it and a glass for her, he made his way out of the storeroom behind the kitchen. A harsh, grinding noise vibrated, reverberating in the pit of his stomach. It took a moment for him to identify it as the anchor chain being winched upward. He stopped long enough to suck in a ragged breath. He'd ignored Sven's and Lucas's warnings. Hearing the same thing from Harold earlier today put a whole new face on things. When a staff captain cautioned you about weather, it was time to straighten up and pay heed.

But I didn't.

Yeah, because I wanted out of there so bad. Besides, by then, I'd met Kayna...

Watching her lithe form make its way across the room had given him a hell of a hard on, which surprised him. He thought he'd moved past spontaneous reactions to female beauty. Brynn reached down and rearranged himself to a less conspicuous position. The pleasant tingle as his fingers brushed engorged tissue might be a reaction to his months of isolation, but he didn't think so. He'd had several veiled—and even a few obvious

—invitations from female cruise ship passengers who wandered around South Georgia, but he hadn't been interested. He'd even had to shoo one particularly bold blonde out of his bedroom after she followed him inside. So much for no locks on the doors.

Kayna was a whole new ball game. Even buried beneath layers of winter clothing, she'd piqued his interest the moment he laid eyes on her. Tonight, her straight-as-a-stick black hair fell to the middle of her back, and dancer's tights covered her long legs. A clingy lavender tunic skirted her hips and outlined generous breasts, a slender waist, and a curvy behind. It was easy to imagine closing his hands around the lush globes of her ass. He took a deep breath, and then another. His current line of thought was doing less than nothing to encourage his cock to subside.

Once he had his libido under tattered control, Brynn arranged the liquor bottle to cover his tented jeans and made his way back to the group. "You're in luck." He placed the whiskey and glass in front of Kayna and slid into a vacant chair right next to hers.

"Thanks." She turned her clear, agate green eyes on him. Her skin was a warm bronze tone, and the finest sprinkling of freckles coated her nose. When she smiled, genuine warmth crinkled the tip-tilted edges of her eyes. Kayna picked up the bottle and examined the wax seal. "Wow. This must be the real deal." She turned the bottle in her hands, reading the label. "Yup!" Her smile broadened. "Bottled in Dublin. Doesn't get much more real than that."

"Do you need a knife for the wax?" Abel asked.

"Now that you mention it..." She extended a hand for the blade he dragged out of a jacket pocket. After she pulled the plastic protector off the cutting end, she held the stainless steel instrument up to the light. "Should I ask where this was last?"

"Probably not." Zach snickered. "Alcohol's a great disinfectant."

"True enough." She cut through the seal, peeled it away, and poured some of the thick, amber liquid into her glass, raising it to her nose and sniffing appreciatively. "Mmm. I could practically eat the smell. It's heavenly."

"Same way I feel about aged single malt scotch." Brynn raised his glass and tapped it against hers. "Cheers."

"Cheers." The others clinked glasses all around and echoed the toast before they drank. "What card game were you playing?" Kayna asked.

"We started with bridge," Ted answered, "but Brynn and I were the only ones who knew how to play, so we got bored and moved on to poker."

"I'm in." She set her glass down and flexed her fingers before shuffling a deck of cards. "Texas Hold 'Em?" Nods rustled through the group and she dealt.

Brynn was much more interested in Kayna than the card game. Watching her slender fingers work the cards, the game's nuances slipped away, and he managed to end up twenty bucks in the hole after a few dollar-betting rounds. Dredging the last of his ones out of his wallet, he turned his palms upward. "You guys cleaned me out."

"We take credit." Abel shot a predatory smile his way.

"I'll bet you do." Brynn poured another finger of scotch into his glass. "Nope, the booze is almost gone, and I'm broke. My great-granddaddy would've said it was a good time to call it even."

"What did he do?" Kayna sipped her whiskey. Her cheeks had developed a rosy sheen, and her eyes glowed in the muted light of the dining room.

Brynn rolled his eyes. "He was about the only member of the whole damn family who wasn't a doctor. He was one of the few investment bankers who came out of the crash of twenty-nine with his nuts intact."

She laughed, a rich mellow sound that warmed him. "You make him sound like a squirrel."

"In a lot of ways he was," Brynn replied. "He hid enough assets to escape the worst of the carnage."

A thunderous crash boomed, and everyone's heads snapped up. "Crap!" Zach muttered. "I remember that sound. It's waves hitting the hull."

"Not that I've done much blue water sailing," Brynn said, "but the boat I caught to South Georgia never made that noise."

"This one has a double reinforced hull to protect it when the water is full of pack ice," Ted explained. Drawing a pen and small notebook from a pocket, he sketched something and flipped it so Brynn could see.

The ship pitched, and Brynn grabbed the scotch. Kayna made a dive for the whiskey, but some spilled before she caught the bottle. "Damn!" She glanced at the dark spot spreading atop the waffle-weave material that sat on all the dining tables to keep things from sliding onto the floor.

"Be glad you didn't lose the whole thing," Zach said. "Maybe we should move this party upstairs to the bar."

"Where's that?" Brynn asked. "About the only places I've been so far are here and my rooms on Deck Five."

"Follow us." Abel stood and gripped the table's edge to stabilize himself. "Better to be up there anyway, at least for us since our cabin is closer."

Kayna followed Abel and Zach out of the dining room, the whiskey bottle clutched in one hand. Brynn chucked the almost empty scotch bottle in the kitchen dumpster. If they were headed for a bar, it stood to reason there'd be more liquor there, except maybe he'd had enough. If the seas were deteriorating as fast as they seemed to be, it might be better to stick with the pleasant buzz in his head and not go for anything more debilitating.

Ted fell into step beside him and motioned toward a steep, narrow set of stairs. "Go that way. If it gets as bad as it was when we left Buenos Aires, about all you'll be able to do is shuttle between your bunk and the john. Booze and a rocking ship are a bad combo."

"Did you get seasick?" Brynn asked as they crested the stairs, and Ted pointed to their left.

"No, but it's damned unpleasant to try to do anything when the ocean's going nuts. Even reading is hard."

"Thanks. I'll keep it in mind." Moving forward in time with the ship's rhythm, he followed Ted's directions and trailed down a long corridor.

"Hey! They made it," Kayna called from one corner of a large, cozy room with couches attached to every wall and round tables bolted to the floor at intervals.

"We're playing twenty questions to get to know one another," Zach said. "It's better than talking about the Russia-U.S. debacle."

"No kidding, and it's too bumpy to play cards," Abel added. "They'd bounce right off the table."

Brynn stabilized himself on the doorframe and glanced around before heading for where the others sat. The space behind the bar was empty. "Where's the barkeep?" he asked.

"It's self-service on the honor system," Ted replied. "Most of the booze is in the back room in crates that are nailed to the shelving. Everything that's not tacked down would end up broken." He grinned. "Guess my Carrie Nation speech didn't influence you."

"It did." Brynn returned Ted's smile and made his way toward the others. "I just like to know how things work."

KAYNA CURLED DEEPER into the corner seat where she'd wedged her body. The booming from waves slapping the hull had developed menacing overtones, and the ship's motion was intensifying. Not only pitching and yawing, but rolling too.

"Princess here grabbed the best seat in the house," Zach noted. "The rest of us risk ending up on the floor."

"You spent enough time there last time the sea really kicked up," Abel teased.

"That is so not funny," Zach groused.

"Do you have your patch on?" Kayna asked. At his nod, she went on, "It's much easier to control motion sickness if you get an edge up on it."

"Yeah, I seem to remember you telling me that a few days ago," Zach muttered.

"He always was a stubborn nelly." Abel rolled his eyes. "Didn't think he'd get seasick."

"Motion sickness is scarcely a moral weakness," Brynn cut in. "It's like altitude sickness. Some people get it and others don't. It's related to your physiology." He dragged a padded chair to the open side of the round table and sat in it. "Damned heavy piece of furniture."

"That's so it won't spill your sorry ass onto the carpet," Ted said and wrestled with a chair of his own. "Except it doesn't always work." He settled into his seat. "A few days ago, I got launched halfway across this room."

Kayna inclined her head in Brynn's direction and waved an expansive hand at the group. "They're all trained in the scientific method, which is sit back and wait, preferably doing instant reruns under multiple conditions. So they adopted a trial and error stance on seasickness, whereas I'd rather have them institute countermeasures before they're needed."

Brynn caught Kayna's gaze and held it. As she suspected, his eyes changed with the light and glowed a soft moss shade with golden flecks.

"The reason it's such a bitch," he observed, "is because it takes way more time and medicine to control something once it has a toehold."

"No kidding." She winked and could've kicked herself. What the hell was she doing?

"How about our game, Doc?" Zach slapped a hand on the table.

"I presume you mean me," Kayna said, still lost in Brynn's eyes.

"He could mean me." Brynn leaned back against his chair.

"Aw hell, look at them." Abel tipped his chin toward Kayna and Brynn. "Maybe we should call it a night and give them some privacy."

"That's really not necessary," Kayna began, but Abel shook his head.

"Nah, it's nearly ten. Past our bedtime anyway." Zach pushed to his feet and winked at Abel. "Coming, sweetheart?"

"Wouldn't miss it for the world. I adore our monkish existence." Abel rolled his eyes. "I bet we got the only bunk beds on this ship."

"My cabin has them." Ted stood too. "But it's only me in there, so I took the bottom."

"See you guys tomorrow," Brynn said. "I'm more or less moved in, so you're welcome to visit my etchings, er cultures." He laughed, but it held an awkward edge, as if joking about whatever was in his lab cost him.

Kayna sharpened her gaze and refocused on Brynn. "Want to tell me about those cultures?" she murmured once the others had cleared the bar. When he didn't answer, she said, "Give me a sec. I've had enough to drink tonight." She walked the Irish whiskey across to a bin behind the bar, struggling to maintain her balance, then returned to the couch.

He moved from his chair to sit next to her. "I'd rather talk about other things. Tell me about yourself. I've had two years with my colonies, but I just met you."

Smooth, he's smooth.

A part of her was glad for any excuse to put off knowing more about whatever he was cultivating in his lab. She twisted to face him. "Not all that much to tell. I grew up in Seattle, went to medical school at U.W., and then did my residency in internal medicine at the University of Minnesota." She dusted her palms together. "See, told you my life was pretty simple."

He closed his hands around hers. The warmth from his body drew her, and she didn't pull away.

"I didn't want the expurgated version. It tells me less than nothing about you, other than you're bright and driven. How'd you grow up? Do you have siblings? How do you like to spend your spare time? Are you part of this ship's staff permanently, or are you headed for McMurdo with everyone else?"

Picking the least personal question she said, "I'm going to McMurdo." Kayna sucked in an uneasy breath. She understood with dismal clarity that outside her immediate family, she'd held virtually everyone except Derek at arm's length. Since he'd spurned her, it didn't exactly engender confidence in baring her soul's secrets again.

"What about your family?" she countered, buying time. While she focused on Brynn, willing him to talk with her—and adding a smidge of a compulsion spell to loosen his tongue—the raven pushed into her mind.

She must've looked startled because Brynn asked, "Are you all right?" Concern shone from his eyes.

"Sure." Kayna tried very hard to sound normal. The raven sat straighter her mind's eye and nailed her with its beady avian gaze. Confused by the bird's presence, she cleared her throat. "Tell me about you," she urged. "When I asked about your family, you didn't say anything."

"Okay." He tightened his hands around hers and scooted closer, so the length of his thigh rested against her leg. "I grew up in the Boston metropolitan area. Both my parents were surgeons, and I went to private schools. Even did a stint at a ritzy private high school in London to enhance the odds of being accepted at a good medical school. I played sports—practically all of them—for the same reason. I was good enough at fencing that I turned down an offer to join the Olympic team." He took a breath, and emotion flashed through his eyes—haunted and sad, but gone so quickly Kayna wasn't certain she'd seen anything.

"I never did any of those things," she said softly. "And I got into medical school."

A wry smile framed his perfect teeth. "Yes, but not Harvard."

"Was Harvard important to your parents?" she prodded, wanting to know more about the man sitting next to her. The raven lifted its head, its beak opening and closing. Apparently, it wanted to know more about Brynn too.

"Important barely covers it." His voice vibrated with bitterness. "It took me a while to find myself, to figure out who I was. My first act of insubordination was getting a Ph.D. in microbiology and working for a while before I went to med school. My second was picking emergency medicine as a subspecialty."

"Why were those things disobedient?"

"My parents saw the Ph.D. as a waste of time and working in the E.R. as bottom barrel medicine."

Kayna drew back. "I'm not liking them very much, listening to you. Surely, they had some redeeming features. They loved you enough to want a decent life for you."

He let go of her hands and shook his head. "To be honest, I have no idea how they felt or what they wanted. We never talked about things like that. Mom's still alive, but we haven't spoken in the two years since I left for South Georgia."

"Oh."

"That's it?" He placed a hand on the side of her face and turned her to look at him. "Just 'oh'?"

Kayna swallowed uncertainty, not sure what to say. "Your life sounds so barren." *A lot like mine, actually.* "Are you married?"

"Why, Doctor." He cocked his head to one side, but didn't stop running his thumb along her jawline. "What a leading question."

"Are you going to answer it?" Her throat was dry, and she'd never been more aware of a man's presence. He was alive, electric. If she closed the few inches between their faces, she could taste his lips. He wouldn't rebuff her. She sensed his interest, but the wife question was important. The raven spread its wings, flew a few feet, and settled again. Approval gleamed from its eyes. Kayna did a double take. Her spirit guide had never shown his beak in all the years she was with Derek, but he was certainly front and center tonight.

It's almost as if he's giving Brynn his seal of approval…

Oh for the love of Pete. I'm extrapolating all over the fucking place.

Brynn's voice took on a husky note. "I had a girlfriend, another M.D. We were together for years. She wanted more than I could give. Eventually, she left me." He glanced down, and Kayna sensed his internal conflict, raw and palpable, before he met her gaze again. "I don't blame her. I wasn't very…present."

"Maybe, she'd still be open to—"

Brynn shook his head. "Too much bad water under the bridge. She told me not to find her after she left. I ignored that wish, exactly like I'd ignored most of her other ones." A muscle twitched beneath one of his eyes, betraying tension. "The row we had once I tracked her down wasn't pretty. Not too long after that, I landed a job with a British bioresearch firm and left for South Georgia Island."

"We have at least a few things in common," she murmured.

"Like what?" He inscribed small circles on her cheek before moving his hand down her neck.

"I had a boyfriend—another doc, like your partner—but he dumped me once I told him I was going to McMurdo for a year."

Brynn looked at her, his eyes brimming with emotions he probably didn't let out to play often. When he angled his head and closed his mouth over hers, she wrapped her arms around his shoulders and drew him close. Hard planes of muscle met her fingertips, and she reveled in how good he felt. His crisp masculine scent, sandalwood and amber, eddied about her. When he ran his tongue along the seam in her lips, she opened her mouth and welcomed him. He tasted sweet like the scotch, and his lips became harder and more demanding as she let him explore her mouth.

Brynn threaded his arms around her and buried a hand in her hair, cradling the back of her head. Her breath quickened, and her nipples hardened where they pressed against his chest. It had been months since she'd had sex. Even before her blowup with Derek, he hadn't touched her for a long time. Need licked at her, hot and urgent, in a rush of hormones all too aware her biological clock was running out of time. Encouragement glittered in the raven's eyes, and she felt him urge her on.

It would be easy to stretch out on the cushions, slide her tights down, and draw Brynn into her. Too easy. Her body screamed for the man in her arms, but common sense intruded and she pulled away. "You're a very attractive man, but this isn't a good idea." Her throat was thick with wanting him, and the words came out garbled.

"Bad call," the raven spoke up.

Holy crap snackers! I've had too much to drink.

Kayna made a grab for rationality, but the raven stayed put, no longer talking, but with his avian attention glued to her.

"I'd try to argue," Brynn said, his voice harsh and raspy, "except I agree." He kneaded the back of her neck. It felt heavenly, and she leaned into his touch. "Not that I don't want to make love with you—" his gaze, dark gold now, bored into her "—because I do. Very much. But I want to take this slow. Get to know you."

His words made something warm and fluttery begin in her belly and spread outward. She untangled her arms from his body and got to her feet. "We'll have time to figure this out."

"Maybe," he said carefully, and something in his voice— perhaps regret—snared her attention.

"Why maybe?"

"You're staying at McMurdo. I plan to go home after a couple weeks there."

With her body buzzing from his touch, and her spirit guide

still making his presence—and opinion—known, she murmured, "One step at a time. We'll see how things unfold."

Brynn looked at her, his hazel gaze unreadable. "It's been a long day. Both of us should try to get some sleep."

She nodded and made her way out of the bar, lurching with the ship's motion. Brynn had his secrets, like she had hers. She sensed his inner turmoil with her paranormal antennae. It was unlikely he could see into her with the same level of accuracy, but none of that mattered. Whether they'd even arrive at McMurdo remained to be seen.

Hell, he may not be able to live with my secrets even if we make McMurdo.

And I might not be able to stomach his.

Secrets aside, why did my raven show up?

Brynn would be a lot easier to accept if his cultures weren't part of the deal. With that unsettling thought scattering her lust like ashes, Kayna plodded back to her surgery, let herself in, and made her way to her bed. The liquor she'd drunk made her head spin, and she hoped no one needed her before morning.

She'd just shut her eyes when the raven formed behind her closed lids. "What do you want?" she asked, but he didn't answer. Instead, an image of the Kiao from her earlier trance state formed. As she stared at the mystical Chinese dragon, she recalled that her father had a tattoo just like it inked onto his upper arm.

Kayna flopped onto her stomach and supported her head with her hands, no longer sleepy. The same questions that had plagued her earlier came screaming back to taunt her. Why would her father show up now? What could he possibly have to do with McMurdo, the southern ocean, or Brynn's accursed samples?

CHAPTER 9

Brynn watched Kayna walk unsteadily out of the bar. It took discipline to hold back from dashing after her and crushing her against him. The intensity of his need shocked him. There'd been a few moments when his normally conservative nature had damn near crumpled, and he'd come outrageously close to tipping her against the couch cushions so he could cover her body with his own. She'd been as aroused as he was. She might've protested, but he didn't think so.

What's wrong with me? Is it that I haven't had a woman in so long?

He rolled the question around in his mind, but his two plus years of celibacy wasn't driving things. Something about Kayna was deeply mesmerizing, and he couldn't wait to pull her into his arms again.

He held the couch's edge in a death grip, but relaxed his hold as he relived how her lips felt pressed against his own. When his imagery summoned the firm points of her nipples pebbled against his chest, he shuttered his mind. It was past time to head for his quarters. If he didn't, he'd end up pounding on her door, once he figured out where it was. The need to hold her again was sharp, insistent, and damn near irresistible.

Brynn worked his way to his feet, almost fell when the ship pitched, and was glad he hadn't had anything further to drink. He made his way out of the bar toward the stairs. Kayna's scent clung to him. She smelled of summer wildflowers, jasmine, and a musky femaleness that made him ache for her.

Another realization intruded as he closed on the stairs. He wasn't anxious to get anywhere near his colonies of archaea, but he needed to check on them. He'd secured the bins, but wanted to make certain the temperature and humidity controls were working properly. Almost as if thinking about them tipped some galactic mechanism, a faint whooshing vied with the waves crashing against the ship's hull. He mounted the stairs, and the sibilant rustling got louder.

Lub-dub. Lub-dub. Lub-dub.

Brynn ground to a halt with his hands curled like claws around the railings lining both sides of the stairwell. It wasn't possible, but the hum pummeling him sounded like a heart pumping blood. His stomach twisted sourly, and acid jetted into his throat, burning like liquid fire.

"Hey, mate," sounded from the top of the stairs. "I'm in a bit of a hurry."

Brynn glanced upward and saw Harold, not hanging onto anything, waiting for him to clear the stairwell. "Sorry." He pulled himself up the remaining risers. "Hold a moment," he said before Harold could leave. "Do you hear anything unusual?"

Harold's features took on a pained look, as if he were trying to be pleasant, but the effort cost him. "It's waves hitting the hull," he explained. "See, this ship's steel frame is doubled to provide strength—"

"I know that part," Brynn broke in, aware his own heart was beating much too fast. "I mean something other than that."

"No." Harold cast an odd look his way. "Don't get your feathers ruffled, but I'd lay off the booze for the rest of the trip, buddy. It's going to get much rougher than this. Sorry, mate, but they need me in the engine room." With a clatter of leather boot heels on linoleum, he disappeared down the stairs.

Brynn stared after him. The slithery, whooshing sound was more distinct up here than it had been lower down. But Harold couldn't hear it. "Christ on a fucking crutch," Brynn muttered. "What the hell does that mean? Have I stumbled into an Antarctic version of *The Twilight Zone?*"

A sinking sensation engulfed him and made his head pound. He knew exactly what he'd done—gone off and left the cultures to fend for themselves in a brand new environment. He'd transgressed, and now a paranormal piper floated in the wings with both hands stuck out for payment.

Brynn slumped against the nearest wall. While his samples didn't seem malevolent like Micah's—at least not yet—having them summon him was so off the wall he could scarcely wrap his head around it. He bit down on his lip until it hurt. No matter what it cost him, he had to get a grip. And damned fast. The slides he'd looked at had been so normal it was scary…

Lub-dub. Lub-dub. Lub-dub.

He would've jammed his hands over his ears, except he needed them to hang on to the bucking ship. Shoulders set in determination, and back ramrod straight, he marched to the first cabin where he'd left his colonies and shoved the door open. All the bins were right where he'd left them, nice and secure in their heat and humidity controlled bays. He flicked on a bank of overheads, hunted down a lab coat, mask, and gloves, and double checked that the cultures had made the transition intact. Midway through the batch of bins he stopped. Something had changed.

The heart sounds. They'd vanished. Just like that. Brynn tilted his head and listened intently, but the only thing he heard was the slap of waves churning against the hull several decks down.

"I'm losing my mind," he said to the bins, but if he'd guessed right, they'd chivied him into taking care of them. Once he entered their environment, acting the role of responsible scientist making certain they'd survive, they didn't need to rattle his cage any further.

Since thinking was counterproductive, he cleared his mind. Brynn worked as quickly as he could, finished in one cabin, and did barebones minimum in the companion pod. It would've been easy enough to fit all his samples into one cabin, but long habit made him split them up. In case something happened in one pod, the other cultures wouldn't be affected. Normally he cared about things like that, but tonight all he wanted to do was finish up and get the hell away from his sample bins, so he could sort out what just happened.

He let himself into his cabin and hunted for a lock on his door. When he didn't find one, he felt like the worst kind of chump. No matter what was amiss with the archaea, there was no fucking way they could creep out of their bins and find their way into his cabin. He stripped off his clothes and stood in the shower for a long time. It wasn't easy because he had to hang onto metal grab bars to stay on his feet. After he hit the mixer by accident with an elbow and the water nearly scalded him, he decided he was clean enough and shut the shower off.

Dry but for his hair, and wearing a fresh pair of dark blue sweats, he stretched out in his bunk. It wasn't long enough, but that worked in his favor because he wedged himself in. The ship weaved, rocked, and rolled. He glanced at the boxes of books he'd tossed into his cabin and left his bunk to break one open. His lifelong penchant for organization served him well, and he pulled both volumes of Harrison's *Internal Medicine* out, chucking them on his bed one at a time.

He was almost certain the books wouldn't have what he needed, but they were the only medical texts he had with him. Propped against a couple pillows, he searched the index, first for delusions and then for hallucinations.

"All right." He spoke aloud to steady himself. "I'm too old to develop schizophrenia, plus I don't have any of the other symptoms of it, like emotional blunting. It's not like I've heard anything else that isn't there." He narrowed his eyes in thought. If he hadn't succumbed to some crazy, atypical mental disorder, he'd have to look elsewhere for explanations.

He dropped the open book across his stretched out legs and tented his fingers in front of him. The pressure of flesh against flesh was reassuring, and he thought about the hypnotic quality of the colonies' vocalizations back on South Georgia—and their ability to appear normal under his microscope when his gut told him they were anything but. He felt like a superstitious fool, but he'd be damned if he wasn't half-convinced the organisms needed something from him, that they wanted to make certain they got to McMurdo. They couldn't get there on their own, so they'd co-opted him.

How was that even possible? He shook his head, feeling bewildered.

He tried to argue himself out of the archaea working as a group to coerce him into transporting them to McMurdo, but the twang of rationality intruded. He'd read enough about quorum sensing to understand the proks were capable of rough group intelligence, but he'd never taken the concept seriously.

Pushing the books aside, he got off the bed and rustled his laptop out of its case, along with the cord to plug it in. There was no Internet to tap into, but maybe if he spent the rest of the night reviewing his notes and measurements on the proks from when he'd first begun to grow them, he'd find the key to their current eccentricity. In the universe he was used to, everything was explainable. This had to be too.

Back in his bunk, he pulled the duvet over his legs, opened his computer, and booted up. Brynn shut his eyes for a moment, and Kayna's lovely face shimmered across his mind. She'd seemed interested in his samples. Depending on what he found in his data search tonight, could he trust her enough to help him puzzle through this?

~

Kayna woke because the ship tossed her against strips of leather lashing her into her bunk. Pale, gray light filtered into her cabin. At least she'd slept until morning. Shaking her head made her temples pound, and reminded her she overdid the whiskey last night. Sleep was one word for how she'd passed the night, but drinking herself into oblivion was closer to the truth.

She stretched her arms over her head and undid the straps that kept her from being tossed onto the floor. Despite her headache, the whiskey's effects had ebbed, and she didn't have to try very hard to sense the same peculiarity that had nicked her nerve endings as soon as Brynn and his samples were stowed on board.

Brynn. God! What a hunk of a man.

She couldn't remember being so attracted to anyone—ever. Before she could stop herself, an image of being cradled in his arms with his lips nibbling and teasing hers filled her mind. Kayna rolled to a sit, planted her feet on the floor, and wrapped her arms around herself. She had to hold onto whatever resolve had driven her from the bar last night. It would be much too easy to tumble into bed with Brynn. Christ! Even her spirit guide was playing matchmaker. What the hell did that mean?

Maybe it doesn't mean a thing. He could be so overjoyed to be in my head after all these years he doesn't want to leave.

Except she didn't think so.

If I'm not careful, I risk getting sucked into the craziness Brynn brought on board.

Maybe he doesn't know.

He'd have to. A person, even one without a shred of paranormal ability, would have to sense there's something bizarre about his cultures. For Christ's sake, Zach and Abel picked up on it over a sat phone connection. Maybe Ted too, for all I know.

"Stop! Just stop!"

She'd held internal conversations with herself since she was a child, and they rarely led to solutions, only mired her deeper in the problem du jour. "I don't know enough to make any decisions." She kept her voice firm. "Preserving an open mind is my best friend."

Relieved to have a direction, and equally relieved her raven hadn't shown up this morning, she made her way into the bathroom, splashed water on her face, and brushed her teeth. Yesterday's sweats were clean enough, never mind she'd slept in them. She yanked the top over her head so she could don a bra, and then pulled everything back into place. She was bending to lace her shoes when someone knocked on the surgery door right before pushing it open.

Chris walked in, looking fairly intact. "Morning, Doc."

"Just a sec." Kayna finished tying her shoes and moved to her drug cabinet.

"Yeah, I guess I still need a chemical assist, but the other reason I'm here is Abel sent me."

She dropped pills into envelopes and turned to face Chris. "Is it Zach?"

Chris nodded. "Guess he had a wretched night."

"Damn!" She handed the envelopes to Chris. "If it's not too far out of your way, could you drop by the galley and get a couple pieces of dry toast and a mug of either weak tea or clear broth?"

"For Zach?"

"Yes. Empty tummies make motion sickness worse."

"Sure, but from the sound of things, I'm not thinking he'll be able to keep anything down." Chris hesitated. "Abel looked really, really anxious. I stopped by their cabin to see if they wanted to come to breakfast, and he sent me to find you."

"Thanks for being willing to help. See you in their cabin in a few."

Chris inclined his head and left, using both hands for balance after he stuffed the pills into one of his pockets. She wondered how he'd manage carrying food, but decided he was resourceful enough to figure it out.

She snapped up Phenergan and a few other things from her supply cabinet, added them to her medical bag, and trotted down the hall to Zach and Abel's cabin. Despite wearing a patch, his seasickness was, indeed, back in spades, and it took a while to get him situated.

True to his word, Chris showed up balancing a plate with both crackers and toast and a covered container of steaming broth. "Need anything else?" He quirked a brow Kayna's way.

"Nope." She flashed a smile. "Thank you."

"No worries." Chris focused on Zach. "You do what the good doctor says, you hear? We need you well to play cards with us."

Zach gave a feeble thumbs up sign, and Chris patted his shoulder and left. After medicine, broth, and toast, Zach looked a little less green.

Kayna dusted her palms together. "Piece of cake. Everything should be fine now. I'll check on you boys in an hour or two, but I'm as close as a holler. If I'm not in my surgery, you can find me in the dining room."

She gathered her bag and headed toward the surgery, intent on dropping off her supplies and finding something for breakfast. Because she wasn't paying attention, she ran right into Brynn. "Ooph! Sorry."

He reached out a hand and steadied her. "Whoa, there." A smile turned his face into something so profanely beautiful, she couldn't look away. "Is doctoring slow enough you're out trolling for business?"

He kept his hand on her, and the warmth of his fingertips caressing her body made her long to launch deeper into his arms. It took gargantuan effort, but she drew back, still fixated on his eyes. Greenish in the muted light of the hall, they flickered with warmth, caring. If she didn't watch it, her resolution to keep her distance—at least until she knew more—would go up in smoke.

He glanced at the bag in her hand. "Guess I was wrong about things being slow. Looks as if you've been working already."

She smiled ruefully. "It's not as if I have a backup crew, so it's a good thing house calls are convenient on this ship. I'm done for now, though, and I was about to hunt down breakfast."

"Excellent." He waited while she opened the door to her surgery, shoved her bag inside, and stood over the sink to wash her hands. Brynn moved to her side and said, "I was coming to see if I could talk you into eating with me."

Kayna's heart did a funny little flip-flop. "I'd love to." She dried her hands before she took a good hard look at Brynn that wasn't totally clouded by wanting him. Smudges darkened the skin beneath his eyes, and his face held a drawn look. "Rough night?" she asked.

"You could say so."

"Did you sleep at all?" she asked. He shook his head, so she went on, "If you need something for seasickness…"

He waved her to silence. "Nah. I wish they made a pill for what kept me up, but there isn't one." He raked a hand through his copper-streaked hair. "Come on. Everything always looks better over eggs and coffee."

"Best offer I've had all day." Kayna closed and locked the door and walked down the stairs with Brynn right behind her.

CHAPTER 10

Brynn watched Kayna, her head bent in thought, steer a collision course right into him. He could've said something, warned her, but wanting to feel her against him, no matter how it happened, outstripped everything. Relieved she hadn't come up with a spate of polite excuses and disappeared into her surgery after he suggested breakfast, he followed her down the stairs to the dining room.

It was closing on eight-thirty, and only a few other passengers still sat over their food. Brynn narrowed his eyes. "They're hanging on to the tables," he observed.

"Indeed they are. Let's settle over there." She pointed at a corner table. "It might be a little less rocky."

Filling a plate with food from the buffet-style serving ledge was moderately challenging. Maneuvering back across the room without spilling it turned out to be a trick and a half. By the time he set his plate on the table and realized he had to stumble across the room again if he wanted coffee, he blew out a breath and mumbled, "This isn't easy."

"No." Kayna slapped her plate across from his. "It isn't, but one more trip should do it. At least that waffle weave stuff on top of the tables keeps the low profile items like plates from sloughing onto the floor." She grinned ruefully. "One morning I made the mistake of mixing up a pot of coffee—of course it's as wretched by the pot as it is by the cup, since all of it's instant. Anyway, I'd no sooner set the pot on the table when the ship danced a jig, and my coffeepot bounced onto the floor."

"I get the picture." He started for the hot water carafe at the far end of the room. He didn't care much for instant coffee, either, but all he'd had on South Georgia was tea. Buckets of black tea. Any coffee was better than none.

Finally, after so long his breakfast was growing cold, he settled into a chair across from Kayna. The chairs were bolted to the floor. So was the table, which made adjusting the gap between his body and the table impossible. He took a forkful of scrambled eggs, chewed, and swallowed. "Gives you a whole new respect for the guys who set sail in those wooden buckets a hundred years ago," he said.

"I'll say." She rolled her eyes. "They were tough. Of course, they didn't live very long. Lots of them were dead before they hit fifty." She munched her way through a piece of toast slathered with butter and jam. "Want to talk about what kept you awake?"

"Yes, as a matter of fact, I do." He set his fork down and took a swallow of coffee. "Even bad coffee's better than no coffee. Try living on tea for two years."

"Last night," she prodded.

He grinned. "I recognize that tactic. They teach it in residency. It keeps patients on track and you on time."

She cocked her head to one side and narrowed her eyes. "True, but you're still sidestepping the question, even though you said you were willing to answer it."

He buttered a slice of toast and used it to sop up some egg on his plate. "Last night, you found out a whole lot more about me than I found out about you. The only personal thing you told me was that you had a boyfriend who dumped you."

"And you'd like to know more before you confide in me?" She quirked a brow. It cut across her golden skin like a startled bird's wing.

"Not exactly the way I'd have put it. I'll admit I'm woefully out of practice, but don't people usually trade histories before they dig deeper?"

She speared a piece of fruit into her mouth, looking thoughtful. "Doctor patient relationships don't work that way. People spill their guts to me without any expectation I'll tell them anything about myself beyond whatever's hanging on my ego wall."

"You're not my doctor." He glanced down and realized he'd eaten everything on his plate.

"That's true, I'm not. Are you still hungry?" She followed the direction of his gaze.

"A little, but not so much I'm willing to traipse back across the room balancing something."

"It's easier for me since I've been on this ship for a few days. What would you like? I'll bring it when I get a refill on my coffee and a sweet roll."

"How about this?" He pushed to his feet, holding the table's edge for balance. "I'll run the coffee gauntlet, and you can bring us an assortment of sweet rolls. I'm partial to cinnamon buns if Cook's made any."

"Done." She stood. "I take cream and sugar, not too much of either."

Once they were settled again, he worked his way through a cinnamon roll, thick with butter, nuts, and raisins. "Your family?" he urged, once he was done chewing.

"What about them?"

"I told you about mine."

She focused on her plate, and he could almost visualize her mind churning as she tried to put the best face on what he guessed was a less-than-pretty picture. He considered saying something encouraging, but kept his mouth shut. She'd have to find the words in her own time.

Kayna shrugged self-consciously. "It's like I said last night. There's not much to tell."

"Maybe there's more than you think." Brynn reached across the table and laid his hand atop one of hers. "You have Asian blood. Where'd it come from?"

"Dad. He was Chinese."

"And your mom?" Brynn traced a finger over the back of her hand.

"Irish. Her mother lived with us, so I was pretty much raised by the Celtic half of things."

"Did your father leave?"

Her mouth twisted before she smoothed her features. "In a manner of speaking. Alcohol got him. He died when I was ten."

"I'm sorry."

"Don't be. It was good in some ways. He held a Ph.D. in environmental biology, which meant he wasn't home much, between teaching and research projects. When he was, though, he was always angry and yelling. Nothing was ever good enough. He —" She shook her head. "Never mind. Mom and Nana had a hell of a time making ends meet once he was gone. Nana took in sewing and Mom cleaned houses, but Kiki and I didn't want for much."

"A sister?"

Kayna nodded. "Three years younger than me."

"What's she doing now?"

"Bad question." Kayna snatched her hand from beneath his. "She didn't make it."

Questions rumbled through his mind. "It's none of my business, but did she develop one of the childhood cancers?"

"No." Kayna set her jaws together so hard muscles flexed in her neck. "Drug overdose when she was seventeen."

"I'm so sorry. It must've been wretched for your mom and grandmother. And for you."

"Gran was dead by then, but yeah, it really tore Mom and me up. Kiki didn't die right away, which made things worse. They kept her on life support for weeks."

Brynn searched for words, but she shook her head, her eyes liquid with pain. "There's nothing you can say." Her voice grated roughly. "Mom and I found ways to keep going, but she's never been the same. I probably haven't, either."

"How long ago?"

"Twelve years. The grief never really goes away, but I've gotten used to living with it." Her mouth twisted, and she looked away, emotion clear on her face.

"If you're done eating, maybe we could move this conversation somewhere more private." At the alarmed look she shot him, he hurried on. "I mainly want to talk. Actually, I need to, but I'm not sure where to begin. You asked why I didn't get any sleep. I spent most of the night reviewing my lab notes and records from my time on South Georgia." Brynn hesitated a beat.

"Did you unearth something you'd missed before?"

"Maybe." Brynn struggled to keep his voice neutral. "I'd like to borrow your scientific training to see what you think before I float my conclusions past you. That way you're coming in clean, without any preconceived notions."

"Wouldn't one of the other microbiologists be better equipped to do that?" She caught her bottom lip beneath her teeth.

"Probably."

"Well, then I don't understand."

"Not sure I do, either," he cut in, "but I want someone whose judgment isn't clouded by standardized training. Let's grab a few more of those cinnamon things before Cook takes them back to the kitchen, and settle in somewhere."

"I need to check on Zach and Abel." Kayna patted his hand, got to her feet, and walked to his side of the table. "Meet me in my surgery in half an hour."

"Do you want more cinnamon buns too?"

A crooked smile lightened the sadness that had coated her features after she told him about her family. "Sure. Carbs are a great hedge against almost everything."

"Do you ever stop being a doctor?" He glanced at her.

"Do you?" she countered, turned, and made her way out of the dining room.

KAYNA LET herself into her surgery, relieved she'd gotten there first. Zach was much better, and she'd sent Abel to the kitchen for boiled rice and more broth. She still couldn't believe she'd told Brynn as much as she had about her family. Derek was the only person she'd ever confided in, and after what happened with him, she'd sworn never to leave herself vulnerable again.

She dropped her bag in its usual place, cleaned her hands with soap and water, and settled at her computer to update her medical records on Zach. A faint knock sounded and she called, "Come in. It's always open when I'm in here."

Brynn ducked inside and pulled the door shut behind him. "I assume it's locked when you're out?" He dropped a white paper bag on her computer table with a small flourish. "Enough cinnamon buns to hold an army."

"Thanks. Unless you're still hungry, maybe we could save them for later. I have a hot pot and both instant coffee and tea here."

"Later is fine. Breakfast caught up with me and I'm stuffed."

"About my door being open." Kayna made a sour face. "I didn't start out locking it."

"Let me guess." He pulled a chair next to hers and sat. "People dropped in and helped themselves to things."

"Oh, yeah." She finished her notes, saved them, and closed

down her computer. "It's amazing how adept the ship's crew—or maybe the Ph.D.'s—can be at picking combination locks."

"It's one of the reasons I went back to biological research," he said, his voice a rumbly baritone that soothed her. This morning he wore the same long-sleeved black top that clung to his muscled torso and a faded pair of jeans. Battered leather, lace-up hiking boots poked from beneath the jeans, and a fisherman's knit sweater was tossed over his shoulders. "I got sick of the endless cavalcade of patients who expected me to feed their habits with pharmaceuticals."

"We have that in common." She spoke deliberately. "A bunch of my friends sold out. It's much easier to give people what they ask for, even if you only prescribe a bare handful. Gets you out from under endless arguments about amorphous concepts like pain."

Brynn blew out a breath. "Exactly. When an accident victim is screaming his head off, I have absolutely no problem kicking morphine into his IV. But when a frequent flyer lands in one of the exam rooms, complaining again about something hurting, that's when I feel backed into a corner. On the one hand, I want to help. On the other, I don't want to inadvertently create an addiction."

Kayna smiled encouragingly. "I thought you wanted to talk about what you found last night."

He sent an earnest look her way that melted her heart. "So I did. I'm stalling for the best of reasons, though. I like you. I want to get to know you better, a whole lot better." He scrubbed a palm down his face. "I'm afraid once I'm done talking you'll think I'm nuts."

She leveled her gaze at him, trying to infuse confidence that he could tell her anything and augmenting it with a jot of magic. "Funny thing," she murmured. "I've had that same problem all my life."

"What problem?"

"The one you alluded to. Knowing if I actually told people what I knew, who I am, they'd cart me off to the loony bin."

His forehead crinkled in confusion. "Are you going to say more about that?"

"No." She drew air deep into her lungs, blew out the breath, and did it again. "How about this for a teaser to get you talking? There's something disconcerting about the colonies you brought aboard this ship."

Air whooshed from him, and he sagged against his chair. "How could you possibly know that?"

"They made Zach and Abel uncomfortable, but it's deeper than that." She extended both of her hands to the sides in a sweeping motion. "Your turn."

"But even I don't know there's anything unusual about them—not for sure," he sputtered.

"It would help me understand if you started at the beginning." Kayna reached for his hand, and he gripped hers a little too tightly for comfort, but she didn't complain. His throat worked as he swallowed, clearly seeking objectivity. Science was rational; emotions only got in the way.

"The beginning, huh?" He sat straighter. "I can do that. I told you last night I signed on with a British bioresearch firm shortly after Rebecca made it clear we were finished. It took a while to make all the arrangements and get to South Georgia, but I ended up there at the very end of their fall season two years ago. The first winter I was by myself. Truly by myself. The Norwegian meteorologists, Sven and Lucas, didn't show up for seven months."

"Was it hard?" A dose of self-consciousness booted her in the ass, but she plowed on anyway. "I've often thought getting away from everyone and everything would be a slice of heaven."

"Hard in some ways." He paused and glanced sidelong at her. "Mostly, and please don't judge me, I missed the Internet. The isolation would've been easier to take if I could've logged on."

She nodded companionably. "I know what you mean. Hell, I've only been on this ship for a little over ten days, and I can't tell you how many times I've wished for Yahoo! or Google."

"A fellow junkie." He smiled and winked.

"Don't tell anyone." She placed a finger over her mouth.

"Your dirty little secret is safe with me." His smile faded. "See how easy it is to skirt the issue? It's almost as if my archaea colonies would prefer we weren't having this conversation."

"I wouldn't doubt that for a moment." She repositioned her hand so she could squeeze his.

"I don't get it." He covered the back of her hand with his other one. "I know you heard me, and you accepted what I said without batting an eye. Most people would have—"

"I'm not most people," she interrupted. "Go on. You were telling me about when you first got to South Georgia."

"Yeah."

He pursed his mouth into a straight line, and she was afraid he'd soft-soap the rest. Her muscles thrummed with tension, and she willed him to go on.

After a few moments, he did. "I spent the first couple weeks setting up my lab and living quarters, and making friends with seals who were clearly used to handouts from the tourists—even though it's against the law to feed them. I walked every inch of the trails and roadways—not that there were very many—got an old Land Rover running, and worked on the generators so they'd put out consistent voltage."

The heat of his hand surrounding hers felt right, like the two of them had been born to be together, but Kayna pushed the feeling aside. "I'm guessing you ran out of busy work pretty fast," she murmured.

"I did. Because winter was close and I was going stir-crazy, I took scrapings off the vegetation running up the hillside behind my lab." He shrugged and glanced at her. "Not long after that, winter set in, and there were days I really didn't want to spend much time outside. Anyway, I started growing cell clusters on agar plates." He offered her a crooked smile. "It's what we biological types do."

"What'd they look like?"

"Archaea. More specifically, prokaryotes. They looked exactly like what they were. I cultured a few strains of bacteria from the plants growing around the buildings you saw between the museum and Shackleton's grave, but they were pretty unremarkable, so I let them go. I suppose I only kept the archaea colonies alive to keep me busy until the weather improved. By then, the bioresearch firm was interested enough in what I was doing that they gave me the green light to continue to cultivate them. They assigned me several other projects too, along the way."

"Why would they be interested in proks?"

"I've suspected for years that they could host a new class of powerful antibiotics. Since they share a structure with most bacteria, they're a natural for fighting disease."

"Interesting." She ran possibilities through her head. "Did you ever test them against any of the common pathogens?"

"Within the limitations of what I had to work with, yes."

The air in her surgery shifted, thickened. Kayna watched Brynn closely, wondering if he felt it too, but he didn't give any indication.

"Eventually, I moved the colonies from agar plates to bins to give them more room. By then I'd taken a stab at aging the cultures and thought they were pretty old."

"Cut to the chase," she said. "What'd you find that kept you up all night?"

"You're right, of course," he muttered. "It's probably easier to get it all out at once."

Kayna pulled her hand out from between his. "You feel wonderful, but I'm going to brew us something hot." She stood, walked to the hot pot plugged in next to the sink, and flipped its switch. "Keep talking."

"The bioresearch firm I worked for is pretty well-heeled. The sample bins were the latest and greatest, and each one had its own temperature and humidity controls."

"Really? That's pretty sophisticated."

He held out his hand for the cup of coffee she'd brewed. "The generator that kept my lab going went a little bonkers, and there was a big power surge. Pretty much anything that was plugged in blew, even through surge bars. I'm lucky I had an extra adapter for my computer."

Kayna dropped the bag of cinnamon rolls between them and sat. She held her mug between her hands to warm them. Brynn was at the crux of his story, and the temperature in the room had cooled perceptibly. He must've felt it because he tugged his sweater closer to his body. She sipped her drink and waited.

"Thanks for the coffee," he said. "I'm still trying to wrap my mind around this, but the bins all got a honking blast of electricity. After that, the colonies grew like I'd given them steroids, and the weird part started."

"Why'd you decide to bring them to McMurdo?" Kayna clenched her jaws tight together. There. She'd gotten her question out on the table.

"The man who runs the base, Jack DeVoe, is someone I've known for years. He called me about a week ago and described some abnormalities with their prok cultures." Brynn gazed at her out of troubled eyes, and their multi-hued tones shaded to brown. "Not that their cultures were doing the same thing mine were, but Jack asked if I could come to McMurdo and bring my colonies along. That way we'd be able to compare and contrast the two."

"There's more," she urged, certain he'd skipped over more than a little.

Brynn nodded. "So much more, it's hard to know where to begin. Scientists live for unusual occurrences, but this is mind-boggling." He gulped his coffee.

Kayna straightened. "You already know something's not right with your cultures—"

"But I don't," he broke in. "After Micah—the researcher at McMurdo Jack introduced me to—sent me screen shots of his stained cells, I scraped some cells and made slides to compare them with his, but mine appeared totally normal."

"I'll bet they did."

Brynn drew back, looking as if she'd struck him. "Are you calling me a liar?"

"Not at all. I'm trying to figure out what we're dealing with here."

The ship pitched in a particularly violent roll, and Brynn steadied himself by grabbing the edge of her desk. "It's starting to look as if none of this will matter," he said, his face pinched and grim. "If the boat sinks before we get to McMurdo…" He let his words trail off.

"It won't," she said dully.

"How can you know that?"

"Your cultures want to join up with their buddies in the McMurdo lab."

Brynn stared at her. "I was worried you'd think I was ready for a straightjacket if I said that, but it's the conclusion I keep coming back to."

"And now you're wondering if I need restraints." She picked carefully through the possibilities and selected her next words with care. "I owe you an apology for being sharp, but there's a lot more to the world than what most people can see and feel and touch—"

Her surgery door swung open. Harold stood in the doorway. "One of the engineers took a tumble in the engine room," he said. "It's nowhere near as bad as the last problem we had, but he's unconscious."

Kayna shot to her feet and lurched across the room for her bag. "Where is he?"

"In his quarters on Deck Two. Follow me." Harold stood aside so she could squeeze past him.

"You shouldn't have moved him," Kayna muttered.

Harold shrugged. "You've seen the engine room. It was a field decision."

"Mind if I tag along?" Brynn asked. "It's rough enough, it might be handy to have an extra set of hands."

Kayna caught the annoyed look Harold shot Brynn's way, but said, "You'd be welcome. I'd love to have help."

"Well, if this isn't my lucky day," Harold countered. "I get two of you overeducated dolts for the price of one."

"I'm going to ignore that," Kayna said, suppressing her anger. "One of these overeducated, what was that you called us? Oh yes, *dolts,* saved your crew member from bleeding to death."

An unattractive red splotched Harold's weathered face. "Sorry, Doc. Don't know what got into me."

I do. You didn't like finding Brynn in my cabin, and you're jealous.

"It's all right. We'll be right behind you."

"Do you have everything you need?" Brynn, who'd walked to her side, tapped her bag.

"Depends what's wrong with him, but one of us can come back here if we need something." As she spoke the words, Kayna nodded to herself. Having another M.D., even one who hadn't practiced for a few years, was a huge boon. When she got an opportunity—and Harold wasn't listening in—she'd tell Brynn so.

CHAPTER 11

Brynn trotted after Harold and Kayna. Harold hadn't been pleased to find him in the surgery, and he recalled the conversation they'd had on the beach. Apparently, it was one thing if Kayna spurned them both, but her chatting cozily with him—and not Harold—didn't sit well.

"Tell us what happened," he called to Harold.

"I'm not sure," the staff captain said. "I wasn't there."

"Well, tell us what you know," Kayna chimed in. "It will save time once we get there."

"I don't know much," Harold huffed and launched himself down the stairs. Once they were all on Deck Three, he turned to them. "When I got there, Mikhail was face down, unconscious. The men said he fell."

"I'm not trying to chew this to death," Brynn said, "but did he slip and fall, or did he fall for no reason?"

"I'll find out more from the other crew once I've shown you where his quarters are." Harold moved rapidly along the corridor and ducked into the stairwell leading to the crew's living area.

Brynn worked his way down a very steep staircase with risers so skinny he had to place his feet sideways. Once he reached the bottom, he glanced around. The hallway for Deck Two was narrower than the ones on the upper decks, and the scents of tobacco, onions, and sweat permeated everything.

Halfway down the corridor, Harold pushed a door open and gestured with one hand. "He's in here," was followed by a volley of Russian, and two burly seamen stepped into the corridor looking rattled. Both curved their fingers into a sign against evil and moved down the corridor, muttering.

"Sorry about that." Harold shrugged. "I told them to leave, but they didn't. Seamen are a superstitious lot, and everybody's upset about two accidents in a row."

"Come back as soon as you can," Kayna said, "in case we need an interpreter."

"Mikhail doesn't need an interpreter, he's unconscious." Harold shot a long-suffering look Kayna's way.

"He may be now," Kayna replied, "but it doesn't necessarily mean he'll stay that way."

"Which do you want?" Harold asked. "Information or my Russian language skills?"

"Both," Kayna snapped.

"Yes, ma'am." Harold did a credible imitation of clicking his heels together, a neat trick on the rolling ship, and disappeared down the hall.

Brynn moved inside the room. Two sets of bunks separated by scant inches filled the small space. Clothes hung from hooks, and a corner basin looked as if it hadn't been cleaned in ages. "Different sanitation standards for the crew," he murmured.

"It would appear so." Kayna dropped her bag on one of the empty bunks and bent over Mikhail's prone form.

"Do you mind if I get into your bag?" Brynn asked.

"Not at all. We need gloves, my stethoscope, a BP cuff—"

"How about this," Brynn broke in. "If I miss something, you can let me know."

"Fair enough. Sorry. Didn't mean to be patronizing." She waited until he handed her a pair of gloves and began her exam.

Brynn gloved up and bent over the seaman. They worked in silence trying to figure out why the man was unconscious.

Harold materialized, taking up what little floor space was left in the cramped cabin. "From what I can tell, he slipped on oil and fell down some stairs."

Something akin to fury flashed from Kayna's green eyes. She stomped over to Harold. "Don't you have workplace safety standards?"

"Of course we do," he said stiffly, "but perhaps not quite to the level you're expecting. This is a working ship, not a luxury liner."

"Fine." She retreated to her spot next to the unconscious seaman. "You might gather the troops and have a day-late-and-a-dollar-short discussion about being careful. The engine room was saturated with oil when I was there. Can't you sprinkle sand or something to mop it up?"

"I'd scarcely characterize a few stray dribbles as *saturated*. You do your job, Doctor—" Harold stressed the last word, by drawing it out into two curt syllables "—and let me do mine." He spun a hundred-eighty degrees and took off at a lope.

"Touchy bastard," Brynn said.

"He's pissed about finding you in my surgery." Kayna rolled her eyes and palpated down the seaman's body.

"Yeah, I gathered that. I'd feel a whole lot better if we could do a set of images of this guy's skull."

"With what?" She glanced at him. "No machinery aboard."

"He could've hit his head," Brynn persisted. "If there's a clot…"

"The only weapon in my arsenal besides aspirin is Coumadin."

"I say we dose him with some."

"If we do, he won't be able to work. What if he falls again? We might not be able to stop the bleeding."

"Surely they'd extend sick leave." Brynn thought about it.

Judging from the state of this cabin, the crew never saw that kind of break from their duties. "Never mind."

"Look here." Kayna had worked her way down to the seaman's feet. "His left fibula's broken. Something we can actually treat."

By the time they set the leg, Mikhail had come around. He wanted to talk, but Harold was long gone. "I'll see if I can rustle up someone from the kitchen." Kayna stripped off her gloves and dropped them into an overflowing trash bin. "Some of them are bilingual."

"I'll stay with Mikhail," Brynn said. "It's important he doesn't put any weight on that leg for two weeks. Do you suppose they have any crutches on board?"

"I have some in my crates of supplies down in one of the holds. We can pick a likely pair once we're done here and give him a crash course in how to walk with them."

KAYNA HIT the code to open her surgery and walked inside, dropping her bag on the floor with a *clunk*. She headed for the sink with Brynn behind her. "Do you think he'll follow our directions?" she asked as she washed her hands.

"I hope so," Brynn said as he washed his hands too. "The gal from the kitchen seemed to have a good grasp of English, so hopefully she did a decent job interpreting."

Kayna dragged a cinnamon roll out of the bag and took a bite. "Knew these would come in handy," she mumbled around the sweet dough. "I need to find Harold and tell him that seaman has to be off duty for at least forty-eight hours."

"And light duty after that." Brynn dried his hands and took a cinnamon roll of his own.

Kayna turned to face him. "You haven't seen the engine room," she said.

"Maybe that's a good thing." He shook his head, his lips pursed into a thin line. "The way you lit into Harold, I'm not sure I want to see it."

"OSHA would dry dock this ship—forever. I'll be back in a few." She dropped the uneaten portion of her cinnamon bun back into the bag, slipped out the door, and tackled the stairs leading two decks up. The likeliest places to find Harold would be either the bridge or the radio officer's tiny room off the bridge, both of which were on Deck Six, or his cabin on Deck Five.

She started with the bridge and got lucky. "Can I talk with you?" she asked.

"Go ahead." He gestured noncommittally. "We're the only ones up here who speak English."

"I speak little." The captain moved toward them. "How my man?"

Kayna glanced at Harold. "Do you need to interpret?"

"Maybe. We'll see."

Kayna turned to the captain and extended a hand. "Dr. Kayna Quan, Captain. I met you when I boarded in Buenos Aires."

He took her hand briefly and said, "Valentin Gorev. Pleasure is mine."

Kayna glanced at the man who, at least according to Harold, exercised supreme command over the ship and everyone on it. He was tall and rangy with longish black hair, a beak of a nose, and shrewd dark eyes. A wrinkled white shirt peeked from beneath a tattered black down jacket with feathers poking through in places. Black pants hugged his legs, and he wore scuffed leather boots. Kayna pegged him at around fifty.

"Your crewman has a broken leg." She made a breaking motion with her hands and then pointed to her lower leg. When the captain nodded his understanding, she went on. "He cannot stand on the leg for two—" she held up two fingers "—weeks, but you can assign him desk duties in two days."

"And after the two weeks?" Harold asked.

"Light duty," she said. "Frankly, he'll have a hell of a time navigating the stairs in the engine room, never mind the ones leading to his cabin, on crutches. And he'll be on crutches for about five weeks."

The captain said something in Russian and Harold answered. He turned to her. "You're free to go, Doc."

Recognizing his words as a dismissal, she turned and left the bridge, sorry she hadn't opted for a Rosetta Stone crash course in Russian before leaving Minnesota. She'd considered it, once she knew she'd be on a Russian ship, but hadn't wanted to cram one more "have to" into her frenetic pre-departure schedule. Besides, she'd assumed most of the crew would have at least a rudimentary command of English.

Guess I was wrong.

McMurdo was a big place. She'd looked at photographs and read up on it. They had to have a library with language tapes. No way in hell would she face the return voyage as underequipped linguistically as she was right now. Assuming she came back via boat and not a plane.

She slowed between the bridge and her surgery, wanting a few moments to process things. When her feet carried her away from the stairs and farther into Deck Five, realization cut deep. Brynn's cabin—and the cultures—were somewhere nearby. The same mild discomfort that had dogged her since she found out about the samples wasn't any worse up here. Maybe taking a peek for herself wasn't a bad idea. It wasn't as if the proks would rise up and attack her. How could they? She shut her eyes and dialed in her psi ability.

Something like a tsunami jammed her in the guts with so much force she was afraid she'd vomit up the few bites of cinnamon bun. She wrapped her arms around her middle and doubled over. No doubt about it, the cultures were two doors down in cabins on both sides of the hall. Kayna tried to tug the glass-bright edges of her power back into hiding. Like a demented form of *Magic Theater*, the curtain that normally shuttered her paranormal side remained stubbornly open. She felt naked, exposed, but forced herself upright in time to see a spectral form take shape, flicker, and appear again a few feet away.

"Garinion." Nana's voice flared deep in her mind in archaic Gaelic. *"Granddaughter. Do not fear your gift. Sure an' the time ye could run from it has passed."*

Kayna took a tentative step toward the ghostly projection, but it dissolved into motes of dust. The pressure that made her want to claw her stomach to shreds eased, replaced by a series of musical notes as ghostly as her grandmother's form had been. Skirting the edges of her hearing, the melody was so haunting, evocative, and poignant, tears formed behind her lids. Everything she'd cut herself off from streamed past in an endless collage of friendships that hadn't gotten too deep, her charade of a love life with Derek, and she and her mother carefully not talking about anything that mattered. They couldn't. Any meaningful conversation would've included the psi gift they shared, and her mother pretended it wasn't there.

Where her grandmother had stood, the raven flickered into being, but only for long enough to flip its beak at her. A cloyingly sweet smell joined the unsettling music.

What's happening to me?

"I'm happening to you." Her father replaced the raven, shimmering into corporeality.

Fuck!

Kayna clacked her jaws shut and straightened her spine. "You're not real."

"Oh, but I assure you I am." The corners of his mouth twisted into the same sardonic grin she remembered from her childhood —just before he backhanded her for some imagined wrongdoing.

Ice sheeted through her blood, and she set her mouth in a hard line so her lips wouldn't tremble. "What do you want? And don't say you want me and disappear like you did last time."

Her father's translucent form turned down the corridor. He

raised an arm and pointed. *"I want what's in those rooms. A single bin will do. You will get it for me, and then we're leaving."*

"The hell I am. I'm not getting shit for you, and I'm not going anywhere with you, either."

"You are my blood. You will respect me." He tossed his head, and long, black hair slapped against a wall.

Anger surged, but before she could come up with a snappy rejoinder, the raven fluttered through a wall and raised his beak in approval. Her grandmother oozed into being right after the bird and started screeching at Guiren in Gaelic. The raven flew at him, trying to peck his eyes out. Magic flared, the air thick with the stink of it. As if it were a macabre accompaniment to the impossible scene unfolding in the fifth deck's corridor, the music became louder—almost deafeningly so. And the smell intensified, reminding her of rotten vegetation.

Kayna shook her head hard to clear it, but it didn't work. What could her father possibly want with Brynn's cultures? *Ach, Christ. This just gets murkier and murkier.*

Her last thought rattled her enough that she screamed at her grandmother. "Screw lambasting him with Gaelic. I need answers."

"Who the hell are you talking to?" Harold called from the stairwell end of the hall.

"Myself." Kayna groaned inwardly. Her words sounded incredibly lame, but at least the battling spirits departed post haste.

Harold stalked down the hall, his gaze never leaving her. He crinkled his nose sniffing. "What's that odd smell? Why are you standing in front of the cabin with Dr. McMichaels's samples? We went to a huge amount of trouble, and hundreds of miles out of our way, to pick them up—"

A wave of fatigue nearly flattened her. "I noticed the odd smell too, and I have no idea what it is." She thought quickly. "It's why I walked down this corridor. To investigate." She took a deep breath. "I'm not the enemy. Stop treating me like one."

Kayna placed her hands on her hips and hurried on before he could ask any more uncomfortable questions. "So long as we're alone, why have you been so irritable? You accused me of impersonating a cactus, but your spines are longer and sharper than mine ever dreamed of being."

The stern planes of his face collapsed. Exposed emotion washed across his austere features. "I wish I could answer that." He looked away. "When I was growing up, I was fascinated by Edgar Allan Poe and others like him. You know, the ones who dragged things out of the dark and scared the bejesus out of everyone by flashing monsters at them." He shut his eyes for a moment. When he opened them, they were filled with desolation. "For the first time…" His voice cracked, and he started over. "For the first time, I feel like I've fallen into a pit with everything I ever feared. It's enough to make anyone *irritable*."

"Go on," she said, keeping her voice soft, encouraging, grateful she'd been able to divert him so easily.

"There have never been accidents on my ships. Now there've been two back to back. I can't explain it very well, but the ship doesn't feel right to me." He drew his brows together. "A man like me gets a feel for his ship. I've spent years aboard this one, and she feels…off beam in more ways than one. Bloody hell." He turned away. "I need to shut up. Some things are better not talked about. It's like tempting fate."

"What about the captain?" she asked, ignoring his last comment.

"What about him?" Harold turned back to stare at her.

"He's been edgy too."

The corners of Harold's mouth twisted into a wry expression. "Sure, but he's superstitious. It's part and parcel of his culture."

"But not of yours?" Kayna narrowed her eyes. "Seems to me we have plenty of superstitions. Television, the movies, and the Internet are full of paranormal phenomena."

"Yes, but none of that is real."

"I wouldn't be so sure." Kayna made a split-second decision to take a chance. "Never discount your instincts. I think there's something very unusual happening too, and it's somehow wrapped up with those cultures. At first I labeled it *bad*, but now I'm not so sure."

Harold screwed his face into a grimace. "Should we jettison the blighters? Lots of ocean out there."

"Somehow, I don't think they'll let us do that."

"Are you feeling all right?" Harold stepped closer to her.

"'Fraid so. It would be convenient if I were a raving lunatic, but I'm not." She spread her hands in front of her. "I don't have any answers, but I'm working on coming up with some." She rolled her shoulders to lessen the tension between them.

He placed a hand on her shoulder, but couldn't meet her gaze. He tried, but his blue eyes skittered away from direct contact with her face. "This will sound as if I escaped from the *Threepenny Opera*, but the ship feels wounded somehow, and there's nothing I can do to save her. The crew feels it too. I've heard them muttering among themselves. They're simple folk, but they're tuned in to this ship. Some of them have sailed her for more than twenty years. After time like that, you get to know every nuance, every creak, every rattle."

Kayna thought about mentioning how a surfeit of magic could make everything feel strange. Instead, she asked, "How long will it take to get to the Antarctic Continent?"

"Normally in seas this rough, it would take better than four days, but the wind is at our back, pushing us. We've been making twelve or thirteen knots. It's little shy of a miracle. If I wasn't so damned worried, I might appreciate it."

She dropped her hands to her sides. "You still didn't tell me how long. Two days?"

"Maybe two-and-a-half, unless the wind shifts and we have to slow down. That only gets us to the South Shetlands, though. McMurdo is thousands of miles farther down the coast."

She moved his hand off her shoulder. "I'm going back to my surgery. Brynn's there and we weren't done talking."

"You like him, don't you?"

Harold's question didn't exactly come out of left field, and Kayna reached for patience. "I'm not sure what I feel. I just met him, but yes, at least so far I like him." She tilted her chin. "I just got dumped after a seven-year relationship. I'm not in a big hurry to leap back into anything.

"But this isn't about Brynn," she hurried on. "It's about you and me. Maybe we could air that part of things, so it's not sitting between us like three-day-old fish. I'm flattered you're interested in me, but have you given any thought to how that might work?"

"I'm sure I don't know what you mean," he stammered, looking like he wanted to sink through Deck Five's flooring.

"So long as I'm being frank, I'm not up for anything as transient as a shipboard romance. Were you planning to stop by McMurdo when you happened to be in the vicinity? How often would that be? Maybe once between now and when my year's commitment is up? What would happen after I went back to the States? I'll end up practicing medicine, probably in a big city. How would that mesh with you being gone at sea most of the time?"

"Stop." He held up a hand. "I didn't think about any of that. All I knew was I found you attractive, and I wanted to get to know you better."

"Again, I'm flattered by your interest, but I can be a flaming bitch. I'm plainspoken, and I call the ball where it lies. Most men don't care much for those traits in a woman."

"Point taken, Doc." He smiled sadly. "I know when I'm not welcome."

"We have bigger problems. Why don't you check on Mikhail? Make certain he stays off that leg to give the bone a chance to heal. It was a clean break, but he could change all that if he misaligns it."

"Sure thing." Harold spun on his heel and faded down the corridor but turned before he got to the stairs. "About the cultures —" he stumbled over his next words "—find me when you know more."

"I will."

Harold didn't answer before disappearing down the stairwell.

What the fuck is wrong with me? I didn't have to hammer him into the ground about being interested in me.

No, actually I did. Otherwise, he'd never have left me alone.

CHAPTER 12

Brynn's head snapped up when the surgery door opened, and he jumped to his feet. "You were gone so long, I was getting worried."

"I had a chat with Harold—and a few other things happened too." She pulled the door shut, fell into a chair, and dropped her head into her hands. "Christ, but I could use a drink."

"Would you like me to rustle something up from the bar?"

"Nah. I need a clear head. Booze will get in the way."

"How about coffee or tea? Lunch might still be out in the dining room." He moved behind her and settled his hands on her shoulders, kneading her tense muscles.

"God, that feels good." She tilted her body into his hands. "I'd probably like a cup of tea, but I don't need it right his minute."

"What happened?" Brynn asked. "Did you have a hard time tracking Harold down?"

"Nope. Found him right away. Look, before I say much more, we need to finish the conversation we were having earlier today. There are lots of things you don't know about me."

The ship pitched left and immediately yawed to the right. Brynn overcorrected and ended up sprawled on his ass. "Goddammit!" He rolled to a sit and then pulled himself upright.

Kayna drew her brows together. "Are you hurt? I swear, you've really got to stay on top of things. I took more than one tumble after the sea turned into something out of *Mutiny on the Bounty.*"

"Nah, I'm okay. I'm really interested in what you have to tell me." He stood behind her and dug his fingers into her shoulders and neck again. It wasn't totally altruistic; her skin was warm and pliant beneath his hands, and he loved the way she felt. Rather than talking, she angled her head back and leaned into his touch. He shifted from foot to foot, keeping his balance by a narrow margin.

The ship lurched, and Brynn went to his knees, cursing. When he was upright again, he said, "This isn't a come-on, but how about if we move to your bed? I can sit behind you and rub your shoulders, which feel like rocks by the way, and you can tell me about yourself. You said you were going to, but you've been pretty quiet."

He could've offered to sit in the other chair, but he wanted— no, make that needed—to keep touching her. She was silent so long, he was afraid she'd ask him to leave, but finally she nodded.

"Sure, we can do that. It's probably not all that comfortable for you standing up with the ship bouncing like an out-of-control merry-go-round."

He walked in front of her and offered his hands to help her upright. Leaning against one another, they made their way through the surgery and into her quarters.

"Sorry," she murmured. "I'll never get a medal for neatness."

"I didn't notice a thing," he lied smoothly as he positioned himself behind her on the bed with his back to the wall. Paying close attention to detail had served him well in both his careers. Kayna's quarters were homey with clothing hanging on hooks and draped over chairs. Books and sheets of paper were scattered about, a few on the floor—casualties of the incessant motion of the ship. Her scent clung to everything, and he felt his body respond. The bunk was narrow, but he tried to keep a slender slice of mattress between her buttocks and his cock.

"This was a good idea. Fighting the ship's rolling gets old." She arched her back into his touch. "Since we're comfy, you'll get the long version of my life story."

"I figured there was more to it than losing your father and sister. Were you a track star? Valedictorian?"

"Right on one count and it's not track star. Seriously, from as long ago as I can remember, I've sensed things most people couldn't. And I've known things were about to happen when there was no rational way for me to have found out. Other things too. The list is long, but the bottom line is I have strong paranormal abilities."

A sinking feeling dragged at his heart. He really liked Kayna. She obviously believed what she'd said, but her depiction of herself couldn't be accurate. Did she have a mental illness with fixed delusions?

"Your fingers changed cadence," she said and twisted around so she faced him. "I know exactly what you're thinking."

"Do you now?" he murmured, not quite meeting her gaze.

She nodded, her eyes pinched and sad. "Of course. It's the same response I get from everyone I'm honest with. When I was a little girl, people laughed it off." She pressed her lips together and then took a deep breath. "Nana took me to secret gatherings of other people like us. We never told Mom. Even though she had the same gift, she hated it. Anyway, I learned to keep my mouth shut, and once I hit about ten or eleven, I started tagging around with psychics and other weirdoes. They accepted me, even used my skills sometimes."

"What about school and friends? Things like that?" Skepticism sparred with wanting to believe her, and Brynn hooked strands of silky hair that had fallen over her face behind her ear.

She propped her head on an upraised hand and smiled

ruefully. "It was like I led two lives. Nana was very strong magically. She taught me a lot about managing my talents."

"You must've loved her," Brynn said, feeling wistful. Having even one supportive adult during his teenage years would've meant a lot. He'd loved his great grandfather, but the old man lived across the country. Another unsettling thought surfaced. Mental illness ran in families. Maybe Kayna's grandmother and mother suffered from the same thing. He drew back a little.

Kayna narrowed her eyes, almost as if she knew what he was thinking. "I did love her. She was an incredible woman. She died a few months before I turned seventeen. Cancer got her. It didn't help we didn't have money for the fancier treatments."

"I'm sorry." He continued to stroke her cheek softly.

"You don't believe me about the magic parts," she said flatly.

He forced his gaze to her face. Her eyes radiated a sharp intelligence, and her brows were drawn together. "It's not easy," he began, "but I'm trying." As soon as he said the words, understanding surfaced. Somewhere between his initial misgivings and when she'd turned to face him, he'd begun to accept her story.

"Do you want to hear the rest?" she asked. "Or would you rather head back upstairs to your own quarters?"

Brynn did a quick inner survey. The thought of leaving Kayna smote him with painful desolation. When he spoke, his heart was behind his words. "I still want to know all about you. Some information takes a little more…immersion than others."

"No kidding." She made a snorting noise. "I need you to be sure, though. Those things—the ones that require *immersion*—once you hear them, they change you forever. You won't be able to kick the door shut on this, or chalk it up to me being deranged, or mentally incompetent." Her eyes invited an answer.

Brynn took a deep breath. "I'm sure. Go on."

Kayna nodded. "Round about my seventeenth birthday, my paranormal ability vanished."

"What exactly does that mean?" He quirked a brow. "How did you know it was gone?"

"There's a place right here." She tapped her breastbone. "And here." She tapped her forehead and then her throat. "They're chakras. There are seven major ones and hundreds of minor ones. They didn't feel…active anymore. I worried about it for a while and finally talked with Mom. She was delighted. I remember her telling me that I could finally have a normal life."

"What happened then? I'm guessing the magic—" his tongue stuttered over the word "—didn't stay gone."

"It did for a long time, or at least it was dormant until one night when I was an intern working in the E.R. I had a desperately ill patient, and I was pulling out every trick in the book to save him. I'd called my attending in, but it was a busy night and he wasn't there yet."

Kayna squeezed her eyes shut; when she opened them, she zeroed in on Brynn's face. "I felt something so cold it raised goose bumps on my arms, and I heard rustling. When I looked around nothing was there, but I knew Death was stalking my patient. Nothing else could feel that ominous—or that hungry."

She tilted her chin, and a defiant expression lit her face. "I won that round. The accident victim I was treating walked out of the hospital two weeks later. I asked some of the other interns if they'd ever sensed Death's presence, and they looked at me as if I'd gone off the deep end. One even took me aside and told me it wasn't unusual for the sleep-deprived to experience hallucinations." She made a sour face. "After that, I didn't mention my more unusual perceptions. It also wasn't much of a surprise when my chakra fields felt alive again."

"This thing you have, how does it work?"

"I can't give you a scientific explanation. When I need to access my extrasensory side, I simply open myself to it, which could lead to my second point, but I need to know how you're doing so far."

Well, how am I doing?

"I've never known anyone with extrasensory perception," he said slowly, "but I have read about cases where the police use psychics. I'm guessing this sixth sense, or whatever it is, is how you knew something was up with my cultures." At her nod, he went on. "What can you tell me about them?"

She laid her hand against his jaw. Her touch felt so electric, he placed his hand over hers to keep her from moving it. "I wish it were that simple," she murmured. "I got a feeling, kind of like a warning, before I even knew about you. One morning at breakfast, Harold roped me into a conversation. Something you told the microbiologists made them gun shy, and he asked if I'd help with the colonies—make sure no stray bacteria got away. Right after that, Zach and Abel showed up. They'd talked with you a second time, and whatever you told them set their minds at ease."

"But not yours?"

She shook her head. "No. My paranormal side had been activated. Once that happens, it's like having someone run their fingernails down a chalkboard, but muted so it's only mildly annoying."

"Does it get worse?"

"Much. Actually, it just did when I was upstairs."

"Turn around," he said. "I love looking at you, but I promised you a back rub."

"You don't have to ask twice." She flipped onto her side, leaving space for him between her and the wall. "Getting back to what happened. Once I left the bridge, I ended up near your cultures. It wasn't conscious on my part, it just happened. I opened up my psi ability, and something damn near flattened me. Nana showed up in a spectral vision. Once she left, the thing that was hurting me withdrew, and something else took its place."

"What?" He settled behind her and kneaded her tense muscles, still maintaining a slight space between their lower bodies.

"I'm trying to figure that out. It was this evocative melody that made me remember every missed opportunity I've had for friendships, family, and lovers."

"Do you think the cultures were responsible?"

She pressed her body back against his, obliterating his safety strip, and he wrapped an arm around her waist. "I don't know. I sure gave them credit for the rush of power that attacked me, but maybe they controlled the other thing too. It was the strangest sensation, almost like once they'd identified me, they wanted to nurture me."

"It's hard for me to admit, but I've felt the same thing from them. Any idea where your grandmother fits into this?"

Her body relaxed against his. "That's easy. She loves me. She's been showing up in dreams and visions ever since I got spun out about the cultures."

He hooked the arm lying against her waist upward and snugged her against him. "I'm jealous."

"Why?"

"I'd love to see my great grandpa again. Too bad this extrasensory stuff isn't transferrable."

"Children have way more ability than most people believe. We drum it out of them when they're very little. If we didn't try so hard to normalize them, we'd probably have significantly more people like me." She made a shrugging motion that pressed her body closer to him. "Look at my mom. She had power to burn, but didn't want anything to do with it, especially after Dad died."

An odd note in her voice cued him and he asked, "What aren't you telling me?"

She stifled a laugh. "Maybe I'm not the only one with ESP. My father showed up outside your lab."

Brynn stopped rubbing her back. "I thought he was dead."

"He is. So's my grandmother. We had a regular family reunion on Deck Five."

In for a penny...

He suspended his uneasiness in the interest of gathering

information. "If your grandmother showed up because she loves you, why'd your dad put in an appearance?"

"He wants your cultures."

Shock pummeled him. "What? Why?"

"I have no idea." Kayna shook her head. She started to turn over, but he held her in place and worked his fingers into her tense muscles again. "I'm no stranger to this stuff, but him showing up spooked me, and I'm still trying to sort it out."

"Can I help?"

"Do you want to?" She leaned against him. "I need to do some more thinking, but if you were willing, I'd love to run my theories past you—once I actually have some."

"Of course, I'll help—any way I can." Brynn brushed his fingertips over the warm planes of her back and shoulders and swallowed. "We should move to the chairs in the other room." He didn't want to, but he'd wriggled back until the wooden edge of the bed pressed against his ass. The length of her body wedged against him made his head fuzzy and his mouth dry. He wanted to kiss her, touch her, brand her. Brynn was glad she couldn't see his face. Where the hell had that atavistic thought about *branding* come from?

What's happening to me? She spun me a tale worthy of healthy skepticism, and I swallowed it hook, line, and sinker.

It's because I believe her.

Not only that, if it were up to me I'd ravish her on the spot.

Brynn took a deep breath. Was he so blinded by wanting her that he'd accept anything? No. The things she'd said held the deep resonance of truth. No matter how hard it was, he had to accept her reality—and work on blending it with his own.

"Yeah, we probably should move," she murmured. "It would be smart, but I don't particularly want to either move or be smart right now." Twisting beneath the arm he had around her, she turned so she faced him again. "I'm surprised you took what I told you about myself on faith."

"So am I. We really should talk more about the cultures, except it would be almost entirely conjecture since I don't know very much, and I won't have a lab to explore the possibilities in any kind of depth until we get to McMurdo. Plus, there are things about the McMurdo proks that we haven't gotten into yet."

He forced his desire back a notch or two. Putting personal needs aside was so second nature, it had practically turned into a religion, and he didn't like that part of himself very much.

"Do you want to kick some of your ideas about them around?"

"Yes, but not right now."

"Me, either." She angled her head and ran the tip of her tongue over his lips.

Brynn groaned and threaded his arms around her, one beneath her neck and the other around her body. He settled a hand on the curves of her ass and pulled her hard against him.

"Damn, you feel good," he said against her questing tongue.

"So do you." Kayna laid a hand against his cheek. "We're not kids anymore. Once this train starts down the track, neither of us will want to derail it."

"I'm okay with that—" Brynn felt his face heat right along with the rest of him "—but then I'm a guy. We do no-strings sex pretty well."

"Ah, but this isn't." She continued to gaze into his eyes. "We're connected somehow. Maybe the cultures have something to do with it, maybe they don't, but if we go much farther, it won't be something either of us can walk away from."

Brynn didn't know what to say. His body screamed for her, and a distant, rational part of his brain—a part that should know better—believed everything she said without question. "So what happens to guys you make love with?" He tried to joke, but couldn't. "Do all of them end up snared somehow?"

"Oh yeah, that's me, the original black widow." She smiled, her green eyes soft with wanting him. "What I was trying to say, and obviously botched, is that you and I are in uncharted territory.

The last thing I thought I'd do was kick the door open to another relationship. Hell, I'm still smarting from the last one ending, but something happened to me upstairs. That second batch of magic, the one that reminded me how isolated I've become, got through to me. And then Nana told me not to be afraid of my magical side. Both things, coming in tandem like that, opened my eyes to how illusory—and pointless—my safety net is."

"I understand better than you might think because I've clung to that same net. Maybe it's past time for both of us to jettison it." Brynn's groin ached, but it was his heart that burst into song when he closed his mouth over Kayna's. She wrapped her arms around him, flung a leg over his thigh, and kissed him back with a fervor to match his own.

He licked and nibbled her lips. As she'd done the previous night, she opened her mouth to his tongue and played with him, sucking, teasing, deepening their kiss until it threatened to drown out the world. She pressed the heat of her center against his leg, and he dropped a hand over her buttocks to snug her against him.

His breath quickened, and his heart beat loudly against his ears. Her nipples peaked where they pressed against him. He tried tugging her top out of the way from behind her, but the angle wasn't right. Kayna tore her mouth from his, her breath warm and sweet against his face. "Let go for a minute." She unwound her leg and pulled away. In one supple motion, she jackknifed her body so she stood next to the bed.

"Did you change your mind?" The place next to him where she'd been felt empty, and it was hard to get words out past a throat thick with wanting her.

"No, silly, but I'm going to lock the door to my surgery. And hunt down a condom." Kayna grinned. "Hold that pose, or maybe you could get rid of some of those clothes. I'd love to undress you, but the bed's pretty small for gymnastics."

He watched the swing of her hips as she crossed her quarters into the surgery. When he heard the snick of a lock catching, he jockeyed his long-sleeved shirt over his head and started to work on his jeans.

Kayna tossed a foil wrapped square on the bedside table and eyed him, her green eyes dancing with merriment. "Want me to do something about those shoes?"

Brynn glanced at his feet. "Oh yeah, it will be a neat trick to get out of my pants, huh?" He laughed, surprised by the sound, and wondered how long it had been since joy spilled from him. "You addle my brain."

"Maybe it needs addling. I know mine does." She knelt at the end of the bunk and unlaced his hiking boots, chucking them one by one on the floor. "There's a method to my madness," she murmured and tugged on his unzipped jeans. Once they were out of the way, she outlined the shape of his erection through his shorts with her index finger.

He struggled to sit, but she pushed him back down. "I already told you there's no escape."

"Your clothes," he panted. "I'm nearly naked."

"Bet I can catch up." She stood and whipped her sweat top over her head, tossing it onto the floor. Next, she pushed her pants down and stepped out of them. She'd been wearing slippers, and he guessed she'd toed them off somewhere between the surgery and her bed.

Brynn gazed at her, delighted by her golden skin. Her breasts overfilled a lacy, half cup bra, and tight black curls spiked from around the edges of matching panties. Black hair tumbled halfway to her waist. Curious tattoos—symbols that looked like primitive writing—trailed across her shoulders. "You're unbelievable," he said, aware of every cell, every nerve ending jangling with need. "Now get back here."

"I was waiting for an invitation." Smiling coyly, she unhooked her bra, dropped it atop her other clothes, and lay next to him.

Brynn knelt over her and traced the lines of her breasts. Full, with coppery nipples, they were so perfect they stole his breath.

He bent and took one into his mouth. She groaned and arched her body, sinking her hands into his hair, while he moved from one breast to the other. When she thrust her hips, searching for something to rub her sensitive center against, he reached between her legs. Her panties were in the way, so he stopped suckling her breasts long enough to shove them down her legs.

He brushed a finger lazily around her engorged nub before exploring farther back. First one finger, and then two, sank inside the heat of her body, while he kept his palm pressed on her vulva. She reached for his cock, but he angled away. If she touched him, he'd come. He was within an angstrom of losing control. He licked his way down her flat belly and held his mouth over her clit, breathing on her.

Her body froze. "Damn!" she panted and placed her hands on either side of his face. "You've got to let me up."

Brynn was so lost in desire, he didn't understand. "Why?" He raised his head to look at her face, rosy with arousal. "Did I do something wrong?"

"Someone's knocking. Got to see who's there."

Groaning, Brynn rolled off her. His balls ached and his cock was on fire, but he understood she couldn't ignore a possible medical emergency.

Kayna was on her feet, pulling on clothes and finger combing her hair. She exhaled sharply. "Damn! I knew this privacy was too good to last. I'll shut the inner door." She favored him with a wanton grin. "While I'd love to keep you naked and at my beck and call, you might want to get dressed."

He wanted to hold her and kiss her and tell her how magnificent she was, but that would have to wait. He tried to infuse what he was feeling into his eyes, but she was already turning away.

"Coming," she called and tugged the door to her quarters closed.

CHAPTER 13

Kayna glanced at her watch. Somehow, it had gotten to be past eight at night. The knock on her door had been a crewman with a cut that required stitches. She'd settled him in a chair, wrapped a pressure bandage around his forearm, and retreated into her bedroom to get into her scrubs. No point getting blood all over her clothes.

Brynn was already dressed and washing his face over the bathroom basin. He'd slicked his tawny hair back with a little more water and asked, "What's cooking?"

Once she outlined the problem, he left to take care of her patient while she set herself to rights, her body still alight from his touch. By the time she re-entered her surgery, a steady stream of patients took up the rest of the day.

"Penny for your thoughts?" Brynn asked and bent to lay his cheek next to hers.

Kayna looked up from her computer where she was dutifully recording who they'd treated and what they'd done. Her face heated. "You probably don't really want to know."

"Since you're blushing—" he brushed his lips over the ridges of her cheekbones and straightened "—maybe I do."

She cleared her throat. "Thanks for all your help today. We treated eight people after the guy with the cut arm. I've never had such a busy clinic on this ship. Mostly the patients have shown up with hours—or days—between them."

"They're starting to trust you," Brynn observed. "Over half the people we treated were crew."

"Crap!" She slapped a palm against her forehead. "Zach. I haven't checked on him in hours."

"He's probably fine. I'm sure Abel would've hunted you down if things went south again."

"Yeah, but I still need to look in on him."

Chris tapped against the open surgery door and walked through, saying, "I'm a little late."

"No problem." Kayna stood and moved to her supply cabinet.

He held out his hand for the tiny envelopes and rolled his eyes. "I'm getting quite a collection of these. I'm sure the Russian gals who clean the cabin wonder what's up."

"Does it matter?" Kayna ran her gaze over Chris and was pleased. He definitely looked better. The hollow-man look had left his face, and he wasn't pale as a ghost anymore.

"Nah." He looked from one to the other of them and furled his brows Brynn's way. "You're an M.D. too, huh? You said that when we met you on the beach."

"Yup. And a microbiologist."

"Here I thought I was over-educated."

"We all are." Brynn grinned rakishly. "We should start a club."

"Speaking of which," Chris said, "you weren't at dinner, but Harold hit every table with some disturbing news."

Something prickled deep, and Kayna folded her arms under her breasts. "Like what?"

"He didn't say much, but they have radio contact via satellite, and the situation in Ukraine is heating up."

"It wasn't good when I left South Georgia," Brynn cut in.

"Russia did something-or-other that involved moving troops there, and the U.S. was threatening sanctions."

"Well, at least according to Harold, it's escalating." Chris shook his head. "Damn it all!" He pounded his fist into a desktop. "Don't they get how fragile the world is?" He cradled his reddened knuckles in his other hand. "Don't even try to answer that one. If the two of you want anything to eat, you'd better hoof it down to the dining room." He turned and left, muttering to himself.

"Dinner?" Brynn quirked a brow.

"I am hungry for something other than cinnamon rolls." They'd nibbled sweet buns through the afternoon, but they weren't a decent substitute for a hot meal.

Brynn kicked the surgery door closed and wrapped his arms around her. "I never got a chance to tell you how much what we did earlier meant to me. Even though we were interrupted, it was incredible." He paused for a beat and nuzzled her neck. "I was teasing when I made that crack about no-strings sex. I've never been able to separate my body from my heart."

"Good to know." She fitted her body against his and arousal, urgent and demanding, surged. He felt it too because his cock hardened where it pressed against her belly.

"If you want dinner, we need to leave." Brynn ran his hands down her back and cupped her butt.

"You're not making it easy." She tilted her head back so she could look at him.

"How about this?" His eyes gleamed golden. "Dinner first. We'll need the fortification for later."

She kissed him lightly and pulled away. "I'm almost afraid to ask what you have in mind. Fortification sounds like hours and hours of—"

Brynn laid a finger over her lips. "We'll be inventive—and pray no one else shows up at the door."

"No matter how creative and imaginative we get, I have to

check on Zach." Kayna opened the door, and waited in the hallway.

Brynn pulled the door shut and set the lock. "I'll run down and get some plates going for us. What do you want to drink?"

"Tea with one sugar and cream."

"See you in a few minutes." He squeezed her hand and turned away.

Kayna watched him go. Something about them felt right in a way she'd never experienced before. It wasn't only the physical attraction, even though it was knock-your-socks-off strong. Working side by side with Brynn was easy. Their medical skillsets complemented one another, and he approached problems with a quiet competence that earned her respect.

She made her way to Zach and Abel's cabin and knocked. Abel opened the door and smiled broadly. "Hey there, Doc. Great to see you."

"I'm guessing our guy's better?" She slipped past him into the cabin and spied Zach sitting on the couch with a laptop balanced atop his extended legs.

"If *our guy* is me—" Zach looked up "—the answer is yes. I have no idea what happened, but that last dose of whatever you gave me did the trick." He clicked a few keys and set the laptop aside.

"Wonderful news." Kayna clasped her hands together. "I wanted to make sure you were on the mend before I went down to dinner. Speaking of which, did you eat?"

"I followed your instructions," Zach said. "No booze, and I was careful to pick digestible things."

"Excellent."

"What he's not telling you," Abel broke in, "is how much he groused about passing on the roast beef in the stew."

"If you're feeling this chipper tomorrow," she said, and smiled, "you can gradually reinstitute your normal diet. I'd lay off alcohol until we get to McMurdo, though."

"Noted." Zach's moon-shaped face darkened. "After what we

heard from Harold tonight, Abel and I have been playing the odds of us even getting to McMurdo. Rough seas aside, this is a Russian ship."

"Yeah, and McMurdo's an American base," Abel said.

Breath whistled from between Kayna's teeth as she exhaled. She hadn't even considered the ramifications of that until Harold's statement earlier in his cabin. "So the Americans who run the base might not allow our ship into McMurdo Sound?"

"Something like that," Zach mumbled.

"It seems unlikely," Abel added. "What with the bad weather and all, I can't envision any country not allowing a ship access to safety for its passengers and crew."

"I didn't study political science," Kayna said slowly, "but it does seem like that would violate a bunch of international treaties."

"We're keeping you from your dinner," Abel said. "Harold's probably still down there. At least he was when we left a quarter of an hour ago. You can ask what he thinks since he heard the actual radio broadcasts."

"Thanks. Glad you're on the mend, Zach. Be sure to find me if anything changes."

"Aye-aye, ma'am."

His jaunty words brought half a smile to her face as she trotted down the corridor and stairwell and made her way to the dining room. Kitchen staff was removing the serving dishes, so it looked as if Brynn had made it in the nick of time.

"Kayna!"

She saw him sitting in the same corner where they'd had breakfast. It was a little easier to make her way across the room, so maybe the seas weren't kicking up quite so badly—for the moment. She missed fresh air and being able to walk about on deck.

"Hey you." She sat and picked up her fork. "Looks great!"

"Hey yourself. I didn't realize how hungry I was until I started eating."

"Have you seen Harold?" Brynn shook his head and she went on, "Zach and Abel did. They were worried about Russia and the U.S. being at odds and how it might impact us landing at McMurdo."

"No matter what happens, it shouldn't have any bearing." Brynn buttered a roll and took a bite.

"Same thing I thought, but the state of the world is damned depressing." She ate quickly, methodically, before forcing herself to slow down. "Hospital duty is really bad for gracious dining."

"Yeah." He pointed at his plate. "I'm almost done. It's because if we don't eat fast, something might happen and God only knows how long it will be before we can get back to whatever meal we abandoned."

She smiled. "You've had a few years to set your bad M.D. habits aside."

"So I have, except I never did." He shrugged. "I've been thinking."

"Always dangerous." She swallowed half her tea.

"What would you say about visiting the cultures after dinner?"

Kayna straightened in her chair. She'd anticipated a sweet suggestion for making love.

Brynn cocked his head to one side and sent a boyish grin her way. "Not exactly what you were expecting?"

"No, but that doesn't mean it's not a good idea." She bent closer to him and lowered her voice. "I could've sworn they were trying to lure me in there earlier. Before my family showed up."

All traces of cheerfulness fled from his face. "If we don't do this, we'll never get any closer to understanding what they want."

His somber mood was contagious. Nana's message replayed in her mind *"Granddaughter. Do not fear your gift. Sure an' the time ye could run from it has passed."*

Brynn reached across the table and laid his hand over hers. "You look as if a ghost walked over your grave."

"That's because one did." Kayna sopped up the last of the stew gravy with a piece of bread, following it with tea. "Was there any dessert?"

Brynn nodded. "I tucked some éclairs in the fridge. Back in a flash. Either I'm getting better at walking on this mother, or the seas are quieter."

She smiled. "Probably a little of both."

~

THE ÉCLAIR WAS a toothsome delight with its blend of custard, chocolate, and fluffy choux paste. Kayna finished hers in record time. When she looked up, Brynn met her gaze, his eyes serious.

"Ready?" he asked.

"Yes. This tête-á-tête with the cultures feels overdue."

Brynn got to his feet and came around the table to offer her a hand.

She took it and led the way up the stairs. Once they reached Deck Four's landing, she turned to Brynn. "I didn't say much about my conversations with Harold. He doesn't understand what he's feeling, but he senses the backlash from the cultures' energy field, and it's made him nervous and out of sorts. At least according to him, the captain and some of the crew are aware of it too, because the ship's not behaving like it, er she, usually does."

"Interesting. After you." Brynn made a sweeping half bow and traipsed up another steep, narrow flight of stairs. Kayna came to a halt about twenty feet from the cabins where his cultures were, facing away from him. "They're a little farther," he said.

"I know. I'm preparing myself." She thinned her lips into a tense line. "I didn't especially like it when my father showed up earlier."

"Is there anything I can do to get ready? I don't have your paranormal edge."

Kayna twirled to face him. He stared hard, trying to sense if anything had changed. If he looked from a particular angle, he thought he could discern a faint glow surrounding her. Brynn shook his head to clear his vision, but the nimbus didn't go away.

"What do you see?" she asked.

"It's probably a trick of the light." His tongue felt thick and stupid.

"Tell me what you see," she repeated.

"You… You're kind of glowing."

"It's my aura. When I open myself to my psychic side, others like me can see it."

"But I have bupkis in the way of psychic ability," Brynn protested. His skin felt one size too small for his body, and his fingers tingled unpleasantly. He recognized the sensation—adrenaline pumping from his sympathetic nervous system.

"Maybe you do, and just don't know it." She walked closer and placed a hand on his shoulder. "Nana told me not to be afraid. I'm telling you the same thing."

"Easy to say, harder to do." His heart slapped against his chest, and the corridor was suddenly so warm he broke into a sweat. "I've spent a whole lot of energy trying to normalize those archaea colonies, so I could continue to coexist with them, especially after that guy at McMurdo mentioned his had turned lethal."

Kayna scrunched her forehead into worried lines. "You alluded to that earlier. What exactly happened there?"

Brynn's gut tightened. "He was convinced the cultures tried to kill him."

"How is that even possible?" Her voice took on a shrill note.

"By bonding to his red blood cells and eroding their ability to carry oxygen." Brynn took a breath and went on. "They've had two deaths recently that the docs attributed to carbon monoxide poisoning, but Micah—that's the guy I spoke with—suspected otherwise. Since they never could locate a gas leak, I assume his theory is right on."

"Crap!" Kayna shook her head. "Even with that, I still don't believe these cultures mean you any harm. Hell, they managed to appear normal when you sampled them, probably to keep you from losing your sanity, and to make sure you got them on this ship."

"I hope you're right." Brynn slipped past her and pushed a door open.

She stepped into the room and stopped with her eyes closed and her hands extended in front of her, palms up. While she was meditating, or communing, or whatever she was doing, he rustled up an extra lab coat, mask, and gloves for her and put his on.

"Here." He handed the items over once she opened her eyes.

"Aren't you going to ask what I found?" She tucked the mask and gloves between her legs while she donned the lab coat and buttoned it. Once that was done, she gloved up and settled the mask in place.

"I'm not certain I want to know. The weirdness increased by a factor of ten, and I suspect we've barely tapped the tip of the iceberg."

"At least you're honest." She touched his arm. "Look at me." He met her gaze over the top of his mask. Something about her expression, vulnerable but determined, tugged at his heart. "My ability scared the crap out of Derek. He made it clear he never wanted to be confronted with it." She narrowed her eyes. "It's part of me. We're a package deal; I can't separate myself from what I am. I did that for Derek, and it turned me into half a person."

He closed the space between them and wrapped her in his arms. "Give me a little while to get used to it."

She hugged him briefly before stepping away. "I like the sound of that. Now let's visit these little guys. For what it's worth, my psi scan didn't come up with anything scary. Did you bring a microscope from your last lab?"

"Sure. It belongs to me. I wasn't about to leave it. It's in the other room, along with slides and stains."

Kayna made her way across the room that was crowded with bins to a small couch bolted to the far wall. She picked a bin from a pod and settled on the couch with it. The box fit nicely on her lap. "Come on." She gestured. "If we're going to figure this out, it will probably take both of us."

Once he was seated, she moved the bin between them. Stabilizing it with one hand, she gently lifted the lid with the other. "Oh, my." She whistled appreciatively. "You never told me how beautiful they are."

Brynn stared into the bin, taken aback. "They've changed." His mouth tasted sour, and his muscles tightened as he grappled with the unreality of what lay before him.

"How?" Her question thrummed with interest.

"Last time I looked, they were a pale gray-green."

"Some of them still are, but look at the range of colors. They're like a forest of exotic sea anemones."

Brynn's pulse accelerated. Kayna's description was accurate. The clusters, which looked like a cross between sea anemones and mushrooms, shaded from pale to dark green, but some were orange, and some pink, violet, and blue. He tried to come up with shifts in biochemical composition that would account for the riot of color before him, but couldn't think of a thing. Seawater hadn't contaminated them, so what could possibly have happened? Maybe they'd gotten chilled, despite him wrapping them well, for their trip from the island to the ship.

Or maybe they're changing into whatever Micah cultured at McMurdo.

"Don't try too hard to explain it," Kayna said. "But I think it would be worthwhile to check the other bins to see if whatever's going on in this one is universal."

Brynn winced. It was such an obvious next step, he felt like an idiot for not coming up with it first. "Once we're done with that," he said, "we can sample the colors and see if they look different under my scope."

"It's a date."

He couldn't see her mouth beneath her mask, but he could've sworn she was smiling. "Kayna."

She inclined her head. "Yes?"

"These cultures are starting to look like pictures Micah sent me. I'm not certain how safe it is."

She set her lips in a determined line. "If they were out to get us, I'd have sensed it."

"You trust your psi ability that much?"

She nodded. "I do. And how it feels about these cultures shifted from when I first heard about them."

"Maybe they're trying to lull you into complacency. The same way they suckered me into making sure they got to McMurdo."

"It's possible," she spoke slowly, "but not likely. I'm willing to take a chance. Let's see what we have here."

CHAPTER 14

Kayna stared at the colonies growing up the walls and along the floor of the bin sitting next to her. Traces of magenta growth medium were apparent beneath the clumps of cells. The same melody she'd heard earlier tweaked the edges of her hearing. "Do you hear anything?" she asked.

An uncomfortable look flitted across his face before he smoothed his features. "Yes, it's like a deep hum, barely audible, but there. Does that mean you hear it too?"

"Not in quite the same way, but yes." She flashed a thumbs up sign. "*Folie á deux!* The best kind."

"Shared madness, huh?" He walked across the room and began checking the other bins. "This is definitely a day for firsts. I'm not only falling headlong into a world I never thought was real, I'm embracing it." He paused a beat. "So they're really vocalizing?" At Kayna's nod, he went on. "Do you suppose that's their way of manipulating their environment?"

She cocked her head to one side. "That's why most of us talk, so why not them?"

Brynn furrowed his brow as he thought about what she'd said. A muscle twitched in his jaw. "When I initially thought I heard them, back on Grytviken, I was certain it was a hallucination from being by myself for so long."

"It's a logical conclusion." Kayna infused calmness into her voice to normalize an experience that was about as extraordinary as anything Brynn had likely come across. "Besides, this is a whole lot easier to swallow than believing the McMurdo colonies turned lethal."

Brynn rolled his eyes. "No kidding. So long as we've segued into LaLa Land, the first night after I brought them aboard the ship, I could've sworn they lured me into making certain they'd transitioned well."

"That was what pushed you to review your notes to try to figure out what was going on."

He nodded. "Exactly."

Kayna placed the lid back on the bin next to her. "We won't figure out why—or even if—we're right about them wanting to get to their cousins at McMurdo until we actually arrive there, but isn't this what scientists do? Search out new worlds where no man has gone before?"

"Captain Kirk, I presume?" He peeked into another bin and shook his head. "Curious. Some of them look like the one next to you, two to be precise. The other three look like all of them used to."

"I'm not surprised, evolutionary biology takes time."

Brynn frowned. "Are you suggesting this is natural selection viewed through a twisted form of time-lapse photography?"

"I don't know any more than you do. Probably less since this is your field, and I only took a couple of microbiology classes. Let's categorize what we know. Aren't archaea really, really ancient?"

"Yes. Estimates peg them at close to four billion years old. They're the oldest life form on Earth, and so ubiquitous it's thought they probably exist on other planets too."

"Oh, yeah." She nodded. "I'd forgotten that part. Aren't there variations that live in really off-the-wall environments, like salt, methane, high heat, and extreme cold?"

"Precisely. Archaea and bacteria probably split off from a common ancestor a very long time ago. They're the only prokaryotes."

"Gawk! I feel like I'm back in medical school. Let's see, those are the single-celled critters that have a tough, rigid cellular wall, and no nucleus."

"You must've been a star student." Brynn grinned approvingly. "Eukaryotes, the ones with nuclei, split off from prokaryotes a mere couple of million years ago. They're the building blocks for every complex life form."

"There must've been an evolutionary advantage for bacteria and archaea to maintain their independence from everybody else." Kayna tucked the bin near her under one arm and stood. "Let's get this show rolling. It takes time to stain slides."

Brynn joined her, leading the way across the hall to the cabin he'd set up as a mini-lab. "There were huge advantages," he said. "For one thing, archaea's cellular wall is so tough it's impervious to pathogens or parasites."

"Probably why they survived." Kayna glanced around the second cabin, which was very similar to the one they'd left, except for a desk at one end. Brynn busied himself opening a thickly padded case and extracting his microscope.

"They've done more than survived, they've flourished." Brynn plugged his scope in and held out his hands for the bin still tucked beneath her arm. "Certain strains love the cold, so they're particularly prevalent in polar waters and plankton colonies. I'm sure that's why it was so straightforward to find them on South Georgia."

Kayna righted a chair that had fallen onto its side and sat next to Brynn. He worked quickly, with a fluidity of movement that spoke to an easy familiarity with his trade. After setting a few slides aside, he placed an unstained one onto his scope and bent over the eyepieces.

"How can you see anything?" Kayna leaned forward.

"This is a darkfield and brightfield scope," he explained. "The darkfield works well for unstained material, if I'm not looking for anything too subtle. Lucky the scope wasn't plugged in when that power surge happened."

After a long moment, curiosity got the better of her and she pressed her shoulder against his. "Well?"

Brynn lifted his head, a thoughtful expression on his face. "Take a peek." He shifted so she could slide into his seat.

Kayna stared through the eyepieces, adjusting them for her vision. She raised her head, turned, and gazed at Brynn, feeling confused. "Maybe it's been too long since I've done much except look at patient samples, but I could swear the cells on that slide have nuclei, which means they're not proks anymore."

"It's exactly the same thing I found," he confirmed. A corner of his mouth twisted downward. "Assuming it's not *folie á deux*, it's good science that both of us came to the same conclusion. Let's check this one." He swapped the slide on the stand for one of the stained ones. "You look, and then I will."

Kayna stared at the slide. This one was easier to see since stain outlined the cell's features, and Brynn had switched to brightfield. Her breath caught as the implications of what lay beneath her vision hammered home. "Your turn." She slid into her original chair.

He laid a hand over hers. "I heard that little gasp, but let me look for myself before we talk about it." Scant moments later, he lifted his head and turned to face her. "This slide came from cells that were the original color, that gray-green. The first one was from a violet section."

"This one looked like I remember bacteria looking," Kayna said. "No nucleus. No organelles."

"Yes, what's on this slide is archaea. It's anybody's guess what was on the first slide. The only piece of good news is Micah's mutant cells are still proks—and they looked nothing like either of these slides. So maybe your instincts about my colonies not having lethal leanings are correct."

The ship pitched, and the slide rattled against the microscope. Brynn grabbed his instrument, moved the slide, and asked her to hand him the microscope's case.

"Pretty delicate, huh?" She observed as she passed the foam-padded case to him.

"It'll be a miracle if it's usable once I get home." He packaged the scope and laid the case on its side beneath the desk. "Too bad. It cost a lot, but beyond that, I'm fond of this particular model, and they don't make them anymore."

Tapping sounded at the door. It might've been a gunshot for the effect it had on Kayna's nerves. She sat bolt upright and spun her body around in the chair to stare at the door.

"Come in," Brynn called.

The door opened and Harold stepped into the room. "If this isn't a good time—" he began, the characteristic hubris absent from his speech.

"Nah, it's fine." Brynn straddled his chair so he faced Harold, and rested his arms across its backrest. "How'd you even know we were in here?"

"I drew deck duty. Actually, I volunteered. We've gotten more radio broadcasts about the U.S.-Russian problem, and it's damned worrisome. Since I didn't think I'd be able to sleep, I've been checking to make sure everything's battened down, and I saw both of you through the porthole playing with the microscope." He shrugged uncomfortably. "Once I shed my waterproofs, I thought I'd see what you found."

Kayna glanced around the room, but there wasn't an extra chair to invite Harold to sit. "What we found was interesting," she began, "but not alarming."

Harold fluttered his hand in a circular motion. "More, Doc. That tells me less than nothing."

"We won't know anything until we get to McMurdo," Brynn said. "I need to run a series of tests to check the composition of cellular membranes, and I can't do that on board this ship. My measurements have to be precise, and the ship's too unsteady."

"Doublespeak," Harold muttered. "What do you think you found? I'm not about to run and tell anyone." He flapped both hands in a disgusted gesture. "Who the fuck would I tell? The captain could care less, and the crew's expertise lies in electronics and mechanics."

Kayna exchanged a quick look with Brynn, hoping Harold wouldn't pick up on it. She felt protective of the cultures. "It may be doublespeak, but it's all we know—at least right now." She stood and picked her way around culture boxes, pulling her mask out of the way to make it easier to talk. "I'm satisfied the contents of these bins don't pose a threat to your ship."

Harold drew his brows together until they practically touched over the bridge of his nose. "Then why does the ship feel odd to me?"

She couldn't tell him what she suspected—that the ship was responding to psi emanations from the cultures. Hoping he wouldn't read the lie in her eyes, she said, "I'm not sure. Maybe it's the bad weather, or the accidents. It's not like we lost anyone. If something truly sinister were afoot, someone might've washed overboard in these seas."

Harold glared at her. "There're things you're not saying."

Oh sweetie, if you only knew.

"Maybe so." She kept her voice low, soothing—the same one she used to calm troubled patients. "But you know the important parts. Your ship's not in danger—at least not from the cultures growing in these bins."

"Do you agree?" Harold shifted his shrewd gaze to Brynn.

"I do. If this ship ends up staying at McMurdo for a space of time, you're most welcome in my lab. I can fill you in on my findings then, once I actually have some."

"Not very fucking likely."

Kayna flashed back to Harold's earlier statement about listening to radio broadcasts. "What'd you hear on the radio?"

"They're all posturing like a bunch of monkeys in the zoo. Only problem is that once a man makes a threat, it's hard to back down without looking like a coward."

"Who made what threats?" Brynn asked.

"Your president—" Harold's voice was laced with scorn "—told the Russian president he'd send troops to Ukraine and impose sanctions on Russian trade unless Russia called its troops home immediately."

"How is that different than what was happening earlier today?" Kayna asked.

"It's not, but no one's hunting for common ground."

"That isn't sounding good," Brynn mumbled.

"Not very bloody much we can do about it," Harold said and screwed his face into a grimace. "Once we pass the South Shetlands—and that could happen by tomorrow morning—I'm certain we'll run into pack ice at some point. We'll need the Americans to send an icebreaker to clear a path for us once we hit the Ross Sea—if not before."

"I can't imagine they'd refuse," Kayna said.

"I hope your confidence is justified." Harold pulled the door open, and then turned back to face them. "In case you've forgotten, this is a Russian ship. I'm the only crewperson, except for the cook, not carrying a Russian or Ukrainian passport. I'll bid you two goodnight. If either of you changes your mind about telling me what you really saw through your microscope, I'll be on the bridge or in my cabin."

Kayna watched Harold step into the corridor and pull the door shut. She took a few steps toward Brynn and opened her mouth, but he shook his head. "We're pretty much done here for tonight."

Warmth added amber motes to his hazel eyes. "Your cabin or mine?"

She smiled broadly. "You're presuming a lot."

"Am I? We need to talk, and for that we need privacy."

"My cabin, then. At least it has the surgery between it and the door. And a storage room on the other side of my bathroom."

"Right behind you." He got to his feet, walked the bins he'd drawn samples from back to the other room, and took a few minutes to secure them.

Kayna took off her lab coat, mask, and gloves while she waited, her mind racing with questions she lacked the scientific knowledge to totally answer. If eukaryotes had branched off from prokaryotes a couple of million years before, it was possible for the more primitive form to spawn cells that made up the building blocks of all living creatures.

"Ready?" Brynn asked, and she started.

"Sure." She did a double take. "Guess I was really deep in thought since I missed you taking off all your lab paraphernalia."

He draped an arm around her shoulders. "Yeah, I've been thinking too." Once they were in the corridor, Brynn pulled the door closed behind them. "I need to stop for a quick minute in my cabin to get a few things."

"Oh-oh." She smothered a smile. "Sounds like someone's moving in."

"Not exactly, but you've got to look out for us men. We're sneaky like that. Leave a toothbrush or a T-shirt, and we've staked our claim to you forever."

"Better watch it," she cautioned from the door to his very neat cabin. "You've seen how I scatter things about. Anything you bring with you is fair game for getting lost."

"You hear that?" Brynn held up a robe and talked to it. "Abandon hope all ye who enter here." With a rakish grin, he walked toward her, the robe slung over an arm and a toothbrush in one hand. "The robe says it doesn't care."

"Breathing life into inanimate objects, huh? Maybe you were too isolated on South Georgia."

Brynn jockeyed her back into the corridor and shut his door. "If cell cultures can hum to me, anything is possible."

They walked down the stairs and into her surgery without saying anything else. Kayna felt alive in a way she hadn't since she'd walked away from her psi ability as a teenager. For the first time, she wished she'd cultivated her magic. While it didn't feel exactly foreign, it was far from second nature. All her arcane, magic sourcebooks were tucked away in the attic of her mother's house.

Unless she ferreted them out and burned them...

Kayna flipped on the overheads in her surgery and dropped into a chair. She motioned Brynn to the facing one.

"Ah, gee—" he pulled a long face "—I hoped we'd fall into bed and pick up where we left off earlier."

"We will, but not quite yet. Besides, you're the one who said we needed to talk. It just so happens that I agree. Tea?"

"Sure." He pushed the door shut.

She reached over and flipped on the hot pot. While the water heated, she popped teabags into cups and added sugar. Once she handed him a steaming mug, she slumped back against her chair and said, "You're going to have to help me with the science. The best I could come up with is that if prokaryotes could spawn eukaryotes once, they can do it again."

"If you're hoping for a bunch of erudite gibberish from me, I'm afraid you'll be disappointed." He sipped his tea and made a small, satisfied sound. "That's the best explanation I could come up with too." Brynn nailed her with his gaze. "Keep in mind, we need to run tests to make sure what we saw was valid. I'm better than ninety percent certain, but still..."

"The McMurdo samples." She fished the teabag out of her cup and set it aside. "Do you suppose they're doing the same thing?"

"I don't think so. From Micah's description, and the slides he scanned and emailed me, they're still proks, but with cellular additions I've never seen."

"I don't suppose it's worth the fifty bucks for five minutes on the sat phone to talk with him again."

Brynn rested his head on an upturned hand. "No on two counts. First off, it would take way more than five minutes, and I'm not certain it's worth a few hundred bucks if all we end up doing is confirming that what we have is different from what's growing there."

"It's unusual for colonies to spontaneously mutate into something radically different." Kayna spoke thoughtfully. "To have two unrelated colonies racing toward different ends is just plain weird."

"Exactly. I came to the same conclusion. So did Jack, the guy who runs McMurdo. Another problem with the sat phone is it's located on the bridge. The crew is mostly Russian-speaking, but it would be impossible to have a private conversation."

"I hadn't considered that." Kayna sipped her tea and set the cup down. "Before we retire to my bed, if we end up doing that, we need to clarify some things."

"Like what?" He drained his cup, set it aside, and steepled his fingers in front of his chest.

"I felt this jolt of—" she searched for words "—instant attraction the second I saw you. I've never trusted things like that." He waited, giving her space, so she forged ahead. "My magical part is screaming at me that you're my Prince Charming, the Galahad I've been waiting my whole life for, but I'm having a hell of a hard time trusting it."

The raven chose that moment to pop into her head, feathers fluffed, eyes shining as if to verify that Brynn was indeed her proper mate. Kayna considered mentioning the bird, but bit her tongue. Pushy spirit guides were a bit too off-the-wall for intimate conversations.

The corners of Brynn's mouth twitched into half a frown. "I'm having the same problem, but I'm so smitten by your considerable charms, maybe it's easier for me to lay my qualms aside. Would you feel better if we'd met under more normal circumstances?"

"What do you mean exactly?"

He waved an airy hand. "Oh, you know. I met you at a scientific convention. We had drinks, dinner. I called you the next week, and we did lunch. Maybe we tossed a few more dinners into the mix, and a movie or two, before I took you to bed."

Kayna exhaled sharply. "Sure, that would feel better."

"Is that how you started with Derek?" Brynn furled his brows. "It's an exact replica of how I started with Rebecca, and look how well that turned out."

"It's not quite how I started with Derek. We were poor medical students. But if you exchange sandwiches in the park for going out, it's close. I see where you're heading, though."

Brynn got up, closed the distance between them, and pulled her to her feet. Once he'd wrapped his arms around her, he kept talking. "So we both did things the traditional way, and it didn't work. Maybe this won't, either, but I've never been so attracted to a woman—ever. You're practically all I think about, Kayna. You're there when I close my eyes, and I've been half-aroused since I first saw you on the beach in Grytviken."

He ran his hands slowly down her back, leaving a trail of sparks in their wake. "Don't get me wrong. That part feels really good. I'd been afraid the sexual side of me was dead."

"You too, huh?" she murmured against his shoulder.

"Me too. Have we talked enough, sweetheart? Can we go to bed now?"

Kayna didn't answer. Instead, she turned her face up for him to kiss her.

CHAPTER 15

Brynn gathered the woman in his arms as close as he could. Familiar hospital smells of disinfectant soap mingled with wildflowers, jasmine, and Kayna's signature feminine scent. He buried his hands under her silky, dark hair and settled his lips over hers. He knew he should be gentle, take things slow, but he wanted to inhale her, drag her to the bed, and claim her in a wild, pagan sexual slide into ecstasy. He'd never felt that way about Rebecca. Their lovemaking had always been tame, even a bit staid. More clinical than passionate. Each knew where to touch and how hard to rub, but the intense wave of desire that weakened his knees had never been part of his earlier relationship. In a rush of self-knowledge, he understood that was why he'd hedged about marrying her.

Kayna hooked her arms beneath his and drew his body even closer. Her breathing quickened against his questing tongue, and her nipples turned into hard little marbles where they pressed against his chest. With their mouths still glued together, he walked them awkwardly toward the bedroom. She dropped her hands to his butt and gripped it hard as she repositioned herself to straddle one of his legs. Heat from her core seared his upper thigh. Between trying to move to where they could lie down and the ship's unpredictable lurching movement, they almost ended up on the floor.

She dragged her mouth from his, her eyes soft with desire and her golden skin flushed with wanting him. "I don't want to let go of you, either, but what do you say we walk to the bed?"

When she turned away from him, he slid his hands beneath her top and tugged it over her head. Once it was off, he unsnapped her bra. "Where do you want these?" he asked, his voice raspy with needing her.

"Doesn't matter." She turned to face him, and he almost forgot to breathe. Her breasts were luscious globes riding high on her sculpted ribcage. His hands itched to close over their perfect spheres. He reached for her, but she batted his fingers away and unzipped the neck of his shirt so she could pull it over his head. With a small sigh, she splayed her fingers across his chest and then traced the lines of muscle covering his shoulders and upper arms.

Kayna met his gaze with her smoky, green eyes. "Has anyone ever told you how damn near flawless you are?"

A flash of heat began in his stomach and traveled upward until his face caught fire. "No—" he shook his head "—no one ever has."

"Hard to believe," she murmured, still running her fingertips over his skin. "Not that I've entertained many men in my bed, but naked bodies are part of what I do. I've seen thousands. Yours is amazing."

"I could tell you the same thing." He reached for the button and zipper on her slacks, and she toed off her house slippers so she could step out of her pants and underwear. Droplets of moisture glistened on the black curls between her legs, and her heady scent intensified, musky with her arousal. His cock felt about to burst, and she hadn't even touched him yet. Hell, he still had most of his clothes on.

"Turnabout's fair play." Her fingers worked the zipper and clasp holding his trousers in place.

"Hold up." He tried to catch his breath, but his heart hammered against his chest. "Shoes."

She glanced at his feet. "We've got to get you something that doesn't have laces."

"Not going to help right now." He brushed his lips over hers and covered the few feet to her bed. Sitting, he unlaced his boots, pulled them off, and moved to the waistband of his pants.

"No! Let me." She pushed him back onto the bed and knelt over him, undoing his pants, but she didn't take them off right away. Instead, she laid the palm of her hand over his achingly hard penis. The heat from her drove him mad. He tried to push his pants out of the way, but she closed her hands over his. "Uh-uh. My game."

Brynn licked dry lips and grinned. "It was your game last time. We never got anywhere near that condom."

"We would've—" she smiled back "—if a patient hadn't shown up. Aw, crap. Speaking of which…" She vaulted off him and trotted into her surgery.

"What?" he called after her, so desperate for the intensity of her pressed close to him, he almost followed her. "Is it midnight already, Cinderella?"

"Gotta lock the door." In moments, she was back by his side, but he'd taken full advantage of them and lay nude on the bed gazing at her.

He drank in her beauty and felt like the luckiest man in the universe. "Tell me what you want."

"Me on top." He nodded and reached for her, but she snapped up the condom that was still on the bedside table and rolled it onto him before coming into the shelter of his arms. "That way we won't have to worry about it later," she murmured before she kissed him.

Her body jammed against his was charged with promise.

Wherever he touched her, his fingertips sent jolts of pure lust to his loins and brain, and he soared higher than he'd ever thought possible as he touched, pressed, and kneaded her pliant flesh.

"I want to make this last," she gasped, tearing her mouth from his, "but I have to have you. Maybe once we get more used to one another, we can slow things down, but not now." Rising to her knees, she straddled his body.

He wrapped a hand around his cock to stabilize it and when she lowered herself slowly over him, he fought for control. Usually condoms had a dampening effect, but he barely noticed the thin sheath. Thank Christ she stopped moving once he was fully encased in her body. Maybe she sensed how close he was to losing it. She tensed her muscles around him once, and then again. He groaned and settled his hands on her hips. If he could control her motion, he'd have a prayer of a chance.

Kayna licked her lips, her gaze never leaving his face as she sat atop him, her body displayed for him to admire, to worship. He moved one hand so he could tease her clit with a finger. She gasped and pressed against his hand, rocking between his cock and fingers. He felt the tension in her vault and also in her swollen nub. Knowing he aroused her as much as she did him thrilled him beyond measure. There was passion in this woman, unbridled lust. He vowed to be worthy of her.

She closed her hand over his, showing him the rhythm she needed. He rubbed harder but in smaller circles. After a harsh, panting gasp, she dissolved in a pool of heat and liquid, muscles convulsing around his shaft. Brynn's balls tightened, and he forced himself to breathe, just breathe. He could come next time she did. Damn if she wouldn't get at least two good climaxes out of tonight.

"Aw, sweetheart." She lay atop him, with a knee on either side of his body, and covered his mouth with hers. The taste and feel of her mouth, lips passion-soft from her climax, fed his soul. He wove his arms around her and held her against his chest, breathing in her glorious scent and kissing her back with abandon.

Slowly, he withdrew a little and pushed back inside. In between kisses, he murmured, "Can we roll over?" She licked his lower lip and then planted a string of little biting kisses across his chin. Taking that for a yes, he jockeyed them onto their sides and then positioned her body beneath his. She wound her legs around his waist, opening herself even more for him.

Brynn supported his body on his arms and gazed down at Kayna. She gripped his hips with her legs, and her body writhed beneath his, her nipples tight buds of desire, her golden skin splotchy with craving. He pulled almost all the way out and made little teasing circles around the opening to her body. She laid her hands along his sides and tugged insistently, clearly wanting him back inside, but he stayed put.

"Please."

Her gaze melted his heart and heated his loins beyond boiling.

Because holding back was damn near killing him, he pushed slowly back inside. Another few long, slow strokes and he was lost. His body undermined the restraint his brain would have imposed, and he slammed into her again and again.

Her legs tightened around him and her fingers dug into his sides. "Yes," she moaned. "Oh my God, yes."

Her rhythmic contractions urged him on. Semen juddered out of him in slow, tantalizing bursts as her muscles milked him. For long moments, there wasn't enough air in the room, and his vision faded at the edges. He let himself down atop her, breathing as if he'd run the Boston Marathon. Her chest heaved beneath his, and her nails raked his back as the last of her orgasm spent itself.

Not wanting to negate having worn protection, he held onto the base of his cock as he withdrew. Hopping off the bed, he tossed the slip of plastic into a nearby trash bin, and then sat back down. "The Russian housekeepers will have a heyday with that one," he said, still breathing hard.

"Well," Kayna put her hands behind her head and smiled broadly. "Can't very well toss it down the toilet. For Christ's sake, we can't even put toilet paper into their sanitary system."

He sat on the edge of the bed. "I don't want to talk about septic systems. That was amazing. I can't believe how good it was. How good you were." He took her hand and stroked her belly and her silken skin with his other hand.

"More than good. We barely know one another, but this…fire that burns between us…" She hesitated, clearly hunting for words. "It's what I always thought sex was supposed to be like, except it never was for me. I figured I wasn't all that responsive, or that there was more hype than reality to sex." She shrugged uncomfortably. "It made it damned difficult to talk with patients —and a whole bunch of them wanted to talk about it."

He grinned ruefully. "I didn't get that quite so much in the ER. Mostly I got the drug-seekers."

"Yeah." She grinned back. "The ones I turned down in my day clinics."

"I'm considering returning to medical practice once I get back to the States."

"Really?" She furled her brows. "Why? Don't you like research?"

Brynn turned the question over. "At first I did, but over the few years I've done it, I've found I miss human interaction. Running my own lab, even back in the States, was pretty isolating. Mostly I delegated stuff to graduate students and post docs. They'd run experiments and then report back in. It's only recently I've admitted this to myself—" he resettled his legs so the wooden edge around the mattress didn't cut into them "—but the grass wasn't greener."

She moved a hand from behind her head and placed it over the one he had on her stomach. "It rarely is. I've been feeling, oh I don't know, maybe avoidant—and guilty—for not working harder to keep my magic up to snuff." She furrowed her forehead in thought. "It's actually a whole lot deeper than that. Between Derek and Mom, I pushed my ability aside. Plus, I was so busy with med school and residency, it was easy to come up with excuses."

"Is that a problem?"

She nodded solemnly. "Yes. I need my paranormal abilities now, and they're rusty."

"I suppose it would be like any other skill," he murmured.

"You'd be right, but I've forgotten lots of things, including most of the spells I used to know."

He crawled over her body and lay between her and the wall in the tiny bunk. She rolled onto her side and fitted her back to his front. "You've seen your grandmother recently," he said. "Maybe she could refresh your memory."

"Good point. You're pretty quick on the uptake for someone who doesn't know anything about psychic phenomena."

"I've read a little. And everyone's seen those psychokinetic guys bend spoons on television."

"This feels nice." She snuggled back against him. "You feel nice."

"So do you. More than nice. It feels like we belong together."

"If I trust my magic senses, we do, but my brain's mush right now. Let's try to get a little sleep. I never know who's going to wake me in the night pounding on the door."

"No kidding." He tucked his body protectively around hers. "It's like working the ER but with no backup and no time off."

"When I signed on with this ship—and agreed to doctor for them in exchange for my ticket price—I was planning on the whole deal only taking about three weeks, but the junket to South Georgia added over a week to the total."

"Are you complaining?" He nuzzled her neck, thinking how incredible she felt wrapped in his arms.

"No. The thing I'm trying to figure out is if you and I were part of the plan."

"What plan?" His mind wanted to drift downward into sleep, but he forced himself to focus.

"For a few minutes, suspend everything you think you know about how the world works." She hesitated, maybe for emphasis or maybe to organize her thoughts. "I figure your archaea colonies have an ulterior motive. They want to be reunited with their distant cousins at McMurdo. Maybe that honking jolt of electricity wakened that need, or maybe it's always been there, but they didn't have a mechanism until you showed up."

"Other scientists have worked out of that lab space," he pointed out.

"Yes, but maybe they weren't studying archaea. They're so common, most scientific types trying to earn their chops would probably focus on something sexier."

"Go on." Brynn recognized truth in her words. His dissertation research and everything that had come after had focused on much more exotic creatures, the zebras of the microbiology world, not the cats and dogs.

"So maybe it was you. Maybe it was the unexpected electrical charge, which could have had a major impact on their cellular membranes, but something activated them." She paused. "We have no idea how they hold ancestral memories. For all we know, they're aware of every other cell like themselves."

"They don't have a central nervous system."

"No, but maybe they have something that serves the same function. Sorry if I'm not making a whole of sense. I'm sleepy. Anyway, you and I could be collateral to the archaea's purpose, but somehow I think we're wrapped up in it. Having my father, who was an environmental biologist, show up and stake a claim to your samples makes me even surer they have untapped potential."

She gave a breathy little sigh before continuing. "I've always lived my life carefully. I'm a planner, and an anal one at that. I've never been one to go off on spontaneous wild goose chases. The idea to go to Antarctica clawed its way out of the blue one day. I quashed it as being ridiculous, absurd, but it bounced back and swatted me in the ass. In a shockingly short time, I'd looked into jobs and landed one, which was little shy of miraculous since M.D. jobs at McMurdo are scarce as hen's teeth."

"You haven't tossed out anything that can't be explained by serendipity."

"No," she agreed, "I haven't. But when too many coincidences pile on top of one another, it looks suspicious."

"So you see the archaea as sentient?" She nodded against his chest. "For the love of God don't spread this around," he said, "but I do too. Why do you suppose they're trying to unite with the McMurdo colonies?"

"Because they're not fighting the trip. They're mutating as if they're getting ready for something."

A chill marched down his spine. "Like what?"

"I have no idea. If the proks at McMurdo have truly joined the dark side, maybe these ones will have some way to neutralize them. The reason your cultures felt ominous to me was because they kicked my psi ability into high gear. It's been a long time since I've been in a hypersensitive state, and what I interpreted as danger was probably my power feeling strange because I haven't called on it, or tried to use it very much, in so long."

"This is fascinating, but I need time to think about everything before I can discuss it intelligently. It's how I process things. Can you stay awake for a little more?"

"Sure. I'm good for maybe ten more minutes before I spontaneously combust."

He chuckled. "That's the oddest description of sleep I've ever heard. What did you think about Harold's concerns?"

"You mean about a war brewing?"

"Yeah."

"I can't imagine two nuclear powers being irresponsible enough to unleash something that has the potential to wipe out life on Earth."

"Yes, but you're being rational," he pointed out. "The Russian president is a real wildcard, and ours isn't a barrel of laughs. I can see things spiraling out of control."

"You're being an alarmist. I'll bet it's not the way you practiced medicine."

He tightened his hold on her, lulled by the warmth of her body despite his grim thoughts. "No, it's not. I'm not sure I can explain it. You have your hunches, probably fueled by magic, and I have mine, fueled by God only knows what, but I have a really uneasy feeling about this."

"It's because we're stranded on a miniature boat in the middle of a raging ocean."

Brynn didn't say anything. It was more than that, but talking about it wouldn't change anything. "Sleep, sweetheart."

"You too. Pray for an uneventful night."

"I stopped praying when I was a child, but I do hope no one bothers us before morning." The sound of her even breathing told him she was sinking toward sleep. He cradled her tenderly, filled with the need to protect her from the uncertainties of the world. No matter why they'd found one another, he'd make certain nothing harmed her. Not now. Not ever.

I guess that means I'm staying at McMurdo.

What if the base tells me no?

I'll figure something out. Between my medical skills and my research ability, I'll make myself so fucking indispensable, they won't be able to imagine life without me.

His body was exhausted, but his tumbling thoughts kept Brynn awake for a long time. Just when he was considering slipping into the surgery to rustle around for some helpful drug, something shifted and the descent into blackness was almost immediate.

CHAPTER 16

Kayna sat at her computer updating her medical records. Brynn had wakened her early when he tried to slip out of her bed undetected, but the bunk was much too small for one of them to leave without the other noticing. He'd kissed her softly and told her to go back to sleep. Almost as if it had been a hypnotic suggestion, she hadn't awakened until seven-thirty.

Between a spate of sore throats, residual seasickness cases, and a wart removal, she hadn't gotten out of her surgery at all and it was the middle of the afternoon. Harold had announced "land ho" over the PA system hours ago, so she assumed they'd made the South Shetland Islands. The anchor chain rumbled and she sat up straighter. Why were they stopping? She'd just scrambled to her feet, intent on searching for Harold, when Brynn strode into her surgery. "Feel like stretching your legs on land?"

"Sure, but where are we?"

"The ship has supplies for Arctowski Station. It's a Polish base on King George Island at the northern end of the South Shetlands. I checked with Harold. We won't be here long, only a few hours, but he invited us to go ashore with the Zodiacs."

Kayna narrowed her eyes. "I wonder if he asked any of the other scientists."

Brynn shrugged. "I can't answer that, but you'd better bundle up. Crew opened the sea doors, and I went out on deck for a stroll. It's bitter out there. Not much more than ten degrees, plus there's a mother of a wind."

She gazed at his Arctic Pac boots, thick pants, wool hat, and unzipped parka and rolled her eyes. "Gosh, my powers of observation are on vacation, or I would've noticed you weren't exactly dressed for another amorous adventure."

"Later. I'll take that as an invitation." He winked suggestively and clapped his hands together. "How about if I close the door and watch you get dressed?"

A laugh bubbled up from her belly. "I have a better idea. Could you run down to the kitchen and find me something to eat, please? Cheese and crackers would do it. I had coffee for breakfast, along with the last cinnamon bun, but that's been it for the day."

"Of course. Back in a flash, but I'd rather stay for the floor show."

"You won't miss much." She headed for her quarters. "Remember, I'm piling things on, not taking them off." When he didn't answer, she realized he'd gone in search of a snack for her.

I could get used to being taken care of. It wouldn't take much.

Kayna stifled a grin and layered up. By the time Brynn came back, she was sweating, but it would be transitory once they left the warmth of the ship.

He untucked his gloves from under his arm and laid a paper bag on her desk. "What do you want to do with the food?"

"Maybe we can take it with us and have a picnic on the beach."

"It's way too cold for that, but it's possible the guys at the station would let us sit inside. Maybe they'll even have coffee or tea."

"Here." She held out a small backpack, and he dropped the

food into it. Angling her arms into the straps, she slipped the pack on. That done, she snugged her hat over her ears and secured her drug cabinet. "I'm ready." She picked up a pair of gloves and worked her fingers into their plush folds.

Brynn walked out of her surgery and waited while she locked the door behind them, struggling to set the lock with her gloves on. He took her arm, and they walked out the gangway door into a stiff breeze that froze the exposed skin on her face almost instantly.

"Whew!" She pulled her neck gaiter over her mouth and nose. "All the cilia inside my nose just froze solid."

"Told you it was cold. Be careful, the deck's really icy. I didn't realize it, because it blends in with the decking, and I damn near fell a little bit ago."

They headed for a small group huddled at the top of the gangway. "Guess that answers my earlier question about whether Harold invited anyone else," she murmured, but wasn't sure Brynn heard her because the wind whipped the words out of her mouth.

"Hey, Doc." Chris waved before hunching his slender body against the wind.

She and Brynn joined the others. "We all get shore leave," Zach said. He might have been smiling, but the lower part of his face was swathed in a balaclava. "Harold made the rounds at lunchtime and told everyone they could visit Arctowski, but we're the only ones who wanted to brave the cold."

"If they think it's cold now, I wonder how they'll do at McMurdo?" Abel mused.

Zach shrugged. "Not our problem."

"Still feeling okay?" Kayna asked. Guilt twinged since she hadn't followed up with him, trusting he'd seek her out if he needed help.

"Better than okay. Guess I found my sea legs."

"That's not all he found," Abel muttered with a pleased undertone.

Chris made a chopping motion. "No dirty talk around me. I don't have anyone to snuggle up with."

"Yes, dear." Abel clapped him on the back.

"Look." Brynn extended an arm, and Kayna saw a Zodiac chugging around the boat with Harold standing in its stern, piloting the craft. "Should we go down the ladder?"

"Not until he ties up the boat," Chris offered.

"Hey! Wait for me. I want to escape this floating bucket of bolts too," Ted yelled. He catapulted around the corner, slipped on the icy deck, and landed on his ass. "Ooph. Kinda knocks the wind out of a guy," he complained as he rolled onto his hands and knees and stood. When he covered the few remaining feet between them, it was at a much more sedate pace.

"Are you hurt?" Kayna asked.

"Nah, too much padding for that, plus I've got all these clothes on top of my blubber."

"The seas really calmed down," Zach said. "Thank God."

"Only because Admiralty Bay is protected," Abel cut in.

Kayna inhaled, enjoying the sharp scent of salt air after the staleness inside the ship. So what if her nose felt frozen. It was exhilarating to be outside. "How long from here to McMurdo?"

"Between seven and ten days," Zach said. "What? You're getting tired of our floating palace?"

"Maybe a little. Oh-oh, Harold's motioning." She started down the ladder. The steps were as slick as the deck, so she held onto the side rails and then Harold's arm when she stepped into the black pontoon raft. The others piled in after her, and they motored across the bay where a sandy beach stretched beneath a weathered, multi-story, wooden structure that looked like it was once a lighthouse.

Once they exited the raft, Brynn moved to her side and draped an arm around her shoulders. "Look at all the whale bones. There was a huge whaling industry all through the Antarctic region until the early nineteen hundreds. I found a couple places on South Georgia with enormous piles of bones."

"I remember the museum on South Georgia with all the whaling paraphernalia." She bent and ran a gloved hand over a three-foot-long bone fragment. "Wow, those guys were huge. That would also explain the deserted lighthouse."

"We'll see you inside," Chris said and trotted after Ted, Zach, and Abel, who were heading down the beach toward a collection of bright yellow railroad cars. When Kayna looked closer, she realized the structures were pre-fab buildings sitting on stilts to keep them above ground level.

She straightened. "Let's walk a little. I hate to waste our time off the boat sitting in an overheated research station."

"Me too. How about if we head that way?" Brynn pointed around a spit of land bordering a frozen body of water. "I spent most of the day after I left you working up the samples I stained last night and making a few new ones."

She fell into step next to him, and he wound an arm around her waist. "What'd you find?" she asked.

"I'm guessing you know stains work by differentially bonding to specific cellular structures depending on their composition. In any event, there are two discrete organisms in those bins: the proks I started with and a much more modern single celled organism."

"Didn't we figure that out last night?"

He pulled her closer to his body. "Last night was the barest beginning. I wanted to see if I could duplicate our results. Once I'd done that, I used different stains to see if I could tease out more differences. I'm far from satisfied, but my curiosity is piqued."

"Did you save any of the slides so I can look?"

He nodded. "I'd welcome another set of eyes. Sometimes we see what we want to see. Not that you're any more objective than me, but still…" His voice trailed off. "I also spent a lot of time thinking about some of the things you said before we fell asleep."

He stopped talking. After a few moments, she prodded, "And?"

"I want to know more about your psychic side."

She skirted two seals skidding around on the ice and barking at each other. "It's not easy to describe or explain."

"Sure, but why do you have it and I don't?"

She stopped walking and turned to look at him. "According to Nana, I inherited my power from her. I already told you Mom had it too. Dad was a Chinese shaman, so there was power from his side as well."

"How about others in your family?"

"My sister had it, and according to Mom and Nana, both Mom's sisters, but they lived in Ireland, and I only met them a couple times."

"They're all women, except your dad. Is magic rarer in men?"

"No, but their magic is different."

"Define different."

Kayna thought about it. How could she explain something that had to be taken on faith? "Let's get moving again. My feet are turning to blocks of ice. How about if we start back? I'd love to see if they have hot coffee to go with whatever you got me from the kitchen before we left the ship."

"You didn't answer me." Brynn draped his arm around her again. It warmed her spirit, but his layers of clothing effectively trapped any body heat that might've migrated through her own clothing to warm the rest of her.

"I know I didn't. It's not easy to explain to a non-believer."

"How about if I'm a wanna-be believer?"

That brought a smile to her face. "Touché. There are lots of different ways humans can hold power. The mode that runs in my family is only one type of magic, and it's specific to people of Celtic origin. I've known men who were shamans, Druids, and mages. I've known male witches too. Each had a different type of power, and some were much stronger than others. I don't think that was linked to the type of magic as much as to the person wielding it." She leaned into him. "I suspect all power has a genetic base, and some people simply have more of their cellular structure attuned to psychic ability."

"You identified your family's magic as Celtic. What'd your father add to the mix?"

Kayna's stomach twisted into a knot. "He was a madman. I was young when he died, but all he did was spout crazed predictions about the world ending." She hesitated. "I'm pretty sure Mom would have divorced him if he hadn't died, because he was doing nothing but getting more violent."

Brynn tightened his hold on her. "Sorry. I didn't mean to bring up something painful." He paused a beat before adding. "Saving the world doesn't seem like a bad thing."

A smile ghosted across her face. "It's not. Probably why Mom fell in love with him in the first place, but he changed. Sank deeper and deeper into delusions. That happens sometimes. The magic twists people, opens the door to madness. Look what happened to my sister."

He steered them around a decaying whale skeleton guarded by a dozen playful, half-grown seals. "On a less personal note, can you estimate the incidence of magical traits in the general population?"

"Oh my goodness, no, but it's a very science-y question to ask."

"Surely you have a ballpark estimate," he persisted. "One percent, half a percent?"

"I really don't know. Why's that important?"

"It probably isn't. But when I can't understand something, I gather data until the picture gets clearer."

"Aw, sweetie. No matter how much time you spent peering into this one, I suspect it would still elude you. Look over there." She jerked her chin toward a signpost with the names of at least fifty major cities around the world nailed to it. "That's funny. Who cares how far it is to Bangkok or Paris?"

"The guys at the station probably have too much time on their hands," Brynn murmured. "I'm actually feeling the cold, started to notice it on the walk back. Let's hurry inside."

They sat on benches in a mudroom and took off their boots. With a wooden floor and every wall lined with well-stuffed cubbies and hooks, the entrance to the station clearly saw a lot of use. The building was stifling after the clear, cold air outside, and Kayna unzipped her parka and hung it on a hook. The rise and fall of conversation swelled from the next room. She caught a word here and there, and her head snapped up. Laying a hand on Brynn's thigh, she bent close. "They're talking about the problems between Russia and the U.S."

"Figures. It would be all over the news. I'm sure these guys get the same radio broadcasts the ship does. Probably other ones too." He stood, spun her to face him, and gave her a quick hug. "Come on. Coffee sounds phenomenal."

"I heard that," someone called in strongly accented English. "Tea. Here we drink tea."

"Why am I not surprised?" Brynn mumbled under his breath. "Anything hot would be great," he called.

DESPITE ITS DRAB EXTERIOR, the inside of Arctowski was surprisingly pleasant. A glass case at one end showcased their research on seals, whales, and seabirds. The remainder of the large room was furnished with well-worn leather couches and chairs. Tables with lamps on them were scattered about the cozy space. Brynn saw another room with long tables and chairs through an open door and assumed it was the group mess hall. Windows were scarce, only two for each module, but it probably helped with heating.

He wandered over to the display case and spent some time reading about seal and seabird studies as well as changes in weather patterns. Kayna joined him. "Look at that." She tapped a finger over a glass-enclosed three-D depiction of how Antarctic ice sheets had retreated in the last fifty years.

"I already did." He shook his head. "It's pretty sobering, but then the Mendenhall Glacier in Alaska is all but gone. So are a lot of the permanent snowfields in the Andes."

"What a mess we've made of things," she murmured.

"Indeed. Feel like that cup of tea?" he asked. She nodded, her eyes sad and thoughtful, and they wandered to the other side of the room where a huge stainless kettle sat atop an electric burner.

One of the station residents dredged up a large bottle of brandy to pour into the tea, and Brynn was pleasantly toasted by the time Harold stuck his head into Arctowski Station. Obviously not up for being sociable, Harold kept his booted feet firmly planted in the mudroom. "Time to go," he said, sounding tired.

"Come on in and have a splash of tea and brandy," Chris called.

"I'd love to—" Harold smiled, except it looked forced "—but the captain radioed me that he wants to get underway. He said something about pack ice thickening by the minute."

"Damn!" Zach got to his feet. "After everything we've been through, we deserve a break."

Harold fixed his gaze on the microbiologist. "It doesn't work that way."

"Have we asked the Americans to send an icebreaker?" Abel asked. He stood and moved toward the mudroom.

"I have no idea," Harold replied, the weariness in his voice back in force. "I'm not responsible for that part of ship operations."

Kayna set her mug aside and left the comfortable chair she'd settled into. "If not you," she asked, "then who interprets for the captain, so he can talk with the Americans at McMurdo? Do they speak Russian?"

"Some of them do." Harold hesitated. "One of the things you'll find, Doc, is you'll have a lot of time on your hands at the base. Many of the residents study languages. They have to do something, especially through the winters when the sun doesn't rise for months on end."

"It sounds like you've put in some time at McMurdo," Brynn said and pushed his way around Harold and into the mudroom.

"I did. I've had ships stuck there for as long as two months." A corner of his mouth twisted into a frown. "I've never been a betting man, but if I were, I'd wager I have another month or so coming up there—assuming the Yanks let us land at all."

"What happens if they don't?" Chris spoke up. He tugged his parka off a hook and got into it, pulling the zipper to his chin.

"Depends on the ice," Harold said.

"I don't like the sound of that." Kayna straightened from having put her boots on and plucked her parka off a hook. "Could we end up like Shackleton, stranded in pack ice?"

"Of course we could." Harold's British accent became even more clipped. "But the ice wouldn't crush us because our hull is steel, rather than wood."

"Yes, but we'd run out of supplies eventually," Abel said. His voice held a rough edge betraying his tension.

"How good a shot are you?" Harold countered.

Abel drew back a pace. "I've never touched a gun in my life."

A distasteful look crossed Ted's rotund face. "I'm anti-guns. Period."

The staff captain shrugged. "There's plenty of food in this neck of the globe, but someone has to be willing to kill it. We have rifles and ammo in a locked space off the engine room."

"That makes me feel so much better," Brynn joked, trying to temper his sarcasm. "We can hold contests. Whoever brings down the most game each week gets extra rations."

"I'll bet you're another one who's not sure which end of a gun is which." Harold stalked out of the mudroom and into darkness.

Brynn stared after him, shocked by the man's reaction to a

lighthearted comment. He started out the door, intent on going after Harold, but Kayna caught his arm and shook her head.

"Let him go," she said. "We'll catch up to him aboard the ship."

"Maybe you're right." Brynn stepped back inside and tucked one of her gloved hands beneath his arm. "Thanks so much for having us." He projected his voice toward the station's cheery living room.

One of the men, a paleontologist who'd spent quite some time talking with Chris, joined them. "I didn't mean to listen in," he said, his voice pitched low, "but you'd be welcome here if things don't go well with our American counterparts."

"Thanks," Chris said. "Good to know. You have my email. Let's chat online about those fossil beds you found. I'm not positive, but there may well be a paper or journal article there." He extended a gloved hand, and the other man—whose name Brynn couldn't remember—shook it.

Night had fallen while they sat in the hut, chatting with Arctowski's resident scientific staff, but an almost full moon lit their way back to the Zodiac. It was even colder than it had been when they arrived, and Brynn wasn't looking forward to the wind tearing at them once Harold got the raft underway.

They loaded quickly, and Harold ferried them back to the ship. "Cook kept dinner warm for you," he said, his tone carefully neutral.

Brynn told Kayna he'd meet her in the dining room and waited until the others filed up the gangway. Once he and Harold were alone he said, "I'm sorry about my flip comment earlier. I didn't mean to upset you."

"Go on in and get something to eat." Desolation hollowed Harold's voice. "I spoke out of turn."

"Yeah, well so did I. If you want to talk about it—"

"I don't," Harold cut in. "Look, mate, I still have to put the boat away, and I can't leave here until you're at the top of the stairs."

"Sorry, again." Brynn pressed his lips together. "There're a lot of rules on this ship that aren't written down anywhere."

"Every business has rules," Harold said. "At sea, those rules are designed to keep you alive. Go. I was working outside while you were at the station, and I'm cold."

Brynn trudged up the gangway, surprised by Harold's abrupt dismissal. As he moved into the warmth of the ship, he replayed their conversation and kept returning to the same conclusion. Harold knew something he wasn't talking about, and that something was eating at him.

He took the steps to Deck Five two at a time, anxious to strip off his layers of outdoor gear and join Kayna at dinner. Thoughts of her dark hair and glowing green eyes made his pulse race. No matter what was wrong aboard this ship—or in the world at large —it would be easier to face because they'd found each other.

And if the worst happens, his somber inner scientist chimed in, *at least I won't go to my grave without having been crazy in love.*

He ground to a halt. He couldn't be in love. It wasn't possible. They hadn't known one another long enough. And then he smiled to himself, remembering the lecture he'd given her about how doing things the "right way" hadn't helped either of them in the past.

For once in my life, I need to go with the flow and tell her how I feel. Even though we're new, raw, she'll understand. Hell, maybe her magical side shoved things between us into high gear.

He knew better, though. It was Kayna. The totality of her lured him with an irresistible song. Magic might be part of that, but it was far from the whole thing. As soon as he shucked his outerwear, he made a beeline for the dining room and the woman he was falling in love with.

CHAPTER 17

Kayna sat at her computer jotting notes into medical records. The seas had kicked into high gear since they left Arctowski, and she'd had a steady stream of patients with everything from seasickness to hemorrhoids.

Coughing in the hall alerted her that another patient was about to appear. Her instincts didn't fail her. One of the Russian seamen trudged into her office and wrapped a hand around his throat. Like many of the crew, he was tall and burly with unkempt dark hair and dark eyes, wearing grease-stained coveralls.

Kayna pointed to a chair and got her stethoscope and a thermometer. He raised his hands and coughed into them. Because she didn't like the sound of his cough—deep, and very wet—she donned a mask in addition to her gloves and proceeded to examine him.

"Any English?" She quirked a brow.

"Little."

"How long for that cough?"

He drew his brows together and flashed an open hand at her.

"Five days?" At his nod, she went on. "Have you been hot—" she mimed fanning herself "—the whole time?"

He nodded again.

"I'm going to prick your arm." She tapped her lower arm, but he looked confused, so she said, "Just a minute. I'll get someone to interpret."

Kayna raced out of the surgery and chugged up the stairs. The seaman sounded to her like he might have tuberculosis, but maybe she was overreacting. She found Harold on the bridge and beckoned to him. "I need you to help me."

He trotted after her and asked, "What's up?"

"One of the crew has a nasty sounding cough. Does anyone else have it?"

"I know who you mean." Harold nodded. "Nope. He's the only one."

Back in the surgery, she explained about a TB skin test and sputum culture with Harold translating. "Normally, I'd wait for the skin test to come back positive before I did a culture, but that cough is bad enough it makes sense to do both together."

After she was done, she said to Harold, "Ask him if he has any idea where he might have come into contact with someone coughing like this. It could be quite a while ago, since it's a slow-growing pathogen."

Russian rattled between the two men for long moments before Harold said, "Unfortunately, he has no idea, but he did say he didn't start coughing until after the ship left South Georgia."

"Doesn't mean much," Kayna said, "since TB has such a long incubation period. Has he been on the ship all along?"

Harold nodded. "We all have. For years, actually."

Kayna blew out a breath. "I'll let you know what my tests reveal. In the meantime, would it be possible for this man to be in his own quarters?"

"That'd be deucedly difficult, unless we bed him down in the engine room." He frowned. "Probably not the best idea."

"No," Kayna agreed. "It's not. Let's start him on these pills." She rustled the strongest antibiotic she had out of her medicine cabinet. "Tell him to take one twice a day with a full glass of water each time. And tell him to shield his mouth with his hands when he coughs and to wash his hands frequently. She handed over a bottle of waterless disinfectant. "Have him carry this around and rub it over his hands after he coughs."

"Will do. Are you done with him?"

Kayna nodded. "I need him back here in forty-eight to seventy-two hours to read that skin test."

"Is it definitive?" Harold asked.

"It's not a hundred percent if that's what you're asking, and I don't have an X-ray machine, so I can't take a chest plate. But if the skin test and culture are both negative, whatever's going on with him likely isn't TB. So long as he's here, maybe I'll draw some blood and take a peek."

Kayna watched them leave and popped the culture plate into a small incubator. Next she ran a few simple tests on his blood. Aside from a mildly elevated white count, the other tests were normal.

"What the hell?" She shook her head and stripped off her mask and gloves, stopping at the sink to scrub her hands.

SHE THOUGHT about the seaman from time to time until he showed up two days later for her to examine his arm. If she'd hoped for something definitive, she was disappointed. The induration was under five millimeters, not enough to constitute a positive reading in anyone. After he left, she checked his sputum culture, even though it probably hadn't sat long enough, but the telltale TB bacilli weren't there.

Because his cough was worse and answers didn't come fast enough, she decided to hunt Brynn down. This needed talking through before she insisted the crewman be isolated. Even though her lab work argued otherwise, she remained uneasy, her instincts on full alert.

She was on her way out the door when the light in front of her took on an eerie glow, and the unmistakable feel of magic pummeled her. The raven formed in her mind, and her father glimmered into a ghostly shape between her and the door. A wave of prickly heat pushed her back, and the door slammed shut.

"For the love of God, leave me alone," Kayna sputtered. "I have enough problems right now."

"You've failed to accomplish the task I set for you." He squared his shoulders and crossed spectral arms over his black-robed chest.

She clacked her teeth together, muttered, "This is bullshit. You're not real," and tried to walk through her father—except she couldn't move.

The raven left her mind and flew at her father, but was met with a volley of Chinese. He shimmered, vanished, and ended up off to one side, presumably out of reach of Guiren's power, with his feathers fluffed and his beak snapping ominously.

Kayna struggled against invisible strands holding her in place. When nothing happened, she pushed harder. Fear churned her gut into a fiery mass, and she bit her lower lip hard enough to draw blood.

Think, goddammit!

She reached for her power, intent on drawing a primitive ward to see if she couldn't distance herself from the malevolent energy pulsing from Guiren in waves. The raven latched onto her shoulder, adding his energy to her own. For the barest of moments, she was able to move a few inches, but then the net she couldn't see tightened around her again.

"I tire of this," her father growled. *"Get me what I requested. Now."*

"Why do you want those cultures?" she countered. So long as she was stuck, maybe she could find out something useful. She clung to a slender wedge of courage to keep from sinking into fury—and despair. The rational part of her said this couldn't be happening.

"You don't get to ask the questions," Guiren sneered.

Weight pounded into her, driving the air from her lungs, and she ended up on the floor, writhing, desperate to breathe. "I'm your daughter," she gasped. "What the fuck are you doing?"

"My point exactly," he rasped. *"You are my blood, and you owe me obedience."*

She started to say she owed him nothing, but consciousness was ebbing, and it might piss him off so much he'd lose it and kill her. As soon as the thought surfaced, she understood how desperate her situation was.

Kayna reached deep, summoning her power. Reluctant and sluggish at first, threads of magic finally wove themselves into something she could use. Because she didn't want to tip off her father and risk having him launch countermeasures before she was ready, she groaned piteously and curled into a ball.

"Good. You've stopped fighting me. If I let you up, will you go upstairs and get one of those bins? We've wasted far too much time as it is. Things are happening, the abacus is counting down—"

Kayna surged to her feet, rewarded by the shock—and grudging admiration—etched into Guiren's austere features. The raven flew at him again, landing a peck in his eye. Guiren roared his displeasure so loud it grated against her magical senses, but she forced herself to shake it off. She had one chance. It was now, and she grabbed it.

While her father battled the raven, Kayna pulled power like a madwoman. Bolting out the door, she scurried up the stairs. Relief at escape made her giddy, and she stopped at the top of the stairwell to catch her breath. And call her grandmother.

"Nana!"

Warmth brushed against her mind. *"I'll take care of it, granddaughter. Leave him to me, but later tonight, we must talk."*

Her grandmother's presence faded as quickly as it had formed.

Kayna sucked in a ragged breath and shambled toward Brynn's lab suites.

BRYNN LEANED BACK in his chair. Over the past several days, he'd spent so many hours in front of his microscope his eyes were crossing. He reached a gloved hand to rub his sandpapery eyes, but stopped once he realized what he was doing. A tense breath hissed through his teeth, and he stripped off the latex covering his hands. He did rub his eyes then, but it didn't make them feel any better.

He stared at the gloves lying beside him on the bench. They were a hodge-podge of colors from various stains he'd used, and he winced at hard evidence that he'd grown sloppy. Usually, he was rigorous about following procedures, but he couldn't shake the feeling he was a hairsbreadth away from understanding something momentous. The harder he tried to pin things down though, the more elusive they became.

At least his up close and personal interaction with the archaea hadn't yielded anything close to him becoming ill, which meant he and Kayna had been correct about his samples being different than what was percolating at McMurdo.

He spun his chair so it faced the cabin rather than his workbench. Maybe looking at something else would ease the unpleasant sensation crawling along his neck.

"I'm missing something," he muttered. "But what?"

He hadn't gotten much private time with Kayna in the six days since they'd left Arctowski. They found each other at night, and their lovemaking was incredible, hotter, and more intense as they got used to one another's bodies, but she'd been even busier than him. So busy she hadn't shown up for most meals, and when he made a point of bringing food to her surgery, she'd nodded brusquely, motioned for him to leave whatever was in his hands, and gone back to whoever she was treating. He'd considered offering to help her, but he wanted to get his own problems squared away first.

They'd discussed Harold's grim aspect, and Kayna was convinced the man had enough latent power to be aware of both her magic and whatever the cultures emitted. Because psi emanations were unfamiliar, Harold lacked a place to pigeonhole them, and the alien sensations made him surly and short-tempered. Brynn shrugged, it was as good an explanation as any.

He turned his attention back to his cultures, annoyed with himself for not doing more weeks ago on South Georgia when he wasn't fighting a pitching, bucking ship. If he hadn't been so disconcerted by the archaea's odd behavior, he would have.

After a perfunctory tap, the door to his lab flew open, and Kayna stuck her head in. "Awk, Christ! I'm glad you're in here. I've got a piss pot of problems."

He was so happy to see her it was almost painful. His heart gave a joyful little leap, and Brynn jumped to his feet. He loped across the room, kicked the door shut, and swooped her into his arms. "I'm glad to see you too. I was starting to feel like your boy toy."

"Because we meet at night, fuck like rabbits, and haven't spent any other time together?"

He buried a hand in her hair and rubbed her tense neck muscles. "I guess so. Men aren't supposed to be emotionally needy, but I miss talking with you. Jesus, you're shaking. What the fuck?" He pushed back so he could look at her. Beneath the golden tone of her Asian skin, she was pale, and her eyes looked haunted.

"I was on my way up here to talk with you about something when my father showed up." She burrowed closer to him. "I know how unbelievable this will sound, but he was furious. I think he would've killed me, if I hadn't broken free of the magical net he snared me with."

Brynn clenched his jaw into a tight line. Her words strained credulity, but it wasn't any less believable than man-eating proks at McMurdo. "Come on." He moved an arm between them, swept it beneath her knees, and carried her to a chair.

Kayna shook her head. "It's been something like thirty years since someone picked me up and carted me around. Put me down. I'll sit on your lap once you're settled. I'm afraid the ship will lurch, and both of us will end up on the floor."

"You lack confidence in me." He set her on her feet, dropped into the chair, and held out his arms. "That seems justified since I'm losing faith in myself, but that's not important. What's all this about your father? I'm not getting how he could be a real threat since he's dead."

She drew her dark brows together and settled into his lap. He closed his arms around her and wished they could stay in that moment—one where neither of their problems intruded.

"We have to figure out why Father's so intent on getting his hands on your cultures."

"If he wants them so badly," Brynn countered, "why doesn't he just show up here and help himself?"

"Because he can't."

"Help me here," Brynn cut in. "If he lacks sufficient corporeality to float through a wall or something and take a culture bin, how the hell could he marshal enough in the way of resources to be a threat to you?"

She tilted back in his arms so she could look at him. "Excellent question. He can bind me with magic because we share blood." A muscle twitched beneath one eye, and she frowned. "It gives me an edge on the other side of things too, though, since I can leverage power against him."

"Is that how you got away?"

She nodded, and a somber note crept into her voice when she said, "The raven helped."

"What raven?" Brynn felt mystified.

"Oh, that's right. You don't know about him. He's my spirit guide."

Brynn's mind reeled, and he opened his mouth to ask more questions, but she shook her head. "We can talk more about what happened to me, but there's something else I need to hash out with you, first. We may have a TB case aboard. One of the Russian seamen."

"Crap!" Brynn's eyes widened, and he understood what a relief it was to have something to deal with that didn't smack of the paranormal. "How sure are you?" He cocked his head to one side. "You don't have an X-ray machine. Did you run a skin test?"

She closed her teeth over her lower lip, and the skin around her eyes formed a network of fine worried lines. "Yes, I ran a skin test. It was nonreactive, but they're frequently inaccurate. I also did a half-assed job culturing sputum. Anyway, I checked the culture under my own scope just now, and didn't find anything."

"Does your microscope have better resolution than mine?"

"You've got to be kidding. Mine is a ninety-nine buck student special from Target." She rolled her eyes. "Not really, but you get the picture. I need to pop a culture plate in one of the bays here where the temperature and humidity are constant."

Brynn dredged up what he remembered about tuberculosis. "He could've become infected months—or even years—ago. Are any of the other crew coughing?"

"No, not according to Harold."

"Don't take this wrong, but it can take six weeks to culture TB bacilli."

"I didn't exactly recall that. So—" she blew out a tense breath "—maybe what I'm seeing is something else. He says he just started coughing after South Georgia."

"I'll take a look and let you know what I think. In the meantime, do you have any of the TB specific drugs?"

"Wouldn't that be convenient? Of course I don't. TB is rare these days. It never even occurred to me to include those meds in my kit. I did start him on an off-label use of another antibiotic, but his cough's gotten worse these last two days." She sagged against Brynn's body. "Do you think I should isolate him until I know what's going on for sure?"

"Mmph. Good question. We saw the crew's quarters. Not much possibility of isolation, plus they all share the same johns."

Kayna scrubbed the heels of her hands down her face. "Let me run my logic past you, and you can poke holes in it." At his sharp nod, she went on. "One. He's been part of this crew for six years."

"I think I see where you're heading," Brynn said, "but go on."

"Two. He's been living in a community environment with his shipmates for a long time. No one else appears to have active disease." She repositioned herself and spread her hands in front of her. "Out here in the middle of nowhere, my take is I dose him with meds, maybe add a spot of steroid to ease his pulmonary function, and monitor how he's doing."

"Maybe we could have Harold warn his roommates and go over some basic disease prevention protocols," Brynn said.

"I already did that." She tucked her head between his neck and shoulder. "I'm tired. I don't understand how seventy people can keep me busy fulltime. Back in Minnesota, my caseload ran into the thousands."

"You had support," he observed. "Nurses, medical assistants, front office staff, other docs to spell you." He cradled her head with his hand. "I've been meaning to help you, but I got lost in slide-land."

"I'd be glad to listen to what's bothering you—" she twisted so she could meet his gaze "—as soon as I get to the end of this problem." She grimaced apologetically. "I made up another agar plate. Do you suppose you could come downstairs with me, grab it, and let it incubate in here?"

"Of course. Maybe I could look at a sample from your first go-round under my scope."

"Aw, Brynn, that'd be great." She brushed her lips over his and scrambled out of his lap. "How are your culture bins?"

"About half are edging toward eukaryotes, but that's not surprising. Whatever drove the first few cells to mutate is catching up with the others. What's been driving me nuts…" He let his voice trail off as he organized his thoughts. "Actually, there's more than one thing, but I've been trying to catch a cell in the process of shifting from one form to another. I want to know if there's something critical that happens prior to the shift. Something quantifiable."

"No dice, huh?" She steadied herself against a wall.

"Nope. Plus, you know how it is when something skulks at the corners of your mind tormenting you? I have this eerie feeling I'm missing something critical, and if I could only get my grubby little fingers around it, I'd understand everything."

"It could be you're reacting to the same thing that's got Harold bent out of shape—an overabundance of magic. I sure feel it and not only when I'm near the proks. Let's plan on dinner tonight." Kayna smiled wanly. "If I don't pitch facedown into my soup, we can kick this around more."

Brynn stood and walked to her. "We need to figure out why your father wants my samples."

"Let's do all we can about my guy with the mystery disease, first. He's getting worse, and I'm worried about him."

He traced the lines of her cheekbones with his thumbs. "You have dark circles beneath your eyes. Aren't you sleeping?"

She shrugged uncomfortably. "Some, not as much as I need."

"It's because we keep each other awake until really late, huh?" He cupped the side of her face. "I'd offer to sleep in my own cabin, but unless you tell me I have to, you're stuck with me. I can't tell you how much I look forward to holding you in my arms and feeling your body against mine."

"I treasure the times we're close too. It's not you." She turned her head and kissed his palm. "I haven't said anything, but a Chinese water dragon's been haunting my dreams. It's related to my father—and apparently to your cultures." Her forehead crinkled with worry, and she hesitated a beat. "I've had the same sensation you described, where I'm manipulating a bunch of puzzle pieces, but no matter how I fit them together, something's not right."

"Maybe that *folie á deux* thing is spreading. Come on." He pulled the door open. "Let me get that new agar plate up here. We can sort the rest out—or try our damnedest—over supper."

KAYNA SCRUBBED the living hell out of her hands after her last patient for the day left. Despite her negative tests, and Brynn's information about it taking weeks to culture, the specter of TB scared the crap out of her.

What I wouldn't give for access to a regular lab with a bacteriological incubator.

If it wasn't TB, what the hell did I see?

She was still racking her brain—understanding the microbe hunt was a diversion, so she didn't have to think about her father—when Chris strolled in. Kayna started for her drug cabinet, but he shook his head. Looking sheepish, he drew several of her buff-colored envelopes from a pocket. "I'm returning these."

Her eyes widened. "You've been stockpiling them?"

He nodded, clearly embarrassed. "Sorry, old habit. Anyway, no more drugs. I'm okay." His forehead furrowed in thought. "I don't understand it, but this time detoxing hasn't been that hard. I've had other things to think about, and when the waves of craving hit I'm able to ride them out."

She took the envelopes and dropped them into her biohazard trash.

Kayna stepped to his side and wrapped her fingers around his wrist. The slow, steady beat of his pulse underscored his words, and she said, "That's wonderful news."

His lean face broke into a smile. "Yeah, I thought so too. I assumed I'd be a junkie till I died of an overdose someday."

"That would've been a true waste." She let go of his wrist.

"Thank you." His smile slipped a notch. "I'm beginning to believe that. Maybe seeing myself as something other than a piece of shit helps."

She focused her gaze on him. "If you ever start to doubt yourself again and need a pep talk—"

"I know where to come. Thanks for having faith in me. It really helped." Chris took a step back and lounged against the far wall. "Have you heard the latest hot gossip?"

Half a snorting laugh blew past her lips. "When would I have had time?"

"Don't let Harold know—" Chris tugged the surgery door shut and lowered his voice "—but I speak Russian. The captain's been in communication with McMurdo, and they're making noises that they expect him to turn the ship around and go back to Argentina."

"Shit! I don't get it. We're not military," she protested.

"I don't know how much history you've studied, but civilians have been collateral damage in every war that's ever been fought."

She tightened her jaw. "Well, I'll be damned if I end up *collateral damage* because of some deranged idiot who wants to play God."

"Hang onto that thought." Chris wasn't smiling anymore. "You may need it. I'm out of here. Couple of things I need to attend to before dinner."

Moments later, Brynn slipped through the door Chris had left open. Kayna stood still as a statue, hands on her hips, staring into space and seething. The warm smile on Brynn's smile changed to a frown.

"What happened?" he asked. "You look like you had a run in with a nine-hundred-pound gorilla."

"Shut the door."

"Yes ma'am." He half bowed and toed it closed until it clicked. "Now will you tell me what happened?"

Instead, she walked to him and wrapped her arms around him. When she did talk, her voice echoed in her ears as if she were talking from underwater. "McMurdo's saying we can't land."

Brynn tightened his hands on her shoulders. "Has Harold been by?"

"Not Harold. Chris. He's been holding out on us. He speaks Russian."

Brynn put enough space between their bodies so he could look at her. "Do you have any details?" She shook her head and watched a muscle twitch along his jaw. "Something else to add to the list," he muttered. "Right after we talk about the mythical creature haunting your dreams, what's on your agar plate, my persnickety samples, and why your father wants them so badly he's willing to scare the crap out of you."

Kayna stepped away from him and glanced at her watch. "It's six-thirty. How about we get dinner and bring it back here? It'll give us privacy and food at the same time." She dusted her hands together. "Maximum bang for minimum effort."

A quarter of an hour later, they were settled in a corner on the floor of her surgery, sitting on couch cushions Brynn had dragged in from the bar. "You're not saying much," Kayna observed between bites.

"That's because you're inhaling your food like a starving woman. You've missed enough meals, I figured you deserved enough peace and quiet to at least finish this one."

"Thanks." She smiled fondly at him and kept eating. "You took my original culture plate with you, along with the new one. I'm guessing you looked at it."

"Yes. Your slides were mucked up with stain, so I took a fresh bit from the agar plate and examined it under darkfield."

"What'd you find?"

Brynn set his fork down, looking troubled. "That's problem

number forty-three. I wish I knew, but I don't. The good news is it's not TB. The flip side is I tried to match it to pictures in one of my texts and came up dry."

"I'm not exactly following you." She swallowed half the glass of red wine he'd poured for her in a few swift gulps.

"I consulted a standard microbiology text that lists virtually all the common bacteria and viruses, not that either of us would be able to see viruses without an electron microscope."

"Go on." She drained her wineglass, hoping the alcohol would mitigate the tension humming along her nerves.

"I could toss out lots of caveats, like the sample wasn't incubated properly and darkfield's not the best for fine work, but given what I had to work with I couldn't find a match in my book."

Kayna clasped her hands together and rested her chin on them. "One more nail in the woo-woo coffin this ship's turned into."

"What do you mean?" he asked.

"You're telling me we have a microbial critter you don't recognize, and it's your field to know virtually all of them. My father's spirit's been activated, I'm dreaming about a resurrection of a Chinese water dragon, and World War III is brewing. Christ!" She squeezed her clasped hands together until the knuckles ached. "Could we possibly have any more problems?"

"Sure." Brynn grinned crookedly. "Your patient zero could've had TB, and the boat could be on its way to the bottom of the southern ocean."

Catching his black humor mood, she quipped, "Yeah, too bad I wasted everyone's time and terrorized the guy's roommates, unnecessarily. Not that I had much of a choice, but still."

"Let me pop back down and bring us dessert. When I get back, your father and the dragon are first out of the box."

Kayna snorted. "I'm sure they'd like nothing better."

CHAPTER 18

Kayna made short work of the Boston crème cake and sipped thoughtfully at coffee she'd brewed in the surgery from instant crystals. Brynn was obviously waiting for her to open up, and she was grateful he wasn't pushing. "At least the desserts are awesome," she said. "It almost makes up for the lackluster dinners." She licked her fork and set it back on the plate.

"You're avoiding the important stuff." He moved next to her and threaded an arm around her shoulders.

"I suppose I am." She pressed her tongue against her teeth and tried to consolidate her thoughts. "When you and the sample bins came aboard, I saw something that looked a lot like a sea serpent, but with an eldritch aspect and intelligent eyes. There were a few nights of peace after that, but it's been in my dreams ever since you and I first made love. In the meantime, I figured out it's not a reincarnation of Nessie, but a Chinese water dragon, or Kiao. My father had one tattooed on his upper arm. It was special to him, bonded to him."

"Do you have any idea what it means? More importantly, it seems to frighten you. Why?"

Kayna leaned her head against his shoulder and placed a hand on his leg. "At first the thing terrified me, but only because I'd never seen anything like it in my dreams or trance states. I'm certain it's linked to my father showing up since it's his spirit guide. I've had guides before, but like I mentioned earlier, mine's a raven."

Brynn blew out a quiet breath. "I need more information so I can understand. Does this apparition talk to you? Do you have any idea what it or your father wants? Did they just show up now because of my cultures?"

"Wish I knew." She shook her head grimly. "No talk, at least not from the Kiao. The reason sleep's been scarce is because I've been trying to figure out what they want and why they showed up." She licked her dry lips. "It's not unusual for spirit guides to be silent. Over the few years when I was deep into my magic, my raven rarely spoke. He didn't have to. I understood him perfectly without words."

"What does he think about your father and the sea serpent?"

"He hates them. He made it possible for me to escape Father earlier." Kayna's mouth twitched into a grin. "The raven really likes you, though."

"You're kidding." Brynn drew back.

"Nope. He was rooting from the sidelines the first time we kissed. Almost like a kinky form of ménage a trois."

Brynn's eyes widened and he muttered, "Incredible."

"No worries." Kayna cocked her head to one side. "He's given us privacy since. But he lobbied hard when I was ambivalent. He was in my head the night I told you about being my Prince Charming."

"You could've said something."

"I know that now, but I wasn't so sure then—that you'd be open to something like that."

"I want you to always be able to tell me anything. No secrets." His voice rumbled against her hair, and he stroked her upper arm with his fingertips. "Tell me how you use paranormal ability to figure things out."

"What do you mean?"

"All I have is my own frame of reference, but like with this epiphany that's floating right beyond my grasp, the harder I try to chase it down, the more elusive it becomes."

Kayna closed her eyes. "Yeah, this isn't like most common problems, where you keep plowing forward until you bludgeon them into submission. Things from the supernatural world come to me in their own time."

"Is being receptive one of the key elements?"

Her eyes fluttered open, and she stared hard at him. "Of course, but how would you know that?"

"How else? I've been reading—in my spare time, so I wouldn't be tempted to throw my microscope out a porthole. Found a general book on spirit manifestations stuffed in a corner of the ship's library. God only knows how it got there, but I was glad to find it. Microbiology texts aren't very forthcoming about paranormal phenomena. Neither is Harrison's *Internal Medicine*."

She gazed into his multi-hued eyes. "I really, really like you. So much it's scary."

"Sweetheart." He shimmied around and placed his hands on her shoulders. "I know it seems premature, but this came to me the other night, and I vowed to tell you but never did." He stopped talking, took a deep breath, and color splotched his cheeks.

"There's no easy way to say this, so I'll spit it out." His hands tightened where they rested on her shoulders. "Kayna, darling Kayna, I'm falling in love with you." She opened her mouth, but he shook his head. "If you're going to say I got sucked in by how great the sex is, don't bother. I'm not a kid anymore, and I know the difference between a woman calling to my body and singing to my soul."

Sudden tears formed behind her lids. She blinked them away. "That's the sweetest thing anyone's ever said to me." She put her empty coffee cup on the floor and gripped his face between her hands, smoothing her thumbs over his cheekbones. "Be warned, I have sharp edges."

"All women who end up in medicine do. If you didn't have ego strength to burn, you would've picked a different career."

Kayna thought back to some of their earlier conversations. "Rebecca was a doctor too, huh?" Brynn nodded, and Kayna smiled crookedly. "So you know what you're up against."

He tapped the tip of her nose with a finger. "Yup. Plainspoken. Cut to the chase. She was a stellar human being, but I never fell in love with her."

Kayna pressed her lips together. "Speaking of not being in love, I wonder how I stayed with Derek as long as I did. Maybe we got comfortable, but it cost me. He made it abundantly clear my paranormal ability scared the crap out of him, and he had no interest in expanding his horizons." She shrugged uncomfortably. "Because my magic was dormant for years, it was easy to ignore its occasional cameo appearances."

"What did that raven of yours have to say about Derek?"

Kayna snorted. "Not so much as a squawk. I never saw him once during the years I was with Derek."

Brynn smiled softly. "I suppose I should feel honored." Color deepened across his tanned skin. "Not that I'm a great expert, but whenever people want to change you, mold you, they can't accept all of who you are. Then it turns into more of a power game than love."

She nodded and exhaled sharply. "You never met Derek, but you described him to a T. He was pretty much lost in the wonder of himself. Not that he wasn't kind and occasionally thoughtful. Medical school and residency were such a grind. There were weeks we hardly saw one another, and it was useful to have an extra person to restock the fridge, and to study with when we had exams coming up."

"More like roommates with privileges," Brynn murmured.

"Yeah. Now that I've gotten a little distance, I realize that. We never had anything close to a grand passion."

"And with me?" He caught and held her gaze. His eyes were hypnotic, mesmerizing.

"You're amazing. I keep thinking something will happen, though. You know, the other shoe will drop, and you'll decide you don't like me."

"The same thing could happen on your side."

He angled his head and kissed her lightly. His lips brushing over hers sent fire trailing down her body.

"Guess it's going to take trust on both our parts," she said against his lips, "even with my raven solidly behind us."

"It's a leap into the unknown. Sort of like your magic must've been for you."

Kayna shook her head. "I grew up with my ability. When you have something like that as a kid, you accept it."

Brynn straightened but kept his hands on her shoulders. "We didn't come up with any answers for the archaea samples, the mystery bacterium masquerading as TB, or your father."

"We sort of did—at least about some of it." Kayna narrowed her eyes. "Lab facilities here aren't adequate to answer much more about the archaea, or whatever I tried to culture from my patient."

"True."

"Maybe you stumbled onto something when you said the answers have to find us," she went on, "but I'd like to hurry the process. It scares the crap out of me that my father's lurking close by. I was grateful when he died. Things got harder financially, but much easier emotionally."

Brynn's expression turned solemn. "Why would a man who's been dead for twenty-two years want cultures of mutating archaea?"

She pressed her tongue against her teeth, thinking. Her next words came slowly. "Spirits can be drawn back from the

Otherworld when something that was very important to them in life comes into play."

Brynn quirked a brow and motioned for her to go on.

"His fanaticism revolved around the world ending and him having a major role to play. He used to say people would immortalize him as a hero."

"Help me here," Brynn said. "I'm not making a connection."

"We've been playing with fire ever since we developed atomic weaponry, and we're teetering on the brink of an international crisis." Kayna twisted her hands together in her lap. "My first guess is Dad's back now because he either suspects—or has inside knowledge—that WWIII is about to break out, and he believes your archaea hold the key to some sort of global cure-all."

"Pretty off the wall logic," he muttered. "Is there a way to verify any of that?"

Kayna rotated her shoulders, displacing his hands. Her joints creaked and popped when she loosened the death grip her muscles had on them. "Nothing about magic is well-defined. It's like dream interpretation, with symbols and layers of meaning that only become clear once you start peeling them away.

"I wish this was clearer, but magic doesn't work that way. It doesn't spring from a logic model—" A frantic pounding startled her, and Kayna scrambled to her feet. "Damn it! I really do not want to see anybody else today."

"If it's an emergency, I'll take it." Brynn stood too. His face held a drawn aspect. The stresses of the last few days had clearly taken a toll.

Kayna opened the door to Zach, Abel, Ted, and Chris. The men's faces were studies in fury. "What the hell happened?" Kayna gestured them inside.

"You tell them." Abel elbowed Chris. "You're the Russian guru."

"Let me get the door first." Brynn kicked it shut.

"I was on the bridge," Chris said, "and the captain was talking with someone on the sat phone—on speaker. It took me a couple minutes to determine McMurdo was on the other end. Anyway, after a few tense rejoinders, the captain started yelling at the guy." Chris exhaled sharply. "Cutting to the chase, McMurdo won't send an icebreaker and won't let us land, even if we can get there on our own. They told us to turn around in no uncertain terms."

"Crap!" Kayna unclenched her jaw. "What happened then?"

"The captain told the McMurdo guy his mother fucks donkeys and slammed the phone down so hard I was surprised it didn't shatter."

"Do you know who was on the McMurdo end?" Brynn asked.

Chris straightened his shoulders. "Yeah. A guy named Jack DeVoe. Christ! It sounds as if they've already declared martial law there. I didn't think McMurdo was a military installation."

"It's not," Zach said.

"Has the U.S. actually declared war on Russia?" Kayna asked.

"I don't think so," Chris replied, "but things are tense. The reason I went to the bridge was because they had a radio broadcast going, and the speaker in the bar was too scratchy to hear very well. I settled into one of those bolted-down stools and looked out the window, pretending I was fascinated by the night sky, but I picked up enough from the broadcast to understand Russia is furious and demanding we move our troops out of Ukraine immediately."

"I know Jack DeVoe, so maybe I can do something about this, but how do you play in?" Brynn gazed from Zach to Abel to Ted.

"We came hunting for Chris," Zach said. "To see if he was up for a hand of cards before bed."

Brynn clacked his jaws together. "I'm sure I can talk sense into Jack. We go back a long way. I met him at Bethesda right after I finished my Ph.D." He shook his head. "I don't get it. He's the reason I'm on this ship."

"No," Kayna cut in. "He's the reason you're heading for McMurdo. I'll bet he doesn't have clue one you're on this particular ship. Beyond that, did you work for the National Institutes of Health?"

Brynn nodded. "Twice. Once as a graduate fellow for a post-doc, and again for my residency to pay Uncle Sam back for floating my med school costs."

"What did DeVoe do at NIH?" Chris rolled his eyes. "Oversee grad student executions? He sounded hard as nails over the phone."

"He has a Ph.D. in biochemistry," Brynn answered. "Because he was quietly competent, they kept promoting him, but he's not cut out to be a desk jockey. He was one of those who truly enjoyed lab-based work. Managing personnel and budgets gave him fits, but he liked the salary. And he fell in love with Antarctica."

"Maybe we should get moving," Kayna said, "before the ship's captain does something rash."

Brynn nodded agreement. "I'll head up to the bridge and use the sat phone to call Jack. It might be best if you four—" he waved an arm to include Zach, Abel, Ted, and Chris "—stayed away. I'm guessing the captain's pretty upset, and I don't want you there to remind him what happened."

"I'm sure he hasn't forgotten," Zach muttered.

"What about me?" Kayna asked.

Brynn cracked a grim smile. "Men always behave better in a lady's presence."

"We'll be in the bar," Chris said. "Come tell us what happens."

"Yes," Abel echoed. "The second you know something." He pulled the door open, and the others trooped out after him.

Brynn chugged up two flights of stairs with Kayna right behind him and strode into the glassed-in bridge. The captain maintained an open bridge policy, so the seamen plying the ship's controls barely batted an eye. On the way, Brynn had decided to simply pick up the phone and settle into a chair. He shouldn't have to ask to use it, and he wasn't going to.

"Captain's not here," Kayna murmured against Brynn's ear. "He speaks a bit of English, and I'll wager he understands it better than he lets on."

Brynn muffled a snort. "How about if you sit over by the windows? I'll join you. In addition to all our other problems, this is starting to feel like *Spy Versus Spy*. Chris speaks Russian, but they don't know. The captain understands English, but isn't letting on to what extent—"

"I don't know that for sure about the captain," she interrupted. "But it's likely because that's how language acquisition works."

"Regardless. Let me get the phone, and I'll join you."

No one said a word when he scooped the phone off the broad chart table. He pulled out his wallet and dropped a fifty-dollar bill in its place. One of the Russians grinned and pocketed the money. Whatever was afoot clearly hadn't rattled the crew.

Brynn punched in numbers and waited through a series of hollow clicks and clacks while satellites communicated with one another. The phone began to ring about the time he perched on an uncomfortable stool next to Kayna. Half a dozen hard, spindly chairs were lined up in front of windows wrapping around the bridge. He clicked the phone's speaker mode and waited. After fifteen rings, Kayna raised her eyebrows and Brynn shrugged.

Two rings later, a harried male voice snapped, "For the love of Christ, this fucking better be good. Oh yeah, McMurdo."

"Jack?" Brynn chuckled quietly. "What are you doing answering the phone?"

"It rings next to my desk, smart ass. If no one else gets it, I answer in self-defense. Who is this?"

"Brynn."

"Why you old son of a bitch! How the hell are you? Getting bored on that afterbirth of an island and reaching out to touch someone? Why aren't you already en route? I'd have thought you'd be on your way."

"I'm guessing you haven't had much of a chance to talk with either Micah or your administrative assistant. I am on my way."

"I've barely had time to wipe my ass," Jack growled. "Why, what would they have told me?"

"That I'm on the ship you just told to turn around." Brynn waited through a silence that lasted so long he was afraid Jack had disconnected, but the reassuring hum of the satellites kept right on droning.

"Aw, shit! Why'd you have to go and do something stupid like that? A Russian ship for chrissakes. With everything that's going on right now?"

"It's the ship your staff arranged for me."

"Crap."

Breath steamed past Brynn's clenched teeth. "There are thirty-five *American*—" he paused to emphasize the word "—Ph.D. scientists aboard this ship, plus another M.D."

"And thirty-five Russians," Jack said, his voice weary.

"Two of the crew are Brits, and a bunch are Ukrainian. Since when is that a problem?"

"Since the White House declared martial law."

"How can they do that? We're not at war." Brynn raked a hand through his hair. Damn, if this wasn't getting worse and worse.

"They can do anything they fucking well please. I'm merely a drone following orders—and I hate it. I didn't sign on for anyone's army."

Brynn glanced at Kayna and placed a finger over his lips. She nodded and remained silent. "Jack, you're going to condemn me and the rest of the Americans on this boat to death if you don't let us land. The crew too. There's not enough fuel for us to circle back to Argentina, or even to make New Zealand the way I understand things. Shit! The Russians are already talking about breaking out rifles to shoot seals or albatrosses or some such thing."

Kayna's eyes rounded into small moons. She obviously recognized Brynn was lying through his teeth since he couldn't possibly have any idea what their fuel status was. Another lengthy silence followed.

"We're going to do the right thing here," Jack said, sounding determined. "I'll deal with the flak from Washington. We've had more…incidents at the base since you and I last talked. Tell Captain Gorev to radio me when he's eighteen hours out. He'll need our icebreaker to get through the pack ice. Is that all?"

"No. You're going to let the crew—all of them—into McMurdo Station too. I don't want them confined aboard this ship. They're human beings, Jack. I refuse to be part of something that's starting to look like a resurrection of Nazi Germany."

"Yeah, yeah, I read you loud and clear. This whole thing was bothering the crap out of me too, except I'm not supposed to have feelings. I'm supposed to follow orders and set an example. Last chance to speak, buddy, I need to get some work done."

"I'm looking forward to seeing you again."

Rough laughter rang through the phone's speaker. "Ditto. It'll be great to have you here."

"Maybe I can tickle your biochemistry skills. My colonies have grown even more intriguing, and I'd love it if you could analyze their cellular walls."

Jack sighed long and low, like a rusty anchor chain. "If I can free up the time, I'd love to. Intriguing how?"

"Different from yours."

"Thank God for that."

The captain stalked between Brynn and the bank of windows. "Tell son of a bitch thanks."

Jack broke into gales of laughter. When he could talk, he rattled off a string of Russian. Valentin Gorev replied and made a chopping motion with one hand. Brynn understood and terminated the call after telling Jack they'd compare notes later.

"Thank you," the captain ground out in his stilted English. "I surprise you lie. Fuel not low."

Brynn set the phone in his lap and turned his hands palms upward. "Whatever works, pal."

"I remember." The Russian sea captain grinned, displaying silver caps on several teeth. "For next time." He spun on his heel and faded into the shadowed bowels of the bridge.

CHAPTER 19

Kayna smothered giggles. "That's just peachy," she said to Brynn, lowering her voice so no one else could hear. "You're teaching him the end justifies the means."

The corners of Brynn's mouth twitched into a boyish grin. "I'm sure Valentin figured that out a long time ago."

"I'm glad it worked. I wasn't looking forward to weeks at sea bouncing our way back to South America—or New Zealand. As long as you've got the phone handy, I need to make a call."

"It's none of my business," Brynn said slowly, "but to whom?"

"My mother. While you were talking, I thought more about my father and the Kiao. A conversation about them is long overdue."

Brynn cleared his throat. "Do you want to say more about that?"

"Not sure what more to say. You already know Dad was a Chinese shaman, and I told you that he had a tattoo on his arm that's a dead ringer for the sea serpent."

"Did he tell you it was a Kiao?"

"Not exactly. I asked Mom about it after he died. When she wouldn't tell me anything, I asked Nana." Kayna blew out a breath. "Dad was strong magically, but Mom never talked about it, just like she never wanted anything to do with her own magic after he died. She and Nana had some roaring arguments after they thought I was asleep. Since they were in Gaelic, I had a hard time following them, but the gist was Nana gave Mom hell for kicking her heritage in the teeth and reminded her she might've lost her shaman husband, but not her Irish magic."

"Where's the Internet when you need it? I'd love to look up that Chinese sea serpent." He handed her the sat phone. "Dial nine-one-nine first, then the country code and the number."

"I'd like the Internet too. My knowledge about Chinese magic is sketchy."

"Maybe your mom can fill in some missing pieces."

"I'm hoping she'll talk with me, but if history is any indication…" Kayna let her voice trail off as she tapped numbers into the phone.

"I'll run down to the bar and let the guys know what happened." Brynn got to his feet. "Besides, that will give you a little privacy."

Kayna eyed him as she listened to the phone in her mother's house start to ring. "You've forgotten Valentin," she mumbled. "He's discovered it pays to eavesdrop."

A wry grin split Brynn's face. "Indeed. I'll see you downstairs when you're done. I'll be in the bar."

Kayna gave him a thumbs up sign about the time a familiar voice said, "Hello?"

"Mom, it's me."

"By Christ and all the blessed saints, sure and is that really you, child?" Moira Quan lapsed into the soft brogue she'd been raised with.

"Yes, Mom. It's good to hear your voice."

"Things have been happening. Fell things from the darkness." Moira choked on the words and tried again. "I've been so worried you were dead. I called the ship company, and they reassured me your ship hadn't sunk, but—"

"Slow down." Kayna sucked in a steadying breath. This wasn't a time to beat around the bush. "If by *darkness*, you mean magic, my power is back stronger than ever. I've seen Nana. Father and his Kiao are threatening me. It's why I called. You have to tell me about Dad."

"Och, *leanbh*," was followed by a long spate of Gaelic.

"English, Mom. My Irish never was very good." Kayna willed her mother not to block her out.

"Sorry." Moira took a shuddering breath that hurt Kayna's heart. "I should've told you long ago, but I had my reasons for remaining silent. You already know your father was a Wu, a shaman. He was a talented healer, and he also foretold the future."

Kayna's stomach twisted sourly. "So that's where I got my second sight from."

"Not entirely," her mother retorted. "His power mingled with mine made yours much stronger. That's what tripped up poor Kiki. Her spirit wasn't powerful enough to contain two magics."

"Is that why Dad drank himself to death?"

"He didn't. Not by choice."

"What?" Kayna collapsed against the metal bars of the chair's back. They cut into her, but she ignored the discomfort.

"Och, child. Where to begin?"

"Hit the high points, Mom. This call will cost over a hundred bucks as it is."

"Oh my goodness, maybe I should write you a letter. Doesn't your ship have email?" Kayna could almost see her mother's pale green eyes widen in dismay.

"Just tell me."

"All right." Moira's voice faltered. "Your father and I wove our magic together. We were strong, the two of us, so strong it might've made a real difference." She hesitated. "Magic has always been difficult to control, and it frequently doesn't jump to commands when you summon it. Guiren and I were working to change that—at least when he was lucid—but my kin and some other Irish mages were horrified because they thought our power, Celtic magic, should remain pure.

"They threatened us, but we didn't pay any attention. Your father was convinced something catastrophic was coming. He saw it in a vision, but never would share the details. He told me over and over we had to master our joint magic before the world imploded."

"Did he foresee the nuclear war that's looming?"

"I have no idea." Moira Quan hesitated. "Like many with strong magic, Guiren gradually lost contact with reality and slipped closer and closer to the edge of madness. It's probably most of what you remember: the rampages and tirades and beatings." A soft sob escaped her. "The man I fell in love with vanished, swept up in grandiose schemes, punctuated by rages.

"It was hard after he died—but it would've been harder if he'd lived. The main thing that kept me going was taking care of you and Kiki. I couldn't think about anything beyond keeping you girls safe. I didn't have the strength. I know you believed I hated my power, but I didn't push it aside totally until after he was gone. I was afraid the magic might eat me alive too."

Moira quieted until all Kayna heard was her breathing. She knew better than to prod; her mother had to find words, and after a time, she started talking again. "I didn't finish telling you what happened to Guiren. One night your uncle and a bunch of his buddies stopped by. Padraig said he was sorry for hounding us and invited Guiren out for drinks to bury the hatchet."

Kayna shut her eyes. Engulfed by a deeply sinking sensation, she already knew the rest. "They poisoned him," she said, her voice flat.

"Och, I'll say your second sight is front and center, child. That they did. They dropped him at our door, barely conscious and reeking of whiskey. I knew something was desperately wrong since I'd never seen him as drunk as that, but it was Nana who smelled the poison. By then it was too late. We dragged him into the car and raced to the hospital, but his heart had already stopped. The doctors were convinced he died of alcohol poisoning. I couldn't request an autopsy."

"Why not?"

"He had to be cremated intact to find his way to the afterlife. If I'd let them chop his body into wee bits, he might've been trapped on this side of the veil, wandering forever like a lost soul. Unfortunately, he's found his way back, despite my efforts."

Tears brimmed; Kayna wiped them away. "I understand why you didn't tell me how he died when I was ten, but why didn't you say something after I grew up?"

"I was trying to protect you." Moira's voice shrilled. "Magic killed him, and it killed your sister. I never wanted it anywhere near me—or you. Nana told me I couldn't run from my destiny—and it wasn't fair to shelter you from yours—but I told her I was damn sure going to give it my best shot." Her mother spoke through ragged sobs. "When your power seemed to recede, I thanked the Blessed Virgin and all the goddesses and tried to move on."

Kayna swallowed hard. Recriminations were pointless. Her mother had made choices, and there was no undoing them. She shuttered the pain. Right now, it was in the way. "Thank you for being honest with me."

"You're welcome, child. After things started happening a couple weeks ago, I've not had a moment's peace. I wished I'd been more forthcoming when I had a chance, but there was no way to reach you. Thank God you called."

"Why were you worried I was dead? What have you seen?"

"Your father. He's been in my dreams. He won't talk to me, but he's there every night."

"He's here too," Kayna murmured. "Him and his Kiao."

"Sure and that doesn't bode well." Moira sounded trashed, but at least she'd stopped crying. "You must be careful. If the world goes to war, he's crazy enough to reach out from the other side to intercede. For that, he'll need a source of living power, and blood's his best bet."

"I figured that part out. It's what to do about it that's giving me fits." Chilly fingers squeezed Kayna's heart, and her hands shook.

"Can you come home?" Moira's voice trembled.

"No. I'm almost to McMurdo Station in Antarctica. If Russia and the U.S. throw a nuclear war party, I may never leave there."

The sound of her mother crying surged through the sat phone again, and Kayna longed to hug her. "Please, Mom, pull yourself together. I'll call you once I'm at McMurdo. They have Internet there, so I'll email you too."

"Don't worry about me, child. Take care of yourself. I know we should hang up, but it's so good to hear your voice."

"Good to hear yours too, Mom. I love you."

"I love you too, child of my heart. You're all that's left."

"No. You have yourself—and your magic. I have a feeling that will become really important, so haul it out and use it. Mine's pathetically rusty."

"You left all your books here."

"So you found them. I figured you'd burn them."

Moira sighed. "I could never do that. I was angry at fate, the gods. They kept robbing me of everything I ever loved, and I needed something to blame. Magic was convenient because it didn't fight back, not like your Nana at all." Her mother tried to joke, but Kayna knew she was holding on by a ragged edge.

"Dust off those books and get hold of a scanner. I may need you to look things up and email them to me. I hate to do this, but I've got to run before I owe more than my first month's pay. I'll call you once I'm off the ship."

"Be sure you do that, child."

"I will. I promise."

"And Kayna. Watch out for your father. He'll use you if he can and never look back."

The green blinking light shaded to red. Her mother had

disconnected. Kayna stared at the phone in her hands for long moments. Her cheeks were wet with tears and her throat clotted with emotion. It wouldn't take much for her to curl into a ball of agony and howl her fear and sorrow to the world.

Can't do that.

Valentin sidled next to her. "You okay?"

She shook her head. "Not even close, but thanks for asking."

He dragged a silver flask from an inner pocket and extended it her way. She took it, unscrewed the top, and took a cautious swallow. What felt like hundred proof vodka set her throat on fire. "Whew," she gasped. "That's some potent hooch."

The captain smiled broadly. "Brother make it. Back in Kiev."

Kayna got to her feet and stared at him. "You're from Ukraine?"

"Me and some of crew, maybe half."

"If so many of the crew are Ukrainian, why does the ship fly a Russian flag?"

Valentin narrowed his eyes. "Long story. Maybe I no have English to tell it. Too much trouble to change. Russia have many ship. Ukraine few. Less rubles too."

Kayna nodded her understanding and said, "You're not even from the part of Russia the U.S. is having problems with."

Valentin took a swallow of vodka. "Ukraine free state. We are victim. In middle." Another big smile. "Thanks to your friend—" he winked knowingly "—maybe we wait out war at McMurdo."

Kayna patted his arm. "If there's a nuclear war, we'll probably all die."

"Like old movie." His smile crumpled. "*On the Beach.*"

"Exactly. With Gregory Peck and Ava Gardner in Australia." The captain offered her his flask again, but she shook her head. "I need to find Brynn. Here." She handed him the sat phone. "What do I owe you?"

"For you, lady doctor, call is free."

"Thank you."

Kayna stumbled from the bridge, still trying to wrestle her ravaged emotions into some kind of order. She wanted Brynn's arms around her and his deep, soothing voice against her ear. Traveling on autopilot, she stopped at her surgery in case he was there. When she didn't find him, she covered the distance to the bar. Everyone was huddled in a corner, sharing wine and playing a card game.

The last thing she felt like was being social, so she caught his eye and motioned to him. Brynn made his excuses and strode toward her. Once he got close enough to get a good look at her face, his expression darkened. He took her arm and steered her back into the corridor where they covered the short distance to her surgery door. "You've been crying. What did your mother say?"

"A lot of things. More than I wanted to hear, actually."

"We have the rest of the night. How about a nice hot shower, and then I'll brew you some tea, and you can tell me everything."

The tears she'd managed to control flooded her eyes, and she clung to him, sobbing. He held her, making low soothing sounds. "Whatever it is, sweetheart, we're in this together. I love you. I'll take care of you. If you need a warrior to do battle with your father and the Chinese dragon, I'll figure that part out too. No one will ever hurt you. Not on my watch."

"I don't deserve you," she choked out between sobs.

"Maybe not." Understated humor ran beneath his words. "But you're stuck with me. Here, let me get the door, and we'll be safe inside your quarters. I'll lock up, so at least the monsters will have to knock."

HALF AN HOUR LATER, Brynn took her empty teacup from her, gathered her into his arms, and carried her to bed. He killed the lights except for one small one. She was still wrapped in a robe, and he set her on her feet to slide it off her shoulders before they lay down. Once she was curled onto her side, he squeezed between her and the wall and snugged her against his body. A flick of his wrist settled the duvet over them both.

"Thanks for listening," Kayna said, her voice wan and drained. "You're taking a whole lot on faith here."

"Maybe not. Your mother obviously believed what she told you, so why can't I?"

"Because magic's not a native element for you."

"It didn't used to be," Brynn corrected her. "Now that you're part of my life, it will be. How are you feeling about your father?"

"Wretched. Scared. He's more damaged than I thought—if that's even possible." She twisted until she faced him and wrapped her arms around him. "How could she have let me believe he was an out-of-control drunk? Why didn't Nana tell me the truth? They colluded and…" Her voice broke. "Aw, what the hell. I wish I'd had a dad growing up. If he could've broken loose from the madness, he might've been able to keep Kiki alive." Bitterness ran beneath her tone, harsh and sour. "Beyond that, it defies credibility that Mom invested so much energy pretending we were normal."

"Your mother was trying to protect you and your sister." His voice wound down and his expression turned grim. "Do you suppose she was frightened you and your sister might be next?"

"What do you mean?"

"It was the blend of Chinese and Celtic magic that offended your kin, right?" At her nod, he went on. "Well, what were you and your sister if not a blend of magical strains, or lines, or whatever the proper term is?"

"Maybe you're onto something. That could explain why no one ever pressed charges against my uncle. And Kiki was next, in a backhanded sort of way." Kayna's voice was small, broken. "Mom was really upset tonight. I'm surprised she managed to get through the parts she told me. Could be that's why Nana has laid low too. Och, as they'd say. I can't go backward. I've got to find a way to live with this."

She laughed hollowly and leaned her forehead against Brynn's cheek. "I have to let all this go. No more anger at either of them. We've got bigger problems than twenty-two-year-old emotional baggage."

Brynn's heart contracted painfully. He wanted to wave a wand and ease her pain, but that wasn't possible. Instead, he laid a hand on her cheek. "Sometimes, we don't get to choose. Your mother did the best she could, even if you'd rather she'd made other choices. I'm sorry you're hurting." He smoothed hair away from her face.

Kayna ran a hand down his back. "Hurting, and sunk in self-pity. I need to pull my head out of my ass. Why am I naked and you still have your shirt and trousers on?"

"You're upset. I thought maybe you might want to fall asleep in my arms."

She kissed him lightly, tenderly. "So you kept your clothes on as a hedge?"

"You know how much I want you, darling. I'm hard right now, but I'm sure you can feel me. Tell me what you need. How can I comfort you? Would you rather be by yourself for a bit? I won't take it amiss."

She drew back and gazed at him. "Do you want to leave?"

He shook his head. "No. Never."

Relief softened her features. "You're the best thing that's ever happened to me. I'm still scared what we have will blow up in our faces, but until that happens, I want our nights together." She tugged his shirt out of the waistband of his pants. "I can't do anything about my past. Who knows what's coming next and when we'll have another opportunity to be together? Please. I need to feel you against me, inside me."

Happiness glowed in Brynn's center, and everything else dropped away. For tonight, it would be him and Kayna and the comfort of each other's bodies. "Give me a moment." He slithered off the end of the bed and undressed, leaving his clothes in an untidy heap. "Where do you keep the condoms?"

Kayna held out her arms. "It will be all right. You hadn't had sex for more than two years before me, and I figure you were careful after Rebecca. I tested myself for everything before I left the States. My IUD is still in place. I'd say we're golden."

Heat licked at his loins, and his cock twitched eagerly where it curved outward from his body. To feel all of her without anything in between tantalized him. His breath quickened, and arousal turned his body into a livewire of anticipation. Maybe she sensed his need because she tossed the duvet to the floor, rolled onto her back, and beckoned with extended hands.

"I don't need fancy—" her voice was husky with desire "—but I do need you."

Brynn knelt between her thighs and rubbed a finger around her slick, swollen clit. Her nipples peaked, and the color he loved splashed across her chest. "You are so incredibly beautiful." He grasped his cock and moved up enough to seat it at the entrance to her body. Her labia parted easily, and he slipped into all her glorious, scorching heat.

Lust etched into her features until she looked like a reincarnation of Aphrodite. She placed her hands on his hips and laced her legs around his back, rocking her vulva against his pubic bone. They'd gotten more familiar with one another, and she came almost immediately, her muscles contracting and releasing around him as she murmured his name. It was sweet, so sweet to hear *Brynn* fall from her slightly-parted lips. Her green eyes burned with twin fires. He could get lost in those eyes, exactly like he lost himself in the wonder of her body.

He lowered himself until he lay atop her and closed his mouth over hers. She clasped her arms behind him, and he thrust his tongue inside her mouth. Their kiss was endless, timeless, as his arousal rose and fell in waves. Kayna pulled her mouth away. "Turn over," she demanded breathlessly.

He rolled so she was on top, and she knelt over him, hair cascading down her body in a dark, silky river. "Watch," she whispered and moved a hand to her sex. Her other hand closed over an erect nipple. She twirled the nipple and rubbed her clit in small, lazy circles, arching her back with pleasure.

Seeing her touch herself was more than he could take. He gripped her hips and plunged himself hard into her body. Control crumpled, and he welcomed the climax boiling up from his balls. She was his woman. *His.* He'd branded her with his touch, and they were joined soul to soul forever. She dissolved in a flood of heat as semen burst from him. Brynn came for a long time, glorying in the feel of her without a condom between them.

Still holding him inside her body, she lay atop him and stretched out her legs. "I love you, Brynn," she murmured. "Don't ever stop being you."

"Darling." He cradled her against him. "There are so many things I want to say, but they all seem inadequate. The important thing is we found each other. Nothing can change that."

"I hope you're right," she mumbled right before the cadence of her breathing told him she'd fallen asleep.

Her words haunted him. He had to be right. Nothing could come between him and the woman he loved.

Nothing.

PART THREE ~~ DESTINATION

The path to our destination is not always a straight one. We go down the wrong road, we get lost, and sometimes we turn back. In the end, it doesn't matter which road we embark on. What matters is that we left at all.

Destinations aren't places, but new ways of looking at things.

Just as a man still is what he always was, so he already is what he will become.
~Carl Jung

CHAPTER 20

A blast of Russian over the PA system startled Kayna from sleep. She looked about the cabin bleary-eyed. Last night came crashing back to her. So did her dreams. Her raven had been front and center, making his dislike for her father and the Kiao known.

At least I got to sleep through until morning.

Nana had shown up too, full of pithy advice, all of it in Gaelic. When Kayna worked to reconstruct the conversation, all she knew for sure was that her grandmother was worried and had cautioned her about setting wards before she did damn near anything. Kayna pressed her lips together. Even if she were in a ward-setting mood, she barely had time to brush her hair. Drawing magic and holding it required extensive time, not to mention energy.

Brynn slumbered next to her, his golden-brown hair tangled across the pillow. The bunks were a tight fit for one. That two of them could actually sleep in such cramped quarters was miraculous. He must've sensed her looking at him because his eyes fluttered open, or maybe the noise had wakened him too.

"Morning already?" He grinned lazily, his face heartbreakingly beautiful.

"Yup. Someone said something in Russian over the PA system. It must've been important since they've never done that before."

"Yeah, I heard it. Would've been hard not to." He narrowed his eyes. "That grating sound. What is it?"

She sat on the bunk's edge with her feet on the floor and tilted her head to listen intently. Now that he'd mentioned it, there was an unusual noise. "Ice," she muttered. "Sounds like ice against the hull."

"Crap! No wonder they want us up."

"Do you suppose we have time for a shower?" At the look he shot her she said, "Never mind. I'll do a quick rinse and be dressed in a flash. We could look out the window in my surgery, but we'll see more from the bridge."

Brynn worked his way around her, got to his feet, and trotted into the surgery. "It is ice," he called. "We're surrounded by it. Damn! I sure hope McMurdo's icebreaker is on its way."

"Didn't Jack say he needed something like eighteen hours' notice? It's barely been twelve since last night."

"Maybe the captain radioed during the night. Besides, we don't know if it takes that long to launch one, or that long for one to get to us, or some combination of the two." Brynn strode past her and stood over the bathroom sink, using a dampened square of terrycloth to wash himself off. His skin gleamed in light spilling from the porthole over the bed. The sight of him drew her to her feet. Because she couldn't resist, Kayna ran her hands down the clean, sculpted lines of his shoulders, back, and buttocks.

"Pretty man," she murmured. "More than pretty. Striking. Stunning. Your body is incredible."

"Aw, I'll bet you say that to all the guys." He turned, swept her into a hug, and kissed her thoroughly. "If we do much more of this —" he dragged his mouth from hers "—we'll end up right back in bed. Some mornings that would be okay, but probably not this one."

She reluctantly left the warmth of his embrace. "The ship's still moving, so it's not as if we're stuck. I'm sure we'll find out whatever's going on over breakfast." Kayna grabbed the washrag, rinsed it, and ran it over her body. When she was done, she bent over the basin and splashed water on her face.

"The dining room is where all the good gossip happens," Brynn agreed from the bedroom where he was sorting his clothes. "Once upon a time, I hung my things up before I went to bed. You're a bad influence."

"Whatever do you mean?" She walked into the bedroom and lifted an eyebrow. "Last night, I could've sworn you called me a goddess."

Brynn stepped into his trousers and turned to face her, the expression on his face unreadable. "Is mindreading another of your more unusual talents?"

Heat swooshed from her chest over the top of her head, and she knew she must be bright red. "Oopsie. Busted. Not always, but we've grown so close, it's easy for me to see what you're thinking, especially when those images are about me."

Brynn cocked his head to one side. "Intriguing. I recall thinking you looked like Aphrodite, but I never said it. What else can you do?"

She started pulling on yesterday's clothes. "I've mentioned it to you, but I've had up close and personal encounters with Death. Not my own, but patients who are hovering at the edge of the veil."

"You've seen him?" Brynn's eyes widened. "What does he look like? Is it even a him? Does he carry a scythe and wear long robes?"

"Whoa there." Kayna held both hands up. "It's more sensation. I feel something intensely cold, and I hear rustling. I've never actually seen anything other than a shadow."

A long, low whistle escaped. "When you told me about that before, I was too wrapped up with the cultures to pay close attention, but it's absolutely fascinating." He gestured with both hands. "What else?"

She tucked her feet into the tennis shoes she wandered around the boat in, and bent to tie the laces. "The ice grinding against the hull seems louder to me. Maybe it's because we're awake, but I want to find out what's up. You can pick through my psi abilities later. Oh!" She slapped her forehead with her open palm. "I almost forgot. I was talking with Valentin last night after I hung up with Mom. The ship only flies a Russian flag because it was a big hassle, and more money, to change it to Ukrainian registry."

Brynn grinned. "Fascinating. One of the points I tried to pound home with Jack last night was that many of the crew aren't Russian." He dug his down slippers from beneath a chair and slid them on.

"The crew are human beings regardless of their nationality. We took an oath to do no harm."

"So we did." He scooped her into a hug. "My fierce princess. One of the many things I admire about you are your principles. If you're ready, we can head downstairs."

"I am."

Brynn followed her out the door and stopped. A shadow crossed his face, and he caught himself against the doorframe.

"What is it?" Kayna asked, instantly concerned. "Are you feeling okay? Dizzy?"

"My own personal physician." He curved his mouth into a grim smile. "Don't get me wrong, it feels great to be cared about. I'm all right, but a dream from last night came screaming into my head." He leaned close to her ear. "That Kiao thing, is it black with golden eyes and a triangular head?"

If she hadn't been standing next to a wall to steady herself, her knees might've buckled. An imaginary fist hit her in the solar plexus, driving all the air from her lungs. When she could manage words, she blurted, "You saw it? I didn't describe it to you somewhere along the way?"

"I saw it. I was in a small sailboat, like the ones I grew up piloting. The Kiao was following my boat, and getting closer. It opened its mouth, and I saw double rows of fangs, glistening with the remains of whatever it had eaten. I thought I should look away, but I couldn't. Its eyes were magnetic, mesmerizing."

Kayna bent toward him. "What happened then?"

"Nothing. You know how dreams are. The scene shifted, and the water dragon didn't show up again. Did you dream about it last night?" He closed the surgery door and locked it.

She nodded solemnly. "Yes, and my raven too." An unpleasant tingling battered her lower spine. "I'm trying to wrap my mind around us sharing dream images. Many cultures hold them to be a part of their mystic traditions."

Brynn angled his head and looked closely at her. "You're looking seriously rattled. I didn't mean to alarm you. It's not as if the thing, the Kiao, hurt me." He laughed uncomfortably. "You can't die in dreams."

"Oh, but you're wrong. If it wanted you dead—" She broke off abruptly and dropped an iron yoke of control over her churning emotions.

"It didn't. Get hold of yourself, Kayna. For all we know, it's your daddy checking out his daughter's lover."

"Spirits don't think that way," she snapped. At the hurt look that bloomed on his face, she winced. "Damn it! I'm sorry. I didn't mean to be sharp. One problem at a time. Let's hit the dining room and find out how serious the pack ice is and if McMurdo's sending an icebreaker to bail us out."

"I'd much rather stay here and educate myself about paranormal phenomena."

Kayna slitted her eyes, trying to decide if he was joking. "You're serious aren't you?"

"You bet I am. It's how I attack problems. I study them until I understand what I'm dealing with. I can't wait to get to McMurdo and their Internet hookup. I'm going to read everything I can get my hands on about Celtic lore and mythology. Chinese, too."

"That makes two of us for Chinese." Kayna pressed her lips together to keep her face from screwing into a mask of resentment. "I'm angry I ignored that half of my heritage. What a stupid oversight."

"We can learn together." He tucked her hand beneath his arm, and they made their way down the stairs, hips squashed together so they'd fit in the narrow stairwell. "At least the ice seems to have slowed the wave action."

"It would," she agreed. "Its weight sitting on the water would be bound to have a dampening effect."

"My little scientist."

"You wouldn't say that if I were a man," she said indignantly and mock swatted him.

"Probably not. I also wouldn't be in love with you if you were a man. Some things cut both ways, sweetheart." They'd reached the dining room, and the buzz of conversation eddied through it. "After you." He made a sweeping motion with one hand.

"Aren't you going to bow and click your heels?"

"Very funny."

Kayna led the way to a table across the room where Chris sat by himself hunched over a cup of coffee. "Mind if we join you?"

He looked up and smiled. "Not at all. I suppose you want to know what that hullabaloo was over the PA system."

"Am I that transparent?" Kayna rolled her eyes.

"Yup. Go get something to eat. We'll have time to talk."

When she and Brynn were settled over steaming plates of scrambled eggs, bacon, toast, and canned fruit, Chris said, "The announcement was we're traveling through serious pack ice. The captain has slowed the ship to avoid damaging the hull. He expects the American icebreaker to meet us sometime this afternoon. Once that happens, we should be docked at McMurdo in about two to three hours."

"Wow! Really?" Excitement thrummed along her nerves. To finally be at their destination felt huge, even though it didn't alter any of their problems.

Chris shrugged. "I was elated too, but there's no reason, except maybe getting off this ship."

"We'll be with a few hundred other people," Brynn said. "Misery loves company, and humans are social animals."

Kayna jabbed him with her elbow. "Thanks. Rain on our parade, why don't you?"

"My pleasure."

She turned back to Chris. "Any further developments on the international news front?"

"None that I know of, but I haven't been back to the bridge. Oh yes, the captain said we should start packing our things preparatory to moving them from the ship to the base. It has trucks designed for snow travel. They'll send the fleet to meet the ship and take whatever's ready to go. I'm guessing it'll take days to transport everything."

"How far is it from where we get off the ship to the base?" Brynn asked.

"I don't know," Chris replied. "Why?"

Brynn sipped his cooling coffee. "My cultures. They shouldn't be exposed to extreme cold for very long."

"It's a scientific base." Kayna jumped into the conversation. "I'm sure they'll have something to protect them."

"If you guys don't need my fledgling language skills anymore," Chris said, "I guess I'll work on packing my duffel. I only unpacked one, so it shouldn't take long, but I like to be prepared. I'm eager to see what the guys and gals have cooking in the paleontology lab."

"I'll second that, but for the microbiology lab." Brynn set his fork down. "My cultures have developed some definite oddities, and I'd love a second opinion. Third and fourth ones too."

"What did Zach and Abel and Ted think?" Chris asked.

"There's been so much going on, we never got around to talking about them," Brynn replied.

"All righty." Chris stood. "I'm out of here. See you guys on the bridge or out on deck."

Kayna hurriedly finished her breakfast and asked, "What do you want to do?"

"Carry you upstairs and ravish your body." He winked broadly.

"I'd like that too, but I had a few other ideas beyond starting to package up my medical supplies, which will take hours. Maybe days."

"I'm all ears." He polished off a scrap of toast and drained his coffee.

"I want to try something to entice the Kiao to talk with us—without my father."

Brynn leaned forward and squared his shoulders. "How do you propose to do that?"

"It's easier to show you than tell you." She bit her lower lip. "It might not work. Or it might work too well, and we'll either get dragged into the Kiao's world, or it will be stuck in ours."

"What are the percentages of each of those things happening?"

"Now who's the scientist? Fifty percent it won't work. Maybe twenty percent it'll escape my control."

"That doesn't add to a hundred," he observed.

"You noticed." She got to her feet. "Magic doesn't work that way."

"Why do you want to separate the Kiao from your father? What are you hoping will happen?"

Kayna held out both hands. "'It's pretty clear my father isn't going to tell us anything. Maybe I can get the Kiao to spill a few beans—or perhaps my raven can. The creatures exist on dual planes: the one where they're bonded to a magic wielder, and another where they live independent lives in the Otherworld— and elsewhere."

Brynn blew out a frustrated-sounding breath. "There's certainly a lot to this."

"Yeah." An uncomfortable sensation shot from the soles of her feet to her head. "And I'm not much better than a neophyte. Probably ought to get moving, before I lose my nerve."

A few minutes later, they cleared the stairs to Deck Four, and she moved toward the next set winding upward. "Aren't we going to use the surgery?" Brynn asked.

"No. For one thing, having someone knock on the door could be catastrophic in terms of my concentration. For another, I want something more neutral than my territory. I thought we'd use one of your lab rooms."

"It won't hurt my prokaryotes and eukaryotes, will it?"

A knowing smile crossed her face as she climbed the last flight of stairs. "I feel protective of them too, which is interesting. Especially considering I viewed them as a threat at first. Something's going on here. It's like having an invisible puppeteer manipulating our strings behind the scenes. Do you care which room we use?"

Brynn shook his head. "All roads lead to Wonderland, so it probably doesn't matter."

CHAPTER 21

Kayna sat cross-legged on the floor with her back against a wall. Brynn sat facing her, so close their knees touched, with his hands resting on her thighs. "Be sure to maintain contact," she said, "no matter what happens, unless I tell you to let go."

"Got it." He sounded mildly rattled.

"Have you ever meditated, or been hypnotized?" she asked.

"Yes to both."

"Use the same breathing pattern," she instructed.

"I'm trying," he muttered. "It's not easy with all this adrenaline humming through me."

"I'm going to chant," she said, keeping her voice low and mellifluous. "It's a simple refrain. Pick up the words and join me. It'll merge our bodies so our hearts beat in a single rhythm. You'll feel yourself drifting. Don't fight it. Magic isn't about control, but about letting go, so it has a route into you."

"When's the last time you did something like this?"

Kayna tapped one of his hands resting on her knee. "Never. If you want to back out say so now. Once I begin, you have to stay until the end—or until things blow up in our faces."

"Will I understand the words in your chant?"

"Depends." She focused her green gaze on him. "Do you speak Enochian?"

He laughed, but it came out more like a grunt. "No, but I watched enough *Supernatural* episodes. Do you mean to tell me it's a real language?"

"Yes. It was developed by John Dee and Edward Kelley in late sixteenth century England. They claimed it came from angels, but it was actually derived from early Celtic mixed with Hebrew. For example, the lines read from right to left."

"Why use it and not Celtic—or Hebrew?"

Kayna blew out a breath. "You're stalling by asking questions, but I'm not all that fired up to crack this nut open, so I'll answer that one. Celtic is simply an early language used by inhabitants in the U.K. Hebrew might work, but my bloodlines aren't right to access it. Enochian is perfect for spells because its words hold power."

"I'm almost sorry I asked."

"You don't have to do this." She shook her head briskly. "I don't, either, but I need to ferret out what my father wants with those cultures—before we get to McMurdo and he has an entire base to sow misery and discontent. He's had ample opportunity to tell us, or Mom since he's dogging her too, but he's chosen to remain silent. I want to know why."

"Do you have any ideas?"

"Beyond my tentative hypothesis about your cultures being part of Father's *save the world* plan? Not really."

Brynn hesitated. "Don't take this wrong, and it might not even be possible, but could you summon your grandmother to help with whatever you're trying to do?"

Kayna slapped a hand across his thigh. "Brilliant. Excellent idea. She'll help if she can. While I'm at it, I'll see if my raven wants a piece of the action. I'll do that first. If they're willing to join us, we'll move to the next step. Ready?"

He snorted. "Let me gather the tattered edges of my dignity.

After all my big warrior talk, how could I possibly leave you alone to face whatever crawls out of the paranormal realm? Any idea how long this will take?"

"Not long. Spirits never stick around. Hush now. No more questions and remember not to move your hands off my legs."

Brynn remained silent.

Her voice rose and fell, stumbling occasionally over the Enochian syllables. Time stopped as she sank into a deep trance. The air around her felt thick, syrupy, but a sense of peace wrapped her like a shroud. The tang of salt air tickled her nostrils, and the same cavalcade of otherworldly creatures that had inhabited her previous trance state marched through the cabin—minus the Kiao.

Damn it!

The one thing she wanted to grill chose this opportunity not to show up. It was possible Guiren was driving the thing. Had her father found a way to quell the creature's independent side?

Nana's spectral form shimmered off to one side. Her deep love bathed Kayna in warmth. The raven joined her grandmother just before Guiren leapt out of the ether, shaking his fists and screaming. It was so like her memories of him, Kayna's insides crawled with the need to run and hide, but she forced herself to keep chanting. She wasn't a child any longer, and she'd be damned if she'd succumb to his bullying.

"War is upon us," Guiren shouted into her mind. *"The war I predicted—the one I was born for. You summoned me, and you will come with me. I need your sister, but you let her die. I should kill you because of that and what your kinfolk did to me. An eye for an eye."* He swiped his hair behind his shoulders. *"But I'm better than that. This is your opportunity to redeem yourself. To buy yourself a place in history."*

Kayna's sense of horror and outrage grew with each word. He truly believed his delusions, and was deranged enough to force them on her.

The raven made a run at him, pecking at his face, but the

Chinese shaman swatted it. Cawing fiercely, the raven tried again.

"Ye'll leave her be Guiren," Nana said. *"'Twas a hard life she had once ye left. Your path will kill her."*

"Out of my way, old woman." Guiren snarled and batted at the raven again.

Nana placed herself squarely between Guiren and Kayna and chanted in Gaelic, weaving her hands into a spell. As quickly as they'd formed, Kayna's spectral visitors vanished, swept into the ether by her grandmother's magic.

BRYNN DIDN'T UNDERSTAND how he knew when Kayna's grandmother joined them, but he sensed a spectral presence, and her abiding love for Kayna. The pitch and timbre of Kayna's chanting shifted lower and became more urgent. Wind rose, rustling through the cabin. With it came the sharp, fresh salt scent of the sea. His heartbeat thudded against his ears, and he shut his eyes. Lights flared at the periphery of his darkened visual field, and he could swear things that hadn't been there before waltzed through the cabin buffeted by a ghostly wind. He tried to pry his eyes open, but they remained stubbornly shut.

The experience was so eerie, the fine hairs on his arms rose as if electrified, and a profound tingling traveled the length of his spinal cord. He straightened his back, but the feeling intensified. Beneath the Enochian chant, he heard people screaming, arguing, shrieking.

Then everything stopped. It was as if a giant rubber band snapped back into place, and the world was familiar again.

His eyes flicked open and he scanned the cabin, but nothing had changed except Kayna. The skin around her eyes was drawn, translucent. Tears streaked her cheeks.

"You can let go now," she said, her voice trembling with strain.

He glanced at his watch. Twelve minutes had elapsed from

when she'd begun chanting.

"What happened?" he asked.

She shook her head, but didn't look at him and didn't move. Concern cut deep, and he scooted next to her and drew her into his arms. She sagged against him, her body vibrating with tension. Pushing wouldn't drag words from her, so he held her and crooned a tuneless song he hoped would soothe her jangled nerves.

Finally, she moved far enough away to look at him, and relief made him weak. He'd been worried she'd gone so far into her trance state, she might never be herself again.

"It was good Nana was there. And my raven too." Kayna's voice sounded rusty, as if she hadn't used it in months. "They took on Dad."

"I'd rather have this in chronological order," Brynn said, "but I'll take what I can get. Did you get to talk with the Kiao? What would your father have done to you?"

"No on the Kiao, and Dad's plan included taking me with him."

Brynn's stomach clenched into a burning mass of acid. "How is that even possible?"

"His magic trumps mine."

Brynn felt as if he'd fallen off the edge of the world into a dizzying madness. "You're his daughter," he said, grasping at something, anything to create order out of chaos. "Why the hell would he want to harm you?"

"To save the world." She squinched her mouth into a moue. "Death hasn't drummed delusions of grandeur out of him."

Brynn tightened his hold on Kayna. "Could we back up, please?"

"Sure." She reached into a pocket, pulled out a tissue, and blew her nose. "Dad said war is a done deal. He's known about it for a long time. That was what he was working on with Mom. Mixing their magic not to stop the war, but to clean the air so everybody wouldn't die from atomic fallout. He'd planned to draft Kiki and me into his master plan, but he died before we were old enough to conscript." Sadness etched into her features. "He's angry with Mom. Really angry."

"Because her brother killed him?"

"That and he blames her—and me—for Kiki's death. He's delusional enough to believe if we'd let my sister embrace her magic, she'd still be alive, but he wasn't there. Mom couldn't have stopped Kiki any more than she stopped me. My sister died because she fell headlong into her magic, not because she avoided it."

Angered beyond words because Kayna was hurting, Brynn dragged her against him. Feral protectiveness surged, heating his blood to molten. If it were up to him, he'd never let go of her again.

She squirmed and moved back enough to keep talking. "Not much point in being angry at Dad. Spirits operate by different rules. My summoning spell might've ended in disaster if Nana weren't there, though."

Brynn sucked in air, blew it out, and did it again to center himself. This was getting weirder and weirder. "How'd you get away this time?"

"Nana stuffed her spectral self between Guiren and me and told him off roundly in Gaelic. My raven tried to peck his eyes out, and Nana chased all of them back to the Otherworld."

"You mentioned that before. What is it?" Brynn wasn't certain he wanted to know, so he added, "Next time you see your Nana, thank her for me. The raven too." His chest constricted, and he felt furious and helpless by turns.

"I will." She wriggled out of his arms. "I wouldn't blame you if you decided this was much too big a mouthful of Dead Sea fruit to swallow. If you want out, I understand totally." Fresh tears glistened at the corners of her eyes.

"Hell no, I don't want out." Brynn pounded a fist into the floor. "What I want to know is how to keep you safe from that son of a bitch. If he'd spirited you off, what would I have found when the trance lifted? You would've been unconscious, right? If that happened, how could I have brought you back?"

She focused her hollow-eyed gaze on him. "Not unconscious. My body would've been gone."

"Son of a bitch." He pounded the floor again, wishing it was Guiren's face.

"That's not helpful," she ventured.

"Probably not." Brynn scrambled to his feet and pulled her upright. "Let's bundle up and go outside to look at the ice. I need fresh air."

She snuffled, still looking trashed. "You were really, really brave to hold your ground once that wind started, and all those creatures marched through here. I've seen them before, but they're enough to send anyone on a one-way trip to the loony bin."

He hesitated, hunting for words. "Do you know what they want or why they showed up?"

Kayna bit her lower lip. "No. I'd never seen them until the trance I summoned around the time you got on the boat."

"Could they be related to the archaea?"

She shrugged. "Maybe. Or to my father. I'm sorry, but I just don't know."

Brynn kissed her forehead. "If it's important, we'll figure it out. I sensed there were…things in here, but I couldn't see them."

"I know. I made certain your eyes stayed closed. Some experiences—" she was clearly struggling to find words "—would change you. They're not meant to be viewed by mortal eyes."

"You're mortal."

"Not the same way you are."

Brynn girded himself so the weirdness wouldn't swallow him whole. "How about going outside? I want to know what the Otherworld is, but not right now."

"Sure. Outside is a grand idea. I'd like some fresh air too, and then I need to start piling things into boxes."

"Piss on the boxes. How can you shift from one reality to another?" he demanded.

Kayna gripped his hand and moved toward the door. "It's not hard. Magical worlds wear many faces, and the other realm, the one you're familiar with, never changes." She closed her hand around the latch and walked into the corridor. "My current problem is it's been fifteen years since I did much of anything with my paranormal side. I don't remember a lot of things, things that used to keep me safe."

Brynn wrapped an arm around her waist and guided her to the cabin where his bunk and clothing were. "I really don't like the sound of that. I need to stop here for outerwear and boots."

She stretched on tiptoe and brushed her lips over his cheek. "I'll run down to my cabin and do the same. Once we get to McMurdo, I'll call Mom. There are chapters in my magic books that I need her to copy and scan into digital form. Some of it's probably available on the Internet these days, so I won't know exactly what I need until we get to the base and I have a connection."

"Before you go." He smoothed hair out of her face, tucking it behind her ears. "I've been meaning to ask how our chest-congestion guy is." The retreat to medicine was familiar ground, and Brynn welcomed it.

Her forehead creased with worry. "About the same. We're well past when the drug should've kicked in. I'm starting to think it's not the right one for whatever he has."

"I suspected as much from what I saw under my scope. I did have an idea, though."

Hope flared in her eyes. "Great. He's fading. If I can't reverse the process, I'll lose him."

"You haven't heard my idea yet. You might not be singing its praises, or mine."

"I'm listening." She closed her teeth over her lower lip and looked so vulnerable it broke Brynn's heart.

"Because we have a bug I can't identify, it's not surprising a stock antibiotic isn't touching it. I've suspected for a long time that archaea hold the key to a whole new class of boutique antibiotics. Drugs we could tailor to address specific infections. An infusion of the archaea that haven't yet mutated into eukaryotes might be just the ticket. Of course, we'd incubate it first with bacteria from his blood to make certain it's effective, but if it was, we could feed the mix into him via an IV—"

"Are you out of your mind? He's a human, not a lab rat. Crap!" She scrubbed the heels of her hands down her face. "Sorry. I'm sorry. Didn't mean to raise my voice. Go on, I interrupted."

"It's okay. Any doctor would've had the same reaction. Think about it, though. The archaea have the ability to mutate. What we need is for them to change into something to destroy the bacteria infecting your patient."

"Okay." Kayna pinched the bridge of her nose so hard it left red marks. "How about this? We can take a better look once we get him into the infirmary at McMurdo. Hell, I'm sure they have an X-ray machine. We can take a chest plate too."

"Sure," Brynn agreed. "We'll rule out the obvious. If the strange mess I saw under my scope is all that's left, you can think about what you want to do. Of course, we'd prep plates with bacteria from his blood and the prokaryotes to see if my theory is right before we introduced anything into his body."

"Thank you."

"For what?" He gazed at her and thought she was the most beautiful woman he'd ever seen. Even with her red eyes and tear-stained face, she carried herself with a simple dignity that touched him.

"Caring enough about my patient to think up something that might help him."

"Old habits die hard. See you in your surgery in a few minutes." He kissed her forehead and walked back into his cabin.

~

KAYNA LET herself into her surgery and stared at its familiar walls. Instead of seeing them, she saw her grandmother. Nana clearly had something in mind to keep her safe, but wouldn't have talked about it in Guiren's presence. If the raven had its way, though, she'd never get within spitting distance of her father ever again.

She moved into her quarters and dragged on layers of clothing, trying not to think about anything.

"Looks like you're about ready." Brynn's voice sounded from the surgery. When she looked up, he was gazing at her, his eyes shining with concern and caring.

Warmth began in her heart and radiated outward. "Guess you decided not to desert me despite my more unusual aspects."

"I told you upstairs that will never happen. I am going to figure out this psi stuff, though, so I'm something more than dead weight."

"You might surprise yourself." She moved to his side and hooked a hand beneath his elbow. "All humans have some latent power. It's a matter of cultivating it. Let me grab my hat and gloves, and we can head outside."

Brynn drew his brows together. "Do you mean I could develop power like yours?"

How to answer that?

Kayna pressed her lips into a thoughtful line. "I won't know until you start working with what you have. It's not likely you have much innate magical ability, but if your genetics match your Scottish name, you might surprise me."

"What does being Scottish—or Irish for that fact, or Chinese—have to do with anything?"

"Genetics 101, sweetie." She tugged a thick, red woolen hat over her head and punched her fingers into black ski gloves. "Certain ethnic groups are more likely to carry particular traits. It just so happens Chinese, Japanese, Scottish, Irish, and Russian bloodlines have a proclivity for paranormal ability. Oh yes, and the Jews. They have a mystical thread running through descendants of the Hasids."

"Someone should've told the Winchesters that," Brynn mumbled.

"Huh?" Kayna moved into the hallway and tugged the door to her surgery closed. Once that was done, she headed for the gangway door with Brynn right behind.

"All that time I was stuck on South Georgia, there were only a limited array of DVDs. I ended up watching nine seasons' worth of *Supernatural*." He rolled his eyes. "It's where the bulk of my information about weird shit comes from. That and *Buffy the Vampire Slayer*. Anyway, one of the *Supernatural* characters had demon blood, but both of the main characters seemed plenty able to manipulate paranormal phenomena."

"Interesting. Maybe they'll have the disks at McMurdo, and I can check them out. Not that I'm expecting to have enough time to… Oh my!" she gasped as she walked out on deck. "Look at all that ice. It's beautiful, but where did it come from?"

"I'm sure the guys in those early wooden sailing ships asked themselves the same thing." Brynn cracked a rueful smile.

"Let's walk all the way around." She set off at a brisk trot, and almost fell, her arms flailing like small windmills.

Brynn closed his arms around her from behind. "Careful. The deck's coated with ice."

"Makes sense." Her heart, which had lurched into her throat, settled into something approximating a normal rhythm.

"Exactly. Let's take this slow. I want to at least do a full transit of the ship."

Kayna walked next to Brynn, and they moved toward the bow. The skies were full of ominous-looking clouds in shades of blue, silver, and gray. Ice stretched as far as she could see in various-sized chunks. Icebergs glistened, some close, some at the edge of the horizon. Because the fresh air had a salutary effect on her jangled nerves, she suggested they keep walking. On their third transit, she stopped and stared at a dark dot. At first, she thought it was another iceberg, but the color was wrong.

"What's that?" She pointed.

Brynn moved his head next to hers. After a long moment, he said, "It could be a random ship, but my money's on the icebreaker that's coming to guide us home."

Valentin glided to their side. "I see you out here from bridge and come down." He clapped Brynn on the back and extended his arm toward the dark dot. "Your friend send boat for us."

"Would we have made McMurdo without its help?" Kayna asked.

The captain shrugged. "Maybe. Important thing is moving. Stop." He doubled both hands into fists and slammed them together in front of him. "Stuck."

"You're not wearing gloves," Kayna observed. "Your hands must be freezing."

The captain grinned. "Russians tough. Very cold there."

"Yeah in Siberia," Brynn cut in, "but Kayna tells me you're from Ukraine."

"Things packed?" Valentin changed the subject.

"Not even close." Kayna nodded. "I know a hint when I hear one."

"Me too." Brynn turned to Kayna. "I'll help with your medical supplies once I have my things squared away."

Kayna realized she hadn't seen the staff captain in a while. "Where's Harold been?" she asked.

"Busy. Many report need writing. He not happy."

"Because he doesn't like paperwork?" Brynn asked.

Valentin shook his head. "He like lady doctor, but she like you." The captain tossed his hands palms up. "Way of world. Who we love not always love back."

A shadow transited his dark eyes, and Kayna wanted to ask who he'd loved and lost, but now wasn't the time. Instead, she said, "See you soon," took Brynn's arm, and walked toward the nearest door leading back inside the ship.

Before she got there, she thought of something and turned. Cupping both hands around her mouth, she called, "Captain."

He strode their way. The icy deck didn't appear to bother him. "Yes?"

"Your crewman with the cough. Once we're at McMurdo, please see he's settled in the infirmary."

"You care for him there?" When Kayna nodded, the captain took her gloved hand, bent over it, and kissed the back. "Many thank yous. He very sick, yes?"

"Don't lose hope," Brynn said. "We have some ideas."

Valentin nailed Brynn with his intense, dark gaze. "He help Harold move your things onto ship. He good engineer. Has wife and four sons. Do your best." The captain twisted his hands together in front of him, almost as if he were praying.

"We will," Kayna said. "I promise."

Valentin nodded sharply and strode past them into his ship.

Brynn frowned. "I remember him. Assuming it's the same man, he was fascinated with my sample bins. Kept up a steady stream of Russian asking Harold questions." His voice trailed off. "Crap!"

"What?" Kayna turned to face him.

"You don't suppose that fellow got his paws into one of the bins, and the archaea felt threatened and infected him?"

A fistful of fear tightened her chest. "I have no idea, but if that's true, could they cure him too?"

"Uncharted waters, Kayna," Brynn muttered. "Uncharted waters."

"I'm going to find one of the kitchen staff who speaks English and go talk with him right now. Packing can wait. By the way, his name is Andrev." She moved around Brynn back inside the ship, determined to figure out if his theory about Andrev touching the prokaryotes was correct.

CHAPTER 22

The day flew by. It was almost dinnertime, and Brynn sat on the floor in the surgery loading boxes with medical supplies. Kayna had joined him half an hour before and described a long and painful discussion with Andrev. Harold ended up translating when she couldn't find anyone in the kitchen. After significant prodding, the seaman confessed to touching the contents of one of the bins. He'd thought the cultures beautiful and hadn't seen the harm in his action.

"At least we probably know why he's sick and no one else is," Kayna muttered through clenched teeth.

"In a lot of ways, that's a relief." Brynn spoke carefully. "Look on the bright side. It means we won't have an epidemic on our hands. It also explains why our cultures didn't match anything in my book."

She blew out a tense breath. "Thanks for the pep talk, but how do we handle his infection?"

"I'm more positive now than I was before that an infusion from the archaea might be just the thing."

"Hair of the dog that bit you?" she inquired caustically and then looked at the floor. "I'm sorry. My temper isn't needed just now."

Brynn patted her hand. "Try not to worry. We'll figure something out. You're frustrated. That can't have been an easy conversation, particularly not through an interpreter."

"It wasn't. Thanks. Harold yelled at Andrev a few times, which didn't help matters." She squeezed her eyes shut and then opened them and finished packing the box in front of her. "We've been following that icebreaker for two hours, and I can see the Antarctic mainland out the window. How long—?"

The rasp of the anchor chain grated loud against his ears. "Hot damn!" Brynn fist pumped the air. "We're finally here."

Kayna snorted. "You barely spent any time on the good ship lollipop."

"Maybe I didn't get sailor genes. It felt like plenty long enough. Did you bring all this stuff with you?" He waved his arms expansively.

"They told me I had to bring my own medications and supplies for the boat. For a poor gal right out of training, it made significant inroads into my meager bank account. I didn't expect to use quite so much of what I brought, but McMurdo will be well stocked. One thing is certain. I'm not bringing any of it back home with me."

"On a slightly different tack." Brynn girded himself. He'd been putting this off, but he really wanted to know. "Could you give me a primer on what you called the Otherworld?"

She glanced sidelong at him and grimaced. "You want to do that on an empty stomach?"

"Well, I have to do it sometime. Hit the high points."

She nibbled her lower lip and sat straighter. "Nana could do a better job with this one, but let's see. It's sort of like a parallel world that wraps around this one. Magical beings live there. It's also where the dead hang out who aren't content to simply, uh, stay dead. I suspect there's more than one

Otherworld, or else it's a much bigger place than the parts I've explored."

"So it's like a psychic launching pad for dead relatives to get back into this world?"

Kayna drew her brows together. "In a manner of speaking, but they generally use dreams as a vehicle. Maybe they have to be in the Otherworld first, though, before they can do that." An uncomfortable look washed across her face. "Like I said, Nana—or even Mom—would know more about this. I was pretty young, and it was a grand adventure to cast a spell and visit there. At the time, I wasn't thinking too deeply about what it all meant—"

"Attention please." Harold's clipped, British accent sounded over the PA system. "As you get your boxes, duffels and suitcases packed, set them outside your door. Crew will ferry them to waiting vehicles. Make certain you have identification tags on your luggage, and that each of your boxes of scientific materials is clearly marked. If any of you have special needs, please see me. I'll be on the bridge or in my cabin." There was a pause and then he added. "Cook's prepared dinner. I recommend you eat aboard tonight. He'll begin dishing up in ten minutes."

Brynn stood and ruffled a hand through her hair. "Maybe we could finish this conversation later. I need to run him down about my cultures. Do you want dinner here?"

"I wasn't aware we had a choice." Kayna looked up from scrawling a label across a box with a marker.

"I expect McMurdo has several mess halls, but Harold's probably right. Our main focus tonight should be finding our quarters and getting situated. I'll be back shortly."

Brynn headed for the bridge, puzzling over what Kayna had told him about the magical realm a hairsbreadth away from his waking reality. The deeper he dipped into supernatural territory, the more it fascinated him.

Who knows? Maybe I do have an aptitude for this stuff.

He stopped and shook his head to clear it before opening the door into the bridge. Harold still clutched the microphone in his hand and was staring out the windows at McMurdo Station. An impressive array of buildings sprawled up and down snow-covered hills. Brynn strode to his side.

"It's bigger than I pictured."

"It holds slightly more than twelve hundred people," Harold replied. "That's larger than many villages in rural England. During the winter, though, there's only a quarter of that number in residence. Scott Base that's run by the New Zealanders a couple of miles away has space for fewer than a hundred."

"About my cultures," Brynn began, but Harold waved him to silence.

"I already ordered a heated transport for them. Never fear, most of your wee beasties should survive. It's only a short distance to the main building. I'll call you over the loudspeaker when the men are ready to collect them, and you can oversee the process if it will make you feel better."

"Thank you," Brynn murmured and added, "In light of what happened with Adrev, I want to make double sure no one touches my cultures."

"That makes two of us," Harold said, following it with, "Hold up a minute, mate, and come with me." He set the microphone in its cradle and trotted out of the bridge. Curious, Brynn followed the staff captain into his cabin. "Thanks for indulging me," Harold said and pushed the door shut.

"Not a problem. What's up?"

"I wanted to thank you personally for finessing your way through that political minefield and pounding some sense into the jackass who runs McMurdo."

"Jack's a decent sort. He hates conflict, and he's probably in way over his head. I'm sure you'll get along fine after you meet him."

"Because I'm a Brit and not a Russian?" Harold made a sour

face. "I hate subterfuge. Now what's the deal with your cell colonies? I asked you once before, and you sidestepped me."

Brynn frowned. "It's hard to explain something I don't totally understand myself."

"I may look like a dumb sailor, mate, but I did manage to finish college. Try me. I'll ask questions if I need to. Why'd they make Andrev sick when he touched them?"

Okay, then.

Brynn squared his shoulders and faced Harold. "They're mutating, and they were protecting themselves."

"Do you have any idea why?"

"Not yet." Brynn paused. "Even with what happened to Andrev, the cultures don't feel creepy and malevolent anymore—at least not to me. Why'd you ask about them?"

"Something still feels odd aboard this ship, but none of my gloom and doom predictions came to pass. No one got swept overboard despite the hellacious seas. We made McMurdo." Harold shrugged uncomfortably. "I operate on hunches. They've saved my bacon more than once. Your science experiment was one unknown still hanging fire. I figured you'd never discuss it spontaneously, so I asked."

"There are a couple things I didn't mention." Brynn blew out a tense breath. "McMurdo is culturing similar organisms, but with very different results. It appears those prokaryotes are responsible for killing some lab workers and making at least one other researcher sick."

"How sure are you that their wee beasties are different from yours?" Suspicion ran beneath Harold's question.

"Very sure. I've been all over those cultures, and I'm not sick. The only reason Andrev is ill is because he reached into the bins, and the proks apparently felt threatened."

Harold whistled long and low. "Fascinating," he muttered and peered closely at Brynn. "That's why you and your samples are here, isn't it? Given you're mates with Jack DeVoe, he probably asked if you could lend a hand with his germs that got away from their keepers."

Brynn nodded. "You're absolutely correct. Otherwise, I'd be on my way back to the States."

"What would've happened to your colonies?"

"Depends," Brynn replied. "If the firm I worked for thought they were important enough, they'd have sent someone else to nursemaid them."

"Thanks for being honest." Harold stuck out his hand, and Brynn clasped it.

"I told Jack to make room at the base for ship's crew." Brynn changed the subject.

"I know. Valentin told me. He also said we're to see that Andrev goes straight to the infirmary. Do you have any idea how to cure whatever your beasties infected him with?"

"I'm working on it," Brynn hedged, not wanting to disclose how desperately ill the man was.

Harold shook his head. "I'm sure you'll do your best. I have to get back to the bridge. It's impossible to oversee the unloading from in here." To Brynn's surprise, he said, "No hard feelings, eh?"

"None at all." Brynn smiled. "See you around the base."

KAYNA FOLLOWED Brynn down the gangway and onto the ice-slick dock. The ship had pulled up to a floating pier. Lights illuminated it, and they made their way to the far end where a truck would pick them up for the final few hundred feet to the main part of the base. She supposed they could have walked, but it was very cold and sleeting from midnight dark skies. "Thanks for your help packing my boxes before dinner," she told Brynn. "I honestly didn't think I'd get done tonight. Hope the guys ferrying them inside don't mix any of them up."

"Even if they do, there're only so many places they could end up," Brynn replied. "Your boxes in the hold were already labeled. It's a good thing we had dinner on the ship. Not that it was anything to write home about, but at least it was hot."

"No kidding." Her breath plumed in the frosty air. "Must be close to ten o'clock."

"I'm sorry you had to wait for me."

"But I didn't. Not really," she said. "I was still packing until five minutes before you showed up."

"Great." Brynn placed an arm around her. "Then I don't have to feel guilty. It took longer than I thought to get my cultures moved into the lab since it felt important to accompany the crew who had my bins. Glad I went along, though. It's a great space. Lots of room for me to work, and it's much better equipped than what I had on South Georgia."

"Excellent. I'm keen to see the infirmary and my clinic, but maybe that can wait until tomorrow. I'm afraid if I show up now, I'll get roped into middle of the night patient care, and I'm well past tired."

A bright red truck rolled to a stop on huge rubber tractor treads, and she climbed into the back seat. The vehicle reminded her of an Army convoy with tarpaulin-covered beds and two rows of seating in a heated cab. The driver, a fiftyish fellow with merry blue eyes, turned to look her up and down appraisingly. His head and the lower part of his face were swathed in wool, so it was impossible to tell what color his hair was, or if he even had any.

"Nice to meet you." He extended a gloved hand over the seat back. "I'm Rover."

She shook his hand. "Is that a nickname?"

"Yup. We have lots of Land Rovers, and I'm one of the mechanics that keeps these babies—" he patted the steering wheel "—running."

"Kayna Quan. I'll be one of your doctors."

"Brynn McMichaels." Brynn shook Rover's hand.

"Are you a doc too?"

"As a matter of fact I am, but I'm also a microbiologist."

"Wow! You can go blind down here from all the letters after people's names. Good that you guys are here. Our main doc's been having…issues. His assistant too."

An alarm rumbled through Kayna's chest, deep and disquieting. "What kind of issues?"

Brynn exchanged a worried look with her, but then he pulled the truck's door closed, and the overhead light went off. "I'd like to know too," he said, "since I might get drafted to help in the infirmary."

Rover cleared his throat. "You're a buddy of Jack's. He said so. I'd better let him tell you. He's waiting in the bar, and I know he's eager to touch base." The engine revved and the truck set off up a hill.

Kayna groaned inwardly. She was so tired her eyes ached. The last thing she wanted was to sit up chatting with someone she'd never met. "Maybe I'll figure out where our room is," she murmured.

"You have to at least meet Jack and shake his hand," Brynn said. "His feelings will be hurt if you don't. I'll tell him how wiped out we are, and I promise we'll make an early night of it."

She leaned against Brynn's shoulder. The heat and motion of the vehicle were almost enough for her to drift off. It didn't take very long before the truck rocked to a stop.

"McMurdo Station," Rover quipped. "End of the line."

"End of the Earth more like," Brynn mumbled, pushed the door open, and got out. Kayna let him lift her over the treads and together they walked into the Antarctic research base. "Bar's that way." He pointed and then wrapped an arm around Kayna, directing her across a large, open foyer toward a door at the other end. Muted lights provided illumination, and considering how late it was, quite a few people moved to and fro.

She stumbled because she was so tired, and Brynn tightened his hold on her. "Hey, Jack!" he called and headed for a slightly built blond man sitting alone at a table in a back corner of the wood-paneled room.

Jack DeVoe bolted to his feet, almost as if he'd been awakened, and hurried toward them. "Brynn!" He pumped his hand. "Goddamn, but it's been too long." He turned his brown eyes on Kayna. "You're our new doc. Glad to have you. More than glad, actually." He grabbed her hand and shook it enthusiastically. "Come. Sit with me. Drinks are on the house."

Jack walked back to the table he'd left, favoring his right leg. About five feet eight, he had a slender, almost feminine, build, and his hair was chopped off untidily at shoulder length. He wore gray sweatpants and a plaid lumberman shirt over a black T-shirt. "Pick your poison," he said. "I'm drinking scotch." He settled back into his chair, and smiled. The expression transformed his haggard face, and suddenly he looked ten years younger than the fifty Kayna had pegged him for. His cheeks were dotted with week-old stubble, and dark circles etched beneath his eyes.

"You look tired," she ventured. "We are too."

"Tired has become a way of life. I waited up for you. Least you can do is have one drink with me." Jack poured from a bottle on the table. "You still like single malt, Brynn?"

"Yup. That's fine for me. I'll rustle up something for Kayna."

"No need." Jack shoved two fingers in his mouth and whistled.

A woman wrapped in a spotted apron materialized from behind the bar. "You rang, oh fearless leader?"

"That I did." Jack looked at Kayna. "Tell her what you want."

"Irish whiskey, neat."

"Bring a glass for my good friend, Brynn, too," Jack said, and then apparently remembered his manners. "This is Sophie. She watches over our booze supply when she's not studying rock samples."

"Nice to meet you." The woman, who looked about eighteen, nodded pleasantly. Long, red hair was pulled into a single braid that hung down her back. Freckles peppered her face, and her eyes were cornflower blue. She turned away before Kayna could introduce herself.

Everything must've been close because her whiskey materialized fast, as did a glass for Brynn. The room was hot after the chill of outside. Kayna unzipped her parka and took off her gloves so she could slip the jacket off her shoulders. Next, she stripped off her hat. Brynn followed suit. The whiskey glass beaded with moisture from humidity, and her fingers slipped on its surface until she dabbed at it with a bar napkin. She took a sip and sighed with pleasure. "That's really excellent."

"We do get good liquor down here," Jack said. "You're almost in time for true winter. Soon you won't see the sun at all, for months."

"Where'd you assign our quarters?" Brynn asked. "Or did you?"

"We'll get to that," Jack said. "In addition to working with Micah to figure out what the hell is up with his cultures, I need you to pinch hit in the infirmary."

"Why?" Brynn drank from his scotch. "Don't you have a bevy of medical personnel on site?"

"Yes on the personnel, but we're light on docs right now, and we have an unusual number of very sick patients."

The same edgy feeling that had buffeted her in the transport vehicle tensed Kayna's muscles into rocks. "What happened to the other docs?"

"Who knows? One's tour of duty is nearly up, but he announced he wasn't working anymore a week or so back. Another's been seeing things." Jack tossed his hands skyward. "Frankly, I don't get it. He's too old to develop one of the mental illnesses where he'd hallucinate. Only thing I can figure is he's hitting the bottle too hard, or sampling his own merchandise."

"Who's been running the infirmary?" Brynn asked.

"We have a physician's assistant and a family nurse practitioner, but they're not supposed to dish out drugs without a physician overseeing their work."

"I'm more interested in the *rash of illnesses*." Kayna shot a pointed look at Jack.

His face turned somber. "We cordoned off one of the micro labs. Thought that'd be the end of it, but it wasn't."

"What?" Brynn cut in. "You alluded to something on the phone. Have you had more asphyxiation deaths?"

Jack slammed back the rest of the scotch and *thunked* the glass on the table. "Yes. Six. Shy of cutting off the ducts, I don't know what to do. But that's not practical because of how the heating system works. Freezing to death's not much better than having some mutant microbe rob your body's O2 supply. At least everyone's been alerted about symptoms to watch out for." He set his mouth in a hard line. "It's why the infirmary's so full."

Kayna set her almost untouched whiskey down. "I'd love to sit and visit with you Jack, but right now I want to see if I can round up either of the other docs so I can talk with them. If you'll point me in the direction of the infirmary, or wherever I might find them, I'd appreciate it."

"Do you want me to come with you?" Brynn asked.

"Maybe not. How about if you catch up on what's going on with the political mess, and we can compare notes later."

Jack furled his brows in Kayna's direction. "Used to triage I see. Your best bet for finding the other doctors is the clinic, the infirmary, or the doctors' lounge."

A man dressed all in black and with a watch cap pulled low on his head raced to their table. He grabbed Jack's arm. "Gotta talk to you, sir. Now."

Jack's face fell. "Aw, crap! There's only one reason you'd roust me out of here. They really did it, huh?"

"Yes. I need you in the radio room. The Pentagon's demanding to talk with you."

"They found out about the Russian ship and want to read me the riot act. Goddammit!" Jack punched the air with a closed fist.

The man's head snapped up. "No, sir, that's not it. It's far worse."

"What could possibly be…?" Jack's voice trailed off, and he rubbed a hand over his stubble-covered cheeks. He capped the liquor bottle, stood, and tucked it under his arm. "Sorry, folks," he said to Brynn and Kayna. "Listen for news over the PA system. We assigned you a room in the wing just past the infirmary on the second floor. Your names are on the door. If you don't like it, you can always move."

"Sir!" The man, who looked like an escapee from *Men in Black*, shook Jack's arm hard.

"Take your hands off me," Jack snarled. "If I'm a few minutes getting to the phone, it won't change a thing. Not now."

Riding on her second sight, which jabbed mercilessly, Kayna asked, "Who dropped a bomb and where?" Her voice sounded garbled, as if she were talking from underwater.

"Go ahead." Jack jerked his chin at the man in black. "Answer her."

"You can't tell anybody." He lowered his voice. "They'll panic."

"Aw, crap, son," Jack cut in. "By midnight, everyone will know. They all have radios, for chrissakes. Besides, people are already panicking about the renegade bacteria." He blew out a tight breath. "How the fuck can you avoid something invisible?"

"I—I suppose you're right, sir. It's just…" Kayna saw his throat work as he battled for control. "So far Russia bombed New York, and we retaliated by bombing Moscow."

Kayna covered her face with her hands. Even if the world's two superpowers stopped there, fallout in those densely populated urban areas would kill millions. Before shock mired her in futility, she splayed her hands on the table and pushed to her feet.

"Where are you going?" Brynn asked, his normally easygoing voice cracking with strain.

"I can't do a damned thing about New York or Moscow, so I'm

going to run down the doctors here and see if I can discover more about what's killing people."

"I'll come with you," Brynn said.

"Keep me posted." Jack nodded sharply. "Adios. We'll catch up in the morning." As he trotted after the man who'd come after him, Kayna heard him muttering, "Why me?" under his breath.

"Do you have any idea which way the infirmary is?" Kayna asked Brynn. She scooped her jacket off the chair back, tucked it beneath one arm, and picked up her hat and gloves.

"No, but I bet Sophie does. Wait a sec and I'll ask her." Brynn made a grab for his outer clothes and headed for the bar.

Even with Sophie's directions, it took a while to find the infirmary. It was staffed by a lone nurse sitting in a well-lighted office. The plump blonde glanced up from typing on a computer keyboard. She had warm hazel eyes and looked about thirty. "May I help you? It's past visiting hours."

"Kayna Quan." She extended her hand. "I'm your new doc." She looped her jacket over a coatrack and dropped her hat and gloves on a small table.

"Brynn McMichaels. I'm here to help any way I can." Brynn offered his hand too.

The blonde broke into a grin. "Awesome! I'm Peggy. God knows we need help. Do you want me to tell you about who's on the floor?"

Kayna squared her tired shoulders. This was exactly what she'd been afraid of, but it couldn't be helped. "Sure, particularly those you're really worried about."

The smile faded from Peggy's face. "I put that new guy, the Russian with the cough, in an iso room just like you requested on the paperwork that came with him."

"Did you schedule him for a chest plate?" Kayna asked.

Peggy nodded. "Yup, and we already took new blood and sputum cultures, but I've had TB patients before, and I don't think that's what's wrong with him." She continued talking for several more minutes outlining the status of the other men and women in the infirmary's beds.

"Great that you're on top of things." Brynn smiled encouragingly. "We don't know their names, but we wanted to find the other doctors."

Peggy waved an airy hand. "No need to say more. You want Doc Stewart and Doc Crowley. Go back out into the hall, turn right, and count four doors on the left. I'll bet at least one of them is in there. It was supposed to be a doctors' lounge, but no one ever used it much. It's also where we keep all the textbooks and journals."

"Thanks, Peggy." Kayna pointed at a glass door leading into the infirmary. "I'll check on everyone first."

"Sure, Doc. Masks and gloves are in boxes on this side of the door."

"While you do that," Brynn said, "I'll run Micah down, and between the two of us maybe we can put part one of my plan into action."

Kayna nodded. "You want to introduce some of your cultures into the renegade colonies here."

"Yes, on a very small scale. We'll take scrapings from the most mutated colonies here, and add a few cells from my proks and my euks. So, two separate plates."

Strands of fear wrapped around Kayna's midsection, and her earlier dinner curdled in her gut. "Be careful. I don't want you infected."

Brynn shot her a wry grin. "Count me nuts, but I think my colonies will take care of me. They have so far. Why would they quit now?"

She nodded briskly to cover her tumultuous emotions. "Hope to hell you're right."

"We'll catch up later." Brynn strode out the door.

Kayna put on a mask and gloves and pushed the infirmary door open. A few patients were reading, but most slept with O2 masks over their faces. She made her way through the group, talking briefly with the ones who were awake and checking the others as unobtrusively as possible. Two were very sick. When she checked their lab results, it was clear their bodies weren't clearing the iron-hungry microbes fast enough. The last thing she did was look in on Andrev. He sent a weak smile her way, along with a thumbs up sign, and she nodded encouragingly.

Kayna made her way back to Peggy's desk. "I turned up the O2 flow for Grimes and Lewey. Have we run chelation drips for either of them?" When the nurse shook her head, Kayna said, "Let's get IVs set up for those two. Tonight if you can."

"You got it." Peggy smiled softly. "Maybe we can finally get back to normal around here."

"Hope so." Kayna tossed her mask and gloves into a biohazard waste can, picked up her coat, hat, and gloves and went to find the other doctors.

She made her way through the corridor to the door labeled *Doctors' Lounge* and stood staring at it. Looking in on sick patients had been a diversion, but she was devastated by what could be the start of World War III. It was unconscionable, unbelievable, and she couldn't believe the U.S. had been so stupid. If they got really lucky—and she sure as hell couldn't count on that—the craziness would stop here. If no one dropped any more bombs, the world might recover. Bile laced with whiskey splashed the back of her throat, as her stomach threatened to rebel.

She swallowed back the stinging in her throat, pushed the door open, and peered into a small, cozy space lined with bookshelves. Three tables with chairs pushed beneath them were scattered about the room. At the far end, two men sat in tattered, leather easy chairs facing one another. The dark haired man was in his mid-thirties, tall, and so thin he might've been anorexic. He glanced up at her with shrewd, dark eyes. His hair was clipped short, and all the bones in his body poked against sallow skin stretching over them. His counterpart looked about forty. Blond hair, thinning at the top, fell to his shoulders. Unfocused, bloodshot blue eyes stared straight ahead.

"Well, lookee here," the dark-haired man said. "We hardly ever get visitors."

"Lost. She's exactly like the rest of us—lost," the blond said, his voice like dull shears grinding through an overgrown hedge.

"Which of you is Stewart?" Kayna asked.

"Who wants to know?" The blond managed to focus his gaze on her.

"I'm Dr. Quan, the new M.D."

"Cool." The blond clapped his hands together in an obscene parody of a child at play. "I can stop feeling guilty now. I'm Stewart, by the way."

"So you must be Crowley." Kayna covered the distance between her and the men.

"Busted. Oops, I mean at your service." Crowley mock bowed from where he sat.

Kayna dragged a chair over and plopped into it. "What the fuck?" she demanded, giving in to a rising tide of anger. "You're professionals. You don't get to check out when the going gets tough."

"Hear that, buddy?" Crowley bent forward and swatted Stewart's knees. "She says we're bad."

Kayna bit her lip so hard she drew blood. She needed a healthy shot of equanimity, but it just wasn't there. She clasped her hands together in her lap so hard her knuckles ached. "Care to tell me your version of what's been going on around here?"

"You never should've come," Crowley intoned.

"Why not?"

"Crazy shit," Stewart answered. "Bacteria I've never seen

before. Antibiotics won't touch 'em. Some bastard bug in the micro lab has it in for all of us."

"But that's not the worst," Crowley cut in. "I'll be the first to admit maybe I'm drinking too much, but Stewart and I are having the same monster dreams. How bizarre is that? I looked up everything I could find on dream states and shared hallucinations. It didn't shed even this much—" he held his thumb and index finger an angstrom apart "—light on it."

It was all Kayna could do to stay in her seat. Adrenaline poured through her, winding her nerves into hot little knives stabbing her from the inside. "What kind of monster?" She was amazed she managed to get the words out without mangling them.

"A fucking sea serpent," Stewart supplied. "Looks a lot like that prehistoric thing in Loch Ness in Scotland. I did my residency in Inverness, so I took road trips around the countryside. Never exactly sighted it, but I did look at pictures."

Kayna's insides felt like broken glass, jagged and sharp. "Describe it," she choked out.

"What are you?" Crowley sneered. "A psychiatrist?"

"Just describe it. You can skip the commentary." Sweat dripped down her body, and she raked a hand through her hair.

"It's black," Stewart said. "Huge. Golden eyes." He shuddered. "I swear, the damn thing looks sentient. Even worse, this Asian dude with really long hair, started showing up with it." He screwed up his mouth as if he'd bitten into something sour. "I've been dosing myself with antipsychotics, but they didn't change a thing and made me feel like crap, so I quit."

"Told you," Crowley leered. "Booze is the drug of choice down here. We were planning to catch a berth on that ship that dropped you off, but this whole U.S.-Russian problem cut the balls out from under us."

"Yeah," Stewart chimed in. "First DeVoe said the ship couldn't land. Then it could, but once it did, it wasn't leaving."

"That's because the ice is bad, and the storm track's about to give us hell," Crowley muttered.

Kayna couldn't sit still any longer. She surged to her feet, feeling like she housed a small cyclone in her belly. After pacing in a tight circle, she stalked to one of the banks of medical textbooks and scanned their spines. She found what she was looking for in short order, tucked it beneath her arm, and plodded back to the men, who were staring at her.

"Here." She dropped the book in Crowley's lap.

He turned it on its side. "What the hell? A parapsychology text? I had no idea this was even here."

"Now you listen." She stood over him and Stewart with her hands balled into fists. "Both of you. I'm not going to waste time telling you why I know these things, but there are a whole lot of elements to the world that are every bit as real as what you learned in medical school. That sea serpent in your dreams is actually a Chinese water dragon. The fact that both of you are seeing it means it wants something from you."

Crowley rolled his eyes. "Yeah. Right. You're worse than we are."

"Where does the man fit in?" Stewart asked as he shot an appraising glance her way. "Say." He drew out the word. "He's Asian, you're obviously Asian—"

"Stop right there," Kayna growled. "You're starting to sound racist. Next thing out of your mouth will be *they all look the same.*"

"Great, just great." Crowley screwed his face into a scowl. "We finally get another doc, and she's not only touchy, but a nut case on top of it."

Kayna lashed her hand out and slapped him hard. Crowley's head snapped back on his neck, and his cheek reddened.

"I resent that." She spat the words out. "While we're at it, I resent you for shirking your duty to your patients. I'm trying to help you understand something that's scaring the crap out of you. If you're not interested in listening, the same way you're not interested in picking up your responsibilities for the patients you've abandoned, there's no reason for me to waste my breath."

She tried to get hold of her temper, but once her Irish was out of the box, all bets were off. More words tumbled out. "There were lots of things I didn't like in my residency. Decisions I didn't agree with. Diseases that tore my heart out. But I never—" she paused for emphasis, and then repeated herself "—*never* said I was going to take my ball and go home."

Stewart's eyes widened. "Maybe your dressing down is well-deserved, but there's no fucking way I can believe you about the Chinese dragon being anything beyond a hallucination." He scrubbed his hands down his stubble-covered cheeks. "Things are bad enough here—bat shit bad—don't go making them worse."

"What he said," Crowley mumbled.

Past the flood stage of anger, Kayna recognized she'd said enough. No need to go into details about the Kiao and her father. She unclenched her hands. "Could you at least chip in with patient care? We have a lot of sick people back there." She jabbed a hand behind her in the direction of the infirmary.

"Of course," Crowley answered. The smart-ass look had left his face, replaced by contrition. "I'm sorry I sniped at you. In truth, I'm feeling ashamed of myself. What part of this book—" he flicked the cover with a finger "—did you want us to read?"

"There's a chapter on shared dreaming and several on mythologies from different cultures," Kayna answered. "Sorry about my temper. That's my Irish half. Once it gets rolling—" she shrugged "—Katie bar the door."

"It's all right," Crowley mumbled. "We needed a good, swift kick in the backside."

She straightened her shoulders. "Sometimes we all do. One of the other ship's passengers who arrived with me is a microbiologist and an M.D. He has some ideas that might defuse the problems with the iron-hungry microbes."

Stewart rose to his feet. "That would be excellent. We've lost eight so far, and I have a couple of folk who won't be here soon if something doesn't change."

"See the two of you tomorrow." Kayna moved slowly toward the door and walked into the corridor. She'd been tired before she stopped by the infirmary, and she'd moved beyond weary to a place she remembered from residency when everything merged into a jumbled landscape, and her brain felt like yesterday's mush.

Resurrecting Jack's sketchy directions, she walked through an interconnecting door into the next prefab module and up some stairs. Next, she wandered down the second floor hall until she saw a room with Quan and McMichaels scrawled on a small whiteboard next to the door. The room held a double bed with a thick duvet tossed over the mattress. Kayna dropped her parka, hat, and gloves onto a chair. She thought about a shower, but pitched headlong onto the bed and was asleep in minutes.

CHAPTER 24

Despite wanting to stay with Kayna, Brynn made his way back to where he'd left his samples. She looked trashed, which was understandable. The news about Moscow and New York, piled on top of whatever menace lurked at McMurdo, was damned unsettling. Because he couldn't afford to get sidetracked, he forced his mind away from everything but the task at hand.

He glanced at closed doors lining the microbiology wing, locating the cordoned off one easily enough from biohazard warnings slapped over the door. A phone sat in an alcove with a list of extensions taped to a nearby wall. He ran a finger down the list until he found Micah Greenwich and dialed the few digits, hoping he wasn't about to wake him up.

Micah picked up on the first ring. "Yeah?"

"Sorry to bother you so late—" Brynn began

"Who the hell could sleep? I've got family on the east coast. Christ! They're probably all dead."

"I'm sorry." Brynn hesitated. "It's Brynn McMichaels. If you want to talk about what's happened—"

"What for?" The other man's voice was choked with suppressed emotion.

"It's an open offer." Brynn marshaled his thoughts. "I understand if you'd rather not, but if you could manage it, I could use a spot of help for the next couple hours."

"You're here!" Micah's tone shifted to muted excitement. "Hell yeah, I want to help. Where are you?"

"Corridor in the micro wing."

"Be there in five. Don't go past the warnings."

"I won't, but it's not safe for you, either."

The other man paused half a beat. "I seem to have developed an immunity. Anyway, it'll be great to meet you."

Brynn leaned against the wall. He didn't have to wait long before a tall, angular young man with shaggy blond hair and a full blond beard loped into sight. He scooted to Brynn and stuck out his hand. When Brynn clasped it, Micah's grip was warm and sure.

"Great to meet you. I can't tell you how much it meant when you didn't blow me off a couple of weeks ago. What's our plan of attack?"

Brynn mapped out what he had in mind. Once he was finished, he met Micah's bright blue gaze. "Why do you think you're immune?"

"Because I've studied my blood. Those of us who wanted to banked our blood—in case something happened and we needed a transfusion, so I had a 'before' sample. When I compared it with my current status, I found some very real composition differences."

"Like what?" Brynn wasn't at all convinced, so he listened carefully. Finally, he nodded. "You may be onto something, which means we might be able to use your blood, and serum from others who've recovered, to help the ones who are still sick. If we get lucky, there'll be matches on blood type."

"Exactly." Micah looked pleased. "No one else agrees with me, though."

"Can't do anything about that tonight," Brynn said. "How

about if you prep two plates from your colonies. Be sure to pick the most mutated cells. Meantime, I'll scrape cells from my archaea and the ones who've transitioned into euks."

"Really want to see those." Micah's eyes blazed with interest.

"Sure. Come on into my new lab. We'll place scrapings on agar plates, and then you can take them into your lab, introduce your cells, and get the whole mess incubating."

Micah was easy to work with. After they finished, they hatched up plans to get together the following day, and Brynn made his way back past the infirmary to where he figured his and Kayna's room was. As he walked, his thoughts turned to the atomic conflagration playing itself out half a world away, and he shook his head.

He climbed a flight of stairs in the next building over from the infirmary and found their room easily. Figuring Kayna would be asleep, he let himself in quietly and gave his eyes a few moments to adapt.

"Brynn?"

"Yes, sweetheart. It's me. Don't get up."

"I need to. Still have all my clothes on, and I need a shower."

"Mind if I turn on the bathroom light?"

"Go ahead." Rustling sounded from the bed as she got to her feet.

KAYNA MADE her way to him and threaded her arms around his body. He hugged her, brushed his lips over hers, and asked, "Mind if I join you in that shower?"

"Not at all, assuming it's bigger than what we had aboard the ship. How'd it go? Did you find Micah?"

"Yeah. He's great. Probably has a brilliant career ahead of him since he's able to think outside the box. Anyway, we got the cultures introduced to one another and incubating, but even better, Micah believes he's immune to his mutant cultures because…"

Kayna listened, taking in Brynn's news. "But that's great," she said, once he'd finished. "It means maybe we can use his blood, which appears to have antibodies, to create something to help the others who are sick."

"Same thing I thought. It's way less controversial than my original theory that would've used material from the proks." He let go of her and started taking his clothes off. "Let's get that shower over with. I'm dead on my feet."

She shucked her outer layers and dropped them on the chair atop her parka. Brynn hung his things as he removed them. She sat to jockey her Arctic Pac boots off and blew out a tight breath. "I didn't tell you about my meet up with Crowley and Stewart, but the weirdest part is they're dreaming about the Kiao—and my father."

"What?" Brynn stopped dead and turned to face her. "You're kidding?"

"Wish I was. Best I can come up with is Dad's rattling their cage because they're doctors. He wants something from them, just like he wants something from me."

Brynn sat to unlace his boots. "Thought he needed you because you share blood."

Kayna nodded. "There is that. Damn! If he was out of control before, he's really going to up the ante now that his prediction about a cataclysmic war finally happened." She finished undressing and headed for the attached bathroom.

"Good news," she called. "Shower's big enough for us both." Flipping on the taps, she stood under water as hot as she could stand. Brynn joined her and coaxed liquid soap from a wall dispenser. Once he had a handful, he washed her hair, and she leaned into his touch. When she got out, inhaling clouds of steam, Brynn wrapped a towel around her before getting one for himself.

She soaked up as much water as she could from her hair and

trudged out of the bathroom. After turning out all the lights, she slid into bed and stretched out her tense limbs. When Brynn joined her, he folded her into his arms and kissed her hard. She understood what he wanted, needed, because she craved him the same way.

There was nothing tender about his kiss, or about the hands he fastened around her body. He gripped her hard, raking her flesh. She bit his lower lip and heard him growl low in his throat. Heat flashed through her, hardening her nipples and turning her crotch into a swamp of desire. He drove a knee between her legs. She reached down and grabbed his erect cock. It jumped in her hand, and she almost came. Keeping hold of him, she spread her legs, hooked them over his shoulders, and guided him into her. Her breath rasped in her throat, and she moved her hands to his hips and pulled until he was all the way inside.

She tilted her body against his until her clit ground on his pubic bone. A climax spooled deep in her belly. Almost there, it wouldn't take much to drive her over the edge. He pulled out and slammed into her again and again. Climaxes rocked her, one after the other, until she was a ball of sensation lost in the wonder of the man in her arms. Brynn uttered a hoarse cry, and she felt him judder inside her. A flood of heat followed.

"Kayna. Kayna. Sweetheart. Darling," he murmured as he collapsed atop her and turned them onto their sides. He stroked the side of her face and kissed her forehead. "Was I too rough?"

"It was exactly what I needed." She held onto him as if he were her only hedge against drowning, realized what she was doing, and loosened her grip digging into his back and shoulders. "My God, Brynn. What are we going to do?"

"Keep chipping away at puzzle pieces until we understand more."

"Maybe that won't be enough."

"You told me once there might be a way to tap into magic of my own."

"I can't give you a crash course in ten minutes, but I have an idea." She wriggled out of his arms and dredged her fanny pack out from beneath her clothing. Reaching inside, she pulled out a small pocketknife, went into the bathroom and washed it with hot water and soap. When she got back to the bed, Brynn was half dozing.

"What are you doing?" he asked sleepily.

"You wanted magic. You don't have to do this, but if you're up for it, we can share blood."

"We're sharing pretty much everything else." He smiled, his face illuminated in moonlight pouring through the window. "How does it work?"

Kayna took his right hand and made a deep, quick slice in the meaty part of the ball of his thumb. After doing the same to her hand, she held their cuts together with her other hand and chanted in Gaelic. "Listen carefully," she said, "and repeat what I say."

When she was done and binding up their cuts with Band-Aids, he asked, "What did I agree to? Did I sell my soul to the devil, or our firstborn?"

"Hush. Don't even talk like that." She lay next to him. "I asked Danu, goddess of the Earth, to waken the magic within you and make it strong."

"Why'd I need your blood for that? Sorry to be question-guy, but I like to understand things." He threaded his arms around her and drew her close.

"My magic is a known quantity. Yours isn't. If this works—and it won't if you have absolutely zero proclivity for magic—my blood will waken your latent power and make it possible for you to see and do things."

"How will I know?"

"There are basic exercises in a parapsychology book I found in the doctors' lounge. Unfortunately, I left it with the other docs. Once we get it back, you might start there." She inhaled thoughtfully. "Meditative states are the base for most magic. You have to empty your mind and open yourself to what you want to happen. Once you're receptive, you ask the goddess to bless you with your desires."

"Is there always that kind of time?"

"What do you mean?" Kayna finally felt her body relaxing, moving toward where she might actually be able to sleep.

"I'm coming from my frame of reference, but in medicine and research usually when things turn to shit, it happens fast, and I'm scrambling. It's not the sort of thing that's conducive to adopting a lotus position and chanting, 'Om.'"

"You're funny." She snuggled closer. "It's wonderful to have a real bed after that bunk on the ship. To answer your question, I haven't been involved in very many magical emergencies. The goddess, or whoever controls the flow of magic, is adept at sensing what her practitioners need. Belief is key. You have to believe in the power running through you. Doubts are the kiss of death."

"Okay. Let me make certain I have this right. Trance state, clear my mind, ask for what I want, and believe."

"It sounds like you're preparing for something," Kayna observed with a sinking feeling.

"I am. Who knows, maybe I'll have another run-in with the Kiao tonight. I want to be ready. One more question."

"Sure." She closed her eyes.

"How does your father access the water dragon?"

"He borrows its shape. Spirits don't have a corporeal presence. It takes energy—and planning—for them to appear to the living. Nana uses the same body she wore in life, probably because we buried her, and the body is accessible. We cremated Father. So for him to be visible on this side of the veil, he needs to borrow a form. Since the Kiao was one of his sacred animals, it's a logical choice. Kiao are shape shifters anyway. No doubt he made a deal with one."

"But when you saw him, he looked like himself."

"No. He looked like a Chinese man." Kayna bit down hard on her lower lip. "Spirits borrow forms. The man I saw was likely one of his dead blood relatives, but one who was buried."

"How'd you know it was your father?" Brynn persisted.

"I'd recognize his energy anywhere."

"Sorry to be a pain in the ass. This next question is indelicate, but wouldn't your grandmother's body have decomposed? Guiren's blood relation's too."

"It doesn't work that way. If you were to dig them up, sure, but this is a magical realm we're talking about."

"Last question, I promise." He tucked her more firmly against him. "What's in it for the Kiao to bargain with your dad?"

"Magical beings love the world of the living. It's brighter, more vibrant, thrumming with energy. Their worlds are dim, shadowed. They leap at any chance to escape."

"Thanks, sweetheart. The more I know, the better prepared I'll be." He kissed her gently. "I love you."

"Love you too," she murmured, right before she drifted off.

CHAPTER 25

Brynn woke to the comforting warmth of Kayna's body. If he'd dreamed, he didn't remember.

"Hey there, sleepyhead," she murmured.

"You're awake."

"Yeah, I've just been watching you. God, but you're gorgeous. I still can't believe you want me."

He pulled her into his arms and hugged her. "Believe it," he whispered against her hair. "Any dreams?"

She pulled away. "Nana showed up. My raven too. The spirit world is all spun out about the war. They draw energy from the living, and they're worried. Nana reminded me of a few protective spells against marauding spirits. My tattoos offer some defense, but they're not enough in and of themselves. Now that Guiren's set his sights on me, further confrontations are inevitable."

"I wondered about these." He trailed a hand over her tats. "How'd you come by them?"

"Nana. She insisted."

"Your grandmother doesn't pull any punches. Is she always that pushy?"

"Usually, she's worse." Kayna grinned sheepishly. "It's not

funny. Things are as grim as I've ever known them, but Nana always was a force to be reckoned with."

Brynn narrowed his eyes. "Will the tats protect you from your father?"

"No. He's my blood. When Nana stenciled the runes on me, she didn't anticipate needing to shield me from relatives." Kayna pursed her lips. "That was before my uncle killed my father."

"Did she tell you anything else?" Brynn left the bed and walked into the bathroom.

"Uh-uh."

Brynn came back into the bedroom and started picking through his clothes and getting dressed. "I sure wish she was still alive."

"Yeah, me too."

Kayna walked into the bathroom for a quick rinse. When she returned to the bedroom, she stood over her own clothes, found her panties, and stepped into them. "What are you thinking?" She gestured with two fingers. "Give."

He shrugged. "When you proposed the theory about my cultures wanting to get to McMurdo, I didn't say much because I'd thought the same thing, and it made me question my sanity."

"Do you still?" She met his gaze, her green eyes serious.

"No." He took a measured breath. "Proks are social creatures. Somehow my colonies on South Georgia knew they were needed here."

"To deal with their cousins that suddenly developed a taste for human life?"

"Sounds even more absurd when you say it out loud," he admitted. "I can toss some scientific mumbo-jumbo out, though. Archaea might be ubiquitous, but the colonies here and in the Arctic are the oldest, purest strains. Geologists have been floating theories for years that polar archaea were responsible for slowing radioactive decay from the Earth's core." He paused. "That's what allowed photosynthetic critters to evolve, along with a breathable atmosphere."

A convoluted look passed over Kayna's face, and she bit her lip. "Maybe that's it," she mumbled.

Brynn waited for a few moments while he finished dressing, but she didn't say anything else. "Maybe what's it?" he finally asked.

"Before Micah mentioned he might have antibodies to attack the problem, you were already thinking your archaea might neutralize the renegade colonies and subvert however they're invading people's bloodstreams. What if some mixture of your colonies and what's here could address radiation sickness?"

Excitement coursed through him. "That's brilliant. You missed your calling. Should've gone into research. That could also explain why your father wanted my cultures." He finished dressing and rolled the idea around in his mind, thinking about how it could move from concept to reality.

Kayna grinned. "It was a logical extension of what you said about polar archaea slowing radioactive decay."

"May have been logical, but it didn't jump out at me. Biologists are a pretty stodgy lot." Brynn pulled his boots on. "Even stodgier than M.D.'s. Getting permission to use base resources to run off-the-wall experiments won't be easy. I'm already girding myself for a fight over turning Micah's blood into an infusion to help the infirmary patients."

She pressed her lips together thoughtfully. "You never know. Desperate times require desperate measures. And if these times aren't desperate, I don't know what would qualify. Don't forget developing a boutique antibiotic for Andrev."

"I hadn't." He walked to her and bent over to kiss the top of her head. "We need to split forces today."

"I was thinking the same thing." She stood and kissed him lightly. "I'm ready to hunt down breakfast and coffee. After that,

I'll pop in at the infirmary, and I'm betting you want to reassure your culture bins that Daddy still cares about them."

He smiled. "You've been reading my mail, sweetheart." She took his hand, and they walked out into the corridor.

Before they reached the stairs, he stopped and turned her to face him. "About that vampiric ritual last night. Am I supposed to feel different?"

She shook her head. "Nope. The only difference would be when you try to draw on something from the paranormal realm. Why?"

"When you've got one foot in fairyland," he murmured, "it's good to know the rules."

"One of those rules—" she moved so she spoke into his ear "—is not to liken anything to vampires."

Brynn narrowed his eyes. "You must be kidding." He made a dismissive motion with one hand. "They can't be real."

"Wanna bet?" She started down the stairs.

Brynn caught up to her, feeling torn about how to focus his time. Now that he'd kicked the door open and discovered a realm brimming with the arcane and the unknown, he was fascinated and wanted to tap every avenue to add to his knowledge base.

As if she could read his mind—and they'd already established she could—she shook her head. "We have enough problems. Let's focus on the mutant cultures and my clinic patients. If the goddess grants us grace, we'll have time for the rest later. Besides—" she grinned knowingly "—there aren't enough vampires left to cause difficulty for anybody."

BREAKFAST WAS A HURRIED AFFAIR, but the coffee was hot, bitter, and strong and the eggs, toast, and bacon expertly prepared. Everyone was talking about the nuclear attack, but Brynn didn't want to get drawn into mass hysteria that could spiral out of control if it were fed. He left Kayna chatting with Sophie and Chris in the cheery dining room and headed for the microbiology wing. When he pushed his way into his lab, Zach and Abel were already there, deep in conversation with Micah.

"Jesus fucking Christ! You never told us about your brain children," Zach cried, clearly too excited to modulate his voice.

"They're not archaea anymore," Abel broke in. "I've been slicing and dicing them nine ways from Sunday, and damn if they haven't morphed into eukaryotes."

"Only some of them," Zach corrected. "Let's not get carried away here."

Ted tromped in from an inner room. "I'm all ears. Keep talking."

"They truly are amazing," Micah said. "I got a glimpse of them last night, and I didn't sleep much after that."

"Welcome to my world." Brynn glanced from one man to the next.

Zach nodded. "Micah showed us computer images from his colonies here."

"Even though it was risky and I had to wear hazmat gloves, I examined a couple of them." Ted pulled his mask down so it hung around his neck. "Most are still archaea—at least from a technical perspective—but others have changed into something I don't recognize." He scrunched his forehead in thought. "They're like a hybrid formation. I need to hunt them down on the Internet."

"Already did that," Micah said. "You won't find anything."

"Last night, Micah and I introduced my proks and euks to the locally grown hybrids," Brynn said and walked to a corner where he grabbed a lab coat off a hook, dug a mask out of a cabinet, and found a pair of latex gloves.

"Walk us through your logic," Ted demanded.

When Brynn didn't answer, only rustled around gathering materials, Zach chimed in. "Whatever this is, we'd like in on it, as second authors of course."

Brynn looked up from the incubator where he'd gone in search of clean agar plates and a marking pen. "We dropped a bomb on Moscow, and you're worried about street creds in scientific journals?" Incredulity underscored his words.

Zach's gaze skittered away. "Makes me look like a petty son of a bitch, huh?"

Brynn slammed the bacteriological incubator shut. "Let's work together to see what we find. If this is as huge as I suspect, there'll be room for lots of researchers."

"Would you at least tell us what you're thinking this will yield?" Zach asked, looking hopeful.

"A couple of things."

"Like what?" Zach persisted. "You never told us your hypotheses."

"Or walked us through your logic," Ted blurted. "Inquiring researchers want to know."

Micah snorted. "Maybe it was a blessing when the other biologists shunned me. At least I wasn't bombarded with questions."

Brynn shot a wry grin his way and considered his next move. Responsible scientists didn't float theories unless they were fairly certain they were onto something, but this was scarcely the protected environment of NIH. "This is going to sound pretty fantastic."

"Try us." Zach tugged his mask down and grinned.

Abel did too. "Yeah, farfetched is where we live. Maybe we could step into the room right next door. It's a little kitchen. We can brew some coffee and talk."

"Grand idea!" Ted tromped toward the door. "I'll run to the cafeteria and get us a few doughnuts. Carbs help me think." The door swooshed shut behind him.

"Do you have any idea where everyone else is?" Brynn asked.

"They've shunned this place ever since my cultures careened

out of control," Micah replied. "And what with World War III brewing, no one's very interested in cell cultures."

"That's a big mistake on their part." Brynn stripped his mask and gloves off. "I was going to set up a few more plates, but coffee sounds great. So do Ted's doughnuts. We can't hurry our plates from last night, so I may as well tell you what I'm thinking."

They sat in a small room lined with bookshelves, and Brynn sipped a steaming cup of coffee liberally laced with powdered milk and sugar. "Let me start with the easy one," he said. "I've suspected for years that archaea could host a new class of powerful antibiotics. Because they share a structure with most bacteria, they're a natural for fighting disease. We have a guy, one of the Russian seamen from the ship, who's got something odd and potentially fatal. It's likely he got it from mucking about in my sample bins."

Brynn drank more coffee before continuing, mostly to buy himself thinking time. "I believe I can create something from my proks—or maybe the ones that have mutated into euks—to treat him."

Zach frowned. "How are you going to distill a new drug? The lab here is decent, but scarcely big time pharmaceutical quality."

"I'm not." Brynn set his cup down. "My plan is simple. I'm going to culture the mystery bacteria from the man's blood, introduce proks and euks on separate plates, and see if either kill off the bacteria. Assuming there's a clear winner, I'll make an IV infusion."

Abel whistled. "Gutsy. You could kill him."

"Nah," Ted cut in. "Proks and euks are so ubiquitous, it's doubtful we'd harm the guy, but we might want to run a few more plates with tissue samples and the infusion, just to make certain we don't end up with mass cell die-off."

Brynn nodded. "I like it. We should start those cooking as soon as possible. Andrev's sinking."

"You inferred that was the easy one," Zach said. "Does that

mean there's more?" He stood and poured himself more hot water, mixing instant coffee crystals into it.

"That's a good segue to my second idea." Brynn gestured at Micah. "Tell them what happened to you."

"…and so, I checked for differences in my blood pre- and post-infection. What I found makes me confident we can create either a vaccine or a treatment for others infected with the iron-hungry proks," Micah finished. "So long as we have blood type matches."

"Sounds plausible," Ted said thoughtfully. "If that's project number two, I'm all over it since I've titrated antibodies from serum before."

"Excellent." Micah grinned. "Let's work on it together. We can begin by harvesting antibodies from my blood. Others have beaten the infection from the mutant proks too, which should give us a ready supply."

"Hold onto your hats, boys." Brynn blew out a breath. "I've got one more idea, and here's where we truly step off into the unknown."

The other microbiologists pulled their chairs closer, faces alight with curiosity.

"Archaea were a key element in modulating the rate of radioactive decay from the earth's core. They're the only organism old enough to be a contender."

"You're thinking they might hold the key to combating radiation sickness," Zach broke in. "Wow, just wow. Give me a minute to get my mind around that."

"Radiation kills by frying you, sort of like a microwave," Abel said. "Surely nothing could protect humans from that."

"Agreed." Brynn nodded. "A few million people in New York and Moscow are either already dead or well on their way. But what about everybody else? The ones who haven't been exposed to radioactive fallout yet because the wind hasn't carried it their way? If we had some way to inoculate them against the worst effects, it would be a win-win."

"We don't have time," Micah protested. "Something like that would have to go through clinical trials. It could take years."

"Do you honestly think," Abel said thoughtfully, "any world government is going to stand on that sort of ceremony given what's happened? Our biggest problem, even if we synthesized something, would be getting it out of Antarctica in the middle of winter."

"No kidding," Ted said. "The whole reason the ship swung past South Georgia was because the weather was too dicey for McMurdo to send a plane for Brynn and his cultures."

"I'm not sure about any of this," Brynn cautioned. "The first supposition about archaea maybe functioning as an *avant garde* antibiotic is the most likely to pan out."

"There's a rodent colony one wing over," Zach said. "After we get the antibiotic and antibody projects off the ground, we could inoculate mice with something, once we ginned it up, and expose them to radiation."

Abel jumped to his feet. "Let's get blood and tissue samples from that Russian seaman, so we can get those cultures growing."

"You handle that part," Ted said getting to his feet. "I'm going to make slides from the cells Brynn has growing on those plates, so we know for sure if something changes."

Brynn glanced from one to the other, shocked the other men hadn't argued his logic model into the ground. "You guys believe what I told you."

"Are you kidding?" Zach rubbed his hands together. "Cowboy science is the best. I love projects I can get my teeth into where I'm flying by the seat of my pants."

"Outstanding." Brynn stood. "Maybe those plates Micah and I set in the incubator will surprise us and cook up faster than I hope."

CHAPTER 26

Kayna made her way to the infirmary. When she'd left the dining room, Chris and Sophie were chatting companionably, and Kayna suspected the beginnings of a blossoming relationship. Sophie was a geologist who moonlighted in the bar and even though she looked young, she was twenty-seven. She and Chris were already holding hands, and neither seemed disappointed when Kayna excused herself.

"Go Cupid," she mumbled under her breath.

A different nurse was at the helm this morning. A stocky redhead dressed in forest green scrubs with pale gray eyes and a cool expression. "Yes?" She raised an arched brow. "Visitors' sign-in book is to your right."

"I'm Kayna Quan, the new doc." She put out a hand, but the nurse just looked at it.

"Elizabeth," the nurse said shortly. "If I were you, I'd mask and glove up. We have some odd illnesses on the floor."

"I know. I had a chat with Dr. Stewart and Dr. Crowley last night."

"Mmph. Well, at least they stopped by here earlier. Probably still in the back if you want to catch up with them."

"How's the Russian seaman? Peggy told me she put him in isolation."

"Still there."

Kayna leveled her gaze at the nurse. "I don't want to get off on the wrong foot with you. You seem irritated."

"Who wouldn't be?" Elizabeth pressed her lips together. "The world's ending, and I'm stuck at the ass end of it." Sudden tears sheened her eyes. "I had family in upstate New York. The operative term being *had*."

"I'm sorry." Guilt smacked Kayna for the relief she'd felt knowing her mother was three thousand miles away from ground zero.

"Yeah. Everybody is, but it doesn't change shit. Go on." Elizabeth made shooing motions with both hands. "I'll manage."

Kayna nodded. "I'm sure you will, but if you need a confidential shoulder…"

"Thanks, now go. I do better if I don't talk about it."

Kayna understood completely. She fished a mask and gloves from the same boxes she'd hit up last night and walked into the infirmary. It was a large, neat space that housed fourteen beds, all with patients in them. Those she'd talked with the previous night smiled or nodded her way. Curtains hanging from the ceiling surrounded each bed and provided a modicum of patient privacy.

Intent on checking on Andrev, she strode down the center aisle and pulled the door to his iso room open. Stewart and Crowley had their heads together, deep in conversation.

"Morning, men," she said cheerily. Andrev raised a hand to her, and she nodded to him.

Crowley inclined his head. He looked better this morning, dressed in a clean smock with his M.D. creds blazoned across an upper pocket. A mask covered his nose and mouth.

"We examined Andrev," Stewart said. He had his professional duds on too, and the frantic look in his eyes had receded. "We upped the steroids and started him on oxygen."

"Did it help?" Kayna glanced from one to the other.

Crowley nodded. "Yeah, his breathing's easier, but if we can't identify an antibiotic to treat him…" His voice trailed off. "I think he has a stubborn bacterial pneumonia."

"Come on." Stewart reached around her and pulled the door open. "May as well introduce you to the rest of the patients. At least one's well enough to return to his quarters today."

"I met some of them last night," she told him, "but I'd love an introduction to everyone else."

A few minutes later, Zach breezed into the infirmary. "Your friendly neighborhood vampire," he announced with a smile. Apparently, the nurse's exhortations for him to put on a mask had fallen on deaf ears.

"Who exactly are you?" Crowley eyed Zach suspiciously.

"He's a microbiologist from my ship," Kayna said.

"Yes, and I need blood and tissue samples from the Russian with the mystery ailment."

"Go back and tell Elizabeth," Stewart instructed. "She's a decent phlebotomist. Run me down once she's done, and I'll help with the tissue part."

"Not much more we can do in here," Crowley said. "Do you have a few minutes, Dr. Quan?"

"Sure." She raised a quizzical eyebrow, but he shook his head.

"Let's dump the masks and gloves and head for the lounge," Crowley suggested. "We have open clinic, but it doesn't start until after lunch. You may as well sit in and learn how we triage care."

"Where's the clinic?" Kayna dropped her mask and gloves into a biohazard waste can and pushed the outer glass door open with her shoulder.

"Far side of the hall," Stewart said. "We'll show you."

They left the infirmary and walked back toward McMurdo's hub with its bar, dining rooms, and other amenities for residents. Stewart stopped in front of an unmarked door and keyed in a code. The door opened into an unadorned waiting room with a dozen hard backed chairs scattered across a linoleum floor. At the far end was a glassed-in enclosure with a sliding window, obviously for patient check in.

"We operate clinic three afternoons a week," Crowley said. "People can make appointments, but we see drop-ins too."

"So you run from one o'clock until?" Kayna asked.

"Until we run out of patients." Stewart shrugged. "Some days are diamonds. Some days we've been here until midnight."

She followed them out of the clinic and back down the corridor to the doctors' lounge. They obviously wanted to talk about something. She suspected it had to do with the parapsychology text. Actually, she hoped they were done with it, so she could take it back to her quarters to review. Plus, Brynn would probably want it for some of the exercises it contained.

Stewart kicked the door shut. "That's a hell of a book you stuck us with," he said and fired an accusatory glance at her as he made his way to the chair he'd sat in last night.

"At least it got us out of our funk," Crowley cut in. "We were up most of the night reading. That Kiao thing is downright terrifying." He strode to his chair and sat. Kayna joined them.

"Terrifying how?" She kept her voice carefully neutral. "My knowledge base about Chinese mythology is pretty thin."

"Not that we believe any of the legends," Stewart put in quickly. "How could we?"

Kayna ground her teeth together in frustration. "What did they say? Or maybe you could pony up the book, and I can read for myself."

"Now, now, don't get testy," Stewart said. "The short version is the thing we saw supposedly houses spirits of the dead. It crosses into our realm to steal the living and burns them out for nefarious purposes. A few nut jobs claim to have been shanghaied by these monstrosities, but most of them ended up in mental hospitals. Oh yes, I almost forgot, the sea serpent is also a shape shifter." He snorted derisively.

"Why the hell would you have us read up on something like that?" Crowley demanded.

"Because you've seen it," Kayna said, making a class act effort to look and sound normal. "I remembered that book from an undergraduate psychology class. I had no idea what it would say about the Kiao." She mimed a shudder. "Creepy, eh? But probably not true."

"The part about shared dreams was much easier to swallow," Stewart said. "Once we were done with that, we started at the beginning."

"I was surprised by how much of that mumbo-jumbo stuff has been quantified," Crowley said. "Of course, it's hard to say how rigorous the science was."

"Any chance I could get it back?" Kayna asked again.

"Not until we're done." Stewart folded his arms across his chest. "But that shouldn't be longer than this evening."

A knock sounded on the door right before it burst open, and Harold walked into the room. "There you are," he said. "I need you to show me where you and McMichaels ended up, so I can route the rest of your bags."

Kayna leapt upright, grateful for a chance to escape. "Sure," she told Harold and then turned back to the doctors. "I'll be at clinic a little before one."

"Make certain you've eaten," Crowley said. "If we're busy, there won't be time to run for anything."

She nodded and made her way to Harold's side. He held the door, and she sidled through. "We're this way," she said and started off at a brisk walk.

He followed her, but remained uncharacteristically silent. After she tapped the door to her room, she turned to Harold. "I have a feeling if I pushed this door open, our stuff would already be inside. What did you really want?"

Color rose from the rounded neck of his T-shirt under his unzipped parka. "Am I that transparent?"

Maybe not. It helps to have second sight.

"I get hunches sometimes," she mumbled. "Are you going to tell me?"

"I get hunches too. Once I had the unloading pretty much knocked, I took a stroll through the complex and along the shore area. There's something I think you should take a look at, but you need to layer up. It's really cold outside."

She glanced at her watch. Eleven. "How long will this take? I have to be in clinic soon."

A muscle twitched in his jaw. "I'm not certain. But if you wait until after your clinic, it'll be dark, and what I want to show you may well be gone."

"Can you tell me more about it?"

"Not really. You have to see it. I might be losing my mind, but it told me to get you." Harold looked as if his skin was crawling with discomfort.

Kayna peeked into his mind, but came up blank. Something was wrong here, but she was damned if she could sort out what it was.

Despite her uneasiness, she was curious too, so she pushed the door to her quarters open and piled on clothes, her Pac boots, gloves, and a hat in record time. Harold nodded curtly and set a quick pace down the stairs and out a side door. The cold hit her like a wall. He hadn't been kidding about the temperature. A chill wind cut through her multiple layers of outer clothes as if they weren't there. She followed him down a hill to where an ice shelf stretched into the ocean. When he reached a rock-and-ice studded beach, he turned left.

Her feet numbed despite nearly running to keep up. In about a quarter mile, he rounded a corner into a protected cove. She glanced back; they were out of view of McMurdo's many buildings. Magic hit her with a blast to the solar plexus that nearly doubled her over. She scanned the beach through ice-crusted lashes and wished she'd thought to wear goggles. Harold motioned to her and said something, but she couldn't hear him over a rising wind that whooshed with such force small rocks pummeled her legs.

The raven blasted into her mind with staggering force, cawing, *"Go back."*

"Kayna," sounded all around her, harsh and strident. At first she thought it was the raven, but the cadence wasn't right, and the bird was still cawing, its shrieks like a dirge.

Harold was obviously trying to retrace his steps to reach her, but he was frozen in place. Since he'd served his purpose, the magic was done with him. Understanding engulfed her, and she threw her power wide open. The world shifted on its axis. Coiled in slushy ice a few feet off the shoreline sat the Kiao, its jaws parted in what might have been a self-satisfied smile.

"What do you want?" Kayna hurried to the edge of the beach.

"You know what I want. The time has come. You must help me, Daughter."

"If *help* means go with you, I won't."

"You don't get to make the decisions."

"Let him go." Kayna extended an arm toward Harold.

Fire flashed from the Kiao's mouth. Freed from its spell, Harold pelted toward her, his booted feet slipping on the icy beach. "Are you all right?" he cried. "Jesus, I'm so sorry. I had no idea—"

His voice terminated abruptly as she was sucked into a different world. Kayna had done plenty of traveling to the Otherworld, but always at her behest. She'd never been dragged there against her will. Nausea rocked her, but at least the profound Antarctic cold receded. She stood in a grassy glade at the edge of a huge lake. The Kiao swam in large, rippling circles, its head and the tip of its tail above the water.

Kayna didn't think it would work, but she marshaled magic and visualized the spot she'd been yanked from off McMurdo

Sound. Nothing happened. The air of the Otherworld didn't so much as flicker.

Her heart raced, and it was a struggle not to vomit. Before she lost her nerve, she stomped through thick grass to the water's edge, unzipping her parka as she went. "This is outrageous." She shook her fist at the Kiao. "You can't kidnap me."

The dragon angled its head until it faced her and spoke aloud. "I just did." Its low voice grated like shards of glass rubbing together. As she watched, the water dragon shimmered, and its edges faded into the lake's surface. In its place, an Asian man with long, black hair emerged and stroked through the water to shore.

Kayna drew back. To give herself time to think and not just react, she focused on something inconsequential. "That's someone else's body," she snarled. "We cremated you."

Maybe it's still the Kiao. They can change form.

"Of course it's someone else's body, but why does it matter?" The man dragged himself from the water and stalked toward her. Water sluiced down his bronze skin.

She locked her gaze onto his face. Seeing her father naked, regardless of whose body he'd borrowed, wasn't high on her list.

"Westerners." He screwed his face into a mask of disgust, and the air about him glowed as he summoned magic to dry himself. Another spell draped his muscular form in a black robe sashed in crimson. A traditional double-edged Chinese blade, the Jian, materialized in his hand. He stuffed it into a sheath that rode across his back and turned in a slow circle. "Is your need for modesty satisfied?"

"I don't give a rat's ass about modesty. I won't be satisfied until you free me to return to my world."

"I cannot do that." Guiren's dark eyes reflected sorrow, determination, and madness. He half-bowed. "I apologize for not being present to train you, but I can no longer wait for you to stumble into your magic. Our task will be much harder since you steadfastly refused to commandeer the biologic material aboard your ship."

Desperation clawed at her. Because she had to do something, Kayna closed her eyes and loosed a different chant that should remove her from the Otherworld. Magic leapt around her, stronger than her first attempt, but nothing happened. No gateway. No freedom.

"I am disappointed in you, but I suppose you had to try—twice," Guiren said.

"You never told me whose body you borrowed." Kayna faced him, her eyes blazing with fury. "Or is it the Kiao in another form?"

"Why does that matter?" He repeated his earlier question.

"In the extremely unlikely event the body's owner is still alive, I need to worry about getting two of us out of this hellhole."

"Whether you get out of this *hellhole*—" Guiren's voice held an edge as deadly as the one on his sword "—will be determined by how hard you work for me."

"And if I don't?" Kayna tipped her chin defiantly and wondered where the hell the raven was. She could use his help.

"Then you will never leave. Even you know enough about the Otherworld to understand your life force will gradually ebb here. In fact, the process has already begun." He glared at her. "I am waiting, Daughter. It is time for you to do your duty for this world."

"What about Mother and Brynn?" Tears threatened, but she cut them off at the source. She could cry her eyes out once she got out of this mess. "Let me go long enough to tell them not to worry."

"Really?" He imitated an eye roll with eerie accuracy. "You actually believe you could tell them the truth, and they'd pat your rosy ass and tell you to have a nice time with your ogre father? I'm not stupid. If you leave, you'll call in that grandmother of yours, and she'll figure out how to keep you safe from my traps."

Kayna unclenched her hands. "So long as you brought up traps, it was really shitty of you to use Harold like that. He may not understand magic, but he's smart enough to know he led me straight into a setup, and he'll be frantic."

"How he feels is of no import. I've wasted enough time. I'm leaving. Either you come along and honor the blood that flows in your veins, or daughter or no, I'll leave you here to rot."

"Fine." She mock bowed, deeply sarcastic. "I'll say one thing, Father. I knew you were crazy, but I had no idea what a son of a bitch you were."

He looked down his nose at her. "Of course you did. You hated me for years for being nothing but a cheap drunk. Now at least you can hate me for something real."

Magic zinged around her, and the lake fell away to nothing.

CHAPTER 27

Brynn was checking the agar plates where he'd combined his cultures with the McMurdo batch to see if his cells were normalizing the McMurdo mutants when Harold burst into the microbiology lab. He was breathing hard, and his face was splotched white where it was frost-nipped. At first, he couldn't manage words. Shocked, Brynn put the plates back into the incubator, stripped off his mask and gloves, and raced to Harold's side. "What happened?"

"You've got to come, mate," he gasped, and then he squeezed his eyes shut. "Mary, mother of God, it won't make any difference. We're too late." He squinched his eyes as if the lab's fluorescent lights hurt them.

Zach and Abel shot out of an inner lab room with Ted and Micah on their heels. "What's going on?" they cried in unison.

Harold glanced at the other microbiologists and shook his head. Brynn understood. "Hey, guys. A spot of privacy, please."

"Sure," Zach said. "We got those serum and tissue samples cooking, so we're done for now, anyway."

"We'll be in the break room if you need us." Abel cast a worried look Harold's way and left the room, flanked by the other men.

"Here." Brynn dragged a lab stool over and pushed on Harold's shoulders. "Sit and talk to me."

Harold sucked in one shuddering breath after another. Brynn handed him a glass of water, and he drained it. That seemed to steady him enough to loosen his tongue because he started a sentence, but quit after the first few words.

"Spit it out," Brynn suggested. "Don't worry if it makes sense."

"Good advice," Harold muttered. "It was all a deception, a ruse. I have no idea how I got suckered into it, but I had to bring Kayna to a place down the shoreline. I was walking there earlier, and this pressure built in me. Something there needed Kayna, and it needed her now." He spread shaking hands in front of him. "So I found her."

Breath whistled from between Brynn's teeth, and he fought a sick feeling in his gut. "After you located her, you took her there?" he gritted out, hoping against all the odds Harold's answer would be no.

Harold nodded. A study in misery, his shoulders were hunched and his face so deeply lined, he looked like an old man. "I didn't have a clue, mate. Not a fucking clue while I walked her down there like a pig to the slaughter. Something closed over me once we hit the beach. I tried to go to her, but I couldn't move. Couldn't even talk." He balled his hands into fists. "This can't be right, but I could've sworn I saw a sea serpent in the slushy water. Suddenly whatever held me let go. I raced toward Kayna." He lifted tortured eyes that made Brynn's heart stutter. "But she vanished. Just bloody fucking disappeared. One minute she was standing there shaking her fist at the serpent, and the next she was gone."

Brynn folded his hand into a fist and punched the nearest wall. Pain lanced up his arm, but he did it again anyway.

"Maybe you should give me something. One of those fancy drugs of yours." Harold's voice was rough, shattered. "What I remember can't be right." He hopped off the stool and wrung his hands together. "Do you suppose I hurt her somehow and I'm not remembering?"

Brynn dragged himself out of the dark pit his thoughts had become. "That's ridiculous," he snapped. "You care about her. You wouldn't have hurt her. I think I know what happened. I have to go."

"I want to help," Harold cried. "This whole thing is my fault."

Brynn spun to face him. "No. It's not. You were duped. If I think of anything you can do, I'll let you know."

He rocketed out of the lab and poked his upper torso into the break room. "Something's come up," Brynn said, amazed he could do anything as prosaic as talking. "I have to leave. Run those experiments we talked about. All of them."

"Sure," Zach said. "You look as if you saw a ghost."

"Is there anything else we can do?" Abel pushed to his feet, his angular face etched with concern.

"Anything at all?" Ted echoed, appearing even younger than usual.

Micah just looked worried.

"Thanks, but no." Brynn pelted down the corridor at a dead run. His first stop was the doctors' lounge where Crowley and Stewart had their heads bent over the parapsychology text. "Sorry, boys." Brynn snapped the book out from under their noses. "I need this."

He ran as if hellhounds dogged his heels all the way to his quarters. A quick look around the room with their luggage piled to one side, told him Kayna's parka, bibs, and Pac boots were missing. "Ach, Christ!" he muttered and sank into a chair. "At least she won't be cold." He dropped his head into a hand, realizing he didn't have clue one whether the place beyond the veil that Kayna called the Otherworld was cold or not.

He clicked off what he knew in rapid succession and came to the same conclusion, no matter how many ways he looked at the series of events. The Kiao had taken Kayna. Because of Harold's weak sensitivity to psi emanations, Kayna's father had suckered him into luring her to where it could spirit her away. Brynn glanced at the book in his lap, feeling frantic. He didn't even have time to peruse the index for something useful, let alone read it.

An idea smacked him between the eyes. He leapt to his feet, grabbed Kayna's fanny pack off a table, and unzipped it. Her cell phone popped out, and he turned it on, grateful she'd kept it charged. He clicked contacts and found her mother's number.

Maybe if he called Moira Quan, she could walk him through how to go after Kayna. At the least, she could raise her mother—Kayna's Nana—to help. Feeling so out of his depth he was swallowing water and sinking, Brynn bolted out the door and hurried toward the central part of McMurdo intent on finding the sat phones. He ran mindlessly with his head down and smacked right into Jack.

"Hold it, buddy." Jack closed an iron grip around Brynn's arm. "What's the rush?"

"Big problems," Brynn panted. "Where are the phones?"

"Second hallway on the left. Hunt me down when you're done and tell me what's got you so riled. I've never seen you break a sweat over anything before."

If you only knew.

"Sure thing." Brynn punched Jack's shoulder lightly and ran on. He couldn't possibly spare the time to explain what he thought was afoot. If he did, there was a good chance Jack would decide he'd taken a short walk off a long pier into crazy-town.

The phones were set up in small, private cubicles, which allayed one of his fears. He didn't want anyone to overhear his conversation with Moira. "Please, please let her be home," he muttered as he fed numbers into the phone after swiping his Visa card.

Let it be the right number. Maybe Kayna hasn't updated her Contacts list.

Stop. All I can do is try.

The delay before the phone rang felt like centuries, but finally the satellites connected. A woman picked up on the second ring, her voice tentative. "Hello?"

"Mrs. Quan?"

"Yes. Who is this?" Her voice sounded strained to the breaking point.

"You don't know me, Mrs. Quan. My name is Brynn McMichaels, and I'm a friend of Kayna's—"

"Something's happened to her," Moira blurted, followed by a cluster of Gaelic words.

"Yes, but I'm going to find her and fix it. I need your help."

Soft sobs came through the phone.

"Please, Mrs. Quan, get hold of yourself. Kayna's gone, and I don't have the first clue how to go after her. I suspect your dead husband nabbed her, except he's in sea dragon form." Brynn stopped. What he'd said sounded so bizarre, he wouldn't blame the woman on the other end for hanging up on him. But she wasn't an ordinary woman. He held his breath and waited.

"What do you need from me?" Her voice sounded stronger.

"First off, do you think I'm right? One of the men here got duped into taking Kayna somewhere, and he said she disappeared. He also said he saw a sea monster. Something paralyzed him, and he couldn't do a thing to help her."

"Guiren would be my first guess." Not only was Moira's voice stronger, anger ran beneath it.

Good. Brynn would take any help he could get. He forced himself to slow his breathing. "Can you reach your mother somehow and tell her Kayna needs help?"

"She already knows. She contacted me before you called. I wanted to go with her, help in some way, but she said it's been too long since I called on my ability." A long, shuddery sigh vibrated against Brynn's ear before Moira spoke again. "I'm certain Mother's hunting for her, but you don't understand how things work on the other side. Guiren will want to hide Kayna from us, and he has the advantage."

"How can I get to where she is?" Brynn glanced at his hand. He was gripping the sat phone so hard his knuckles were purple.

"Do you have magic of your own?" Moira asked.

"I don't know. Kayna did some sort of ritual where we shared blood."

A gasp ricocheted against his ears. "Och, so she must think you have power." Moira paused as if she were girding herself. "My daughter must be very special to you, because what you want to do holds huge risks."

"I don't care. Time's sliding away from me like sand in an hourglass. Kayna said something about emptying my mind and asking the goddess for guidance. Is there more?"

"Och, *buachaill*, laddie. If you only knew. Be very certain." She lapsed into an even heavier brogue. "Even if you manage to blunder your way through, there are no guarantees you'll make it back in one piece. Some spirits are hungry for the warmth of living things. Kayna has protections tattooed in key locations. You probably don't have any such thing."

Brynn squeezed his eyes shut. A lifetime of care and caution blew up in his face and shattered everything he'd ever known to bits. When he opened his eyes and stared at the four walls of the phone cubicle, he was a different person.

"I told her once if she needed a warrior to stand between her and the Kiao, I'd figure it out. I'm not trying to be rude, Mrs. Quan, but if there's anything else I need to know, tell me now."

A quiet chuckle tickled his hearing. "If the radiation doesn't kill me, I'm looking forward to meeting you. That last boyfriend of hers was a simpering wimp who thought he was God's gift to the planet. Are you ready?" Without waiting for him to reply, she forged ahead. "Listen carefully. Write this down if you have to. My mother's name is Bridget Hawkins. You'll need her name to find her on the other side. The two of you together have a much better chance of locating Kayna than either alone."

Brynn pulled a pen from his pocket and wrote *Bridget Hawkins* on his palm. "How do I get there?"

"You may not be able to. The harder time you have, the less likely it is you'll find your way back. Go outside to a place you won't be bothered. Clear your mind. Call Danu. Tell her you are Kayna Hawkins Quan's intended, and you need to save her from fell powers in the Otherworld."

"That's it?"

"That's it," Moira concurred. "Do that and wait. If it works, it'll work quickly. May God and all the blessed saints protect you."

Brynn swallowed hard. "I thought you prayed to pagan deities."

"Och, sonny." Moira laughed, but there wasn't a scrap of warmth in it. "Sure and I hedge my bets. Now off with you. Time grows short."

"Thank you." Brynn started to say more, but the line went dead.

He didn't want to take the time to return to his room for outerwear, but he couldn't go outside in what he wore. He'd freeze to death in short order and not be any good to anyone. Not feeling particularly good about the compromise, he made his way to one of the mudrooms, swiped a likely pair of bibs and a parka and Pac boots that looked close to his size. In less than five minutes, he let himself outside and looked right and left to determine the quickest path to a deserted location. Moira had said he shouldn't be disturbed, and he was so green he didn't think he could afford to ignore any of her advice.

The part about maybe not being able to return was unsettling, but he didn't want to live without Kayna and if the Kiao took her, Brynn was afraid the thing would wring her dry. That Guiren had been stalking her didn't bode well. Father or no, Brynn recognized fanaticism in the man's fixation on what he'd labeled as his mission in life—and death.

Brynn stopped between two deserted warehouses and listened. No voices or any sign anyone was nearby. Cold rolled through him in waves, some from the minus temperature and the rest from frantic concern for Kayna. Thinking metal or any of civilization's trappings might interfere, he stood in between the two Quonset hut structures and did his best to clear his thoughts of his fears for his beloved. He waited through long moments and called Danu's name in his mind.

Minutes dribbled by. His feet turned to blocks of unresponsive flesh in the cold, but he ignored them. Finally, he gave up and started over. This time he made a point of taking deep, slow breaths and focused on counting them to keep rising panic at bay.

"Please." he heard himself talking aloud, but didn't stuff the words back inside. "I love her. She's a part of me. I don't know zip squat about this magic stuff, but I'm willing to learn. I'll dedicate my life to learning if only you'll help me this once. Please, Danu. Christ!" Brynn shook his head in disgust. "I've never been any good at this prayer stuff."

He bowed his head and clasped his hands in front of him. "I have to find Kayna Hawkins Quan. She's in trouble. She needs me. She was taken to the Otherworld against her will—"

"Enough, human," reverberated through his skull. Brynn was afraid it was a hallucination and froze. Brittle laughter tinkled around him, or it might've been icicles jangling against one another in the stiff breeze. *"Beware what you ask for. You tread a dangerous path and pit yourself against things you do not understand. Do you undertake this journey of your own free will?"*

"Are you Danu?" Brynn's mind reeled.

"What do you think? You summoned me, but you've yet to answer my question."

"I'm asking of my own free will."

"You have never done this before. For long moments, there will be no air. Do not fight the sensation."

On the heels of Danu's words, something like an electric charge built around him until he was afraid he'd be crushed. Darkness swirled, thick with menace and the unknown. Part of him wanted to call the whole thing off, but a bigger part was committed to the path he'd chosen. Kayna was worth any sacrifice. After all this, he hoped to hell he'd make it to her in time. His lungs burned, seizing from lack of oxygen. This must be what drowning was like, minus the water blocking his airway.

When he was as close to blacking out as he'd ever been, the pressure released him and he fell onto rocky ground. At least there was air, blessed air. He lay on his stomach where he'd fallen and sucked it hungrily into his lungs. He had to be up and on his way, but he couldn't do a damned thing until his oxygen-starved cells recovered.

As soon as his head stopped spinning, he pushed himself unsteadily upright. He was in a thick forest. It was cold, but nothing like Antarctica. More like New England on a crisp autumn evening. He was bruised where rocks had dug into him when he fell, but as far as collateral damage went, it was minor.

What now? I'm in an impossible place, a place people go in dreams, a parallel universe next to my waking reality.

He looked around, searching for a path or any indication of which way he should go, and then he shook his head. Things probably didn't work like that here. He called, "Bridget Hawkins." Nothing happened, so he called her name twice more.

On the third try, a slender, white-haired woman wearing an old-fashioned gingham skirt and white blouse strode out of the gloom toward him spouting Gaelic. Her hair was drawn behind her head into a substantial bun.

"I'm sorry." Brynn extended a hand, but Bridget ignored it. "I don't understand Irish."

"What I was sayin'—" she gazed at him out of green eyes that were dead ringers for Kayna's "—was now that every shade in this world knows I'm here, ye can well and truly shut up."

"But your daughter told me—" he began and shifted gears because it didn't matter. "Where's Kayna?"

"Aye, sure an' we'd both like to know that, wouldn't we?" Bridget walked to his side and laid chill fingers over his wrist. She might look alive, but her touch said otherwise. Brynn didn't flinch, and the old woman twisted her head to nail him with shrewd eyes. "Ye rolled the dice and managed to come up with aces."

"What do you mean? There are no aces without Kayna."

"Maybe not," her grandmother countered, "but ye would like to get out of here alive, wouldn't you? I have welcome news. Ye hold enough power to be findin' the other side again."

"I'm not leaving without Kayna."

Bridget let go of him and moved so she faced him. Despite being a foot shorter, she commanded his attention. "Now ye listen up. We have no idea what we'll find. If I tell you to leave, ye will do so with no questions. It'll take you years of practice to hone mage craft. Danu told me ye promised her your undyin' allegiance."

Bridget stopped talking, but it obviously wasn't to take a breath because she'd moved beyond the need to feed her body with air. "Ye made a covenant, a promise, to the goddess. She'll expect you to honor your vow with action."

"Yes, yes. I've never welched on anything. Let's get moving."

"We will, but I'm not done." The lilt of Ireland fled and her words were like rough stones. "If ye study hard, there will come a time ye can afford to ignore those like me. That time is years in the future. For now I want your absolute word ye will do as I say no matter how much ye wish to do something different."

"What happens if I say no?"

Bridget narrowed her eyes. "That would be a very bad decision. It will take both our blood ties to my granddaughter to locate her. If ye don't agree to my terms, I'll leave you here and search on my own. Not because I expect to find her, but because it is the right thing to do."

"All right," Brynn said. "I agree." Now wasn't the time to stand on ceremony. Not in an environment he knew less than nothing about. He felt trapped, but he wasn't anywhere near as trapped as Kayna. "Tell me about her father."

Bridget's cold fingers sought his hand again. She must need the contact to link with him. The old woman shut her eyes, chanted a few notes, and scented the air.

"Touching you was a great help. More than I imagined it would be. Kayna is this way—" Bridget pointed "—and not all that far. Ye asked after Guiren. He was a strong mage with a good grasp of Chinese power, but he had an obsessive edge when it came to his savior complex. He only married my daughter to access her magic and create children with mixed magical bloodlines. I tried not to interfere, but once I found out he beat both her and my grandchildren—and forced them into magical prisons—I made it my business to step in…"

CHAPTER 28

Kayna stood in an open spot in thick woodlands before a primitive altar. A selection of blades was scattered across it. Some fine as a scalpel, others thicker and cruder in appearance, as if they'd been cast by some aboriginal tribe. Her father, or perhaps an earlier mage bent on leveraging his power after death, had hewn the rough altar out of two downed tree trunks. As was usual in the Otherworld, dim light softened the landscape, and a low hum filled the air. Not birds or insects because they didn't live here, but the sound of spirits fighting their way back from various stages of death collided with fairy melodies in a discordant jangle.

"Why do you want the archaea?" Kayna asked, but it was probably her hundredth question, and Guiren wasn't inclined to answer any of them.

"Silence." He didn't raise his voice, but his tone cut into her.

"What are all those tools for?" She waved a hand toward the blades.

"What do you think?" His handsome features took on a nightmarish cast. "Sometimes spirits need a bit of assistance escaping their living body."

Aw, shit, shit, shit!

Terror iced her bones. Who was he planning to kill? Surely, he didn't expect her to stand by and assist him. Her entire body thrummed with outrage, but the best way to deal with bullies was to sling a little attitude around.

"Now you look here." Kayna might not be able to leave the Otherworld, but she sprinted to the far side of the clearing, twirled to face him, and crossed her arms beneath her breasts. "Whatever you have in mind, you can't force me. If you're carrying a grudge for what I believed as a ten-year-old child about you being a drunk, that's absurd. Any youngster would believe what their caregivers told them. No matter how I felt about the way you died, it was goddamned hard growing up without a father. Money was scarce, and I ended up taking care of Kiki because Mom and Nana were always working."

"You didn't do a very good job," he broke in viciously. "She turned out too weak to survive."

Kayna swallowed hard. In her dark, secret places, she'd always blamed herself for her sister's addiction and death. To hear the words roll casually from her father tore old wounds wide open, and the fight ran out of her. "What do you want?" She spread her hands in front of her.

"Your power. I need a boost from my own blood. Being dead now that the apocalypse has finally struck is worse than inconvenient. This is my battle, what I was born for. I tried to light a fire under some doctors and scientists by appearing in their dreams as the Kiao—and as myself—but modern men ignore such signs." He spat into the dirt. "Pah! It's tempting to let the world self-destruct, but I'm better than that."

She straightened her shoulders to shake off inertia and understood how tired she felt. The Otherworld dragged on the living. The longest she'd spent here was a few hours, and at least two had already passed. "Let's get to it," she forced the words out, "so I can go back to where I belong."

"You might return," he sneered, and an eerie light blazed hot behind his dark eyes. "It's likely you won't have enough strength left to light a match. That would be when the implements you were so curious about will come in useful."

Kayna's eyes widened, and she drew back as understanding kicked her in the chest like a runaway mule. It wasn't some stray her father had targeted for death, but her. "You wouldn't," she choked out, the taste of ashes coating her tongue. "I'm your daughter."

"You're here, aren't you? And you can't leave unless I release you. The game pieces are in motion, the abacus clicking." He eyed her like a predator focusing on intended prey.

Powered by a sudden flood of adrenaline, Kayna bolted from the clearing with her heart hammering in her ears. Her father would bleed her power to augment his own as he cast spells. Once she was empty, he'd cast her aside and cut her up to salvage every last iota of her psi ability. She'd read about the dead, particularly powerful mages, doing such things. It was why Nana had insisted on tattooing her. She tried to draw a ward around herself, and she screamed for her grandmother in her mind. Nana might be here somewhere. If not, could she possibly come in time?

The raven fluttered into her mind. His beak snapped open and closed, chiding her for not listening on the Antarctic beach when he'd told her to run.

"It was already too late," she told the bird. *"How can I get out of here?"*

"Your father must release you."

"That's not going to happen."

"Then you must destroy him." The bird ruffled its feathers and cast an appraising glance her way.

Kayna cursed her clumsy boots. They slowed her as she chugged through thick brush. She tried to sense her father behind her, but he didn't seem to be there. For one wild moment, she let herself believe maybe she'd escape. Once she was alone, she'd pull out all the stops to leave the Otherworld. If she could find the fairy folk, they'd remember her from when she was a carefree teenager dancing with them in hidden dells. Despite the raven's grim prediction, maybe they could help. Not everything in the Otherworld was dead and menacing.

Brynn flashed through her mind. He'd be desperately worried. She hoped to hell he wouldn't do anything stupid—like try to follow her. He was plenty bright enough to figure out what had happened, but even if he possessed magic—and that was an unknown—he was naive, untrained. To place himself square in harm's way to save her would be like him, though.

Don't do it, she exhorted silently.

Gasping for breath and with sweat streaking her face and sides, she stumbled into another clearing and ground to a halt. Guiren stood at its far side blocking her path. "Enough," he growled. "You squander energy. Critical energy that I need. Either return with me peaceably, or I'll institute other measures."

"Like what?" She panted and bent forward, resting her hands on her thighs as she inhaled as much as she could of the thin air. "Last time I asked you what would happen if I didn't cooperate, you said you'd leave me here to rot."

He shrugged. "That was a ploy to encourage you to come with me. If you don't, I'll render you unconscious. At least it will force you to stay in one place."

"Noooooo!" Kayna's scream filled the otherwise silent landscape, so primal and hysterical it shocked her. She had to remain awake. If he zonked her with magic, she'd be as good as dead.

The air flickered and sizzled. When it settled, she was back in the glade with the altar. There had to be a way out of this, but she wasn't seeing it. She was still dizzy from her sprint through the woods, and it was hard to think. Guiren extended a hand toward her, chanting in Chinese. Kayna did everything she could to block him, but her energy ebbed by the minute.

I can't just stand here and let him kill me.

"Relax," he suggested silkily. "You'll last longer if you're not fighting me."

"What are you doing with your spell?"

"Gathering your energy to augment mine. Once I have enough, I'll create barriers around the bomb sites to contain the radiation."

"You'll kill everyone inside," Kayna protested, aware her voice was weakening.

"They're as good as dead anyway. I'll be the hero who saved everyone else. They'll create ballads and sing my praises. Every man has a task. This one is mine."

Kayna recognized deep-seated madness in his words.

No one could use magic to build an impenetrable wall around somewhere as big as New York or Moscow. Arguing would only antagonize him, but words fell from her anyway. "No one will *sing your praises*. For Christ's sake, you're a lunatic. No one will have any fucking idea you did anything. There's no way in hell you can stop radioactive fallout with a magical shield. Even if there were ten of you, it'd never work."

"Silence! You are my child. You will obey without question."

"Bullshit. I'm thirty-two years old and no one's child." Her vision grayed at the edges, and she swayed before sinking to her knees. Horror filled her that she'd die in this alien landscape, but even that took on a muted quality as consciousness retreated. The raven loomed in her mind, like an ancient, winged sentinel, urging her to fight back.

"Child! We are almost there."

Nana. It's Nana.

Kayna clung to the familiar voice, but Guiren must've heard it too. The invisible funnel connecting them upped the ante sucking psychic energy from her, and she sprawled in the dirt before the altar.

BRIDGET HALTED SO PRECIPITOUSLY, Brynn collided with her. "Kayna knows we're here. Unfortunately, so does Guiren. Once we clear these trees, we'll be upon them. Ye will stay in the shadows and let me handle this. Trees have friendly spirits that will watch over you."

"What if you need help?"

"Your task, which was to help me locate my granddaughter, is done. Your command of power is too fragile to assist me. Don't make things harder by giving me two of you to rescue."

Brynn clamped his jaws together and mumbled, "Got it."

Ten long strides brought them into a clearing that looked like something out of *Deliverance* minus the river. An Asian man swathed in black robes stood tall behind a rustic altar scattered with rocks and metal weapons. It took Brynn a second to zero in on Kayna lying belly down in the dirt. He started toward her and then remembered his promise to Bridget. Their rescue attempt was fraught with danger, and he might compromise her efforts if he disobeyed.

The old woman vanished from his side only to reappear standing between Kayna and her father. She raised both arms in front of her, and lightning bolts flashed from her hands. Guiren rocked back on the balls of his feet but didn't fall. A raven formed from the ether, enormous and menacing. Wings spread, it flew right at Guiren, but the shaman blasted it with something invisible and it disappeared, reforming a few feet away.

"You dare challenge me, old woman?" Guiren snarled, his features shifting into the Kiao's head and then back into a man. The raven dive-bombed him again; he repulsed it with magic.

"Ye have no right to the livin'," Bridget cried. "Unhand my granddaughter. My blood ties supersede yours."

"Not in China they don't..."

Brynn had given his word to remain out of the way, but Kayna lay so still he was frantic she was already dead. His throat was so dry he couldn't swallow, and his heart crashed painfully against his ribcage. He didn't wait for the last of the exchange between Bridget and Guiren to play itself out before launching himself to Kayna's inert form. He crouched next to her and placed a hand on her neck, relieved beyond words when he found the beat of her pulse. It was weak, thready, but at least it was still there.

He gathered her into his arms, using his body to shield her. "I'm here, love," he crooned. "We'll get you home." He thought her lips might have moved, but it could've been wishful thinking on his part, or a trick of the flat light in this place. Bridget had said the trees were protective. He staggered to his feet with Kayna in his arms and carried her to the edge of the grove where he tucked her tenderly between two large evergreens. Guiren ignored him, probably because he and Bridget were deeply engaged in trying to blow one another to bits. The raven was doing his damnedest, but the closest he'd gotten was a few pecks to the back of Guiren's head while evading magic zapping through the air.

"Please," Brynn prayed to long forgotten deities. "Let Kayna be all right."

When he glanced up, the air between Guiren and Bridget blazed so bright, it made his eyes ache, and the raven was wreathed in fire. It had to be illusion because air couldn't burn, but thick flames and smoke rolled his way, scraping savagely at his already-raw throat.

"I banish you from this clearing. You interfere with what doesn't concern you," Guiren shouted at Bridget, his face contorted with rage. Bridget's form flickered and then vanished. "The same applies to you." Guiren turned his unsettling dark gaze on Brynn. "Unhand my daughter or die." The burning raven flew between them, cawing.

"I don't think so." Brynn sprinted from where he'd left Kayna and bulldozed his way to Guiren. He scooped up a lethal looking rapier from the altar and charged the Chinese shaman. A shocked look blossomed on Guiren's face, but he recovered fast, and a blast of energy lifted Brynn off his feet and slammed him to the ground twenty feet away.

Air whooshed from his lungs when he hit the ground, but Brynn held onto the slender sword and shot to his feet, intent on burying it in Guiren's brain. Even if he was already dead, something like that had to slow him down.

I hope.

Jesus fucking Christ, I know less than nothing.

The gods protect children and fools. Maybe Danu will take pity on me.

Guiren moved from the far side of the altar and reached behind him to sweep a long, lethal-looking sword from a sheath he wore across his back. He brandished it at the raven, no longer surrounded by a fiery nimbus, and the bird fluttered to the ground next to Kayna, nudging her with its beak.

Brynn stared at the double-edged, steel blade. Two feet long and four inches across the top, it tapered to half that at its end. "You want combat?" Guiren growled. "I admire your spirit, and I could use a bit of entertainment. When you're dead, I'll nick your essence too."

Brynn squared his shoulders. Talk about an unlikely warrior. Beyond college fencing, he'd never done anything remotely resembling this. But once upon a time, he'd been a damned good fencer. Some of that had to still be locked in his muscle memory. He thought quickly. Maybe he could outsmart his opponent with flattery. "I'd like to admire you."

"You will once you're dead." A grisly smile split Guiren's face. "Since we'll both be here, we'll have centuries to replay what you should've done to beat me."

"Not what I meant." Brynn grasped at rising anger, knowing he'd need its energy. "I'll fight you, gladly. But for it to be an even match, you can't use magic."

Guiren narrowed his eyes. "Done. You'll still lose."

"We'll see about that." Brynn gripped the rapier tighter in his hand. He glanced down and realized his heavy, winter clothing would be a serious impediment. "I've watched traditional Chinese combat," he said, and forced himself to bow slightly, but not so much he took his gaze off his opponent. "With respect, I suggest we remove our clothing."

Guiren nodded tersely and untied the sash holding his robe in place. Brynn retreated deeper within the trees and shucked his parka, bibs, and heavy boots. He eyed the raven and murmured, "Take care of her." Brynn could've sworn the bird nodded its feathered head.

Down to a stretchy top and trousers, he strode back into the clearing, weapon in hand. He hefted it, relieved to find it well-balanced. Guiren had a loincloth affair wrapped around his genitals and nothing else.

He quirked a brow. "I knew Westerners were outrageously modest, but is that your idea of removing your clothes?"

Brynn shrugged. "It'll do." He raised his hands in front of him. "Ready."

Guiren lowered his head and charged. Brynn sidestepped him at the last moment and the shaman, driven forward by his own momentum, somersaulted through the air but ended on his feet. The motion was worthy of an Olympic gymnast, and fear bit deep into Brynn's innards, congealing his blood. All the years he'd spent hunched over a microscope, his opponent had been honing his physical abilities.

Don't think about that. I have to win. If I don't, Kayna will die here —right along with me.

Guiren danced around him in half a circle, light on his feet. His sword flashed out. Damn, but it had a long reach. Brynn skidded sideways, but not fast enough to avoid getting nicked in the thigh. The Jian was so sharp it sliced through his trousers as if they weren't there. The cut burned like fire, and blood dripped down his leg. Not seriously injured, but he was seriously outclassed. Only a bold and unexpected move could end this in his favor.

Guiren charged again. This time his sword caught Brynn's forearm, cutting deep. Blind fury swept Brynn into its maw, and bloodlust ignited his spirit with the need for revenge. Anger lent him courage. When Guiren came at him the next time, Brynn sliced out with the rapier and caught the dead shaman in his ribs. Smoke rose from the wound, which puckered around its edges.

"You can't hurt me," Guiren taunted. "I'm already dead."

"Inconvenient," Brynn wheezed, "but I've always welcomed a challenge." He watched the flesh where he'd stabbed Guiren. It continued to draw apart, bubbling as if something had poisoned it. Whatever was in the rapier was mildly toxic—so long as it pierced Guiren's skin. All Brynn had to do was strike something vital. He danced from side to side, trying to anticipate Guiren's next move. His cuts throbbed, but adrenaline pushed the discomfort to a distant place, one he could ignore.

"I weary of this."

Guiren circled behind Brynn, and he spun to keep him in view. Gathering nerve he didn't know he had, Brynn raced right at Guiren, veering to the right at the last moment. As he'd hoped, confusion marred the dead man's smooth, Asian features. In that moment when Guiren was off guard, Brynn hurled himself atop the other man, leveraging his weight advantage and driving the shaman to the ground. Guiren reached up and closed his hands around Brynn's throat. He gasped for air, his lungs burning with the need to breathe.

He squeezed the man's ribcage between his knees. All it elicited was a grunt. He tried to loosen the man's chokehold with one hand, but didn't make a dent. Thoughts slipped away as consciousness receded. While he still could, he slid his grip lower on the rapier and drove the blade through Guiren's eye and into his brain. The eye spewed fluid, showering Brynn with wicked-smelling gunk.

Because he didn't have to hold onto the rapier anymore, Brynn closed both hands around Guiren's and raked his nails down their backs. The shaman's chokehold finally loosened, and Brynn staggered upright, sucking air into his lungs like a fire-starved forge. Smoke poured around the dagger buried in Guiren's eye socket. The air took on a fiery edge, and Guiren's human form shimmered into nothingness. In its place, the Kiao flickered, and then formed with the same dagger sticking from its eye socket. It opened its mouth and disgorged a weak gout of flame, but missed Brynn by feet.

"Maybe I can't kill what's already dead," Brynn snarled, "but you're looking pretty done in." He hauled off to kick the water dragon's inert form and then remembered he'd left his boots next to Kayna. Bending, he dragged the blade from the Kiao's eye and swiped it against a bush to clean it.

Bridget floated in front of him, less corporeal than before. "Hurry." She gestured with both hands. "Ye have an opportunity, but it won't last long. Take my granddaughter and leave while Guiren is immobilized." She flashed a feral grin his way. "Solid work on your part, laddie. Among other things, it neutralized the spell Guiren used to force me from this clearing."

Heedless of his injuries and the blood soaking his shirt and trousers, Brynn hurried to Kayna's side. The raven stood watch next to her, its amber eyes savage. Bridget spoke a few words of Gaelic, and the bird fluttered to her shoulder. "Hurry," she said once more.

Brynn moved as fast as he could. He stuffed his arms into his parka, dropped the blade, and stepped into his boots, not bothering to lace them. He gathered Kayna's boneless body into his arms. If anything, her respiration had slowed further, which alarmed him and underscored Bridget's exhortations.

"Tell me what to do." He eyed the old woman who was looking progressively more transparent. The raven still sat on her shoulder, its talons hooked deep enough to make divots in her clothing.

"Open your mind to me. I'll forge your way back."

Brynn started to thank her, but the still, dead air of the Otherworld exploded around him. When he could see again, he was exactly where he'd started, between the two Quonset hut warehouses at McMurdo. It was night and the cold slapped him like a live thing. Wind blew so hard, he bent double against a particularly vicious blast. His toes and fingers numbed instantly.

He got his bearings and forced himself forward with Kayna in his arms. He had to get her to the infirmary where he could figure out what was wrong.

One step at a time. If I think too long or too deep about what happened, I'm afraid I'll go mad.

CHAPTER 29

Brynn carried Kayna inside McMurdo Station. It must've been very late because he didn't pass a soul between the main door and the infirmary. His injured arm ached, and he limped to take pressure off his leg. It felt like a long way, but he pushed himself to keep going. Despite his exhortations not to think about it, his mind returned to the Otherworld and the battle he'd waged. What happened was so far beyond believability, it strained his already-battered senses, pummeling them mercilessly.

Brynn shouldered the infirmary door open with Kayna clasped firmly against him. Peggy leapt to her feet.

"What the hell?" she cried. "Where'd you find Dr. Quan? For that matter, where have you been? We've turned the base upside down looking for both of you. Search and Rescue teams are out right now with dogs."

Brynn opened his mouth to craft some kind of reply, but words spewed from Peggy effectively cutting him off.

"Jack was afraid she fell, hit her head, and froze to death, and you got lost looking for her and froze too. The other thing we were afraid of was you'd fallen prey to the iron-crazed microbes, lost your minds, went outside, and were frozen in some snowbank we hadn't checked yet."

"Call off SAR," Brynn said hoarsely, "and then help me."

Peggy came around her desk. "Is that Dr. Quan's blood?" She looked him up and down.

"No. It's mine. I'll fix myself up once we've got Kayna situated."

Peggy bustled past him and held the door open. "Lay her down. I'll make a quick call and let the boys know you're all right, and then I'll be in to help."

So tired he was almost beyond speech, Brynn carried Kayna to the only empty bed and spread her atop it. He pulled her parka and boots off, and then grabbed a blood pressure cuff and a stethoscope.

Dr. Stewart hustled in. "What the hell?" he repeated Peggy's question. "Where'd you find her? You're bleeding. What happened to you?"

"Long story," Brynn said. "Could you take her BP again? It's got to be higher than what I came up with."

"Sure. By the way, I'm David. We didn't get around to first names that day in the lounge." He bent over Kayna and busied himself checking her vitals. When he looked up, his eyes were grave. "Let's get a vasopressor on board and an IV going. She's looking pretty dehydrated."

"What do you need?" Peggy hovered on the other side of the bed.

"The rest of her clothes off," Brynn said, "so we can check for trauma. Hot blankets too."

Half an hour later, Kayna was swathed in heated blankets and had an IV drip going. Brynn hadn't found any obvious trauma, which was an enormous relief since he'd transported her in his arms. If she'd had any sort of spinal cord injury, he might've crippled her.

"Sit down before you fall down," David said.

"Huh?" Brynn pasted bleary eyes on him.

"I want to take a look at your arm and leg. There's blood all over the floor, which tells me every time you move, you're opening up whatever happened to you. I'm going to examine your injuries, debride them if I have to, and put in stitches. Come on." David placed a hand on Brynn's shoulder. "Nothing more we can do here, and it'll give housekeeping a chance to clean the floor."

Brynn followed the other doctor across the hall. His mind was foggy as he first sat and then laid on an exam table, and he didn't remember how clean sweats materialized.

"Would you like to talk about it?" David asked once he finished stitching Brynn up.

"Not particularly." Brynn eased to a sit and then moved to one of two chairs in the small exam room.

"Let me phrase it another way." David Stewart took a deep breath and narrowed his blue eyes. "I recognize knife wounds when I see them. From the amount of blood, I was expecting you'd been bitten by a seal. Even that would've been damned remote. Another problem is you should show signs of exposure from being out in the cold, but I'll be a sailor's uncle if I can find any. Then there's the trifling matter of bruising around your neck congruent with someone trying to choke the living shit out of you."

"Well, aren't you a reincarnation of Perry Mason."

"That isn't helpful. If you must sling television characters about, I prefer to see myself as Dr. House, Antarctic style." David flashed a mouthful of teeth, but he wasn't smiling, and he didn't show any sign of backing down.

Brynn held up a hand. "Could you say it was a seal? Please."

"You're asking me to lie." David stripped off his gloves, tossed them into a waste can, and scrubbed a hand down his face. "Give me one good reason. Or better yet, tell me the truth and let me make my own decision."

"You wouldn't believe any of it," Brynn muttered.

"Try me. I know I looked like a burned out schmuck when Kayna first met me, but I've had time to rethink that."

"What do you think is wrong with Kayna?" Brynn switched gears.

"I'm not sure. She's obviously had a hell of a shock, and she's retreated into a coma to deal with it. Nothing wrong with her physically that I can detect, beyond her blood pressure and core temp, and those should be back to normal soon."

"We should run an EEG," Brynn said.

"We will if she doesn't come around in twenty-four hours. Back to you, pal. What happened? If I knew, I might have a better feel for what's going on with Dr. Quan."

"Patient privilege," Brynn stated flatly.

"Of course." David leaned against the exam table and folded his hands across his stomach.

"Remember—" Brynn smiled grimly "—you asked for this." He took a deep, steadying breath. "Kayna's father was a mentally unstable Chinese shaman who was convinced his life's work was to save the world from a nuclear holocaust. It was mildly inconvenient the nuclear war didn't start until he'd been dead for twenty-two years. He needed an infusion of power from his living bloodline to fight the battle he was convinced he was born for, so he nabbed Kayna, took her to a place called the Otherworld, and drained her essence. If her grandmother and I hadn't shown up when we did, she'd be dead. Oh yes, and that Chinese water dragon in your dreams was actually Kayna's father borrowing its form."

"You want to play that one again from the top?" David asked, his voice soft and soothing. Brynn recognized that voice. It was the same one he'd used with deranged patients. "How could her father have been any sort of threat if he was dead?"

Brynn stood and gazed across at David. Not much point in mentioning Kayna's grandmother was dead too. "I didn't think I'd get through to you. I'm sure you think I'm insane, but I'm not.

Until I met Kayna, I had no idea anything like a spirit world existed beyond the minds of Hollywood producers and novel writers."

He pressed his lips together, wondering where to go next. "Not everything has a rational explanation, and the boogeyman under the bed is real. What happened to me was devastating, shattering. I'll never be the same, but I have to figure out how to keep going. It's going to be goddamned hard if Kayna doesn't make it." He started for the door.

"Where are you going?" David asked.

"To sit with Kayna. If anything happens, I want to be there."

David walked to Brynn's side. "I'll write my report and say I stitched up seal bites."

Relief, gratitude, and exhaustion weakened Brynn's knees, and he faced the other man. "Thank you."

David grinned. "My complicity doesn't come cheap. Once you've had a few days to get over this, I want the long version of what you told me. I figure it'll take a while, but the little you said rang true for me, despite my questioning the part about Kayna's father. It's too bizarre for you to have made it up."

"You got it." Brynn tugged the door open.

"Would you like me to spell you watching Kayna? You're dead on your feet."

Brynn shook his head. "No. But if things turn to shit, I'd like to be able to call you. It might take two of us to keep her alive."

"Of course. I'll sack out in one of the rooms right next door. Peggy will know where to find me."

Something struck a chord in Brynn's befuddled brain, and a few clumps of neurons connected. "I know it's cold here, but is it common to send out a SAR team immediately?"

An odd look washed over David's face. "You were gone more than three days. Particularly in light of all the asphyxiation deaths we've had, everyone here was certain both of you were dead."

Brynn caught himself on the doorframe. Time obviously

passed differently in the Otherworld. No wonder he felt so disconnected. One thing was certain, if he'd spent much longer, the transition back to normal might've been impossible.

"How long did you think you were gone?" David asked, his voice neutral.

"It doesn't matter. I'm going to look after Kayna." Brynn walked slowly out the door. He wanted to move faster, but his body would fragment into a million pieces if he pushed it.

He made his way out of the clinic and back across the hall, nodding to Peggy as he passed her workstation. Someone had indeed cleaned the floor, and the faint odor of disinfectant burned his nostrils. Brynn bent over Kayna's inert form and checked her vitals noted on a clipboard. Both core temperature and blood pressure had stabilized. Thank God. He sat on the edge of her hospital bed and took her hand.

"You're back, darling," he murmured low, his voice aimed only for her.

Brynn drifted in and out of consciousness as he sat on Kayna's bed talking to her. He was aware of Peggy from time to time, and of David Stewart, but neither disturbed him. At some point during a long night that morphed into the next day, he pulled a chair close, sat on it, and fell asleep with one of Kayna's hands gripped in his. Bridget came to him in a series of disjointed dreams, trying to talk, except she spoke Gaelic, and he couldn't understand her.

He was certain he still dreamed when a hand stroked his hair. Because it felt like Kayna's touch, he leaned into it, his eyes still closed, pretending the nightmare he'd dragged her from hadn't happened. Someone shook his shoulder. Brynn ignored it, wanting nothing more than the emptiness of sleep where he didn't have to think about anything.

"Dr. McMichaels," a woman said in a voice that wouldn't take no for an answer.

Brynn lifted his head and felt a weight slide off it. He was bent double with his butt in the chair and his head on the bed next to Kayna. His eyes snapped open as understanding surfaced that Kayna's hand had been on his head. She'd moved it there while he slept, which meant her coma must've lifted.

Relief so poignant that he felt the bite of tears coursed through him. He met Elizabeth's gray eyes, and she beckoned with a finger. When he forced his body upright, he felt stiff, like a very old, arthritic man. Brynn let go of Kayna's hand and followed the nurse to the end of the ward.

"She's better," Elizabeth said. "She woke early this morning before shift change, but only for a moment or two. Peggy said to let you know right away, but it looked to me like you needed to sleep."

"I want to get back to her." Brynn turned away, but Elizabeth closed a hand over his arm, forcing him to look at her.

"Kiss her, tell her you love her, and then Jack wants to see you. Dr. Stewart and Peggy held him off all night, but he's expecting you in his office as soon as you're able."

"Okay. Take good care of her for me. She's a very special woman."

"I gathered that." Elizabeth smiled softly. "You're pretty special yourself. Wish I could find a man who'd camp out by my bed."

Brynn patted her hand and walked back to Kayna. As he moved around, his body felt more normal. Sore and bruised, but at least it didn't feel like it belonged to a stranger. He sat on the bed and stroked Kayna's hand.

Her eyes fluttered open, right before they sheened with tears. "I don't know how you did it," she rasped, her voice barely there, "but you found me."

"Anytime, ma'am." Brynn tried for humor, but his throat was too choked with emotion to pull it off. He bent forward and gathered her against him, careful of her IV. "God, I love you. I was scared. So scared. All my warrior talk was crap. I killed there, never mind what I killed was already dead…"

"Hush, shush." She stroked his back. "I never saw the Otherworld as a threatening place before. We can talk, but not here. I love you too. More than words. You risked an enormous leap into the unknown for me." Tears roughened her words until they were nearly unrecognizable. "You were courageous and dumb. Didn't you realize—?"

"Quiet, darling. It will be all right. We'll figure things out. I know all those things. I called your mother. And your Nana showed up too. Both of them told me I was stupid and necessary. It's a hell of a combination."

"What part of *report in* don't you get?" Jack's voice boomed from behind Brynn.

He disentangled himself from Kayna and twisted to meet his friend's brown-eyed stare. "Sorry." Brynn got to his feet. "I've had a bitch of a time here, and I've been worried sick about Kayna."

"I figured that part out on my own." Jack narrowed his eyes. "I also understand she's on the mend." He inclined his head Kayna's way. "Glad to hear it. Wouldn't want to lose you quite this soon."

"I don't want to lose me, either," Kayna said.

When she smiled, Brynn's heart cracked with relief, right before it took flight.

He ran a hand down his borrowed sweat top and looked at Jack. "Elizabeth said to meet you in your office. I'm glad to do that, but would you like me to shower first? I'm sure I don't smell that great."

"I have lunch waiting," Jack said. "Talk with me, eat a little, and then you can shower and change."

"It's fine," Kayna said, sounding more like herself. "Maybe they'll spring me from here soon."

The doctor in Brynn took over. "Not until twenty-four hours after your vitals are normal."

Kayna rolled her eyes. "I'll take it under advisement."

Jack laughed. "Love it when women have spirit. Now follow me, soldier."

Brynn threaded his way out of the ward. Jack was waiting in the corridor. He didn't say anything, just set a course for his office. The smells of coffee and tuna hit Brynn the second Jack opened the door, and he realized he was famished. Jack left him alone until he'd downed a sandwich and a full cup of coffee.

"Care to tell me what happened?" Jack asked.

"Wasn't most of it in Dr. Stewart's report?" Brynn met Jack's shrewd gaze, keeping his own eyes guileless.

"I read the report, but I don't believe it," Jack said flatly. "We go back a long way, Brynn. Fifteen years. I want to know where you and Dr. Quan disappeared to for three days. For Christ fucking sakes, you should be dead. You didn't have survival gear, and it's been minus thirty out there with a wind chill factor. Plus, I've never known a seal to bite a human at this base. Your outer clothes are thick enough they'd have a hell of a time getting through the fabric unless they chewed the fuck out of you. Then there's the minor problem that you didn't have storm pants on when you carried Dr. Quan back inside the base. And a flaring nimbus of light surrounded you when you walked out of nowhere and materialized behind that Quonset hut."

Brynn blew out a tight breath. "How would you know that?"

"Security cameras. I studied the disks." Jack pursed his lips in a tight line. "You can stonewall me, but I don't suggest it."

"You wouldn't believe me if I told you."

"I've run into a lot of odd things in my life." Jack flexed his fingers in front of him and then picked up his coffee cup. "Dead things that somehow rejuvenated. Biochemical impossibilities I saw under my scope. Real tales that rival anything you've seen on spooky television shows." His voice softened. "We haven't talked about it since, but I'm sure you remember all the times I went to bat for you and some of your more unusual research projects back at NIH."

Brynn nodded and looked into Jack's eyes. "I haven't

forgotten." He smiled gently. "Your support meant a lot. You always were a hell of a scientist, and I respected you."

"Respect me enough to tell me the truth."

Brynn got to his feet and poured a fresh cup of coffee. He waggled the pot in Jack's direction, but he shook his head. Because sitting felt impossible, Brynn paced, cup in hand, and started at the beginning, with Kayna and her psi ability.

The story took a long time. Jack didn't help by interrupting with questions. Finally, Brynn released the death grip he had on his long-since-empty mug and set it on a table. "I guess you're going to send Kayna and me packing on the first ship or plane out of here."

"Not at all." Jack nodded as if to himself. "I figured it was something worthy of the *Twilight Zone*, although I have to admit parts of what you relayed rivaled even my fertile imagination. You don't have to worry about me saying anything. I won't. We have bigger problems than the paranormal world."

Brynn exhaled sharply. "Did the war escalate?" He looked longingly at a chair, but figured if he sat he might not get up.

"No. Thank God. At least for now both parties seem cowed, and Russia pulled its troops out of Ukraine. In exchange the U.S. lifted its trade sanctions."

"I bet everybody's scrambling madly for a cure for radiation sickness."

"You'd be right about that. While you were gone, the microbiologists from your ship told me about the experiments you'd mapped out." Jack rolled his eyes. "It's a formality, but I have to approve all research on the base."

"What'd you think?" Brynn asked, holding his breath. Jack's support was a lynchpin. Without it, his research would be DOA.

"Brilliant. That's what I think. Of course, you always were too smart for your own good. Now get out of here. Convince yourself Dr. Quan will be all right, and then go to your quarters, clean up, and get some shuteye."

"Those sound suspiciously like orders."

"Oh, they are." Jack cracked a grin. "And I'm used to being obeyed."

Brynn walked out the door intent on returning to the infirmary. Having food and coffee on board helped, but he still felt like an extra in *Night of the Living Dead*. David had put a dozen stitches in his leg and maybe fifteen in his arm. Brynn lost count after the Novocain numbed him. The bits of polymer thread pulled when he moved, and his wounds ached.

He rounded the corner into the infirmary, waved to Elizabeth, and walked into the ward. Valentin and Harold were standing next to Kayna's bed talking in low, earnest tones. Brynn joined them. Harold extended a hand and held on for a long time after Brynn clasped it. There was desperation in his touch and relief so palpable Brynn could almost sense how much Harold had suffered and blamed himself.

"I was explaining how sorry I am," Harold said. He looked like hell, with deep circles beneath his eyes and lines in his face that hadn't been there before. "I've been out with every SAR team hunting for both of you. Haven't slept since I rousted you out of your lab." He lowered his voice. "I wanted to tell everyone exactly what I'd seen, but Valentin talked me out of it. Said if I did, they'd never let me be part of the search teams."

"It wasn't your fault," Kayna said, sounding stronger. "Really. Don't give it another thought."

"Nice try." Harold returned his gaze to her. "I've never felt as helpless as when I tried to cross that stretch of beach to you and couldn't." He inhaled deeply and blew out the breath. "Valentin and I discussed it. There are Russian myths and legends of similar happenings, but I never would've believed them if I hadn't ended up with a starring role."

Valentin Gorev bent and laid a hand over Kayna's. "I glad you alive, lady doctor. Plenty worry."

"Thank you." Kayna smiled warmly. "We'll have time to talk, but Brynn's dead on his feet, and I could sleep for days."

"We can take a hint." Harold looked down as he searched for words. "Not that you have to tell us a thing, but Valentin and I, we're good at keeping secrets, if you ever feel like talking about it."

"See you once I'm up and about," Kayna said, neatly sidestepping the invitation for show and tell. "One of the things I want to do is learn Russian. Bet you'd practice with me, huh Valentin?"

"Ship be here long time. Too much ice to leave. I look forward to teach Russian." Valentin walked toward the door with Harold behind him. "Maybe I work on English," he shot over a shoulder right before the door closed behind them.

Brynn sat on the edge of Kayna's bed. She scooted into his arms and snuggled against his chest. "Go to our room and get some rest."

"I will, but I wanted to hold you again first. Dear God, when I realized I had to do something drastic or you were going to die, it kicked my butt into hyper drive. Never knew I had that kill or be killed mentality in me."

"When you scratch the surface, we all do," she said solemnly. "We'll get through this. Christ, Brynn. If we could survive what happened, we're bulletproof."

He cradled her head beneath his hand and threaded his fingers through her hair to stroke her neck. "What happened is too fresh and I'm too raw to know how I feel. The only clear thing is that I love you. Every moment I can hold you like this is precious."

She pushed back and looked at him. "I'm so lucky. Not every woman has a prince who's willing to lay down his life for her."

"It wasn't just me. Your grandmother and raven helped. Your mom too." He kissed her forehead. "You may want to study Russian. I plan to study magic. No way in fucking hell will I be as unprepared as I was earlier today. Which reminds me, apparently we were gone for three days."

"I'm not surprised. Time is different in the Otherworld. Sometimes shorter, sometimes longer. Figures it would've been shorter this time around. Once I'm out of here, I want you to tell me everything. I have no idea what happened after I blacked out."

"I'll be back as soon as I get up." He brushed his lips over hers.

"By then, maybe the requisite twenty-four hours will have passed, and you can escort me back to our room."

He snorted. "It's a mess. All our duffels and suitcases are crammed in there."

"I know. I'll help you put things away."

"We can crawl over them. I was hoping to retire to our bed and not surface—ever."

"Hang onto that thought, tiger." A lovely rose deepened the gold in her skin. "I'll hold you to it."

CHAPTER 30

Brynn rubbed his eyes and set tests to run one more time. In the two weeks since he'd returned from the Otherworld, he'd spent most of his waking hours in his lab. If everything checked out, the current mixture would go into an IV infusion for Andrev.

"So far, so good?" Micah asked.

Brynn started. He'd been concentrating so intently he hadn't noticed the other man come in. He spun his chair to face Micah and nodded. "I probably didn't need this last set of checks, but they'll make me feel better."

"Know what you mean." Micah cracked a crooked grin. "We're in uncharted territory—for damn near everything."

"Isn't that the truth? But we've gotten lucky."

"Either that, or we're bitchin' competent."

Brynn laughed. "Maybe a little of that too. I'm just glad my mutated cultures stopped whatever was going on with yours."

"I'd feel better about that if I understood what got into mine in the first place."

"That's been bothering me too. Who can understand why organisms change that radically?" He frowned "It flies in the face of selective adaptation, but then my colonies did the same thing—without the lethal overtones."

"Tincture of time." Micah shrugged. "Usually if you give something enough latitude, it becomes more understandable."

Brynn bit back a snort. "That hasn't been my experience. Sometimes things just get murkier."

"Maybe I need more miles under my belt. On a positive note, the last patient with carbon monoxide poisoning left the infirmary yesterday. Ted was a genius creating an antibody infusion from my blood. Between me and a couple other volunteers who'd recovered, we had all the blood types we needed."

"Thank God no one else died."

"No kidding. I still feel wretched about the half dozen we lost after we should've known better. The symptoms are subtle." Micah shook his head. "When I felt lightheaded and generally like crap, I ignored it. Figured I hadn't eaten enough. Walking in and finding those two women dead on the floor of my lab was a definite wakeup call. Even then, I didn't figure things out until the doc forced me to take some downtime in the infirmary."

Brynn eyed the other researcher. "When things fly in the face of our training, we try to force whatever's bothering us back to familiar ground."

Micah shrugged. "Ain't that the truth? Downplaying my symptoms didn't help, either." He folded his arms over his chest. "You'd have thought some sort of innate survival mechanism might've sounded an alarm, but it didn't."

There was a time when Brynn would've written off intuitive logic like that, but not anymore. Not after what he'd lived through. "Whatever the reason, I'm glad you got it checked out. Once those receptor sites on your red blood cells start carrying something other than oxygen, it's a quick downhill slide."

"Are you at a point where you can leave what you're doing?" Micah quirked a brow.

"Sure. What's up?"

"I wanted to show you the latest results from the radiation experiments."

Brynn got to his feet and stretched. "Good news, huh?"

"How'd you know?"

"Otherwise, you'd still be in the rodent lab."

Micah rolled his eyes. "You're worse than having a wife."

"Don't tell Kayna. I'm ready when you are." Brynn gestured at his workbench. I have time to kill before I do my very last set of checks and balances and prep Andrev's infusion."

He followed Micah out of the lab, down the corridor, and into the animal lab in the next building. The musty scent of rodents hit him the moment he got past the door. "Whew. Never quite got used to that smell."

"Funny. I don't even notice it anymore." Micah tilted a computer screen. "Take a look at these numbers."

Brynn peered at the display and smiled. "Excellent. So this last batch didn't produce liver or kidney problems?"

"Yup. The previous mix kept them alive, but when we did bloodwork, it appeared that while we may have saved them from a fast death from radiation, we opened them to a slower one from metabolic syndrome."

"Have you replicated these results?"

Micah shook his head. "Abel and Zach are working on that right now."

Brynn felt quietly pleased, but knew better than to declare victory on the basis of one successful experiment. "Keep me posted, okay?"

"Will do."

Brynn made his way back to his own lab, deep in thought. When his latest batch of tests checked out, he created a sterile field and set about mixing what would go into Andrev's IV bag. Even though he felt mildly uncomfortable, he offered up a short prayer to Danu to watch over his efforts. He'd promised to dedicate his life to the goddess, and he wouldn't welch on the deal.

KAYNA WALKED out of a treatment room where she was conducting clinic and gave instructions to the medical assistant, a young Chilean male. He winked at her with his liquid, dark eyes and disappeared into the room. Time had passed since Brynn hauled her out of the Otherworld, and she was mostly recovered. At least her body felt close to normal. It would take far longer to heal the scars pitting her mind. That her father was narcissistic enough to assume she owed him her life festered like a sore that refused to stop oozing. It was infinitely worse than when she'd chalked him up as being a crazy drunk.

She'd talked with her mother several times. Moira rethought her antipathy toward her power and was studying to make up for lost time. Apparently it hadn't sat well when she'd wanted join Nana in the Otherworld and been vetoed. Kayna smiled to herself. Nana pestered her almost every night in her dreams wondering if she'd married the "wonderful young man" who'd rescued her yet. The raven, clearly delighted she was still alive, popped in at odd times. Kayna hadn't realized she shared the bird with Nana—and her mother. Once Brynn told her the raven had responded to her grandmother's command and perched on her shoulder, she'd asked Nana about it and learned the bird was linked to her family.

So much I don't know...

Kayna made her way to the front desk and peered at the computer screen to see if she was done for the day. A sharp rap on the glass started her. She straightened and looked into Brynn's striking hazel eyes. Today they held amber tones with golden flecks. She pushed the glass aside and grinned. "Sorry, you're not on the schedule."

He held up an IV bag full of beige liquid streaked with violet and red. "I can't believe you forgot."

She clapped a hand over her mouth. "I didn't. Not totally. Give me a sec. I want to come with you. I'll go out the back way and meet you in the hall."

He was waiting for her when she emerged from the clinic. As they walked across the hall and into the infirmary, Kayna thought about Brynn's experiments. Against what she saw as steep odds, he and the other microbiologists had produced an antibiotic that was truly a powerhouse. Unlike commercially prepared antibiotics, it took time to tailor these to target specific bacteria, but the archaea had proven wonderfully adaptive—and cooperative. Almost as if they understood the stakes and rose to the occasion.

After many tests, today was the day they were going to hook Andrev up to an IV. If his body responded the same way bacteria cultured from it did, he should be hale and hearty soon.

The men had also developed a serum-based antibody injection that cleared the iron-hungry proks from people's bloodstreams far more quickly than supplemental oxygen. But the best news was Brynn's gamble that his colonies would neutralize the mutant McMurdo microbes had paid off. Micah's colonies were back to normal, and there'd been no new cases of carbon monoxide poisoning.

Kayna smiled warmly and said, "If your preliminary work here pans out, multidrug resistant strains of bugs could become a thing of the past."

"It would be awesome if it worked that way—" Brynn hooked his foot around an IV tower and attached the bag to it "—but the big drug companies will fight us tooth and claw."

"Why would they?"

"Because I'm using natural substances that can't become proprietary blends. There's no money in it for them." Brynn frowned. "That's their problem. I'm in this to save lives."

"Don't care about getting rich, huh?"

"I am rich." His smile lit her world on fire. "I have the best woman in the entire world. Come on, let's do this." He pushed the door to Andrev's room open.

The Russian seaman broke into a wide grin and flopped his arm out for them. Using Harold to interpret, Kayna had already told Andrev what they were doing and what to expect. He'd said he was sick of lying on his back and would welcome anything to make him whole again.

The IV slid in easily, and she adjusted the flow. "I'll have the nurse look in on you," she said, even though Andrev might not understand. "This will take time." She pointed to her watch and he nodded.

"Time okay," he said and flashed her a thumbs up sign.

They left Andrev's room and walked back through the infirmary. Kayna checked on her patients while Brynn waited. Once she was done, she hung her smock on a hook and walked out into the corridor where she reached for Brynn's hand and said, "The antibiotic experiment is looking like an unprecedented success, at least in the lab. I can't wait to see how our patient responds. How are your nuclear rats doing?"

"Mice." He corrected her, looking thoughtful. "We've only done one complete round of tests with the latest combination, but the mice we treated with our cocktail—blended from my mutated cultures—didn't get sick, despite exposure to enough radiation to kill their counterparts. And we seem to have the side effects under control."

"Wonderful news! What happens next?"

"What always happens with science? We replicate our results, to make sure they weren't a fluke, and then we move up the food chain to make certain the protective effect extends to living creatures other than rodents."

"How long are you thinking it will take?"

He shook his head. "It won't happen fast enough to help the

worst hit in New York and Moscow, but we should have this choo-choo heading down the track in plenty of time to inoculate everybody else before the fallout gets to them. Assuming we can come up with a way to transport our special blend out of Antarctica."

"Can't it be created with archaea from somewhere else?"

"I suspect we need cells from a direct line to what's already cultured here. Archaea are everywhere, but these Antarctic ones are special, older, more plastic. We wouldn't get the same results if we cultured them from other locales." He snorted. "Just try finding prokaryotes that spontaneously morph into eukaryotes."

She scrunched her forehead in thought. "Maybe transport won't be a problem. Every major government in the world will want to get their hands on your mix. Today's kind of a red letter day, and it certainly answers some of those questions we had."

"Which ones?" he asked with a smile.

"Somehow—and don't ask me how because I don't know—your archaea understood they needed to be right where they are—in position to neutralize the threat from the cultures here at McMurdo. Via ancient knowledge or shared memories, or some type of engram we don't understand, they recognized the power, and the necessity, of mutating to combat what was going on here. It was the mutated strain that forced Micah's colonies back into line, wasn't it?"

Brynn nodded. "The mutated strain also forms the substrate for the anti-radiation mixture. I never could've synthesized it on South Georgia. My lab was too primitive. A few months back, I'd have signed myself into a psych ward if I started to believe my cultures could communicate." He rolled his eyes, managing to appear sheepish and wise all at the same time. "Do you suppose it's why they sang to us?" He arched a brow.

"I do." Kayna snorted. "Good thing we paid attention. I hate to think what their next move would've been."

Brynn chuckled. "I never even considered that angle."

"Let's hear it for my ability to come up with a creative spin on almost anything." She smiled broadly. "I still think this is a special day. Do you feel like a celebratory dinner?"

"Actually, I'm one step ahead of you. I have a surprise."

She clapped her hands together. "Really? What?"

"It's back in our room."

She cast a knowing look his way. "You're trying to lure me off alone to ravish me."

"Yeah, that too. Guess you've got my number." He grinned, looking young and carefree, but she wasn't fooled. Shadows danced behind his eyes that hadn't been there before. It would take much longer than a couple weeks for him to come to terms with the world he'd discovered courtesy of her.

She tucked a hand beneath his arm. "Lead out, Galahad."

"Aw, come on. I don't call you Guinevere."

"She was King Arthur's consort." Kayna elbowed him in the side. "Get your mythology straight."

"Who was Galahad's wife?"

"I don't know that he had one. He was part of the search for the Holy Grail. Being gone that long isn't conducive to keeping wives happy."

They reached their room, and Brynn pushed the door open. Kayna gasped in delight as she saw a table set for two complete with unlit candles. "Oh my God, you did this for me. You sweetheart." She spun and wrapped her arms around him. Brynn hugged her back and kicked the door closed right before he balanced himself against a wall and toed off his boots.

"I would've scattered flower petals, but they're in rather short supply down here."

"No kidding. I'm amazed you came up with decent china. The stuff they have in the dining room is serviceable, but this is lovely." She walked to the table and turned a plate over. "Spode. Wherever did you find it?" She sat in a chair and unlaced her boots, tugging them off.

"Valentin and Harold. They had it on the ship and were more than happy to loan it to me." He tossed her boots to one side and dropped to one knee in front of her. "I'll keep this simple," he said, his marvelous eyes never leaving her face. "Would you do me the honor of becoming my wife? I promise to love, cherish, and protect you until the end of my days."

Kayna felt the hot, quick bite of tears behind her lids. Her throat thickened with emotion and deep love for the man before her. "The honor would be mine." A tear slithered down her cheek, and she brushed it away with a thumb. "Now get up, silly," she said. "I'm guessing those covered containers are our supper, but I'd rather crack that bottle of wine, drink a toast to us, and have you remove my clothing very, very slowly."

"I like the way you think." He rose, plucked the wine off the table, and worked a corkscrew into it. "Not only could I not find flower petals, jewelry stores were also in rather short supply. Once we get back to the States, though, I'll buy you whatever engagement ring you want."

"That's a year from now." Her eyes twinkled with merriment. "You just proposed, and I accepted. I was sort of hoping we'd be married by then."

"Okay, so I'll owe you two rings." He tipped the wine bottle and poured claret-colored liquid into her glass. "To us," he murmured, filled his own glass, clinked it against hers, and drank.

"I'll definitely drink to that." Kayna stood, glass in hand, and took another swallow before setting her wine down. She held out her arms and he came into them, all hard muscle and lean, sculpted lines. She closed her arms around his back, reveling how he felt against her body. He hooked his arms beneath hers and splayed his hands across her back, crushing her against him.

"I never can decide what I want to do the most with you," he murmured, his voice muffled against her hair. "Looking at you is a study in art, touching you is sheer delight, but being inside you is about as close to heaven as anyone stuck on Earth can get."

"I feel the same about you," she said. "Every time you take your clothes off, I wish I were a sculptor or a painter. Your body is perfection." She tilted her head back, knowing what would come next. Brynn didn't disappoint her. He slashed his chiseled lips over hers and kissed her hard. It was the kiss of a man who knew what he wanted and would slay the world to get it. His tongue dipped into her mouth and she sucked on it, hungry for all of him. He tasted like the Cabernet they'd shared, smoky and enigmatic. No matter how many times they made love, she never got enough. Leaving him in the mornings was torture, but joining with him at night made up for it.

He ran his hands beneath her top, teasing the bare skin of her torso with knowing fingertips. Her nipples peaked where they pressed against his chest, and her breathing quickened. Desire clawed at her belly, and her sex slicked with need. She tore her mouth from his. "Time out," she panted. "Let's get rid of these clothes."

"It's always like this with us," he said, his voice husky with wanting her. "We're so desperate to have each other, we hurry. Tonight, we're taking all the time in the world. I want you so much, I can barely breathe, but you called it when you asked me to remove your clothes slowly."

As if to demonstrate, he took a step back and tugged her stretchy black top over her head. His eyes burned like gemstones, amber with golden highlights, and he ran his hands reverently down her body, starting with her face and moving to her neck, shoulders, and breasts. She reached back intent on unhooking her bra, but he batted her hands away.

Kayna's nipples rubbed against the black lace of her bra, shooting sparks to her belly. Brynn filled his hands with her breasts. Sensation flooded her, and she reached out with a hand to steady herself on the table. He moved his hands down her ribcage and stopped at the elastic waistband of her scrubs.

She wriggled beneath his touch, expecting him to push her

pants down her legs, but he kept his hands curved around her hips. Slowly, deliberately, he let one stray lower until he cupped her vulva. She bucked against him, desperate for contact.

"My God, you're the most enchanting creature." His voice was even thicker and lower than it had been before. "I still can't believe you're mine."

She shook hair out of her face and said, "I might not be if you don't get moving," but he laughed, obviously not taking her seriously.

He bent and ran his tongue from the vee between her breasts up her collarbone. Shivers cascaded down her body, and she reached for the bottom edge of his shirt, intent on pulling it over his head. She wrestled it off him and tossed it aside. Kayna stared at the planes of muscle carving across his shoulders and running down his arms. She moved her gaze to his tightly budded nipples with their fine scattering of coppery hair and then lower, where his abs and obliques disappeared beneath the waistband of his belled out pants.

Desperation to see all of him buck-naked speared her, and she made a grab for his zipper, but he danced beyond her reach. Brynn grabbed her from behind and wove his arms around her, closing his hands over her breasts. His erection jutted against her backside. He dipped his hands under the edge of her bra and rolled her nipples between thumb and forefinger. Nuzzling beneath her hair, he teased her neck and ear, biting, nibbling, sucking.

Desire tore at her and she reached behind herself, jimmied her hands between their bodies, and made short work of the button and zipper holding his pants together. They slid to the floor, and she pushed the elastic waistband of his boxers after them. It was tempting, oh so tempting to close her hands around his hot, ridged flesh. Instead, she pushed her own pants out of the way. They puddled around her feet, followed by her thong, and she butted the bare skin of her ass against his cock as she stepped out of her clothes.

"Hussy," he breathed against her ear. "You were supposed to let me worship your body. It's hard enough to hang onto shards of control when we have clothes between us."

"And now?" She spun in his arms and raised a brow.

"Impossible." His eyes blazed like twin infernos. "I give up. Get on your hands and knees on the bed. You've got the finest ass in Christendom. It frames your sex to perfection."

"What happens after I'm there?" Her mouth was dry. She wanted him so much it was hard to form words.

"I'll admire the view."

"Bet you twenty bucks you do more than that." She sauntered past him and crawled onto the bed, her butt in the air.

"Aw, sweetheart, you could've bet a thousand and come out ahead. You must know how irresistible you are."

The bed shifted as he knelt behind her, and she felt the heat of him where he pushed his thighs against her. His cockhead fit snugly at the opening to her body, and she arched her back to give him better access. Feeling him push slowly inside nearly carried her over the edge, but she hung on by her toenails. His cock was magical, long, hard, and thick. And it did astonishing things to her body.

Once he was seated inside her, he unhooked her bra and reached around to cup her breasts, skin to skin this time. Between him twirling her nipples between his fingers and twitching his cock deep inside her, an orgasm caught her hard, twisted her, and spit her out in a blazing gale of ecstasy. He nipped her where her shoulder and neck joined, licked the spot, and nipped her again.

The sound of their breathing was harsh against the silence of the room. She shoved back toward him, wanting him to move, wanting the elation of his body joined to her. He straightened, moving his hands from her breasts to her hips so he could stabilize himself. Once he had hold of her, he withdrew until the tip of him swirled around her opening, igniting her nerves as if her earlier climax hadn't happened. Kayna couldn't wait for more. Bracing herself against the mattress, she bucked upward until he was deep inside her, then withdrew and did it again.

He groaned, followed by a deep, almost purring noise as he caught her up and met her thrust for thrust. She came and came again, her entire body vibrating. When it got to be too much, she cried out, grateful they didn't have close neighbors. In the midst of her fourth climax, she felt Brynn release, his cock shuddering. They swayed for long moments before collapsing onto the bed where he rolled them onto their sides and kept his arms firmly around her.

"You don't follow directions very well," he gasped.

"Do I hear a complaint?" Talking was still a struggle.

"No. No complaints. You're the most incredible woman ever. Eve had nothing on you. Neither did Cleopatra or Aphrodite or—"

"Mmm. You're pretty amazing yourself, and it's lovely to be appreciated." Kayna wiggled free of his penis and rolled over so she faced him. "Say, do you suppose our dinner's ruined?"

"Worked up an appetite, did you?" He grinned and looked wonderfully mischievous with his tawny hair askew and framing his face.

"Nah. I'm practical. We'll need fuel for the next round."

"A lady after my own heart. I'll get you a warm washcloth if you'll see to our supper."

"It's a bargain." Kayna kissed him warmly, then moved off the bed. Her body felt alive, as if she glowed with a thousand tiny lights. If this was what being in love was like, she'd take it any time, hands down. Brynn strode to her side and handed her a warm, damp cloth.

"Thanks, special guy." She swiped it between her legs and then snugged into the robe he handed her.

By the time he emerged from the bathroom, she'd dished up

their cooling dinner and refilled both wine glasses. She placed his in his hand. "To us. Forever."

His eyes took on a solemn light and he clinked his glass against hers. "Forever. Not only do I like the sound of that, I'll hold you to it."

"You're on, buddy." She tipped her glass and drank.

PART FOUR ~~ AN END OR A NEW BEGINNING?

I only went out for a walk and finally concluded to stay out till sundown, for going out, I found, was really going in.
~John Muir

Forget not that the earth delights to feel your bare feet and the winds long to play with your hair.
~Khalil Gibran

Do not dwell in the past. Do not dream of the future. Concentrate your mind on the moment and live it fully.
~Budda

Life isn't about finding yourself. Life is about creating yourself.
~George Bernard Shaw

CHAPTER 31

Three months later

Brynn tossed his parka hood over his head and zipped the garment up past his chin. He shoved his hands into mitts and glanced at Kayna, who'd dressed for the outside too. "About ready?" he asked.

"Yes. Are you certain you want to do this?"

"No, but I have to. That old saw about facing your fears is true. Besides, if I don't, there won't be any point in all the work I've done developing my power." Brynn clenched his jaws together. "To be honest, I'm scared, but it's the summer solstice—even though June is high winter down here—and according to everything in the stuff I read online and the materials you got from your mother, this will be the easiest time for me to test my mettle."

"It is," Kayna concurred and tugged the door to their room open. "Magic is strong during the solstice and the veils between the worlds thin. If you're going to batter your way through to the Otherworld under your own power, tonight is definitely the night."

"Last time Danu took pity on me." Brynn blew out a tight breath. "This time I have enough knowledge to be dangerous."

"Spoken like a modern warrior." Kayna clapped him on the back. "You never know, maybe you'll find that grail after all."

He cast a thoughtful glance her way. "The grail myth is personal for each man—or woman. Tonight is personal to me."

Her eyes shaded to emerald. "For me too. Because of you, I've reclaimed my magical heritage, and I feel whole for the first time in a long time."

"Too bad the price was so high."

"Nothing worthwhile comes cheap." She smiled ruefully.

"Ain't that the truth?" He strode into the corridor and led the way down the stairs and out a side door. It was midnight on the shortest day of the year in the southern hemisphere, but short was relative because they hadn't seen the sun in four weeks. Darkness reigned in Antarctica, but Brynn figured the Otherworld would be bathed in the half-light he remembered.

He patted his side, reassured by the subtle clang of metal against metal from the oversized pockets of the cargo pants he wore beneath his bibs. This time he wasn't going empty-handed. Even though Kayna thought it unlikely they'd run into her father again, Brynn wasn't so certain. He'd dipped his blades in a deadly poison he'd created with a spell that required his blood. If it worked—and Guiren would have to show up to find out—it would strip Kayna's father of any existence at all.

Once he'd begun hunting down spells and incantations, Brynn had been flabbergasted by their diversity. He'd found recipes for everything from love charms to wasting spells. There were so many spells to manage pesky shades who refused to remain dead, he'd had quite a choice.

"I've finally acclimated to the cold," Kayna said as they emerged into the night. Her voice shook him out of his thoughts. "It's still a shock when I first go outside, but once I'm out here for a little bit, I don't mind it as much."

"Yeah, it's the same for me." Brynn positioned an arm around her shoulders and headed them toward the deserted stretch of frozen rocky shoreline where Kayna had disappeared. "I've pretty much decided to accept that offer from the Canadian company."

"It's a good call," Kayna said. "Their idea to create a nasal preparation for the anti-radiation drug is much better than an injection. Makes it more practical for everybody but especially third world countries." She hesitated. "That was an awful lot of money they offered. What are you going to do with it all?"

"The question," he murmured, "is what are *we* going to do with it? And there won't be as much as you think. I'm only accepting developer fees and first year research support. I was correct about needing cells from a direct line to what's already cultured here. These Antarctic ones truly are special. We wouldn't get the same results from archaea culled from other places."

"What happens to the project after we leave Antarctica?"

"The money goes to NSF to continue to support research in the lab here. Jack's really excited about the project. He was considering going home, but I think he'll stay another few years to see this thing through. Zach, Abel, and Ted aren't going anywhere, either. Neither is Micah. They say this is the most exciting thing they've ever stumbled across." He paused for a beat. "Something else nice happened yesterday that I didn't get a chance to tell you about."

"What?" She nudged him. "Turn left here or we'll miss the entrance to the cove."

"My mother ran me down via sat phone. Somehow, she got wind of my research projects. Anyway, she came as close as she could to apologizing and said she was proud of me."

"How does that feel now that you're almost forty?" Kayna's voice was suspiciously devoid of intonation, as if she didn't want to influence him.

"Honestly?" She nodded, so he went on. "It would've meant a

hell of a lot more when I was a kid. You keep an eye on me once our own babies start coming, okay?"

"What kind of eye?" She grabbed his arm and turned them so they faced a full moon. "We can stop here."

"If I start sounding like an authoritarian jerk, kick me."

"How about if I drag you to bed and fuck your brains out?"

"That could work. Okay." Brynn straightened his spine. "Now remember, don't help."

"I won't have to. You're stronger than you think."

"No help from the raven, either."

Kayna laughed. "No worries on that front. He may have marked you as my one true love, but you'll have to find your own spirit guide."

Brynn cleared his mind. He'd found when practicing that he was more effective if he had a focal point in the natural world. Tonight he picked the moon, an obvious choice since it dominated the night sky. He chanted, the magical words feeling more like an extension of himself than they ever had before. His body expanded until he sensed every cell, every morsel of blood pounding through his veins and arteries. Magic was an incredible high. It raced through him like high voltage and intensified everything. Colors tumbled around him before everything shaded to black. Moments later, the Otherworld formed.

"Nicely done," Kayna said. "Elegant. You made it look easy. Quick too. We weren't in the airless part long enough for it to bother me."

Power blew through him like a runaway train. "It felt easy, natural, like I stumbled onto a destiny that's been here all along waiting for me."

"That makes me feel a little better." She unzipped her parka and tossed her hood out of the way.

It wasn't minus fifty in the Otherworld, and he mimicked her motions. Brynn still felt overdressed, plus if Guiren showed up, the heavy clothes would slow him down. He shucked his parka and slid his bibs off his shoulders, bending to step out of his Pac boots so he could take the bibs all the way off. Along the way, he added his gloves to the growing pile of clothing.

"What are you doing?" Kayna asked. "I know it's warmer here, but wasn't the whole purpose to see if you could get here on your own? You look as if you're planning to stay a while."

"Getting here was one goal." Brynn spoke carefully and then switched gears. "What did you mean about my affinity for magic making you feel better?"

She bit her lower lip. "I've been feeling guilty as sin. If it weren't for me, you'd never have found out about the Otherworld, and you'd have gone right on believing magic wasn't real." Kayna dropped her parka and gloves atop his. "Even though you knew less than nothing about the paranormal, you risked your life to save me."

"I'd do it again in a heartbeat. I take care of what's mine." Once the words were out, sitting in the pale, thin air of the Otherworld, other realizations hammered him. "My life wasn't complete without magic. It was as if I was on the outside looking in, trying to figure out what was missing, but it always eluded me. Remember when I told you I felt as if I was on the edge of an epiphany while we were on the ship?" When she nodded, he continued. "That was it. The revelation was about magic completing me in a significant way. If it weren't for you, I'd never have found out."

"Thank you. You're such a sweetheart, I love you to pieces." It might've been a trick of the light in this world, but her eyes glowed, intense emotion flickering in their depths. "Come on." She crooked two fingers at him. "As long as you got comfy clothes-wise, I'd like to introduce you to the fairy folk. I used to have friends among them."

Brynn moved to her side, aware his feet were cold. He sent an experimental thread of magic to see if he could warm them and was tickled when it worked. "Where are we going?"

"To a glade with a huge lake. Actually, there are several lakes in the Otherworld, but the fairies' castle sits at one end of this one, and they're usually out and about frolicking."

"Do they really spend time in our world? I read that they did, but since I've never seen one…" He let his voice trail off.

"You may now that you're attuned to different frequencies. Fairies aren't always helpful, though. Some play pranks."

Iridescent lights flickered through the trees and illuminated a faint path beneath Brynn's feet. "Is the Otherworld always the same?"

"Excellent question. No. It shifts and changes, but I figured out how to find my way around by sensing things. It's like a psi map, as opposed to the kind you're used to. Once I have an image of where I'm going firmly in hand, a path like the one we're on lights up, and all I have to do is follow it." She glanced about and frowned. "We're almost there. I wonder why no one has come to greet us. The fairy folk post sentinels. Surely they know we're here."

"How big are they?" Brynn asked. "I read accounts of everything from Tinker Bell-size to taller than humans."

"The ones I knew look a lot like us," Kayna answered, "but Nana told me about the small variety. I guess she worked magic with them back in the Old Country."

Thick tree cover fell away, and a lake shimmered in the half-light of the Otherworld. Brynn wondered if the pearlescent, gray-hued ether ever grew lighter or darker. He opened his mouth to ask Kayna when she gasped.

Brynn's head snapped up. With all his senses, magical and human, on full alert, he scanned the glade and the lake, zeroing in on a Kiao inscribing lazy circles as it moved closer to them.

"We have to leave." Kayna tugged his arm. "Forget our clothes. Let's get the hell out of here." Panic shrilled her voice.

"It's your father, isn't it?" Brynn asked, surprised by the deadly calm that descended over him like a well-worn cloak.

"Of course it's fucking him," Kayna cried. "Not that there's only one Kiao in Chinese mythology, but what are the odds? Plus the lakeshore's deserted, which means the fairies barricaded themselves inside their castle."

"What castle?" Brynn peered through the gray gloomy air above the lake.

"They've shielded it. They want nothing to do with the Chinese water dragon or its magic."

Brynn inhaled deeply, blew out the breath, and did it again. He shrugged his shoulders to loosen them and danced from side to side on the balls of his feet.

"No!" Kayna tugged harder on his arm. "You are not going to take on Chinese magic."

"Why not? I came out on top before, and this time I have more knowledge—and better tools."

"What? You should've told me." Her voice grated like pebbles grinding together.

"I did. When we talked about it, you said it was unlikely your father would be here." He bent close to her. "Return to our world. I'll meet you once I'm done."

"I don't bloody well think so. If you insist on doing this, you'll need my help." She straightened her spine in a motion that filled him with pride and broke his heart.

"It's your father. You shouldn't see this."

"That son of a bitch tried to kill me. He would have if you and Nana hadn't shown up. Even worse, he was going to slice me to bits to capture my magic once I was too weak to be of any further use."

"You never told me that part." Brynn heard a dangerous edge in his voice and marveled at the thin line between civilization and a retreat to his atavistic roots.

The Kiao was only fifty yards from shore. The air around it

darkened into a glistening nimbus. Guiren shot from its center as if a cannon had discharged him. He somersaulted through the air and ended in a crouch in the lake's shallows. When Brynn scanned the lake, the Kiao had disappeared.

"Good. He'll be easier to deal with in human form." Kayna pitched her voice low. She drew magic of her own; it eddied about her in waves that collided with Brynn's casting.

"Doesn't matter what the thing looks like. It's all powered by your father's energy. Last time after I stabbed the human shape, it shifted back into the water dragon."

"I was so out of it, I must've missed that part. Let's get this show on the road."

Brynn blinked in surprise. He recognized Kayna's strength, but she'd sounded positively feral. "Are you certain you don't want to go?" he asked again, worried she'd be damaged by witnessing what he had in mind.

"Touching." Guiren rose from his crouch and sauntered toward them naked. His long black hair shrouded his golden skin, and his penetrating dark gaze never left them. The same double-edged sword hung from his back in a sheath. Guiren pulled the Jian, said a word, and fire ran up both sides, illuminating black runes carved into the metal. The symbols pulsed in a mesmerizing rhythm almost as if they called to him, and Brynn forced himself to look away.

"I'm not leaving," Kayna growled.

Brynn dug into a pocket in his cargo pants and handed her a sheathed bayonet with a wicked-looking six-inch blade. She threw the sheath aside and glanced at the brilliant crimson coating the knife's cutting edge, but didn't say anything.

"Only use that if I fail." Brynn placed his body between Kayna and Guiren. He reached back into his pocket, and a twin bayonet materialized in his hand. Unclipping the sheath, he tossed it aside. He'd pilfered the weapons from the base armory and doubted they'd be missed.

"Ever the gentleman protecting his lady," Guiren sneered and swung his sword hand wide. "I'm surprised you want a rematch."

"My recollection is you didn't exactly win." Brynn tried pushing into Guiren's mind, but the shaman repulsed him easily.

"Not as strong as you think you are, college boy." With no warning, Guiren rushed him from the side.

Brynn spun out of the way, but the Jian sliced into his ribs. Damn, but the shaman was quick on his feet. His long blade helped because he didn't have to get very close to inflict damage. Blood splashed down Brynn's side, but he ignored it. His heartbeat accelerated as he tried to anticipate Guiren's next move.

Kayna raced from behind him, intent on burying her blade in Guiren. He laughed and sidestepped her so easily, her body spun in place.

"I told you to stay behind me." Brynn ground out the words.

"Yeah, like I'm going to stand back and watch that bastard kill you." She was breathing hard, and she twirled to face her father, knife balanced in one hand as if she'd been born with it there.

"Excellent." Guiren's wide mouth gaped, and he showed his teeth in a parody of amusement. "I get two for the price of one. The old woman's not here. At least she was a worthy opponent." He swung his sword lightning fast, nicking Brynn's upper arm.

Brynn pivoted, backing beyond the Jian's reach. His ribs ached, and an alarming amount of blood dampened his side. At least his arm wasn't injured. One thing hadn't changed since his last go-round with Guiren. The other man was a trained fighter. Brynn wasn't. He threw himself at his opponent, but the shaman twisted away.

Kayna's green eyes held a fey light, and she raced toward her father's shade again. This time, her raven took shape next to her and charged Guiren too. While Kayna's father was intent on neutralizing their attack, Brynn launched one of his own. Moving behind Guiren's back, he locked an arm around his neck in a single, fluid movement. Once he had the shaman pinned, Brynn didn't hesitate. He plunged the poison-tipped bayonet into his neck, dragging it forward to sever both jugular and carotid. Blood geysered, showering them. It smelled old, rancid. Brynn blinked the stinking liquid from his eyes. Guiren twisted the Jian behind him and sliced deep into the side of Brynn's thigh.

"Goddammit!" Brynn sawed through Guiren's neck intent on decapitating him.

Greasy, dark smoke rose from the ragged hole in Guiren's neck, and the shaman took on an insubstantial aspect. Something bright erupted from his mouth and homed in on Kayna. Using both wings, the raven chivied the glowing sphere right toward Kayna's blade. She caught it on the tip of her knife, driving the metal deep. "Die, you bastard," she snarled. "Die and never come back."

The raven screamed its approval.

"I'm your father," sounded all around them.

"You lost that right when you tried to kill me." Kayna pounded her bayonet into the earth of the Otherworld, and the bright, white light clinging to its tip dimmed, and then faded into nothingness. Guiren's body slumped against Brynn, made a popping sound, and disintegrated into wispy threads that floated away.

Brynn stared at his knife freed from its burden. Even though Guiren wasn't there anymore, the blade still dripped red-black blood. The thrum of magic receded; bloodlust departed along with it. Maybe because Brynn had prepared for it, what he'd done this time didn't devastate him like his first go-round with the shaman. Coolly, as if carnage were second nature, he located the scabbard, wiped the blade on his pants, and dropped both back into a pocket after he'd sheathed the knife.

"Why didn't the Kiao show up after I skewered your father?" he asked.

Kayna raced to his side. "Because you captured my father's spirit with whatever was on the knives, and the Kiao beat a hasty retreat. Never mind that. You're bleeding. A lot. We have to get you back."

"Another thing I've been working on is directing magic to heal wounds," Brynn said through clenched teeth. Now that adrenaline wasn't running hot, his thigh and ribs felt as if someone had poured lighter fluid on them and set them on fire.

"I still want to look at them and stitch you up," she said, sounding so fierce and protective it made him smile.

"Fine. Get your knife, and let's collect our clothes." Grunting with effort, he plucked the Jian from the ground. "It's had enough of a taste of my blood, I can claim it."

"That is how it works." She stifled grim laughter. "At least now I know what you were doing all those nights when you didn't come to bed until past midnight." She scooped up the sheath and dropped her knife into it. "Base armory?"

"You guessed it. Let's get out of here." He grimaced. While he understood the cellular underpinnings of healing, focusing power to undo the damage to his body wasn't as easy as what he'd read suggested.

Kayna shot a sharp glance his way. "You going to make it, Galahad?"

He grinned crookedly. "You bet, Guinevere."

Brynn wanted to take them home, but Kayna wouldn't let him. She helped him with his boots, got his parka and bibs on, and summoned power to transport them back to McMurdo. Threading a strong arm around him, she supported him until they got to the clinic and clucked over him like a mother hen while she cleaned, stitched, and bound his wounds.

"They aren't as bad as I expected they'd be," she murmured. "There, all done."

"That's because I used power to knit some of the broken parts together. Given time, I'm sure I could've done a better job. I have the knowledge. It's just a matter of applying it in a different way."

He hopped off the exam table and scooped bloody debris into the biohazard waste can.

She pursed her lips and stood before him. "Let's hope you never get another opportunity to practice that particular skill. What kind of poison was on the knives?"

Wincing because his ribs still ached, he reached for her and drew her into his arms. "You're smart. One of the many things I love about you."

"You didn't answer me."

"A spelled toxin to make sure he stays dead. Do you know if it worked?"

She leaned into his embrace and felt so damned good in his arms, his spirit soared.

"Yes," she said. "It worked. That glowing thing I pinned to the dirt after you killed the body again was his essence. It's also why the Kiao never reformed. It was smart enough to know the gig was up."

Brynn stroked her hair. "I said it before in the Otherworld, but I would've spared you that."

"I know, and I love you for it, but he wouldn't have stopped." She tilted her head into his touch.

"Why not? The radiation threat has cooled. Let's walk while we talk. I'd love to lie down, but we need to detour past the armory, so I can put those blades back before we go to our room."

"Can't we do that tomorrow?"

"Tonight's better," he said. "Less chance of anyone noticing us. I'm okay. Walking around is probably good for me." He untangled himself from her and stepped in front of the sink to rinse the residue from his spell off the edge of the borrowed blades. That done, he dried them and placed them back in their sheaths.

"Ready?" He made a sweeping motion that set his side on fire.

"Ready." She gathered their discarded outer clothes into a pile in her arms, and led the way out of the exam room where she'd patched him up.

Brynn snatched up the Jian and turned it this way and that as light sparked off it. "Too bad the scabbard disappeared. I'm sure I can make another, though."

Kayna shot him a look. "Something decorative to hang on the wall."

"Of course." Brynn kept his tone bland. Tonight probably wasn't the best time to mention he planned to learn how to fight with the weapon that had drawn his blood.

"As long as we're talking about Father's sword, I've had a few frank conversations with Mother. Nana's suspicions about him wanting Mom to breed super-children was right on. Anyway, if he hadn't died, she planned to leave him and take Kiki and me as far away as possible."

Brynn ducked into the armory and put the bayonets back in line with the others before rejoining Kayna in the darkened corridor. "The immediacy of the nuclear holocaust has retreated. I wasn't at all sure we'd find Guiren in the Otherworld. Why do you suppose he was still there?"

"Because he tried to control me and botched things. He also wasn't able to manage the radioactive fallout the way he wanted. Even in death, he couldn't accept either of those failures. He lost face, needed a fall guy, and it was me."

They lapsed into silence for the rest of the walk to their room. Brynn used his uninjured side to push the door open. Once inside, he propped the Jian in a corner. Dropping his shirt, trousers, and boots along the way, he slid into his side of their bed, sighing with pleasure to be off his feet. Kayna bustled around the room, hanging things up and turning out lights. When she finally slipped in beside him, he was pleasantly drowsy and held out his arms for her.

"Are you certain I won't hurt you?" she asked.

"Never."

"Next time you plan something like this—" the teasing note vanished from her voice "—tell me."

"I didn't plan anything," he protested. "I came prepared."

"Bullshit. You planned enough to activate the spell to douse those knife edges with a tincture. As I recall, it's plenty complex—and required your blood."

"Okay, so maybe I planned a little." He tightened his arms around her. "I love you Kayna. I take care of what's mine."

"What if I feel the same way?"

"I'd welcome it, darling. We can take care of each other."

She snuggled closer. "I like the sound of that."

"Good, because I could no more not protect you than I could not breathe. Mmm, you feel amazing against me."

"You feel pretty damned good yourself. Promise me something."

"Anything." Brynn felt himself slipping toward sleep.

"Next time you feel the need to play knight errant, talk with me first."

"That's easy. I promise."

"Sleep, love." She stroked his neck and back. "We're having dinner tomorrow, or maybe it's tonight since it's well past midnight, with Harold and Valentin."

"Great. I like them both."

"The political climate—and the weather—have cleared enough, they'll be leaving soon, despite it being the dead of winter, and they want to know what really happened to me. No matter how many times I've told him to stand down, Harold still feels responsible. Because he was involved, I think it's only fair to tell him the truth."

Brynn snorted. "Let's see, that will make Jack and David and probably Crowley, since I'm sure David told him—in confidence of course—and now Valentin and Harold who know about our adventures on the shady side of the veil. Why don't we write a book and tell the world?"

Kayna laughed. "You never know," she said, "maybe someday

we will. Under pen names, of course." She kneaded his shoulder muscles with strong fingers. "Sleep, love. Doctor's orders."

"Are you always this pushy?" His voice slurred from weariness.

"Not always. You're special." She kissed his forehead and his eyelids and cheeks. By the time she settled back against him, he was almost asleep.

CHAPTER 32

Brynn and Kayna stepped off a plane at Sea-Tac International Airport and made their way into the terminal with its rain-spattered windows. Kayna took a deep breath of the filtered air and made a face. "I miss Antarctica already."

"Know what you mean. No pollution there. Plus it held such a pristine quality." Brynn took a measured breath. "When I left South Georgia, I was convinced I was done with that part of the globe, but damn if it didn't grow on me, get into my blood."

"Maybe it got better because we had each other."

He grinned. "I'm certain that played a major role."

"The year we were there sure went fast. In the end, it was actually hard to leave." She locked gazes with him, and he nodded his understanding.

"We can always go back. Jack and everyone else made that abundantly clear."

She flashed him a smile. "Good to keep all our options open."

"Indeed it is." Brynn hooked an arm beneath hers. "Let's hurry over to customs, so we can get through this next part. I never enjoyed press conferences, but this one is essential."

She leaned closer and kissed his cheek. "I'm so proud of you.

What you and the others created in Antarctica saved tens of thousands of lives. Maybe even more than that."

He smiled, and tiny lines formed in the corners of his eyes. "You helped. I'm just glad it worked."

"And it's still working. That nasal preparation has found its way all over the globe, and world health organizations are still inoculating everyone they can lay their hands on."

"Good to be part of a growth industry. It should also help pad the funds they pay me for developer's fees. I ended up opting for a share of profits."

"Yeah." She elbowed him. "Smart man. I wanted you to take the fixed amount up front."

"That's what husbands are for," he informed her archly. "We handle the family finances."

She laughed. "Yeah, and you get to take out the trash and mow the lawn too. Right after you're done balancing the checkbook and doling out my allowance."

"Would you mind very much if we never had a life like that? Not the male-female dominance part, but a normal stint in suburbia?" Curiosity underscored his questions.

"I don't think we'll ever have that kind of life, and I'm fine with it. No white picket fences for us, at least not for quite a few years."

Swept up by the crowd, they followed arrows to the customs stations. "I still can't get over how close our nation came to wiping out the entire world," Kayna muttered.

"There would've been something left," Brynn replied thoughtfully, "but the way things turned out is ever so much better."

She leaned into him as they stood in line, waiting their turn to get their passports stamped. She'd slept a little on their various planes, but they'd been traveling for almost a week, and she felt like a road warrior. Or maybe the sky version of the same thing. First, there'd been the plane to the South Shetlands. Then the one to Ushuaia. From there, they'd routed through Buenos Aires and Panama City to Mexico City.

"Penny for your thoughts." He bent and brushed his lips over her cheek.

Kayna shrugged. "Just replaying our journey back to civilization. I would've liked to catch a ship as far as Ushuaia, but it would've taken too long."

He rolled his eyes. "After all that talk once we finally got off the *Vladimir*, I can't believe you're lusting after more shipboard life."

A snort blew past her lips. "I miss our cozy sleeping space."

"I'm certain we could book passage with Valentin and Harold again." He skewered her with a meaningful glance. "They've been texting me, or Harold has, anyway."

"Hey!" She pointed. "Our number just popped up."

The bored-looking customs agent—a man in his forties with short, brown hair and a slight build—didn't even look up. "Passports, please."

Brynn shoved his through a hole beneath the glass-fronted cubicle, and Kayna followed suit.

The agent did look up then. After the briefest of pauses, he sprang to his feet and snapped off a salute. "Dr. McMichaels. It's truly a pleasure to meet you, sir. You've been in all the news media for months."

"Thank you." Brynn said gruffly. "Would you have any idea where the conference center is located?"

The man grinned, and it lit his brown eyes from within. "We were expecting you, sir. Let me make a call, and your escort will be here in no time." Still on his feet, he tapped something into his computer terminal, scanned their passports, and handed them back.

"Thanks," Kayna said.

"Will you be needing help with your luggage, sir?" the agent inquired. "There might not be time to wait for it before the scheduled press conference."

"I was going to handle that part," Kayna informed him.

"Yes, we only look trashed." Brynn tried to joke. "We've had days of traveling to work out the fine points of our arrival."

"Of course, sir. Only trying to help."

Brynn eyed the agent. "Please stop calling me sir. I appreciate the thought, but it's totally unnecessary."

"You got it, sir. Uh, sorry." Looking flustered, the agent sat back down. "That dark-haired man heading toward us will see you make it to the conference."

Brynn took Kayna's arm, and they walked toward the uniformed security guard. He was tall and lean, with the hard-eyed look common to most policemen.

Once they'd shook hands all around, Kayna asked. "Where will Brynn be? I'm going to round up our luggage and get it into some sort of secure storage. Once I've done that, I'll listen to whatever's left of the press conference."

"I figure it will still be going strong," the guard said. "Representatives from every major venture capital firm known to western man are here—along with all the media outlets." He trained his shrewd blue eyes on Brynn. "You've got quite a reputation to live up to."

"I'll do my best."

Kayna muffled a laugh at the dry undertone in Brynn's words. Rising on tiptoe, she kissed his cheek. "See you soon. We're still headed to Ottawa day after tomorrow, right?"

Breath whistled through Brynn's teeth, and he shut his eyes briefly. "Yes. I'd actually be looking forward to it, if I wasn't so tired of planes. Regardless, I have to have a face-to-face with Ultimate Pharmaceuticals since they're the ones we partnered with to create the nasal spray."

Kayna wanted to spirit both of them away from everything, but it wasn't possible. "Just double checking. I'll do what I can to hold most of our stuff here. There's not much point in flying with twenty bags and assorted crates if we don't have to. We'll be back in Seattle once we're done in Ottawa."

"Good plan. Glad one of us is on top of things."

She blew him a kiss, and loped through the terminal. If felt good to move after all their hours in cramped quarters. They'd discussed where to set up at least a temporary residence in the U.S., and Seattle won, mostly because her mother was there.

Interestingly, both of them had relegated their personal effects to storage lockers. Hers was in Minneapolis and his in Baltimore. He'd cleared out his house and put it on the market before he left for Antarctica. It sold while he was gone. All she'd had was a rental flat, and it hadn't made any kind of sense to pay for it to sit empty for a year.

They'd be starting fresh.

Kayna grinned wryly. If what she suspected came to pass, they'd be on their way back to McMurdo in the fall. It was April, and winter was descending on Antarctica. Come October or November, the journey would become more doable. Jack had married them on July fifth, and he'd made it clear he expected them back for their second anniversary, which meant they'd have to arrive well before winter and stay several months.

She checked the kiosks for the one linked to their flight from Mexico City, and settled in to wait. Her mother had wanted to meet them at the airport, but Kayna suggested they wait until she and Brynn were back from Canada. She wanted to settle in for a long visit with Moira Quan, now that they could finally do something other than make meaningless small talk, and the few hours between flights fighting jet lag wouldn't be conducive to a long overdue reunion.

The conveyor belt lapped noisily around its endless circle with nary a bag in sight.

Her thoughts turned to Brynn and today's media circus. He was in line for a Congressional Gold Medal, and he was also a nominee for a Nobel Prize in medicine. They'd have to travel to Washington D.C. at some point for the Congressional Medal, but fortunately, that didn't have to happen immediately. He, along with Abel, Zach, Ted, and Micah, had authored numerous journal articles chronicling their hypotheses and findings. At times, the satellites servicing the southern ocean had become so jammed with traffic from other researchers calling and emailing, the system shut down entirely.

Smiling to herself, Kayna wedged herself in closer to the conveyor belt and began plucking familiar items off it as they flashed by. She'd maintained her anonymity, but Brynn had moved beyond where that was possible.

Lucky for me, no one knows we're married.

She could only imagine the crowd clamoring to talk with the famous researcher's wife, who was also a doctor.

In short order, she was surrounded by a veritable sea of duffels, suitcases, and crates. The same guard who'd met them upstairs made his way to where she stood. "Dr. McMichaels thought you might need a hand."

"Thank you. I do." She fished out their personal suitcases from the welter of things. "All we really need until we get back to Seattle are these two items."

He nodded crisply. "Fine. I'll see to it that everything else finds its way into storage." He spoke into a microphone clipped to his uniform. "We'll just wait a few moments until one of my associates comes to collect all this."

"Not that I don't trust you, but where will everything be?"

"We've secured an airport storage locker for you."

Kayna couldn't help it. She laughed.

The guard took a step back. When he spoke, his voice was carefully neutral. "This is none of my business, but what was funny about that, Dr. Quan?"

"It appears storage lockers are the story of my life—Brynn's too." She held up her hands in the universal gesture for no-contest. "I'm very grateful for your help. I'd have had to figure out how things worked at this airport, otherwise."

"You're most welcome." His eyes glowed warmly. "Dr. McMichaels is a hero. The world owes him a lot. Making certain his things are safe is nothing by comparison."

"Do you mind if I get a cup of coffee from that vending machine while we wait?"

"Not at all. In fact, you sit tight. I'll get one for you. How do you take it?"

She started to ask for one cream and one sugar, but decided she needed all the caffeine she could muster. "Black."

"You got it."

Kayna watched his retreating back. She was dead on her feet, but rest could wait. She wanted to join Brynn and be there to see him receive his due. He truly was brilliant, and his ability to think outside traditional boxes was a rarity in today's scientific community.

The guard made his way back to her and handed over a steaming cup. She was just nodding her thanks when another man wearing the same pressed, buff uniform hustled to them dragging a large wheeled cart. He hucked everything into it and passed her a printed sheet with the location of the locker and the code to access it.

"Ready to join the press conference?" the first guard asked once the other man disappeared tugging the overladen cart behind him.

Kayna nodded and made a grab for one of the two remaining suitcases, but the man waved her off. "I'll get them."

"Did they finalize the new international peace settlement?" Kayna asked as they wended their way up elevators and across walkways. She polished her coffee in a few gulps and tossed the cup in a waste bin.

"Just yesterday. It's been months in the making, but it holds enough safeguards we should be able to breathe easier."

"Guess I should've taken advantage of our downtime in Mexico City to hunt down an English language paper, but Brynn and I were so tired, we fell asleep at the gate waiting for the flight here."

The guard pointed toward the end of the hall. "The conference is just behind those doors."

Another uniformed man stood guarding them. He took the suitcases and wheeled them to a nearby wall. "No worries, ma'am. I'll watch after your things."

Kayna turned to thank her escort, but he was already fifty feet away, moving through the crowded corridor. She pushed the door open and slipped into the back of a desperately overcrowded space. Perhaps two hundred were wedged into a room designed for half that many.

Brynn stood at the front of the room and used a laser pointer to highlight a presentation he'd put together before they left Antarctica. He'd had it on a flash drive in his pocket, working on the assumption they'd provide the computer and projector hookups he'd requested.

Kayna knew the presentation by heart since he'd practiced it in front of her, and she recognized it was drawing to a close.

"...Partially, I got lucky," Brynn said. "But my belief in archaea providing the substrate for boutique antibiotics helped. I'm hoping at least some of you venture capital folk can see your way clear to help fund further research along those lines. We also need continued support for the anti-radiation inoculation. Ultimate Pharmaceuticals is a very small Canadian firm, but they are publicly traded, so there are a number of ways to support them ranging from direct donations earmarked for particular research projects to outright stock purchases."

"You've been offshore too long, doctor," someone called. "UP's stock price went through the roof as soon as it was clear their nasal preparation would be a success."

Brynn laughed pleasantly. "Your funds, ladies and gentlemen. How you allocate them is up to you."

Over the next half hour, over fifty million dollars hit the table, pledged for a variety of research projects. McMurdo got some funds, as did Ultimate Pharmaceuticals. Kayna let the rear wall prop her up, watching with amazement.

"…Think about our offer," a man reiterated.

"I will. While having my own fully funded, completely equipped lab has its seductive aspects, it's likely my wife and I will return to Antarctica. Now if I could use the funds there…"

"Wife?" a female journalist called.

"Kayna." Brynn gestured her way.

She would've waved him to silence, but it was too late. The cat was out of the bag. She threaded her way around the room's periphery and joined Brynn on the podium. Never one for public displays, she felt her cheeks heat as she faced the collection of journalists and businessmen.

"Did you have a role to play in Dr. McMichaels' discoveries?" someone called from the back of the room.

"Yes. How did you meet him? Have you known him since his NIH days?" another voice queried.

"We're not going to get into anything personal," Brynn inserted smoothly. "Kayna Quan is an M.D. Her bright, inquiring mind helped jumpstart mine on more than one occasion."

Rippling laughter spread through the room.

"Thank all of you," Brynn said once everyone quieted. "Kayna and I need a spot of downtime. We leave for Ottawa day after tomorrow, and quite frankly we're tired. Thank all of you for your generous contributions. We'll be in touch."

The room erupted in applause spattered with more questions, but Brynn shook his head. "No more today."

Kayna got the hint and made her way off the dais with Brynn behind her. They worked their way through the crowd and out the double doors. Kayna extended an arm toward where their suitcases rested against a wall.

"Do you need me to call you a taxi?" the guard inquired.

"Thanks, but we'll manage." Brynn grabbed the handles of both suitcases, and they made their way one building over to ground transportation.

"I can't believe how much money you raised," Kayna said, keeping her voice low.

"To be honest, neither can I. Where are we bunking tonight?"

She cast a sidelong glance his way. "My bad. I didn't make reservations. Maybe we should sit somewhere and start calling hotels that aren't too far from the airport."

"Good idea." When he looked at her, layers of weariness fell away, and hunger, bright with sharp edges, danced at the back of his eyes.

"I love it when you look at me like that."

"Like how?" he asked, his voice guileless.

"Like you want to rip my clothes off and ravish me."

"So what are you waiting for?" He retreated to a bench and sat. "Let's get that hotel room cooking."

ALL IT TOOK WAS Brynn's name to get them booked into a suite at the nearby Radisson. The hotel offered the room at no cost, but Brynn demurred. He kicked the door shut and swept her into his arms once he'd let go of their suitcases.

"All this hero and sir stuff is getting really, really old," he muttered.

"Better get used to it." Her voice was muffled against his chest. "We've barely gotten back."

"No one bothered us in Mexico City," he pointed out. "Or anywhere else along our journey home."

"Because no one knew it was us, or rather, you." She pulled

away long enough to look at him. "You blew my cover at the press conference. Before that, no one knew you had a wife."

"Misery loves company." He tightened his hold on her. "Besides, I'm proud of you, and I wanted to show you off."

Something warm opened inside her and cracked wide open. Tears threatened, but she blinked them back. "I love you too."

Before she could say more, he covered her mouth with his and kissed her, plumbing her mouth with his tongue. Despite how tired she was, desire wove a path through her, heating her blood with wanting him. Sandwiched between them, his cock hardened against her belly.

After an endless, breathless time, Brynn tore his mouth from hers. "That mutual masturbation under blankets on the Panama City flight—"

"It was the Buenos Aires one," she corrected, suppressing a giggle.

"Whatever." He made a very male sound. "It was titillating, but I'd much rather have the real thing."

"How about in the shower?" She quirked a brow. "We both stink, and there's enough room in there for an army. I peeked."

"Excellent idea!" He toed off his shoes and began to strip off his clothes.

She shook her head.

"What?"

"I must be exhausted. I can't decide whether I want to get the water going for us, or watch you undress."

"We can have it all, sweetheart." He unbuttoned his shirt and undid his pants. Once they pooled around his feet, he stepped out of them and pushed his shorts out of the way. His cock stood out from his body, engorged and ready for her.

Swallowing around a suddenly dry throat, she tugged her sweater over her head and bent to unlace her shoes, which she slithered out of. Her pants followed.

Brynn unhooked her bra and slid her panties down her legs. "See?" He grinned. "Teamwork. Gets the job done every time."

She made a grab for his cock, but he sprang out of the way. "You can only have me in the shower. Your rules. Your game."

Laughter bubbled from her as she sprinted after him. By the time she stepped over the high rim of the tub, he already had water jetting from multiple shower heads. He opened his arms and she sank into them delighted to be with the man she loved.

Much later, when they emerged damp and sated, she cupped his face in her hands. "It doesn't matter where we live."

"Where'd that come from?" He smoothed her wet hair over her shoulders.

"Home is where our hearts are. So long as we're together, wherever we are will be home for us."

He wrapped a towel around her. "Just a couple of vagabonds, huh?"

"For now. Maybe not forever."

Brynn grabbed a towel and started drying himself. "Each day as it happens, huh?"

She nodded. "Yup. I do want to go back to Antarctica, though."

"Me too. We'll make it happen in a few months."

Kayna unwrapped the towel and swatted him with it. "I'll hold you to it."

"Yeah, you, Jack, Valentin, and Harold. I mentioned this earlier. Harold's been texting me about joining their November resupply run out of Ushuaia."

"Resupply for whom?"

"For places like Arctowski and the other research stations."

"Go ahead and tell him yes. I kind of miss the *Vladimir*." Kayna plucked a robe off the back of the bathroom door and wrapped it around herself.

"Where are you going?" Brynn asked.

"To check out the room service menu. I'm starving."

"Get two of everything," he called after her. "Possibly three. And a bottle of cabernet."

Happiness bubbled up, surrounding her with warmth as she perched on the edge of the bed, room service menu open across her lap. Dreams truly did come true. Deep in her mind, the raven formed, opening and closing his beak in agreement.

ABOUT THE AUTHOR

Ann Gimpel is a national bestselling author. A lifelong aficionado of the unusual, she began writing speculative fiction a few years ago. Since then her short fiction has appeared in a number of webzines and anthologies. Her longer books run the gamut from urban fantasy to paranormal romance. Once upon a time, she nurtured clients, now she nurtures dark, gritty fantasy stories that push hard against reality. When she's not writing, she's in the backcountry getting down and dirty with her camera. She's published over 50 books to date, with several more planned for 2018 and beyond. A husband, grown children, grandchildren and wolf hybrids round out her family.

Keep up with her at www.anngimpel.com or http://anngimpel.blogspot.com

If you enjoyed what you read, get in line for special offers and pre-release special reads. Newsletter Signup!

If you liked Kayna and Brynn's story, you might enjoy *Alphas in the Wild,* an anthology of paranormal and science fiction romances set in the world's wild places. A teaser from *A Run For Her Money,* one of the books in the anthology, follows.

A RUN FOR HER MONEY

Book Description:

Sara's day begins like any other. A routine extraction in tandem with a local Search and Rescue team. *Routine* crashes to a halt when she ends up trapped in a hut, high atop Muir Pass in the Sierras. Four days later, running out of food for herself and her dog, she makes a bold dash for safety.

Jared's walking the Muir Trail when all hell breaks loose. After hunkering beneath a boulder pile for days, he dares a difficult cross-country route, hoping it'll put him into position to approach a backcountry ranger station. Surely one of the rangers will know what happened, because he sure as hell doesn't.

Jared locates the cabin, but it's locked tight. He's getting ready to leave the next morning when a helicopter lands, with Sara at the helm. There's no time to trade war stories. It takes a leap of faith, but they throw in their lot together. Can they face the impossible and come out the other side unscathed?

CHAPTER **One**

My name is Sara Holcomb and I'm a Ranger for the U.S. Park Service, a post I've held for better than twenty years. There are those who say I should've transitioned to a desk job long ago, but somehow I don't think I'd like that nearly as much. See, I've loved the backcountry ever since I was a little girl, probably because my daddy was a Park Ranger too. He used to tell me stories about the forest creatures from the saddle we shared while he patrolled Yosemite Valley. I'm sure you couldn't get away with dragging your daughter along on horse patrol now, but things were different back then. Another thing is I don't really like people all that much, so wandering the trails in the national parks is about as perfect a job as I'm likely to get...

Her forehead furrowed in thought, Sara read over what she'd written as she absent-mindedly swept a strand of greasy hair out of her eyes with grime-crusted fingers. It didn't stay put, though, and she found herself looking through the lank, black strands again almost immediately.

"Well," she muttered, "this doesn't have to be a literary masterpiece. I'm just writing it so people will know what happened to me if they find my body."

She cleared her throat to flush the thought of her possible death out of her mind and picked up her pen again. That was one of the good things about the Muir Hut, there were lots of pens and paper as well. Too bad some desperate traveler had chopped up the only table and burned it for firewood years before. The Park Service debated replacing it, but in the end they decided not to. If one table could burn, a replacement might meet the same fate. Besides, it wasn't easy to get supplies to the beehive shaped stone hut sitting atop twelve thousand foot Muir Pass.

Blowing air out through her pursed lips, Sara frowned as she considered what to write next. She'd planned to dive right into the meat of things, but whoever read her journal really needed to know how she'd ended up trapped in the Muir Hut, so they could understand all the rest.

...I'm getting ahead of myself here. I've been stationed at the McClure

Meadows Ranger Station for the past few summers. Sometimes there's another Ranger with me, but usually there's not. The Park Service has had some cutbacks in recent years. McClure Meadows is in Evolution Valley, and it's my favorite of all the backcountry stations. It even has a geothermal spring so I don't have to heat water for baths. At ninety-six hundred feet, it's below timberline, so there are lots of trees around it— not just granite and shale. Incredible wildflowers dot the meadows all summer.

About six days ago, I got a radio call for help late in the day. A climber was stranded on Mount Darwin, and things weren't looking good. I put in a call for the rescue chopper, packed up what Jake and I would need, and started on the five mile trek to Evolution Lake. Jake is my coal black, search-and-rescue German Shepherd the Park Service finally agreed to let me keep in the backcountry.

It was pretty much a mess when we got there. Suzy, the missing climber's wife or girlfriend, was hysterical and it took me over an hour to get anything useful out of her, like which route her significant other had taken. By then the chopper was circling to land. There are some flat areas at the south end of the lake that are perfect for that...

A chill seeped into Sara from the cold, stone floor, so she changed positions. As she rubbed feeling back into her butt cheeks, she wished again for the missing table. She could've sat on it. A stone bench leaned against the wall of the hut outside in bright sunshine, but it was safer if she didn't go out there. Benches lined the hut's walls inside too, but they probably wouldn't be much warmer than the floor. Stone was a real heat-sink unless it had a chance for the sun to warm it. She gazed back over what she'd written and shrugged. Pushing to her feet, she stretched, rotating her torso first in one direction, then in the other.

Fingers pressed against the ceiling, she blessed her height and her strength, shaped by years of grueling, manual labor. She could do anything a man could, and she was proud of that. Though frequently the object of admiring glances, she'd been very selective in that regard. The occasional co-worker had possibilities but, while the Park Service said *relationships are fine so long as you're not in a direct line of command* on paper, Sara didn't think they were especially open-minded in that regard, so she kept her dalliances brief and private.

Sometimes it was a lonely life, but it was the one she'd chosen. Her hours and time away from home wouldn't have played well with most men, anyway. Children were out of the question. Not if they ever wanted to see their mother.

"Crap, my thoughts are really wandering," she said wryly as she reached over to stroke Jake's soft head. When she'd come to her feet, the Shepherd did as well. "Not much point in telling whoever might read this about the rescue," she went on, talking to her dog. "The climber was dead when I got to him, so the main problem was figuring out how to get the poor son-of-a-bitch out of there."

Jake whined as if he understood exactly what she was saying.

The actual extraction had taken hours. The SAR volunteers—God only knew where they'd been trained—had been less-than-useful. They were competent enough as climbers, but one began puking at the sight of the dead guy's mangled remains, and the other had a hell of a time forcing himself to actually touch the corpse. Since she ended up doing most of the packaging-up of the body herself, Sara was exhausted when she slithered down the last steep talus slope above the southern end of Evolution Lake. Nearly twenty-four hours had passed since she'd started on the rescue mission, and she was surprised she was still capable of sentient thought.

One thing that still bothered her was an unusual amount of rock fall during her descent. Not that she could see anything, but explosions boomed around her. Usually if you heard rock avalanches, you could see them, but not this time. One of the SAR dudes had asked what the fuck all the noise was, but she'd been too tired to have much of an answer.

It had been a relief when the chopper left, and she and Jake were alone again.

In the few hours she'd been high on Mount Darwin, autumn had attacked the aspens around Evolution Lake with a vengeance, and fall colors blazed from every hillside. That was the way things happened above ten thousand feet. Winter lasted a really long time, while the other seasons came and went in the blink of an eye.

After feeding Jake, she'd keyed her radio to report in, finding a small pleasure in hearing Lonnie's cheerful voice. He was her boss, and he ran the dispatch service from Park Headquarters.

"How's it going, pumpkin?" he'd asked. In his sixties, Lonnie didn't pay much attention to the latest governmental directives about not using words that might be construed as sexual harassment.

"Not bad," she replied. "But I'm tired. I'll camp here tonight and head back to McClure tomorrow."

"Now that you mention it," he drawled, "think you might have enough energy to run up to the pass?"

Sara didn't feel like *running up to the pass*. It was another four miles and fifteen hundred feet of climbing. "Uh, not really," she murmured. "At least not tonight."

"Come on, Sara," he'd urged. "We've been getting odd reports from that area. I'd like some firsthand data. You move fast. You could be there in well under two hours." There was a pause, then Lonnie added, "It won't even be dark by then, princess."

Maybe it was the *princess* that did it—her father used to call her that. Sara gathered what she thought she and Jake would need for a few days, stashing all her extraction gear behind a boulder pile. Then she shouldered her pack and struck out for Muir Pass. Lonnie was right, she did move quickly over the trails, her long-legged stride capable of eating up over three miles an hour uphill, more if she was coming down.

Distracted as she replayed the tragedy on Mount Darwin, Sara was surprised how quickly she reached the hut. It was still twilight. Plenty of time to get herself situated.

She dragged herself back to the present, settled on her spot on the floor, and picked up her pen again.

...The extraction was long, but uneventful. No point in describing it here. Once it was over, my boss sent me to Muir Pass to check on reports he'd been getting of unusual activity. While I wasn't anxious to do more traveling that day, I do know how to follow orders. Jake and I reached the hut around six-thirty. I pushed the door open and, as always, was greeted by whichever of the resident rodents chose to take a stand. Jake made short work of them while I shoveled last season's snow into poly bags so we could melt drinking water. Dredging my tent out of my pack, I smiled at the small, satisfying clicking sounds the segmented poles made as they nested into one another.

I didn't know then it might be one of my last smiles ever.

So much of setting up camp is automatic, I'm surprised I even noticed. What did grab my attention, though, was Jake. While he sleeps next to me after I turn in, he usually prefers roaming about when I'm getting our camp set up. Not that night, though. Oh, he started wandering all right, but before I was even done with the tent, he was back by my side whining, with his ears back and his tail tucked low.

"What's the matter, boy?" I asked, but of course I didn't get an answer.

Some of you reading this might wonder why I didn't just bed down in the hut. Well, huts are always, always cold. It's actually far warmer in my down bag and my double walled tent than in a stone hut. In a winter snow storm, I might use one of the widely-spaced huts that dot the Sierras, but never in the summertime or autumn.

Just as I was settling in to melt some of the snow I'd gathered for water and dinner, the light—or what was left of it—began to look really odd, all flickery with iridescent fingers reaching down out of the sky. Searching for a reason, I glanced up and froze. Right above Jake and me was this really large thing that could only have been a spaceship. It was oblong with blue and green lights lining the long sides, and white lights at either end. It was huge, maybe over two hundred feet, though it's hard to measure things when they're in the sky. Jake clung to my side like a shadow as I stared upward in utter and absolute disbelief. He head-butted me toward the open door of the hut, so I told him he could go inside if he wanted. Pretty silly to tell a German Shepherd that. They're trained to die by your side, so, naturally, he didn't go anywhere.

The ship altered course. It had been heading pretty much due east, but it began circling and getting lower and lower. In the meantime, I'd grabbed my radio but, for some odd reason, I couldn't get anything out of it. Usually, high places like the pass have great reception. I checked the battery indicator, and it said eighty percent, so that wasn't the problem.

At first, the ship looked exotic and, well, fascinating. I majored in ecology and wildlife management eons ago. As I studied the ship, I tried to tap into some of that scientific training to figure out how something that non-aerodynamic could fly.

I should probably tell you I'm—or, I used to be—a helicopter pilot. I got my training during a brief stint in the military right after college. I'm pretty sure that's why the Park Service hired me in the first place since they were short of Rangers who could fly back then. Anyhow, I'm getting off track here. I'm not sure how long I spent gawking at the thing in the sky. It was mesmerizing in a weird sort of way.

As it got lower and lower though, I began to get scared. Really scared. At one point I crooked my fingers into a sign against evil I haven't used since I was a child. Then one of those unnatural light beams sweeping the ground found a pica and vaporized it. One minute the little guy was there, looking hopefully at me as I pulled dried food packets out for dinner. The next he was gone in a poof of smoke, leaving this icky, burned smell.

Well, that certainly mobilized me. I dove through the door of the hut and huddled next to Jake on one of the benches. I did leave the door open a crack, though, so I could still see. As soon as I was inside the hut, the damned thing altered course again. It stopped circling and resumed its easterly trajectory, despite being, probably, a thousand feet lower—too low to clear the passes next to either Wallace or Echo Cols. Even though I willed it to crash, I'm sure it didn't. I would've heard something...

Sara skimmed over what she'd written. She wanted to make sure she hadn't missed anything important, at least up until when the ship appeared. Laying the paper aside, she shivered. It was nearly as bad reading as it had been to live through. It also shed a whole new light on what she'd labeled as rock fall when she was descending from Mount Darwin. Maybe it had really been some kind of detonation.

She bit her lower lip. No point dancing around the issue. Not *detonation*, a dry rather clinical term, but bombs. The noise on Mount Darwin sounded like bombs, and maybe that's what they'd really been.

"Crap. Crap. Crap. What the hell is going on?"

Jake whined sympathetically and moved closer to her. She arranged her sleeping bag, laying it out on a foam pad on the hut's floor, before leaning into the dog's warmth. Things had only gotten creepier since her retreat into the hut. Another shudder racked her, and she got inside the bag, trying to regroup.

She'd been in tough situations before. Hell, backcountry life was one tough situation after another, but she'd never felt so out of control.

Right after the ship left her line of sight, she'd retrieved her mostly-erected tent and shoved it sideways through the door of the hut. Once it was upright on the stone floor, she'd gone back outside and tossed her other belongings—scattered on the dirt, snow and rocks—after the tent. It didn't take a genius IQ to understand there was something about the stones of the hut that masked her presence from whatever was in that ship.

The next day, Sara packed up at first light and headed anxiously down the trail with Jake at her heels. She hadn't gotten a quarter of a mile, though, before the dog began to whine. Scanning the surrounding mountains, she didn't see a thing— until she glanced upward. The ship, the fucking abomination of a ship, was on its way back. With the memory of the vaporized pica fresh in her mind, Sara sprinted up the switchbacks toward the hut. Fear clawed at her, making her stomach ache. As she ran, she fought against a helplessness that threatened to immobilize her. Once she and Jake got back to the hut, she sat inside it for a long time, trembling.

They'd beaten the ship to Muir Pass by the narrowest of margins, not an experience she was anxious to repeat.

Days passed.

Four long days, where it required every ounce of Sara's willpower not to simply take her chances and make a dash for freedom. Despite trying the radio regularly, it never came back to life. There were other things that worried her too. Like no other hikers on the Muir Trail. It was only mid-September and there should've been at least twenty to thirty backpackers on that part of the trail each day. She remembered the wilderness permit rosters transmitted via satellite to McClure Meadows daily. Yes, there certainly should have been hikers. There weren't any airplanes, either. This part of the Sierra was on an east-west flight trajectory across the country. Normally, planes passed over regularly.

Sara experimented. The longest she was able to stay outside, before the ship reappeared on the horizon, was sixty-five minutes. Sixty-five minutes wouldn't even get her back to Evolution Lake. She needed at least two hours to make the nine-and-a-half miles to McClure, and that would have to be running, not walking.

Lying in her sleeping bag at night, she wondered if it was the same ship. If there were more than one of them, what did that mean? Had the United States been attacked by alien life forms? Was that why there were no other hikers and nothing else in the sky?

...I tried to leave, but the ship chivvied me back. I don't mind telling whoever may be reading this, I've never been so frightened—ever. And I don't scare easy. If it hadn't been for Jake, I would've really lost it. By the

fourth day, I was running out of food and fuel for my stove. No fuel meant no water. Jake was out of kibbles. He was pretty handy at catching rodents, but I had to do something. And that something meant leaving the hut. I didn't know if I'd be smarter making a run for my cabin at McClure, or if I should head for the LeConte Ranger Station, two-and-a-half miles closer. If I got lucky, I just might be able to make the seven miles downhill to LeConte in ninety minutes. My other option was to climb out over Echo Col and head for Lake Sabrina where there was a paved road and, maybe, people.

I thought about it a lot that night. The next morning thunderhead clouds brewed on the western horizon. I didn't know if the alien craft could see though cloud cover, but I packed up everything to be ready and, for the first time since I was a child, I prayed. Not to any sort of organized type of deity, just to whatever might be out there listening to a forty-something woman, who desperately needed help.

By ten, the clouds were thick, and it started to snow. This weather might give us our only chance to escape. We'll be heading toward LeConte since it's closest, and likely to have food. I'll bring these pages with me and add to them as I can...